Mermaid in Manhattan

Jessica Gadziala is a *USA Today* bestselling author and the author of *My Big Fat Vampire Wedding*. She lives in rural New Jersey with her parrots, dogs, and an ever-growing collection of houseplants. A lifelong dreamer, she's been writing stories since childhood and published her first book in 2015. When not at her desk, she's usually feeding backyard birds, rewatching crime dramas, period pieces, and 90s supernatural TV shows, or adding to her towering stacks of unread books.

PRAISE FOR *MERMIAD IN MANHATTAN*

"I was hooked from start to finish and
never wanted to come up for air."
Emma Lucy, bestselling author of *Live, Ranch, Love*

"An enchanting romp with all the charm of a classic
rom-com!"
**A. T. Qureshi, *USA Today* bestselling author of
*The Baby Dragon Café***

"Witty, swoony and completely bingeable."
Nadia El-Fassi, bestselling author of *Best Hex Ever*

'I loved Finn and Iris . . . It's a version of
New York I would happily live in'
Athena Carstairs, author of *There's Pumpkin About You*

"Utterly addictive"
Annabelle Slator, author of *The Launch Date*

"Gadziala has taken something as chaotic as the sea and
made it seem warm and homely. 'I loved Finn and Iris . . .
It's a version of New York I would happily live in."
Athena Carstairs, author of *There's Pumpkin About You*

READERS LOVE *MERMAID IN MANHATTAN*

"I flew through it whenever I had the chance."

"Snarky and often laugh-out-loud funny while also
romantic and a bit steamy, a bit of everything all woven
together and it totally works!"

"I beg everyone to read this. I loved it so, so much."

"Absolutely hilarious, there was not a single page that went by that I didn't giggle or highlight a quote."

"This book is unexpected in the best way and pure joy."

"Jessica delivers an effortlessly easy to love heroine."

"This book is unexpected in the best way and pure joy."

"A really fun and cozy read. Five stars."

"If you're looking for a read that is a mixture of sweet and spicy and amusing then this one is for you."

"I devoured this in one go, and really enjoyed it!"

"I had such a fun time reading this story."

"Completely addictive!"

"Had me kicking my feet and screaming."

JESSICA GADZIALA

Mermaid in Manhattan

avon.

Published by AVON
A division of HarperCollins*Publishers* Ltd
1 London Bridge Street
London SE1 9GF

www.harpercollins.co.uk

HarperCollins*Publishers*
Macken House, 39/40 Mayor Street Upper
Dublin 1, D01 C9W8, Ireland

A Paperback Original 2026
1

First published in Great Britain by HarperCollins*Publishers* 2026

Copyright © Jessica Gadziala 2026

Jessica Gadziala asserts the moral right to be identified as the author of this work.

A catalogue record for this book is available from the British Library.

ISBN: 978-0-00-878566-6

This novel is entirely a work of fiction. The names, characters and incidents portrayed in it are the work of the author's imagination. Any resemblance to actual persons, living or dead, events or localities is entirely coincidental.

Set in Sabon LT Std by HarperCollins*Publishers* India

Printed and bound in the UK using 100% Renewable Electricity at CPI Group (UK) Ltd

All rights reserved. No part of this publication may be reproduced, stored in a retrieval system, or transmitted, in any form or by any means, electronic, mechanical, photocopying, recording or otherwise, without the prior written permission of the publishers.

Without limiting the exclusive rights of any author, contributor or the publisher of this publication, any unauthorised use of this publication to train generative artificial intelligence (AI) technologies is expressly prohibited. HarperCollins also exercise their rights under Article 4(3) of the Digital Single Market Directive 2019/790 and expressly reserve this publication from the text and data mining exception.

*To the sea, for being dramatic, salty,
and occasionally murderous—an inspiration, really.*

Iris

Iris broke the surface with a flick of her pearlescent green tail, sending droplets scattering like diamonds in the morning light. Humming softly, she pulled herself up onto her favorite sun-warmed rock, arching into a lazy stretch that set water rolling down her arms, the salt water glistening on her skin.

Was there anything better than a refreshing swim in the summer sea? Perfect temperature. Perfect lighting. Zero responsibilities.

She reached back to wring the water from her hair and felt something crinkly in the strands. Not seaweed—unless seaweed had started using packaging.

With a sigh, she pulled out a plastic wrapper, the logo faded to oblivion by sun and salt.

"Seriously?" she muttered, crumpling it up. She reached back into her hair, this time encountering a length of broken fishing line. Once again.

"Oh, come on." She carefully untangled it from her pink waves with the patience of someone who had done so *way* too many times, then folded it up with the wrapper like she was collecting ocean-trash trading cards.

For the life of her, she couldn't understand why it was so hard for trash to make its way into a garbage can.

Humans.

Flopping back, Iris closed her eyes and tried to forget the trash as the sun dried the water on her skin.

There was a flutter above her, interrupting her perfect solitude. Sure, it could be a random gull. But nope. She didn't even have to open her eyes to know who it was.

Montague Featherington.

Monty, for short. Drama, for long.

Iris had named him herself when she'd been eight and going through her 'everyone deserves a ridiculously formal title' phase. Right before she'd stolen an enchanted pearl—that she totally wasn't supposed to take—that, when gifted to the pelican, granted him the ability to speak.

He had been loving the sound of his own voice ever since.

"Hey, Monty," she said, shading her eyes with one hand. "How are you doing?"

"How am I doing?" he repeated, already winding up. "Emotionally adrift. Spiritually soggy. And some thieving seagull stole my favorite thinking rock. What does he have to contemplate? Which human he's going to mug today? The gulls have no interiority. I've said it before, and I'll say it again." He nodded his giant beak for emphasis. "But I am hanging on by a feather. And sheer spite. Allow me a melodramatic sigh."

Iris smiled. "You can borrow this rock if you promise not to monologue at it."

"Tempting, but I prefer the acoustics by the cliff. Better echo." He ruffled his feathers. "Shouldn't you be with Her Majesty?"

"My mother?" Iris blinked. "Why?"

"Because, dearest sea spawn, you mentioned a *super important* meeting last week. With capital letters and everything."

"That's today?" Iris yelped, the edge of her tail slapping the water and sending droplets flying.

"According to my internal calendar and innate sense of dramatic timing—yes. And you're thirty-two minutes late. Not that anyone's counting. Except me. And your mother."

"For Triton's sake!" Iris yelped, vanishing beneath the waves like a startled fish and launching into a desperate, splashy sprint.

Her mother, Tatiana, was a lot of things: powerful, elegant, and entirely over Iris's shenanigans. Being late to a meeting she'd had a week's warning about was just another notch against her.

If she was *lucky* she would be sentenced to eel duty again. The royal singing eels were a barbershop trio who couldn't harmonize to save their slimy lives and never, ever slept.

If she wasn't lucky, she'd be forced to massage the crabs at the royal spa. And they were entitled *and* pinchy.

By the time Iris reached the seafloor, her stomach was in knots as she pictured her mother seated on her seashell throne, tapping her fingernails against her arm in irritation.

"Hey, Carl," she called to the palace gate guard, who pulled open the massive whale-boned gates with the weary look of a merman who'd seen too many late princesses in his time. "Don't say it," she added.

Carl said nothing. His eyebrow, however, spoke volumes.

She shot past the palace's lush kelp gardens, where electric-blue gobies darted between fronds, blissfully unaware that they were being watched by snarly kelp dragonettes.

"Nice stripes," one dragonette heckled. "Did you lose a bet with a zebra fish?"

Up ahead, the bioluminescent coral towers stood proudly, inviting merfolk and sea creatures alike.

Say what you would about maternal expectations and unending royal pressure, but the palace? The palace was magic.

Coral spires, glowing towers, water that hummed with music—this was home.

As she glided through the halls, she ignored the pitying looks from those she passed.

"I'm sorry, I'm sorry!" Iris sang as soon as she swam into the throne room, breathless and trying for repentant but likely landing somewhere more along the lines of 'guilty puppy.'

Queen Tatiana didn't even blink. Her icy-blue gaze swept over Iris like a glacier.

"I do not have time to be kept waiting, Daughter."

Translation: you're in *so* much trouble.

Her pink hair danced in the water around her as her cool blue eyes took in her daughter. "But, indeed, your dedication to shirking your royal responsibilities ends today."

Great.

Crab pinches were definitely in her future.

Or maybe a squid-ink graffiti cleaning detail.

"It is time for you to marry."

Well, then.

Iris blinked.

"I'd rather take the eels."

Her mother didn't flinch. Not even a twitch. Which made it *so much* worse.

As a princess, Iris understood that marriage was a non-negotiable. And likely heavily influenced by her mother. That said, she was young; she had time. Hopefully, by then, all the obnoxious mermen who thought it was appropriate to comment on her seashell bra would be married off to others.

"It's going to be Osiren, isn't it?" Iris asked. Her mind conjured up images of the last time she'd seen him—bench-pressing a defenseless manatee to show off his bulging biceps for a group of giggling mermaids. Iris loved her people, but she had to admit, they could at times be a tad superficial.

Unfortunately for Iris, that gene had skipped her. She didn't particularly care about the size of her potential partner's muscles.

That was probably why she spent so much time reading the pressed-kelp, shell-bound books in the royal library. Even if there was an extremely limited supply thanks to a general preference among the merfolk for socializing rather than reading.

But those books were full of complex men and women who had motivations outside of sensual escapades and decorating their hair.

That said, she'd known for many years that, politically, her marriage would be to someone important.

Like it or not, Osiren was the son of her mother's closest confidant.

And, sure, Osiren had abs for days.
But he also had the personality of wet driftwood.
She'd rather marry the manatee.
"It is not," Tatiana said.
A chill ran down Iris's spine.
Oh, no.
That meant it was someone *worse* than Osiren. Which shouldn't have been possible, and yet, here they were.

But for the life of her, Iris couldn't think of a single councilman who was anywhere near her own age. The prospect of being forced into marriage with a man old enough to be her own father made her heart sink.

Sure, she knew that no matter how much her heart ached for a real, genuine love connection, she was always meant for an arranged marriage designed to further a political agenda. The best she could hope for was to learn to care for her spouse.

"Who is it?" Iris asked, sounding like a sea urchin was caught in her throat.

"Finn Westrock," the queen announced.

Finn Westrock?

Iris blinked.

"I'm sorry—who?"

That wasn't a name; it sounded like a brand.

Was he one of the mysterious, brooding finfolk? Or, perhaps, one of the deeply emotional selkies?

Iris might not mind a marriage with one of them if a union between sea creatures was what her mother was seeking.

"What is he, then? Selkie? Finfolk? Siren with a tragic backstory?"

"He is a human."

Iris stared. "A *human* human?"

"Yes. A land-dweller. Bipeds. You've seen their trash."

Iris couldn't stop the laugh from bubbling up and bursting out.

"Oh, thank you, Mother. I was in desperate need of a laugh."

"I assure you, this is no laughing matter."

Iris's heart sank. "You want me to marry a *human*? On *land*?"

"Yes, darling. That is where the humans live."

"But that's not where I live! I sunbathe on rocks; I don't collect husbands from them!"

"You know just as well as I do that you are more than capable of living on land."

Capable? Yes. Willing? Absolutely not.

"Mother . . ."

This could not be happening. She loved the ocean. It was her home. It was all she ever knew. She'd never technically even been on land. The closest she got was sunning herself on a rock. But she always panicked when she dried too much and started to see skin replace her lovely scales.

"I'm afraid this is non-negotiable, Iris."

"Why can't Shelly marry this Finn man?"

Iris's younger sister notoriously loved the land. She dreamed of little else than stepping out of the ocean for good and living among the people and creatures above sea level.

"You know Shelly is too young."

"She's not that much younger than me. It can wait a year. Even two."

"It cannot."

"Why?"

"It will be too late by then. There is an election going on in the surface world this fall. Your betrothed has promised to create legislation that will make the ocean safe from land pollution. As such, this marriage must take place in ninety days. Before the upcoming election."

"Ninety days? Mother, please, I beg you, choose someone else."

"That is not an option. It must be someone who can represent all merfolk. As a princess, that is you. Tomorrow, you will go on land, and you will meet your groom. I won't hear any more arguments about it."

Iris had to try one last time. "You're really sending me to live on land. With a stranger. For . . . for politics?"

Tatiana simply raised one elegant hand.

That was the end of it.

And maybe Iris had known, deep down, that her protests were pointless.

But that didn't stop her heart from plummeting like a shipwreck.

She knew her mother could be unbending when her mind was made up. She would not be swayed by the emotions coursing through her middle daughter right then. And Iris would rather not cry in front of her mother.

She swam off, rushing through the halls, out the doors, past her beloved kelp gardens, and through the gates.

She didn't stop.

Not at the spiraling reef towers where she and her sisters used to play tag. Not at the swirling sandbar where the dolphins came to dance. Not even when she swam past a current singer whose haunting melody faltered midnote as Iris rushed past with tears clinging to her lashes.

She just kept going.

The pressure in her chest built with every stroke, like her ribs were tightening around her heart. Her tail flicked harder, faster, until the water around her blurred. She passed a jelly lantern, its tendrils pulsing with light.

She didn't look back.

When she finally slowed, her breath caught on a sob.

She curled up by an old coral graveyard. The dead reef felt like her soul: bleached, picked over, and completely out of its element. Its wasted potential, the evidence of the harm the humans had inflicted upon her people, called to her as she folded forward, burying her face in her hands.

How could her mother ask this of her? To leave not only her home, but her homeland, the only thing she had ever known and loved, the people she had been committed to serving. Albeit a couple of minutes late. She wasn't perfect. But she *cared*.

The fish found her soon enough, as they always did.

A sleepy trumpet fish twined gently around her wrist. A pair of pygmy seahorses nestled in the crook of her arm like living jewelry. Even a spiny lionfish hovered, not close enough to sting, but near enough to lend its quiet, comforting presence.

They brushed against her skin, teasing through her hair-like strips of seagrass, offering comfort she hadn't asked for but desperately needed.

She hadn't summoned them. But heartbreak, in her, always echoed through the currents. And so the fish came, determined to comfort her through it. It was a strange phenomenon that didn't happen for either of her sisters. Iris always felt a little guilty, feeling like her emotions removed their free will. It felt like a cruel sort of irony that they would gain theirs just as she was losing her own.

There had to be a way out of this.

She could try speaking to her mother again. Maybe if she caught her in her private chambers, not on the throne, she might be able to appeal to her mother, not the queen.

It was a long shot, and Iris had little faith in her mother bending.

But if she couldn't get her mother to call off the contract, and she was unable to do it herself, that did leave her with one other option.

She could get her prospective husband to call it off.

The more she thought about it, the more genius it seemed.

The fish, satisfied with a job well done, swam back to their lives as Iris straightened.

It could just work.

She would have to be careful.

If it got back to Tatiana that she'd been deliberately difficult or hostile, she would be in a world of trouble. If, however, she simply made herself undesirable to her new fiancé by being . . . aggressively mermaidian—insisting on absurd rituals, making up wildly exaggerated mermaid customs that they *must* follow, mentioning impractically extravagant living accommodations—she might just be able to get this human to rethink his desire to marry one of her kind.

She was going to make this Finn Westrock guy regret the day he asked for a marriage contract with a mermaid.

Operation: Horrify the Human was officially underway.

Finn

"Remind me why I'm doing this again?" Finn asked.

He moved in front of the massive mirror leaned up against the wall in his office to smooth a hand down his suit.

It was blue.

It was always blue.

Blue evoked feelings of trustworthiness and approachability to constituents. Or, at least, that was what decades of research had concluded.

Black was too somber, tan too casual. And gray was often the color worn by lawyers. And no one wanted to be associated with lawyers.

Blue hit the sweet spot, especially when paired with a crisp white shirt and a lighter blue tie. Not red, which was too aggressive and power-hungry. Or even striped, which people couldn't put a finger on why they didn't like but didn't, regardless.

'Color theory' was just one of the many strategic moves being used by Henry, Finn's campaign manager. And only friend in the world.

What that said about Finn, he chose not to think about.

Finn's gaze moved over the rest of his appearance to check for anything out of place: neatly styled brown hair, his cleanly shaven square jaw, and the green eyes that Henry insisted were just the right shade—not too dark to seem like he'd gone to a witch for an enchantment spell on them, but not too light that they made him look like a revenant.

"Because you are falling behind in the polls," Henry said. He was slouched on the couch in the corner of the room, one of his long legs crossed over the other at the ankle, his pants riding up to reveal socks printed with some amorphous cat character from an old cartoon.

Finn had to wear white socks, no exceptions. And he could never miss a trim or teeth-whitening appointment.

Henry's own light brown hair was brushing the collar of his suit jacket. And he'd never gotten his crooked eye tooth fixed.

"I'm not the politician; you are," he'd reminded Finn when he'd mentioned it.

"It's early yet," Finn insisted.

"That is the exact type of thinking that is going to have you losing this race." Henry snapped the newspaper closed and stood as he folded it. "You need an advantageous marriage to a prominent member of one of the supernatural royal families. You know as well as I do that it's important to make it clear we respect their dedication to stick to their old ways while also existing within a larger democratic rule. Marrying a member of one of the royal families will send that message of mutual respect loud and clear."

"Fine. But why a mermaid?"

"Well, a mermaid would certainly look nice on your arm," Henry said. Finn's nose wrinkled at that. He was willing to concede that an arranged marriage would be good for his image and career. But he didn't love the idea of choosing someone just because they were beautiful. "And they were the only family who asked for a reasonable request in exchange for the union. The vampires wanted the removal of bite consent cards."

Finn ignored that sticky subject.

"What did Tatiana ask for?"

"Tighter pollution regulations around the city."

"That was already part of my campaign."

"Exactly. We are winning here." Henry's golden-brown eyes were bright at not needing to give in on anything.

Henry was experienced and knowledgeable, but he could (at times) be a bit cutthroat for Finn's liking.

"What do we know about my potential bride?"

"There's not much to know. Yet. She's the second-born daughter."

"Second?"

"The firstborn is automatically meant for the throne," Henry explained.

"Right. Anything else?"

"Her name is Iris Lanae Marivelle. She's a princess. And she likes to read. That is all I've got."

"Really?" Finn's brows knitted. It wasn't like Henry to have such little information. He'd once compiled an entire fifty-page document about an important sorceress whom he'd only needed to shake hands with. Now he was supposed to marry this woman without knowing anything about her?

"Stop fidgeting." Henry swatted him with the newspaper. "It's just brunch."

"You're sure she's coming alone?"

"From my understanding."

"And you're sure you can't come?"

"I have that speech to write for your press conference."

Finn's eyes narrowed at Henry, suspicious. Henry was the definition of a micromanager. He'd once crashed Finn's personal training lesson to inform the trainer that Finn's shoulders weren't wide enough and that the situation needed to be remedied.

Sure, Finn did appreciate his stronger, wider-looking shoulders. They did fill out a suit nicely. But Finn was forever concerned that Henry might drop in on his next haircut appointment or during his yearly physical.

"I'm not buying it. You never miss an opportunity to stick your nose in."

"Fair enough," Henry conceded. "But that is about politics. This is about your personal life."

"You forced me to take up archery and take an interest in plays."

He wasn't even going to mention the piano lessons. That had been a disaster both of them wished to forget.

"Besides, in your eyes, my marriage is political."

"Sure. And there will be discussions and media training for your bride-to-be, but I figure I can trust you to handle a simple meeting by yourself." Henry checked his watch. "You need to get going if you're going to get across town in time. Be charming. Ask her questions. Remind her how advantageous an arrangement this is for the both of you."

"Quite romantic," Finn drawled.

"Never claimed there was anything romantic about politics," Henry said. He flicked his wrist, checking the time. "You need to get going. Be the charmer we both know you can be."

Finn said goodbye to Henry and made his way to the subway. It would shave off time and frustration simply to take a cab, but Henry thought it was important for Finn to be seen as a 'man of the people.'

And given the positive press that had come from some other passenger snapping a picture of Finn while he'd been standing, one arm holding on to the bar, the other holding a book he was reading on interspecies relations after giving up his seat to a young fae woman, Henry was right about that.

The subway platform buzzed with its usual chaos—commuters dodging harried pixie couriers, a warlock softly muttering into a runestone, a bored centaur chewing something that looked suspiciously like a travel-sized hay bale.

Finn sidestepped a spill of what he suspected was a glamour potion—pink and sparkling on the floor. The last time he'd accidentally touched a glamour potion, he'd taken no fewer than fifty duck-faced selfies.

Just another Tuesday in Manhattan.

Still, he barely made it to the restaurant on time.

True to form, Henry had chosen the best possible spot for the first meeting.

Vino on the River perfectly bridged both their worlds. It was squarely in Manhattan but was a waterfront establishment.

Finn was led toward the table on the patio, and he couldn't help but notice the archway behind it, covered in green vines and vivid pink flowers, and how it would make the perfect backdrop for a photo op.

Finn winced at that train of thought, wondering when he'd started to view every single moment of his life through a media lens.

"Can I get you anything to drink?" the waitress—a human, if his instincts were correct—asked as she handed him a menu.

"I'll have a negroni." It was his knee-jerk order. Heaven forbid he be caught drinking some brand-name soda or a drink deemed too 'feminine' by the press. "Do you happen to have anything on the menu a mermaid might enjoy?"

"A mermaid?" the waitress asked, eyes filling with wonder. "Here? At the *table*?"

Finn couldn't fault her for her awe. It was a rare occasion anyone saw a mermaid at all, save for maybe sunning themselves on a sandbar at the beach. You certainly never saw one in the city itself.

He'd wondered himself more than a time or two why a mermaid, of all species, would want to marry a human political hopeful. They were known for never straying far from the sea, if they ever bothered to surface at all.

"Yes."

"Oh, my goodness. Oh, that is so neat. I've never seen a mermaid before! Um, I don't think we have anything technically on the menu for mermaids. You know, since they never come on land. But I will talk to the bartender, and we will make up something super special for her. Him?"

"Her."

"Right. Her. Okay. I will go get right on that," she said. Then, voice a little lower: "I'm *totally* voting for you, by the way."

Before he could even thank her, she was off. He watched as she rushed behind the counter, bouncing on her heels in excitement as she filled in her equally astonished-looking coworkers.

The three of them brainstormed for a moment before one produced a fishbowl-sized glass from under the counter. Then there was an almost alarming amount of preparation going on, as Finn silently worried he shouldn't have ordered for Iris.

Admittedly, mermaids were one of the species he knew the least about. Mostly because of their aforementioned aversion to being on land. He wasn't sure if they were more traditional, like the vampires and werewolves, or if they were more modern like many solo-practicing witches and warlocks, or demons.

Oh, well.

The decision had already been made.

Finn ran through conversation points in his mind for a few more minutes before, about fifteen minutes late, he heard the hushed whispers followed by the restaurant patrons craning their heads toward the door.

There were many supernaturally beautiful creatures in the world.

But Finn was willing to bet that this reaction was to a rare sighting of a real, live mermaid. Without her tail. An even rarer sight.

Finn was ready to scoff at their over-the-top shock and awe.

Until he laid eyes on her himself.

His tie felt too tight as he tried to swallow down his saliva, so he didn't drool all over himself.

Sure, he'd seen paintings of mermaids. He'd even seen drawings of them in a biology textbook.

But nothing compared to the real thing.

She was soul-crushingly beautiful with her cascading pink waves over her tall, fit frame, clad in a flowing blue dress that hugged her every curve. Her face was soft, feminine perfection with generous lips, high cheekbones, a dainty, lightly upturned nose, and eyes the decidedly un-human shade of sea glass.

There was a shimmery quality to her skin that must have been a mermaid trait, along with a small smattering of pearlescent scales up near her hairline, and what at first appeared to be scars on the sides of her throat, but logic told him must be where her gills would be when in the water.

He fully understood why everyone was gawking, why they were taking out their cameras to snap pictures. He never wanted to look away.

Belatedly, he remembered to rise to his feet and offer her a smile.

"Iris?" he asked. As if there would possibly be another incredibly rare mermaid in the same restaurant.

She opened her mouth to speak.

But just as she did, her foot wobbled.

Then she was falling, quite literally, right into him.

His arms went out automatically, wrapping around her. He was overwhelmed with salt water and citrus—the scent that seemed to cling to every inch of Iris. He couldn't help but notice how her body seemed to perfectly melt against his—all her soft curves against his hard lines.

Iris's arms had gone to his arms, fingers grabbing the material of his shirt. It conjured up images of her hands peeling it off of him, of her eyes bright with desire and—

No.

He couldn't let his mind go there.

This wasn't even meant to be a *real* marriage. At least, that wasn't how Henry pitched it to him.

"It's all on paper, of course," had been his exact words. "Unless the two of you want there to be more."

"You all right?" Finn asked, wondering if Iris could hear the breathlessness of his voice just then. Because he could hear it. Loud and clear.

This wasn't supposed to feel like . . . anything. This was meant to be a diplomatic move. A photo op. A partnership on paper with clear political boundaries. He wasn't supposed to notice her curves pressed to his chest and imagine . . . anything else.

Yet for one mindless moment, his body betrayed him.

He cleared his throat.

He needed to focus.

Be charming.

Ask questions.

Don't ogle the mermaid.

"Yes. Yes, of course," Iris said, stiffening and pulling away.

He'd heard stories about the voices of mermaids. They'd never been described on the same level as sirens, but it was said that there was a certain sweetness and a sing-song quality that made you want to lean closer to hear more.

Finn pulled away before he could do something that absurd.

"I'm still . . . getting used to my land legs."

Finn reached to pull out her chair, getting pinched brows from Iris, who was likely not familiar with the human custom. Or, you know, chairs. After a moment, she slid in so he could move to his side and sit.

"I'm so glad you were willing to meet with me today."

For just a moment, there was a flash of something across her face. It was sharp and cutting. But gone so quickly that Finn was almost sure he'd imagined it.

When Iris spoke, it was almost as if her voice got even sweeter, more musical.

"Oh, of course. I have *so* many plans for our courtship."

He wasn't sure why, but Finn felt like he'd somehow just stepped into some sort of trap.

Though he was relatively sure that he wouldn't mind being trapped with someone like Iris.

Or so he thought at the moment.

Iris

"You are so lucky." Shelly punctuated the statement with a disarmingly effective pout. Iris had stopped falling for the look ever since the whole octopus incident that had left her punished for a month and Shelly walking free, despite being just as guilty as her big sister.

"Yes. So lucky. Who wouldn't want to be bartered off to a stranger? A human, nonetheless."

"You can't say things like that," Juna, Iris and Shelly's older sister—the heir to the throne—scolded. "Not on land, anyway. It sounds speciesist."

Juna held out Iris's bag.

"If Iris screws this up, can I marry the human?" Shelly asked.

"She's not going to screw anything up. And that is not appropriate language for a princess. You know you are too young to marry."

"Can I at least go with Iris? She knows nothing about the land or people."

"And you do?"

"I've been studying them my whole life."

Shelly might have been one for dramatics, but on this, at least, she was telling the truth. Shelly was constantly missing dinners, parties, and important council meetings because she got so engrossed with watching the humans at the beach.

Iris suspected that Shelly might have even done more than merely watching from the water. Sisterly affection kept her from tattling to their mother. Even if she did worry that Shelly idolized people that she couldn't possibly relate to, the way she did to the other merfolk.

"Mother wants you nowhere near the land," Juna said. Her chin lifted in that regal way that reminded Iris so much of their mother.

"It's like she wants us to suffer," Shelly grumbled. She threw herself backward, arms folded over her chest.

"Don't be ridiculous," Juna said.

"She does! All I have ever wanted is to go on land, but she's keeping me here. All Iris wants is to be in the sea, and she's forcing her to go on land. It makes no sense, unless she just wants to hurt us."

"Or," Juna said, her tone taking on a frustrated edge, "she is an incredible ruler who knows what is best for her people. And sometimes what is best requires a sacrifice."

Iris was starting to feel just like that: a sacrifice. Someone handed over to a man she'd never met, knew nothing about, on a silver platter.

Here. Isn't she pretty? She'd look lovely standing silently at your side.

Iris shook off those thoughts, knowing she wouldn't be able to play her part even halfway convincingly if she let herself get too bitter about the whole situation.

"Anyway," Juna said, looking at Iris. "You remember where you are going?"

"You've told me four times already."

"Mother has it all arranged. There will be a change of clothes for you. And you will need to *bathe*."

Juna tripped on the word. It wasn't one most merfolk were familiar with. They didn't, after all, need to bathe.

"Which, again, is a process—" Juna started.

"Where one submerges in water then rubs a slippery substance known as 'soap' all over their bodies." Then, as she understood it, the water went down the drain. It sounded like a monumental waste of water to her.

"Precisely. If you struggle with dressing, the woman, Maria, who is taking you to the hotel can assist you."

How hard could dressing be? Sure, she still had no idea how she was going to handle the whole legs situation, but she didn't imagine it would be hard to slide fabric up over them.

It was actually the only part Iris was a little bit excited about. She'd never worn clothes; she couldn't even imagine what they would feel like. Though she was reasonably sure that if the standard attire for humans involved that lower-body garment that slipped between women's butt cheeks, she wasn't going to enjoy that.

"I'm sure I can handle getting dressed." She had to not only accomplish that but also tamp down all of her anger and resentment about the situation so she could come off as overly excited about it.

"Remember that while you are on land, you are

representing not only our family but also all our kind. Conduct yourself appropriately," Juna said, reaching out to tuck some of Iris's hair behind her ear in an uncharacteristically gentle gesture.

"I know what I'm doing," Iris assured her sisters.

She just went ahead and didn't tell them that what she was doing was making her potential fiancé run screaming.

She said her goodbyes and started her swim toward the surface.

"What do we have here?" Monty called from the sky as she broke the surface on a sandbar. He landed with the grace of a swan and the drama of a disgraced duchess.

"You didn't hear the news?"

"News? What news? I do hate to miss some juicy gossip."

Iris plopped herself on the sand, knowing it would be a few minutes before the water would dry and her tail would slowly disappear. She couldn't pinpoint why the potential of seeing her land legs filled her with so much dread.

"I am being sacrificed to the gods of politics," Iris told the bird. "I'm getting married. To a human."

"Betrothed? You're betrothed? To a man with *knees*?"

"So it seems. I have to go meet with him today."

"I have *just* the outfit for an Upper East Side brunch." At Iris's raised brow, Monty fluffed his feathers. "I'm obviously coming with you. I've always felt I was meant for city life. Do you think a cravat is too much?"

Iris had no idea what a cravat was but was almost certain it would be too much. Like most things Monty.

"Is there some sort of clause in this marriage contract for your emotional support pelican? Because there should be. Anyway, tell me everything. Does he have a penthouse? Does he have . . . breadcrumbs?"

Leave it to Monty to somehow lighten her mood, despite everything.

"I don't know where he lives. I don't know much about him. Apparently, his name is Finn Westrock—"

"The mayoral candidate?" Monty gasped. "We're going to be political royalty. I want a sash! No, a tiara. With diamonds. We might be invited to galas! And be in the tabloids! I do hope they will catch my good side. I mean, they're all good sides, but still. This is fantastic. We might be one step closer to my real dream: Broadway! Which, of course, I could segue into a long-running reality show. I could interview people every week. And give my opinion—"

"How do you know he's a mayoral candidate?"

Looking down, Iris watched as the glitter of her scales dimmed, shimmer by shimmer, leaving unfamiliar skin in their wake.

"By his flyers, of course."

"Wait, you can read?"

"Of course I can read. How else do you think I keep up with gossip? And seafood recalls."

Monty, it seemed, had a whole life outside of listening to her complaints and humoring her with tales of the things he witnessed at the beaches.

"Don't get too excited, Monty," she said. Her tail was almost completely gone, replaced with two long legs and feet. She spread her toes, seeing the slightest bit of webbing between them—seeing a flash of the green there, the only remaining trace of her tail left.

"Why ever not?"

"Because I don't plan on actually marrying the man. I am going to get him to break off the engagement."

"But why? You finally get your fin in the door of high society, and you want to slam it shut? Are you having a quarter-life molt?"

"I don't molt. And he's a *human*, Monty."

"A human. With a job. And health insurance, most likely. That's more than we can say about half the bachelors in the reef. Neptune's beard, do you have any idea how many kelp cakes I've stress-eaten at the idea of you winding up with Osiren?" Monty did a whole-body shiver at the very idea.

"My home and life is in the ocean," Iris told him. Looking down, she saw more flesh-toned skin creeping up her belly, her chest. And her shell bra—once fused seamlessly to her skin—had fallen off. Thank goodness for her long hair that provided a bit of modesty.

"And now you can have a new life on land! With all-you-can-eat sushi bars! And reality television! What's not to love?"

"Well, these for starters," she said, waving down at her legs.

"I've seen a lot of legs. Those are some nice ones. Though, we might need to go with closed-toe shoes," he clucked. "Just a friendly reminder—the humans and other creatures on land aren't quite as free about nudity as the ocean folk are." His gaze moved down her bare body.

"I think there are clothes in here." Iris produced a bag and pulled the zipper down to reveal several articles of clothing in plastic bags. Juna, true to her obsessive nature, had labeled everything inside.

'Outfit A' was meant for wearing to the hotel.

'Outfit B' was for the brunch.

There were also bars of soap, a toothbrush, and . . . "What kind of torture device is this?" she asked.

"That, my dear, is an eyelash curler. A medieval torture device repurposed to assist with flirtation."

"Why would I need to curl my eyelashes?"

"Oh, my dear, I keep forgetting you have lived in a world devoid of fashion shows. Or, you know, the internet. We have so much to go over. Why don't you slip into something less comfortable while I get started?"

He draped his downy white wing over his eyes as Iris held up Outfit A like it might bite her. What even was this fabric? And how was she supposed to know which part of her body it belonged on?

She struggled into her clothes as Monty launched into a rambling monologue about makeup and beauty standards that made Iris's head spin.

"Hmm," Monty said as she struggled to her feet after dressing. "We're going to need to work on that."

"Work on what?"

"I hate to be the one to tell you this, but you walk like a newborn giraffe. I don't know if I should chuckle or call animal control."

"What does that mean?" she asked, feeling wobbly on her land legs.

"Well, it means you're walking like the ground personally offended you, and your legs are trying to file a complaint."

"Gee, thanks," Iris grumbled.

She took a few more steps, her body rocking side to side.

"Stop looking at your feet," Monty demanded. "You're giving . . . sea spaghetti."

It was an awkward ten or fifteen minutes before she felt like she was getting the hang of it.

"Better, right?" she asked, overcome with a strange, swirling sensation in her stomach that she knew from her books to call insecurity.

"You're wobbling like kelp in a riptide, darling. But it's . . . endearing."

She wasn't sure she believed him.

"Monty," she said, shoulders sagging. "I hate everything about this." She dropped back down onto the sand, pulling her knees into her chest, wrapping her arms around them, and lowering her head.

Monty exhaled hard before moving to stand beside her, his big wing wrapping around her back.

"I know none of this is your choice, my sweet sea fairy. But I am here for you. To teach you the ropes. Or to lend a listening ear. I'm just trying to make the best of things, since, right now, there is no changing them."

He was right.

It was useless to keep bemoaning her fate.

She had to get through this part.

Then she could slowly and methodically dismantle her engagement.

"You're right," she said, exhaling hard.

"When am I not?" Monty asked.

"We should get going."

They'd already wasted too much time. Her mother would not be happy if she was late for the meeting.

"Why is everyone looking at me?" Iris asked, brushing her sun-dried hair off of her neck.

They'd made their way off the beach and were heading

toward the parking lot where their transportation was supposed to be waiting.

"Because you're a mermaid, darling. Practically the stuff of legend."

"What are you talking about? There are tons of us."

"But never on land. And on land, you, my dear, are a ten out of ten."

Iris had no idea what to say to that, so she turned her attention to the little glass box painted a vivid cerulean blue. "What is a 'Modesty Box'?" she asked, reading the sign.

"That, my sweet sea fairy, is for the land shifters. They are full of cheap articles of clothing saved from landfills, washed, and stored inside for anyone who accidentally shifted and found themselves suddenly in desperate need of covering. Several shifter nonprofits set them up all around the city."

There was so much Iris had to learn about the land, so many customs she was in the dark about. There was only so much she could learn from her textbooks, and she had almost no contact with any supernaturals outside of those who lived in the ocean.

"Princess?" a woman called, making Iris's head whip over. She was tall and lithe, with a cat-like face and long golden-brown hair. Iris wasn't entirely sure if she was human or another paranormal.

"Yes?" Iris called. A wave of uncertainty washed over her. She'd never really conversed with anyone except for fellow mermaids—and Monty, of course—before. She wasn't sure how to interact with this stranger.

"My name is Maria. Your mother sent me to escort you. Who is this?" she asked, looking down at Monty.

"Montague Featherington," Monty answered. "Head of Surface Affairs. It's a very niche field. Highly specialized."

If Maria thought a talking pelican was odd, she made no comment on it. Iris couldn't help but wonder if talking animals were more common on the surface than she'd realized, if this woman seemed so unperturbed about Monty.

"Of course," Maria said, opening the back door for the two of them to slide inside her car.

"Roomy," Monty said, wiggling around on the seat.

Iris thought it was quite cramped, when she was used to the vastness of the ocean, but kept her opinions to herself. Once the car started moving, she was too busy trying not to get sick to make any sort of conversation. Not that Monty noticed. He kept a one-sided conversation going the whole drive. Iris stopped trying to listen when he kept throwing out words she didn't understand.

She watched out the window as more and more cars started to flood the streets. They crossed over a giant bridge, and she watched the water slipping away behind them, replaced by hard, cold, solid concrete.

Her heart sank as her very blood screamed for her to turn back, to go home.

But she couldn't do that.

They drove over the bridge, and Monty declared—with his usual enthusiasm—that they'd entered The Big Apple!

Though, from what Iris could see, there weren't any apples anywhere.

Her gills might have vanished, but the instinct remained. The air felt too sharp in her lungs, too dry. Her skin itched under her new clothing, too warm in the places it clung, yet too bare in the places it didn't.

Outside the windows, the streets pulsed with magic and

metal. Glamours flickered on paranormals and humans alike, just the barest shimmer giving them away.

There were no currents here, no bioluminescent coral towers. Just concrete and strangers who didn't even look at the cars as they passed by. The noise had her shoulders creeping up near her ears. The rumble of car engines, the shrieks of sirens, honks of horns, and the occasional thump of music. She was so used to the quiet calm of the ocean, interrupted only by the occasional whale sound and the soft whooshing of the water.

Iris pressed her hand against the cool glass window, longing for home.

They quickly pulled up in front of a towering building. Though in this city, it seemed as if each of the buildings was in some sort of competition over which one got to be tallest.

There were humans and creatures everywhere, their shoulders brushing as they moved through the congested, noisy streets. There was a chorus of horns, conversation, sirens, and music that had Iris wincing as pressure built across her temples.

"We'll be brunching at Four Stars with A-listers in no time," Monty declared, waving a feather at a restaurant as they passed. "I do hope Drach and Violetta bring the twins . . ."

Iris had no idea who those people were, but Monty's enthusiasm was starting to become contagious, despite her previous plans to hate everything about this city.

She wanted to stop and take it all in, but Maria was in a hurry to get her to a room once they reached their first destination—the limestone and glass hotel.

"I will wait out here if you need anything," Maria said,

insisting on standing in the hallway as Iris and Monty made their way into the room a few moments later.

"Oooh, this is nice," Monty declared. "Those better not be down pillows," he said, waving a wing toward the bed. "I mean, I'm not a fan of geese. They're nasty little sky demons. I once got mugged for my sandwich. I'm still in therapy about it. If I wanted to be chased around and snapped at, I'd go visit my Aunt Cora again. Still, we can't support any bird-plucking industry." He gestured down at his own pristine feathers. "Well, what are you waiting for? You need to bathe. You still have seaweed in your hair, for Triton's sake."

"How do I turn on the water?" Iris asked.

With a long-suffering sigh, the pelican led her into the bathroom, turning on the tap, showing her how to adjust the temperature, demonstrating how soap and shampoo worked, then explaining she must dry herself with a towel afterward.

Iris ran the water while stripping out of her clothes.

As she slipped into the water, her legs fused, familiar magic stitching her back together. She let out a breath she hadn't known she'd been holding.

The moment her legs vanished, she nearly wept with relief. The tight, uncomfortable awareness of them had made her feel like someone else entirely, foreign and exposed. But as her tail curled beneath her as it always had, she felt some of the tension slipping away.

She lingered longer than she should, soaking in the quiet. The hum of the water pipes was no ocean song, but it was better than nothing.

She had to admit, there was something quite nice about the citrus soap and the sudsy shampoo. Her only regret was having to drain the water and dry off, watching her beloved tail disappear, when Monty knocked at the door to remind her that this was real, that her time was up.

She combed her hair before opening the door to the other room and walking out to find Monty . . . wearing a crown. More precisely, her crown.

"Why, yes, I do look quite dashing," he said, speaking to an invisible audience. "But that is no sur—oh . . ." He trailed off, seeing Iris.

"Having fun?" she asked. "That is a priceless family heirloom, you know." She was a little surprised to find that Juna had packed it. They typically only wore their crowns for special occasions. "I feel like it might be too much for a meeting, though."

"I operate under the belief that a crown is *always* a good idea. But the decision is yours. Even if it is the wrong one."

After some fiddling, the two of them figured out how the gown was supposed to go on, and she slipped into it. It felt a bit like wearing a jellyfish—soft, clingy, and probably going to sting her if she moved wrong.

Once dressed, Iris moved in front of the mirror on the back of the closet door.

She didn't recognize the girl in the glass—hair sleek, eyes wary, mouth set in a line that didn't belong to someone free.

"Do I look . . . human?"

"Not even remotely. But that is not a bad thing. Come here. Let me smell you."

"Smell me?" she asked. But the bird was already making his way over, ducking his giant beak down and sniffing her.

"Good. Not a hint of seaweed. You smell . . . citrusy. Like a very expensive cocktail. Or a scented candle named

High Maintenance. Yes, I do believe you are presentable enough."

"As always, your praise is truly humbling," she quipped.

"I *am* a giver. Come on. Let's go snag you a husband."

"I'm not going to marry him, remember?"

"Sure, sure. Let's go ruin your engagement with the devastatingly handsome, perfectly groomed politician with the award-winning smile. I stand with your right to terrible decision-making, Iris."

She thought Monty was being dramatic, as usual, about her would-be fiancé's appearance.

But after she convinced him he couldn't come in the restaurant and mustered the nerve to do so herself—touching the coral charm she still wore under her dress, just once, quick, like the breath she suddenly couldn't take—she followed the hostess's directions down the back path to the last table.

Where Finn Westrock was waiting for her.

And, if anything, Monty had been *underselling* his good looks.

Merfolk were known for their beauty. And Iris was sure she'd seen the best of what male beauty had to offer.

She was incredibly, fully, monumentally wrong.

Because Finn Westrock was devastatingly handsome.

He had to be six-two, seemed fit beneath his stuffy blue suit, and had bone structure that seemed to be carved out of coral limestone—sharp, defined, not meant to yield. And his cheekbones could cut like shale ledges—high, angular, beautiful. And his eyes, well, they glowed green like algae at midnight.

She never expected to be seeing so much of her homeland in his face.

Surely, her surprise over that was to blame for how she lost her footing and literally tumbled into him.

His strong arms went around her as his scent enveloped her. He smelled dry and steady—like driftwood that's been polished smooth by years of waves.

Interest washed through her—heady and familiar—but deeply unwelcome. She'd barely resisted the urge to turn her face into his neck and press her lips to the pulse of his heartbeat there.

Then he spoke, breaking the spell.

He had an appealing voice—smooth and clear like crisp fall waves, but with just a hint of gravel beneath it. It was the kind of voice that made you want to lean in. So, naturally, she stepped away.

No matter how handsome he was—or how good he smelled—she was determined not to be charmed by him.

He was just a man.

With a stupidly perfect face.

An easy target.

It was time to make him regret ever agreeing to the marriage contract.

Iris

"I'm so glad you were available to meet with me today," Finn said as soon as they were both seated.

Iris bit back her real thoughts that ran along the 'It's not like I had a choice' direction and pivoted to the complete other way.

"Of course! I was so intrigued by your offer. It's not every day a land man wants to endure the rigorous courtship of a mermaid."

Doubt flicked across his green eyes, making her hold back a smile.

He was a master at controlling his emotions, though, tamping them down and replacing them with something more manufactured. Even the smile he shot her seemed practiced and disingenuous.

"This union could be historic," he said. "A royal mermaid has never married a surface-dweller before, let alone a human." That voice that just a moment before had been so appealing felt suddenly fake. Too clean. Too careful. Like someone had focus-grouped his vowels. "A real step forward for both our kinds. And who better than us to set the example?"

Oh, he was smooth all right.

He was the kind of man who could convince you to sell him your coral bed and thank *him* for the privilege.

Iris's eyes narrowed.

But before she could respond, a peppy woman came bouncing over. In one hand was a small glass that she set silently in front of Finn. Then, with a flourish, she set a glass the size of her head in front of Iris.

"We made you a saltwater cocktail!" she gushed. "Salt water infused with just a splash of gin, muddled with nori, and garnished with pink Himalayan salt and ground kelp!"

They'd even put a little fake fish inside the cup.

"It looks lovely," she told the waitress, even if she'd never had 'gin' before.

"And we have a massive seafood menu. Just flag me down when you're ready to order."

With that, she bounced away.

"She was very excited to get to make you a drink. And serve a mermaid."

"I feel like there are a lot of eyes on me," Iris admitted.

Out of the corner of her eye, she saw a flash of white. Turning, she saw Monty landing on the railing near an abandoned table. Hopping down, he started eating leftover crab cakes off a plate.

"Can you blame th—Is that a pelican?"

"Seems like it. So, Finn, what made you decide you want a mermaid wife?"

He reached as if to loosen his tie before he lowered his hand to the white tablecloth instead.

"Well, to be honest, you represent a key demographic. Your background will add great diversity to my platform."

He sounded like he was reading off a script.

Had his campaign manager coached him on what to say? Or, worse yet, did he truly feel that way?

"We don't need to be in love, obviously," Finn kept prattling on. "We simply need to put on a convincing show for the media, and—"

"Shoo! Shoo!" someone called from her side, making Iris turn to see one of the servers trying to get Monty to leave. She was so amused by the show Monty was putting on, pretending to try to bite the woman's arm, that she lost track of what Finn was saying. Not that it was hard to drift off during Finn's press release disguised as conversation.

"The optics of a single male candidate aren't great. Not even with how much progress we've made as a society the past few decades. The people—both human and not—like the idea of strong family values."

"I see," she said when it seemed like Finn was waiting for a response from her.

"It is, unfortunately, a lot to accomplish in a small amount of time. But I'm confident we can curate something believable. After all, a picture-perfect couple is curated, not happened upon."

How romantic.

"You'll be amazed how quickly the press will take to you. Once we . . . tweak a few things."

"Tweak a few things?"

Iris was quickly losing control of her composure. If she

wasn't careful, she was going to blow up at him. Then there would be no avoiding her mother's wrath.

"Oh, I don't mean to offend you. Your look might just need to be . . . refined a bit. Nothing dramatic, just polished. We all have to sacrifice a bit of individuality for the sake of public image. We might just need to tone down the . . . mermaidness."

"But I *am* a mermaid."

"Yes, which is an important factor. Polling suggests that the fae, vampires, and shifters—in particular—would prefer a candidate who has close ties to one of the paranormal communities, so they know we understand their specific concerns. However, polls also suggest that they like their politicians to be relatable. Voters wouldn't be able to see themselves in us if we are too . . . unique."

"So we can't be individuals."

"Sure we can. For example, I practice archery, go to plays, play golf—"

But did he enjoy any of those things?

"Look, I can see you're getting a little . . . tense." She wasn't sure what word he'd been going to say before he settled on that one. But even if it was unflattering, she would have preferred something real. "Try not to let your emotions lead."

Try not to let her emotions lead? She was a mermaid. Everyone knew that mermaids were known for accepting and embracing their emotions.

And he was, what, calling an important part of her identity a flaw?

"Politics are all about calm and control. If we give in to feelings, we lose credibility."

Iris could feel her pulse quickening with each word he was saying.

"And the last thing we need is an emotional outburst in front of the cameras."

She was out of her seat before she could even process what she was doing.

Her giant drink was in her hands one moment.

The next, it was poured over his head.

As the salt water ran down his face, there was no anger in his expression. Not even surprise. Just a quiet kind of resignation. Like he'd expected the worst and was relieved it was only seawater.

For a man who seemed so obsessed with perception, it was almost unsettling how little he cared about how he looked in that moment.

He simply blinked the salt from his lashes, the tiniest sigh escaping as if he'd just surrendered to her fury.

It made her stomach twist.

He was still sputtering on the salt water as she turned and walked away.

How was *that* for an emotional outburst?

"Shoo, you dumb bird!" she heard from somewhere behind her.

By the time Iris burst out of the restaurant, Monty was flitting over to her, his feathers literally—and figuratively—ruffled.

"You dump a drink on a politician's head, and *I'm* the one who's banned from the restaurant?"

"The *nerve* of that man!" Iris stomped forward, finding her gait was a lot steadier when she was angry. "He was basically calling my entire persona political suicide, but he still expects me to want to marry him?"

"Back in my day, we didn't need to arrange marriages," Monty said. "We just fought over sardines. Like adults."

"Not a single word that came out of his mouth seemed like a unique thought that he'd had. It was all off some script or something. The man is absolutely devoid of character."

"He looks like he wears boat shoes unironically," Monty declared.

"Dammit," Iris said, stopping mid-stride, head tipped up to the sky. "My mother is going to be livid. I'm going to be cleaning barnacles off sea turtles for the next thirty years."

"Oh, what do you have to be sad about? I'm the one who's losing his chance at fame and fortune."

"Maybe this won't get back to my mother."

"I wouldn't be so sure about that. Didn't you see that pack of gulls hanging about? They're your mother's personal spies. She's probably getting an earful as we speak. I should have eaten them instead of those crab cakes; they're repeating on me," he said, tapping his chest.

"Don't even try to be comforting," Iris grumbled.

"Technically, I am your emotional support bird. Emotionally, I am struggling."

"What are you struggling about?"

"I was having dreams of penthouse apartments or brownstones with some order-in sushi and eighteen seasons of *The Real Lives of Desperate Minotaurs*."

"I fully support you going out and getting that dream life for yourself."

"And leave you all alone? The woman who gave me life?"

"I gave you a voice," Iris clarified.

"Same thing! Do you think I enjoyed squawking and grunting? Like some . . . some animal?"

Iris smiled down at her old friend. "I'm sorry to destroy your dream. If it makes you feel any better, I am *going* to suffer for it."

"A platter of anchovies would make me feel better."

"You got it. If I'm not grounded like a child, that is."

By the time she and Monty made it back to the hotel, gathered her things, and drove back to the beach, Iris had rehearsed a long speech to give her mother. Then revised it half a dozen times.

"You're going to need to go and face the music eventually," Monty said as the two of them sat on the sandbar, watching the sun lower down on the horizon, casting pink and purple slashes across the sky.

"Yeah," Iris said, flapping her tail in the water. "I guess, so long as it isn't the singing eels, I can deal."

She sucked in a deep breath and slipped further into the water. For the first time in her life, all she felt was dread as the water enveloped her.

"I'll see you tomorrow, if I can get away," she called to Monty.

She dipped under the surface, humming to herself as she swam slowly back down to the seafloor.

The subtle headshake from the gate guard was all the evidence she needed that the word had already gotten back to her mother.

It was time to face the consequences of her actions.

"Where is she?" Iris asked Juna as she swam past her sister. She chose to ignore the judgmental eyes.

"In her room."

If possible, Iris swam even slower as she neared her mother's quarters.

"Come in," Tatiana called before Iris could even lift her hand to knock.

Iris's brows knitted when she didn't hear any sharpness

in her mother's tone. But she pushed open the door and swam inside.

"Mother, I can—"

"That arrived for you," Tatiana said. She waved her hand toward the table where her jewelry collection was set.

Iris moved closer, brows knitting when her gaze landed on it.

"What is this?"

"A book."

"A book? Like . . . a land book?"

She'd come across many a land book in her time—ones that had likely been left by careless humans on the beach and had been swept away in the tide. But by the time they made it to the seafloor, there was nothing left but a soggy clump of paper.

"Yes," Tatiana said, head tilted as she watched her daughter's eyes brighten.

"But how?"

"My best guess is it has been spelled to survive underwater."

Her hands shot out, grabbing the tome with eager hands. She ran her fingers over the cover, amazed at the smooth feel of it.

The cover shimmered faintly beneath her touch, humming with subtle enchantment. It was a leather-like material, not fish leather, nor kelp-pressed pulp. It was something foreign. Something from the land.

Her fingers trembled as she flipped it open. The pages were bone-pale and unmarred, each line of text as crisp and perfect as the day it had been printed.

It smelled different than sea books too. Faintly metallic,

with just a subtle hint of candle smoke, from whomever had spelled it to survive the deep.

Iris swallowed hard.

Maybe it was a PR stunt. Maybe it wasn't. But the book was here, it was real, it was new, and it was personal.

Iris couldn't remember the last time someone had given her something that wasn't about education or duties.

"I didn't know that was possible," she said, looking up at her mother.

"Nor did I. But you know who did?"

"Who?"

"Your fiancé."

Fiancé?

"Finn? Finn sent this?"

Why would he do that after what she'd done? Was it some sort of apology?

"He did. Even after you dumped a drink on his head."

"Mother, I—"

"I don't want to hear your excuses, Iris. You had one job to do: to represent not only this family but also all of your people by being a kind and gracious brunch date. You failed even the most basic task set forth at your feet. You have embarrassed me, your sisters, this kingdom, and all of our kind. I am ashamed to have not only a daughter but also a princess to this great kingdom behaving so atrociously. Your behavior today was selfish. You may not have *meant* harm, but intent does not outweigh perception. Perception is everything in politics, and today, you projected pure chaos."

Each word was a piercing sensation to Iris's chest.

Her mother was right. She'd been selfish in her actions, thinking only of her own unhappiness, not the image she'd been projecting of all merfolk. She hadn't even taken a sip of that lovely drink the server had prepared for her.

"I wouldn't have blamed Mr. Westrock if he'd held a press conference explaining your reckless and rude behavior. But no, instead, he visited a bookstore, found a witch to enchant a book, then had it sent here for you. His graciousness seems boundless."

Graciousness, Iris wanted to scoff. It was probably some carefully curated public relations move.

"I'm afraid your behavior is forcing my hand."

"What do you mean?"

"Tomorrow, you will take your belongings, pack them in a suitcase, and go back to the surface."

"My belongings? Why?"

"Because you are moving in with your fiancé."

"What? Mother, I—"

"This is not up for discussion. You should count yourself lucky that Mr. Westrock still wishes to marry you. Because you would not have liked your punishment if this arrangement had fallen through."

"But—"

"If you insist upon taking that insufferable pelican with you, I suggest you teach him proper restaurant etiquette. Now go. I am quite tired from all of the stress today."

"Mother—"

"Iris, darling, I believe you have tried my patience enough for one day. Go. Take your book. Reflect upon the kind of man who would give you a gift after such blatant disrespect. Maybe you will conclude what I have known all along—Finn Westrock will be a considerate and forgiving husband for you. Now go. I need to rest. I have a council meeting in the morning."

Considerate and forgiving.

Those were not exactly the qualities Iris envisioned for a life partner.

She wanted heat and passion.

She wanted a love that scalded and soothed in equal turns.

But she was going to get consideration and forgiveness.

Something she shouldn't need just for her very nature and personality.

Her heart felt as fragile as a seashell picked up by a careless hand—beautiful but bound to be broken.

Having no choice, Iris took her book and swam down the hall toward her own room.

Her mind was consumed with all she was losing: her home, her friends, her family, her beloved ocean, her *tail*. Even the annoying singing eels. And the squid ink that would stain her skin for weeks.

Still, she couldn't seem to stop herself from turning her attention back to the book Finn had gifted her. Though she suspected Finn himself had nothing to do with it. The man didn't appear to have a singular, unique thought. It was more likely a peace offer from his campaign manager.

Regardless, it had been the perfect gift for her.

There were only fifty fiction books in the royal library. Iris had read each of them a hundred times, getting swept away in intrigue and romance. There was something comforting about revisiting already loved characters. But it had been many years since she'd gotten a chance to fall in love with new ones.

So, despite knowing she should be spending her night packing, mourning, and trying to come to terms with her future, she opened the cover and got lost in a new book.

Iris

"What is that?" Iris asked as she surfaced at the sandbar, eyeing the absurdly large suitcase Monty was perched on.

"My belongings."

"But why?" Iris asked, hefting her own luggage onto the sand.

"Because I'm coming with you, of course."

"So, you heard."

"Shelly was sitting on a rock this morning, ranting and raving about your move and how ungrateful you are."

"Ungrateful," Iris scoffed. She pulled herself up onto the sandbar. She'd been up all night reading, getting swept away by a grand romance between a princess and the knight from an enemy kingdom. Then she'd spent the morning swimming, trying to soak up as much of the ocean and the things she loved in it while she still could.

When she couldn't stall any longer, she grabbed her

luggage and left her home. She hadn't said a single goodbye, since her mother was in a meeting, Shelly was off sulking, and Juna was MIA—likely too angry with her sister to offer a proper goodbye.

Perhaps that was for the best. If she had to look in their eyes, knowing she might never live under the same roof as them again, would not be able to sneak into their rooms at night to gossip, to share in their inside jokes anymore . . .

Yes, better not to have to face her sisters. She wasn't sure she would be able to leave if they were there. And she was in enough trouble already.

"Stop gloating," Iris grumbled, brushing wet hair from her face.

"I prefer to look on the bright side of life. And on the bright side, I am going to be living in the lap of luxury. Do you think your betrothed has the silver spoons I'm always hearing about?"

"I'm not going to be a fun companion today," Iris warned him.

"You'll come around. There are so many things to love about city life."

He launched into a list of those things, but Iris was distracted, watching her tail and scales shimmer once—twice—before they vanished completely.

Before she was bare, she slipped into the same shorts and shirt from the day before.

"Hmm," Monty said, giving her a disapproving look.

"What? I'm . . . covered."

"Did your mother happen to send you with a clothing budget?"

"Oh," Iris said, brows furrowing.

She'd never had to consider clothing before. But even in her books, the characters spent a lot of time thinking about and discussing clothing. Iris couldn't figure out what was wrong with the bodies everyone was born with, though. Why they felt the need to cover up so fully at all.

"I know what you're thinking, but you have to wear clothes. Land folk get real weird if they see a nipple in the daylight. Instant pearl-clutching scandal. I mean, flash a fin, fine. Flash a boob? The mayor resigns, the stock market crashes, and someone's grandma writes a furious letter to Congress.

"Besides, if that naked body is yours, they'll arrest you, worship you, or propose. Possibly all three."

At Iris's eye roll, he flapped his wings.

"You don't get it. You're a mermaid. You're not just pretty; you're ethereal. You've got the flowing hair, the mythical glow, the skin shimmer. Beauty influencers would pay a fortune for that shimmer, by the way. But what do you think the land folk would do when a living fantasy saunters around the city with no pants on? They'll crash their cars. They'll start new religions. And don't get me started on the poetry—it'll be terrible. Odes. Limericks. Maybe a few tragic musicals." Monty cringed. "You have to put on clothing. For the good of all mankind."

"Okay, okay," Iris said with a small smile. "I will wear clothing. But why can't I just wear this?"

"It hasn't been washed."

"Washed?"

"Laundered. In a machine that swooshes the clothes around with soap. Also, if you wear the same thing every day, they'll start whispering. They'll assume you're unwell, that you've given up; they'll crowdfund money to buy you a new wardrobe. And it'll be full of beige. Beige!" Monty shuddered at the thought.

"Well, Triton forbid that," she teased.

"That's what I'm saying. Besides, darling, you are not just normal land folk now. You are going to be political royalty. There will be entire gossip columns and 'hot or not' social media posts about what you wear."

Iris let out a sigh, already exhausted just at the thought.

"Let's get going before I change my mind and run away to live as a rogue mermaid off the coast of Antarctica with the penguins."

"I don't know why you're so grumpy," Monty declared after they caught their ride into the city. "I mean, doesn't this just give you many more opportunities to sabotage your engagement with Mr. Tall Dark and Press-Conference-Ready?"

She hadn't considered that.

She thought that if Finn wasn't completely turned off by being splashed with a huge cup of salt water, nothing she could do would get him to change his mind. But actually *living* with him would give her many unique opportunities to make him regret the day he agreed to the arrangement.

"You know what, you're right," Iris agreed. "It's not over."

It wouldn't be over until she was free to choose her own future once again. Or, at the very least, to choose a compatible merman who would allow her to continue to live in her beloved ocean.

"This is it," Maria, who seemed to be some sort of employee of her mother's, declared as she parked outside of a towering white and gleaming glass building. "Your mother wanted me to give you this." Maria passed a small bag between the seats. "And to advise you to use it wisely."

Before Iris could even think to do so herself, Monty was unzipping the bag and letting out a whistle.

"What is it?" she asked, looking at all the green and white sheets of paper.

"Luxury, darling, that is pure luxury."

He didn't elaborate, just slung the bag across his chest, then opened his door to exit.

"Thanks, Maria," Iris said before exiting.

Monty stood on the sidewalk, gaze angled up at the building.

"I suppose it will do," he said. "I do hope he has the penthouse, though. I had my heart set on a penthouse."

If the people passing on the street thought a talking pelican was an odd occurrence, they made no show of it, just brushing past them as if they weren't even there. Except, of course, for a few men who stopped and stared.

"It's positively nauseating, isn't it?" another voice asked.

Turning, Iris saw a woman standing to her side. She was tall, almost statuesque, with rich, warm brown skin, and long deep green hair.

There was something . . . not quite human about her—an otherness in her posture, in the steady, grounded way she blinked.

"What?"

"All that glass and stone," the woman declared, shivering. "Though, it doesn't make me quite as woozy as all this concrete," she said, rubbing the soles of her shoes against the sidewalk. "You're a mermaid, aren't you?"

"Yes," Iris said. She was pleased that even out of the water, surface people could still see her for what she was.

It made her feel a little more herself in this big, strange new world. "Iris," she introduced herself.

"Willow," the woman introduced herself, then added, "dryad."

"A dryad? In the city?"

Dryads were tree fae. They typically lived in dense forests where they were free to live both inside and outside of their trees.

Iris had only ever seen a handful of trees in her life, usually off in the distance when she surfaced near a seaside town. She had a hard time imagining an entire forest of them.

"I've always lived here," Willow told her. "I was rooted right there." She gestured to the space where Finn's building now stood.

"Wait . . . did they . . . did they cut down your tree? To build . . . that?"

"They did."

Iris's stomach twisted. She could only imagine what it would feel like to have a bit of your soul bulldozed for someone else's skyline.

"How are you still alive?" Monty piped up.

"Monty!" Iris scolded.

"It's a valid question," Willow said. "Just as they were cutting it down, a seed capsule flew loose. I found it, saved it, and planted it in the small courtyard in the back of the building. Do you need to get in the building?" she asked, shifting a netted bag full of fruits onto her shoulder.

"We're moving in," Monty declared, puffing out his chest. "With Finn Westrock."

"Oh, Finn! He's a nice guy," Willow said.

A nice guy? Iris just barely resisted the urge to snort at

that declaration. Maybe surface people and merfolk had different definitions of 'nice.'

Willow produced a small oblong piece of plastic as she walked toward the door, then held it up toward a screen near the door.

"Keyless entry," Monty said, nodding. "Fancy. We're moving up in the world!"

While Iris didn't agree with his sentiment, she had to admit that there was something beautiful about the interior of the building. In its strange, straight lines, and in all of its stone, tile, and glass. Nothing in the ocean was so uniform. Things grew wild and often shapeless there. And even she could appreciate the beauty of something the complete opposite.

"Are you . . . related to Finn?" Willow asked as they moved inside a small square box. As the doors slid closed, Iris felt like a hand had closed around her throat, squeezing tighter with each heartbeat.

"She's his fiancée. Ah, which floor are we going to?" Monty asked as he studied the panel of numbers.

Willow offered him a knowing look as she pressed her finger into the one at the very top, set apart from the others by location, but also because it was a letter, not a number.

P.

"Penthouse! I knew it! I just *knew* I was meant for the high life."

Willow shot Iris a smile as she shook her head at the pelican's materialistic glee.

"I didn't realize Finn was engaged."

"Oh, it's all new. Very hush-hush," Monty explained. "There will be a whole press conference and such about it.

Montague Featherington," Monty said, offering his wing. "Head of Surface Affairs."

Willow awkwardly took the bird's wing and gave it a small shake.

"That sounds like a very important title."

"Indeed," Monty agreed. Iris didn't think it was possible for his head—or massive beak—to get any higher than it was right then.

"Well, this is me. It was so nice to meet you, Iris. Mr. Featherington."

Monty missed Willow's smirk toward Iris.

"You too, Willow."

"If you need anything, that's me right there in 5B. But you will usually find me on the roof or in the courtyard."

Before Iris could say anything else, the doors slid closed, and they continued their ascent toward the penthouse.

Beside her, Monty seemed to be trying to stretch himself taller with each floor they moved past.

The floor numbers blinked higher. Iris swayed slightly, clutching the wall like the box might tilt sideways.

Until, finally, the elevator dinged, and the doors slid open.

"Welcome to our new life!" Monty cheered, strutting out of the elevator car, pulling his rolling suitcase behind him. "Look at this! They're pulling out all the stops!"

Iris glanced over to where a long, rolling rack was sitting in the hallway beside a door. Dozens of articles of clothing hung there. There were intriguing silhouettes and strange fabrics that made Iris want to reach out and run her fingers over.

"Only two beige outfits. These guys know what they're doing." Monty had a wing raised, rifling through the material. "Huh. Not a single thing for me. That's . . . disappointing."

"To be fair, I don't think Finn could know you were coming."

"That certainly makes more sense than forgetting about me," Monty decided.

Before either of them could knock on the door, it flew open.

"There you are," the man declared, gaze tracking over Iris in a way that made her squirm. It wasn't lecherous but clinical. "Yes, I think you will do nicely."

"Monty Featherington," Monty said, stepping in front of Iris to offer the man his wing.

The man, unruffled, took Monty's wing. "Mr. Featherington, good to meet you. Henry Hadden. I'm Finn's campaign manager."

So this was the man responsible for Finn Westrock.

He was less manicured than Iris had imagined. His hair was just a bit longer than seemed fashionable among the humans, and he had a strong shadow of a beard.

"I'm Iris's Head of Surface Affairs," Monty declared. He was really leaning into his fictional role.

Iris resisted the urge to point out that he'd made up the title himself.

"Of course. Please come in. We are heavily in preparation mode. May I?"

He didn't wait for her answer, though, taking her bag and bringing it into the apartment.

"Preparation for what?" she asked, following behind.

Iris had no frame of reference for what a penthouse would look like, but she certainly hadn't expected for all the windows to go from the floor to the ceiling, giving panoramic views of the city as well as the water of the bay just beyond. But it looked more like a backdrop than something real, something alive, something that sang in her veins.

The sprawling space was sun-soaked, lighting every corner of the very bland decor.

She knew it was wrong to judge too harshly, given that Finn came from a very different culture than her own. But she couldn't help but long for the bright colors of the sea—the pinks, yellows, and purples of the coral, and the vivid yellows and blues of the schooling fish.

Everything in Finn's home was gray. Not just the paint, but the mood. Even the couch looked like it might sigh when you sat on it.

There were no curves. No motion. Just edges. Sharp corners. Soulless.

Iris wandered toward one of the enormous windows, placing her palm against the glass. Outside, she could see the bay glimmering in the distance. But she couldn't *feel* it anymore. The barrier had dulled it. Separated it from her.

It was beautifully displayed. But locked behind something clear and cold.

Like her.

"Oh, this will do," Monty declared, waddling into the apartment. "This will do just fine. Where are our rooms?"

"Uh, about that," Henry said, reaching up to rub the back of his neck. "We were only expecting Iris. Finn only has one bedroom."

One bed?

Of course, there was only one bed.

The surface world had a sick sense of humor.

"But Finn does have a small office we can outfit for you, Mr. Featherington."

"I suppose that will do."

"Wait," Iris said, brows pinching. "If there's only one bed, and Monty gets the office, where am I sleeping?"

"In the primary bedroom, of course."

"Where is Finn sleeping?"

"In the same bedroom."

"Where is Finn? Can I speak to him?"

She didn't *want* to speak to him, not really. But his absence rankled regardless.

He'd invited her to move into his home—technically dragged her into it by political contract—and he couldn't even be bothered to be around to answer her questions?

Part of her wanted to be angry. The other part . . . wasn't sure if it was disappointment or relief.

Maybe both.

"Finn is at a meeting with the werewolf construction workers' union. He will be home later."

Iris's gaze moved around the space, her eyes landing on the enormous L-shaped couch. She supposed that would do. Or she could insist on sleeping in Monty's room. Or, if she got her way, in the bathtub. She had to pick her battles.

"You mentioned preparations," she said, looking at Henry. "What are we preparing for?"

"To turn you into a proper political wife."

Iris didn't know whether to laugh or bolt back to the sea.

Finn

Finn was having a hard time concentrating on what was a very important meeting. If there was one demographic you wanted to get to back you on a political campaign, it was the unions.

Yet all he could focus on was if Iris had gotten his gift, if she was going to come and move in with him like her mother's spokesperson claimed.

He'd realized his mistake the second the salt water cascaded down his head.

Finn had been regurgitating talking points that he and Henry had discussed in private in the cold, clinical way they always talked about optics.

He hadn't taken Iris's feelings into account.

When he'd run back the conversation in his mind, he'd seen all the parts that she may have found insulting.

The regret had been instantaneous.

Henry had been quick to go into crisis mode when he'd

found out, insisting that they had to make it right, to salvage the situation.

"There's simply no time to try to find another wife for you. We have to fix this. Or we have to accept that you're going to lose this election."

Losing was not an option.

So, Finn took the one thing he knew about Iris—the fact that she liked to read—and came up with a plan. From what he understood about mermaid books, they were few and far between and printed on kelp paper.

One trip to a local witch-owned bookstore later, he had his peace offering to hand off to Tatiana's spokeswoman, Maria, to bring to Iris with his message that he still wished to move forward with the contract.

Then all he could do was hope for the best.

Henry seemed convinced that the plan would move through. Enough that he'd been in planning mode all morning: ordering wardrobe selections, making plans for Iris at the salon, setting up etiquette classes, and preparing his plans for rigorous media training.

"I agree," Finn said after the union leader had spoken. Truth be told, he had only caught every other word. He'd been too busy remembering the look of hurt and outrage on Iris's face just before she dropped her drink over his head.

There was a bit more back-and-forth before the meeting was finally over. And, for once, Finn had no idea if he'd secured their vote or not. What's more, he didn't particularly care.

All he wanted was to get back to his apartment to see if Iris had responded to his gift.

Not because, as Henry feared, it was their only shot at securing the mayoral vote. But because he genuinely felt remorse and regret for upsetting a woman who did nothing wrong except agree to marry him. Likely with immense pressure from her mother or the mercouncil.

They were both cogs in a political machine.

He often wished his own feelings could be a factor in his life and career, so the least he could do for Iris was to be mindful of hers. Especially seeing as they were in his world, not hers. She had to be feeling unsure and vulnerable. Yet all he'd offered her so far were polls and optics.

Finn was sure they could still provide Iris the proper training while taking her comfort into account.

That thought was what had him rushing across town, worried that Iris might have shown up and been subjected to Henry at his most gung-ho—overwhelming her with charts and demographics and the thousand and one things he was going to put on her schedule for the coming weeks.

When he got to his apartment, there were several voices inside, making him sigh as he pushed open the door.

Sure enough, there was Henry in the living room with Iris, the two of them engaged in some sort of argument as she attempted to rip a book back out of Henry's hands.

"It's just a book," Henry insisted.

"It's *my* book. And I'm tired of it falling on the floor because you think I walk funny."

"Funny, I could work with. You're walking like it's some sort of . . . mating ritual."

"Mating ritual?" Iris sputtered. "I'm a *mermaid*. Everything about us is very . . . fluid."

"Fluid is fine. Sensual is not going to work with our voting demographics."

"I'm kind of sick of hearing about demographics and polls and—"

"That's the whole point of all of—"

"What's going on here?" Finn asked, closing the door behind him as he moved inside.

Iris looked over, her shoulders slipping from up by her ears to a more relaxed posture. But she took advantage of Henry's surprise and yanked the book out of his hands. She hugged it to her chest, and Finn couldn't help but feel a warm sensation spread across his chest when he saw the cover. It was the book he'd gotten spelled for her.

"Finn. Good. We are trying to do some training, but your fiancée here is being—"

"Call me 'difficult' one more time," Iris grumbled.

"Now, now, we're all getting our feathers out of place," another voice said, tone calming.

Turning, Finn saw a large bird standing on his kitchen island.

"Is that . . . is that the pelican from the restaurant?"

"That reminds me," the bird said, "I need to give them a scathing review. Can I borrow someone's phone?"

"Since when do you know how to use a phone?" Iris asked. Finn guessed that *she* didn't even know how to use one.

"Not all of us have been living under a rock—or under the ocean," the bird told her. "Of course, I know how to use a phone. You know, in theory."

"Finn, this is Mr. Montague Featherington. He is Iris's Head of Surface Affairs." The pitch of Henry's voice and slight tug at his lips told Finn that they shouldn't take the bird's position too seriously. "He will be staying in your office."

"Of course. I'm happy to have you, Mr. Featherington."

"You can call him Monty. He's being pretentious." Iris shot a fond smile toward the pelican.

"Am I being pretentious, or am I simply committed to the gravitas of my role?"

"What, exactly, is that role, Monty?" she shot back. Her sea glass eyes were dancing.

"Well, I am your handler, of course. Your buffer. Your first line of defense against scandal, bad lighting, and subpar crab cakes. Speaking of, shouldn't we be breaking for lunch?"

"Of course. We can order anything you want," Finn said. His gaze slid around the apartment. "Henry . . ." he said, tone frustrated.

"What?" Henry asked, avoiding eye contact.

"Where is he?"

"Where's who? That hell-beast you call a companion?"

"A hell-beast?" Iris asked, stiffening.

"He's talking about my *cat*," Finn explained. "A cat he made me adopt, I might add."

"Pets soften your image. Adopted pets speak to the masses who worry about overcrowding in our shelters. The optics were all there. It's not *my* fault you picked the nastiest one of the bunch."

Finn had to admit that Checkers was a bit . . . spirited. And the animosity went both ways when it came to how Checkers felt about his campaign manager.

"Did you lock him in the bathroom again?"

"I'm not a monster. I locked him in the office."

"In *my* room?" Monty balked.

Finn just barely held back a laugh at that. Iris didn't bother.

"It wasn't your room when he locked the cat in there," Iris reminded him.

Finn opened the office door, and Checkers came barreling out, making a beeline for Henry in a flurry of calico rage.

"Hey, no," Henry scolded, jumping to get his legs away from the cat's claws. "This is designer, you monster."

"You brought this upon yourself," Finn told him. "I hope you're not allergic," he said to Iris, feeling another pang of guilt for not knowing more about her. Even if their arrangement wasn't a love match, he should at least know about any allergies or other medical conditions she might be dealing with.

"I hope he likes me more than he likes Henry. Though, there were several times today that I wanted to claw at him too, so I get his reaction."

"Ha ha," Henry said as Iris shot him a saccharine smile.

Checkers, seeing Monty, leapt up onto the island, trying to decide what he thought of the giant bird.

"Hello to you, sir," Monty greeted him. "Do you speak?"

"No, he's just a normal cat," Henry told him. "Thankfully. Can you imagine what he would have to say?"

"Monty!" Iris hissed.

Finn looked back to find the pelican attempting to see if Checkers would fit in his beak.

"I wasn't *really* going to eat him," Monty said with a fluff of his chest feathers.

No one in the room seemed overly convinced of that fact.

"Maybe we should order some food," Finn offered.

"Yeah, that might be a good idea," Iris agreed.

As he reached for his phone, he caught Iris sending the pelican a stern look.

"Well, I'll get going. I have a lot to set up."

"I told you I'm not getting my toes snipped."

"Toes snipped?" Finn asked.

"It was a whole thing," Henry said, sighing.

"I'm not deforming myself because you don't like my feet."

"Anyway," Henry went on. "I have to set up Iris's spa treatments, her etiquette classes, and get the ball rolling on the wedding plans. We are cutting things dangerously close. You and me, tomorrow, nine."

"What's tomorrow at nine?" Iris asked.

"The gym. He also wants to change *my* looks," Finn told her.

"Just your calves. Shorts season is coming. We can't have you caught on the golf course with subpar calves."

"I don't understand," Iris said. "I thought you managed his campaign, not his appearance."

"They are one and the same. Welcome to politics," Henry said.

With another reminder of the next day's itinerary, he was off.

Finn led him to the door, and when he came back, he heard Iris hiss, "Triton's beard, Monty, what is *wrong* with you?"

When he rounded the corner, he saw her lifting his cat into her arms and *away* from the pelican, who had a bit of fur clinging to his beak.

"I'm impressed. He won't even let me pick him up."

Iris said nothing to that as she sat down on the sectional, trying to put the cat to her side, but he climbed back onto her lap and immediately started to purr.

"He's vibrating. Is that a good thing?"

"That's a very good thing. He likes you. And that," he said as the cat started to press his paws into her thigh, "is called making biscuits. I only know that from the extensive cat research I had to do when Henry made me take him home, not because he's ever done it to me."

"Henry is . . . a lot. And that is coming from someone with an older sister who is taking her future on the throne with a grave sort of determination and thinks everything I say or do is embarrassing or inappropriate."

"Did he insult you?" Finn asked. He was surprised by the way his stomach boiled at the idea.

"Oh, only about everything about me," she said, sighing. "I'm too fluid. My voice is too wishy-washy. My toes are weird. I don't know what talk shows, town halls, or diners are . . ."

"Your voice is not wishy-washy. It's a little sing-song, but in a charming way. I think your gait is like night and day from yesterday. Talk shows, town halls, and diners are on his mind because they're on my itinerary in the coming weeks and months. But there is plenty of time to learn about them. As for your feet," he said, moving to sit on the coffee table in front of her. "May I?" he asked, gesturing to her feet.

She offered him a shrug, so he reached down to pull one foot onto his leg.

"Wow. Your toenails are naturally pink?" he asked, looking at the shimmery nails.

"That is something Henry liked. He said it would save a lot of time on pedicures. Whatever those are."

"Then what's the problem?" She had perfectly nice feet. Petite, even.

Iris sighed and spread her toes.

"Oh," Finn said, surprised. There, between each of her toes, was a small amount of light, pearlescent webbing.

He couldn't stop his thumb from moving out, teasing across the webbing, finding it warm and smooth.

A gasp escaped Iris, making his gaze shoot up.

Was that surprise?

Was she ticklish?

Or was it something else entirely?

He knew he needed to keep his hands to himself. He didn't want to overstep a line. Especially when he didn't know how willing a participant she was in this arrangement yet.

Yet, there was no stopping himself from letting his finger do one more innocent swipe.

Iris stiffened as she sucked in her breath.

Watching her face, he saw the furrowed brows of confusion, but the hooded lids of desire.

"Are your land legs new to you?" he asked, his head tipped to the side.

"Yes. Yesterday was the first time I've ever really used them."

And then there was Henry, forcing her to walk around his apartment because he didn't like that she had a 'fluid' walk. He knew his campaign manager well enough to know that when he said 'fluid' what he truly meant was 'sexual.'

But she was a mermaid.

She couldn't help that.

It would be like being frustrated with a vampire for having a menacing air about them.

"Are they killing you?" Finn asked, running both thumbs up the center of her foot.

The moan that she let out was giving his body all sorts of ideas that most men thought about their fiancées, but he couldn't let himself think of his. At least not as things stood right then between them.

"I don't understand," Iris said, her voice sweeter than before. He couldn't help but wonder if that was what pleasure did to her, what she might sound like if his hands were drifting up her thighs, if his face was turned into her neck, breathing in that citrus salt scent to her skin . . .

"Don't understand what?" he asked, hearing the husky edge to his own voice and needing to cough to cover it.

"My tail never hurt," Iris said. "Why do land feet hurt?"

"I would say it's because they're new, but my feet can hurt me too. I don't have a good answer for that. Though, I suspect shoes have something to do with it."

Iris relaxed back against the couch, her eyes drifting closed as his thumbs pressed into her arch. A little moan escaped her that had desire pinging off his nerve endings.

"Feel good?" he asked, though he already had his answer.

"Yes," Iris said, her voice even more hypnotic with her pleasure.

"So . . . did we just forget about the food, or . . ." Monty's voice broke in.

A snorting laugh escaped Iris as her eyelids fluttered open.

"You have talked about nothing but food all day."

"You're not excited because you don't know what land restaurants have to offer."

"I know, I know. Seafood buffets."

"Not only that. Pizza. Pasta. *Soft pretzels*."

"Sounds like I need to order a little bit of everything for you to try," Finn said as he reached for Iris's other foot.

Monty counted on his flight feathers all of the dishes he wanted to try as Finn pressed his thumbs into Iris's other arch.

She melted into the touch—and the couch—her back arching, her eyelids drifting closed.

He took advantage of her distraction, allowing himself to study her stunning face. Even in stillness, she shimmered with the kind of magic that artists could spend lifetimes trying to capture. She was luminous in a way that made him feel suddenly dim, but, God, he would never want to dull her shine.

He was so entranced by the curve of her mouth—and all the images it conjured up in his mind—that he hadn't noticed her eyes had opened again until he was caught looking at her, the hunger, no doubt, plain on his face.

He'd been expecting immediate discomfort, if not outright disgust, but Iris's head tipped to the side, watching him with those sea glass eyes—their depths unreadable.

"Don't mind me," Monty interrupted, flopping onto his side with a long, pained groan. "I'll just nibble my own wing while you rub toes and forget your loyal, underfed companion."

"I guess we need to feed him," Finn declared, giving both of Iris's feet a gentle squeeze.

"You'll be fishing Checkers out of his beak if you don't," Iris agreed, pulling her legs off his lap.

The moment, it seemed, was over.

There was no accounting for the churning disappointment in Finn's chest as he started to take the order for Iris and Monty before listening to the bird's list of demands for his bedroom. It included Egyptian cotton sheets, a sound machine, and a TV with every subscription channel available. Apparently, he had a lot of catching up to do on his 'stories.'

Iris was mostly silent through the whole process, save for the occasional question about an item Monty was asking for.

She was a lot more sheltered than he—and he ventured, Henry—had realized. Finn had been operating under the assumption that mermaidian royalty would have had many occasions to leave the ocean and experience the surface.

That was clearly not the case.

Monty had needed to demonstrate to her how to use a fork to eat her food. What a dishwasher was for. How the television worked.

Finn let the pelican take the lead, not wanting it to seem like he was condescending to Iris. She had a poor enough impression of him since brunch; he was going to attempt to win back her favor.

Because despite the arrangement being only on paper, Finn couldn't help but hope for it to turn into something real. Sure, he would do what needed to be done for his career. That said, who didn't want to fall in love with their partner? To have someone to share all the highs and lows with? To lean on? To create warm memories with? Maybe, if he was lucky, to build a family with?

By the time he'd gotten out of the shower later that night, he'd found Monty asleep, perched on the end of his desk in the office. Iris passed out on the sectional. He wasn't prepared for the rush of warmth that flooded his chest, this strange, bone-deep *rightness* he felt filling him at seeing her there, in his home like she belonged.

"That's not gonna work," he murmured to Checkers,

who was keeping watch over his new favorite person from the back of the couch.

Finn slid his arms under her slowly, not wanting to disturb the first moment of peace she'd known all day.

She jolted hard as he lifted her up, but he just pulled her more tightly to his chest. "You're okay," he murmured. "I've got you."

As he walked, she seemed to go more and more lax against him, likely from a lifetime of the comfort of currents in her sleep. He couldn't help but wonder if her sleepy mind confused his arms with those same currents, like something safe and steady.

He placed her gently down on his bed, pulling the covers up over her body. He was incapable of fighting the urge to swipe her soft pink hair from her pretty face.

But he didn't let himself linger; he just gathered his pillow and then went to sleep in the living room.

Where he drifted off with the scent of her in the cushions and all over him, giving him vivid, steamy dreams he had no right conjuring up for a woman who clearly wanted nothing to do with him.

He wanted to believe that could change.

Not because of polls or favorability ratings.

But because every time she let her guard down—even a little—it cracked something open in him too.

And he didn't want to close it again.

Iris

Iris woke up slowly, then all at once, jolting upright in an unfamiliar bed in a strange room, all of it washed in that aged driftwood smell that clung to Finn like a second skin.

How had she gotten in his bed?

For one horrified moment, she worried she might have followed her desire right into his room. She felt a wave of relief when she realized she was still fully dressed, tragically.

Sure, some part of her was A-okay with the idea of getting naked and glandular with Finn. Especially after that delicious foot massage and the way such a chaste touch somehow managed to spark little fires of need to break out through her body. She was a mermaid, after all. They were sensual creatures. She enjoyed getting warm and steamy with a partner as much as the next person.

The other part of her, though, that still found Finn—even after hours in his company—stuffy and stiff, constantly bringing the conversation back to politics and surface-level observations, wanted nothing to do with some base, biological response to a man she was being forced to marry.

"That's enough of that," she mumbled to herself as she climbed out of bed, feeling aches in her land legs she hadn't anticipated. She went into the bathroom to brush out her hair before changing into one of the outfits Henry had left for her—long, flowing pale blue pants in a material he'd called 'linen' and a tight, white, silky top he'd called a camisole, though she couldn't quite remember what else he'd said about that particular garment.

There was a rich, thick scent in the air as she made her way into the common area.

"What is that?" she asked, sniffing the air.

"That, my sweet sea spawn, is ground-bean juice," Monty declared, producing two mugs (gray, of course, like everything in Finn's home). "The humans call it 'coffee,' and I find it is best served with a lot of cream and sugar. Enjoy."

She took the mug, the heat teasing her fingers, making a shiver rack her system. "Why is it so cold in here?"

"That is what the human women call Women's Winter."

"Women's Winter?"

"That's when the temperatures outside skyrocket, so the men set the internal temperatures to frigid. And the women freeze."

She certainly felt like she was freezing. Little bumps had pebbled up all over her skin.

"Monty, do you have any idea how I wound up in Finn's bed?"

"Seeing as he was asleep in the living room this morning when I came out to look for Check—a snack . . ." the pelican caught himself ". . . I would assume he did the thing every swoon-worthy romantic lead would do. He carried you to bed."

She went ahead and ignored the way her chest warmed, and her belly swooped at the idea of that.

Too many romance novels, giving her subconscious all sorts of silly ideas.

"I can't believe I have to tell you this again, but you can't *eat* Finn's cat."

"I haven't touched him," Monty declared, but the way the cat hissed at the pelican when he looked over told Iris all she needed to know.

"Didn't you eat enough last night?" she asked. Her mind wandered back to all those foreign meals and the pleasant explosion of strange new tastes and textures across her tongue. She'd particularly enjoyed the pizza and fries, even if Monty declared they were 'very bad' for them.

"Apparently not," another voice said as the apartment door closed. "Because he had me order break—"

Finn broke off with a choked sound as he came into the kitchen and his gaze landed on her.

His whole body language had changed.

He'd gone from uncharacteristically relaxed to ramrod straight, his shoulders spread, chest broad, and his pupils blown wide in a blink.

Her own gaze moved down, confused by his reaction.

That was when she remembered what Henry had said about the camisole. That they were for being worn *under* other tops. To 'protect her modesty.'

At the time, she hadn't understood his meaning. But in the freezing apartment, her nipples had hardened into points that pressed against the tight material.

Her gaze flicked back to Finn, finding his lips slightly parted, his breath coming quick and shallow.

When she took a breath, making her breasts press even harder against the material, an almost pained sound escaped him.

For a moment, she was helpless but to follow the urge to track her eyes down his body as well.

Gone was his stuffy suit. In its place was a white T-shirt that hugged his toned body and showed off surprisingly strong arms. His pants were different, too. They were a flowing gray material that showed off his outlines.

One outline in particular.

Surprised by the tightening of need in her core, her gaze shot back up to his face just a second before he forced his to rise as well.

"Iris, my sweet, innocent, adorably naive little mergirl," Monty—who'd likely witnessed the entire encounter with his sharp eye for details—started. "Remember how we discussed needing another layer of clothing? I'm partial to a flowing evening gown, but I suppose a sweater would suffice."

"Oh, right. Yes, he did . . . Henry mentioned that," Iris said. She was suddenly too aware of her own body, finding herself almost . . . uncomfortable with it. That was a first. And the swirling sensation in her stomach was not a welcome one. "I forgot. I, uh, I will change . . ."

"Wait," Finn said. His voice was choked, making him clear his throat before continuing. "No," he said, shaking his head. "Don't change. This is your home now too. You should be in whatever makes you comfortable."

"For goodness' sake, Mister Mayor, sir," Monty said, eyes bugging. "Don't say that to her. What is most natural to a mermaid is near nothing at all."

"I'm not a fool, Monty," Iris said, feelings bruised. "I know humans have to wear clothing."

"Iris, don't worry about it. You look . . . fine."

Fine?

She looked . . . fine?

A word so aggressively neutral it might as well have come with a shrug. Was this some sort of political tactic? Downplay her, make her doubt her own beauty? To what end? What purpose would that serve his campaign? To make her more relatable?

Henry's words from the day before came back to her on a loop. He'd made constant comments about how she was, essentially, 'too much' and how they would need to 'tone her down' to cater to mass appeal.

Was that what Finn was attempting to do?

Because she had clearly seen the proof of his desire when he'd been looking at her.

So instead of celebrating her beauty that he clearly appreciated, he wanted to make her question it, if not outright start to think less of herself?

The hurt that had started to pool in her chest began to churn and flow until it became a tsunami of rage.

How dare he make her doubt herself?

Him with his salt-slick smile and his manufactured personality.

Iris dropped her mug back down on the counter with a loud click before turning and striding back to the bedroom, slamming the door for good measure, before walking to the closet to pull on one of the many tops Henry had provided.

Not because she felt suddenly less beautiful, but because she no longer wanted Finn to notice it. He had no right.

This was good, she told herself as she buttoned the

long-sleeved top. She needed the reminder of why this marriage could not go on.

It wasn't just the marriage she resented; it was the quiet reshaping of herself she hadn't even noticed happening.

A little less shimmer. A little less sway in her step. A little more fabric, a little more resilience.

She hadn't agreed to be edited.

And if she let this go, let them go on correcting her voice, her walk, her wardrobe, she wouldn't be Iris anymore.

She'd be some shimmering shell of a woman she didn't even recognize anymore.

She couldn't allow that to happen.

By the time she made it out of the bedroom, Finn was gone, and Monty was looming over the cat with his beak spread wide.

"Monty!"

The pelican snapped his beak closed, turning with a guilty look. "Pure instinct, I assure you," he said, lifting his head. "I am far too refined to actually eat a cat."

"I'm not so sure of that," she said. She scooped up the cat and hugged it to her chest. His little body started to vibrate, the sensation immediately calming her frayed nerves. "Where did *he* go?"

"Henry came to take him to the gym. But not before he left that for us," Monty said, gesturing toward a stack of little square cases of plastic.

"What are they?"

"Documentaries. But not the ones about the tragic backstories and scandals of the elite. Oh, no. They're documentaries about humans."

"Humans?"

"Henry said he was concerned about your lack of

understanding of how the world works. So he brought these for us to watch. I'm sure they won't be dry enough for us to choke on," he mumbled. His gaze took her in. "Yes. That is much more appropriate. Even if it won't make your fiancé pitch a tent like the cami did."

"What does that mean?" Iris asked.

Monty cleared his throat a bit as he waddled over to the kitchen.

"Well, um, let's see if the documentaries explain it," he said with an uncharacteristic amount of discomfort. "I will get them all queued up. You bring all the food over to the coffee table. It looks like we are having an inside day."

With that, the two of them sat down on the sectional with a spread of French toast, pancakes, hash browns, bacon, and eggs.

"Not fish eggs," Monty was quick to explain when Iris's lip curled. That was the one seafood she could never bring herself to eat—something about the texture making her gag—but her mother liked to have them served at all their royal meals. And, apparently, it wasn't becoming of a princess to try to discreetly spit the eggs into her hand and feed them to the snails that always hung under the table, hoping for scraps.

She didn't let herself remember the time she'd tried to hide the eggs in her seashell bra. Only to have them come floating out when she'd been dancing with an important selkie political figure.

Iris poked dubiously at the eggs. Even though they were yellow and fluffy and didn't resemble anything close to fish eggs.

On the screen, a generic-looking man with a hangover tummy and round glasses moved into frame in his tweed suit.

"Did you just swim to the surface? Crawl from the

depths of the Earth's core? Come screaming through another dimension? Welcome. This is *The Surface World: A History and Survival Guide*."

Iris's eyes went wide, surprised such a thing existed. But also a little comforted that she wasn't the only creature to feel much like a fish out of water—flopping around helplessly.

"In this series, we will examine the core behaviors of human beings: movement, communication, mating rituals, beliefs, and recreational habits . . ."

"Oh, B-roll," Monty declared as the narrator appeared beside two human beings, naked as the day they were born, standing there with blank expressions as the man used a stick to point to the various points of their bodies.

The lessons went on from there. Until Iris not only knew the proper words for all human organs but also why so many felt shame at their nakedness.

She could hardly believe what she was hearing. The parts that made humans who they were—breathing, pulsing, needing—were considered . . . inappropriate?

It was no wonder they covered everything up in so much stiff fabric and scrambled to look away at the sight of nipples.

It was all so fragile, so performative.

She missed the salt and softness of merlife. The honesty of bare skin. The comfort of the water to carry you away when things felt too heavy.

And everything on the surface felt like too much to carry on her back.

"But more on this topic in *Disc 7: The Laws and Lawlessness of Humans*," the narrator went on before launching into an explanation of strange human habits.

"I still don't understand the human obsession with

television," Iris declared a few hours later, flopping back against the cushions, bored out of her mind.

Even if she had learned a lot.

"That, my sea fairy, is because you have yet to experience," Monty declared, reaching for the remote control, "soap operas."

"Why would anyone write an opera about soap?"

To that, Monty did nothing but groan and declare she would see soon enough.

To his credit, she was deeply engrossed in the make-believe characters within two episodes, no matter how absurd their storylines.

At some point, Iris was vaguely aware of Henry and Finn in the apartment but decided to ignore their existence completely.

It wasn't until Finn declared to Henry that he was going to take a shower before they headed out that Iris declared, "Don't forget to thoroughly wash your penis."

You could have heard a pin drop in the silence that followed.

It took every bit of control Iris possessed not to burst out laughing.

"Wh . . . what?" Finn asked.

Looking at him right then, Iris was pretty sure she understood what Monty meant when he said someone's 'flabbers' were 'fully gasted.'

Iris schooled her face into a mask of wide-eyed innocence mixed with genuine concern.

"Monty and I have been learning all about your anatomy," she declared. "And it is apparently *very* important to keep your genitals clean. And if you happen to have a foresk—"

"I don't . . . I, um—" Finn fumbled.

Beside her, Monty was hiding his laughter by pretending to preen the feathers under his wing, his body shaking enough to vibrate through the couch.

"I think that's enough documentaries for today," Henry declared, walking over to gather the plastic cases. "Or, possibly, all time."

"Did I say something wrong?" Iris asked, pressing a hand to her heart, lips curving into a pout that would make her little sister proud.

The twin masks of shock on their faces were making it hard to keep her own features flat.

"Let's just . . . not bring up the cleaning of one's genitals from here on out," Henry said, tone tight.

Iris was pretty sure she could read the regret on his face as he reached up to yank the collar of his shirt off his neck.

"Understood," she agreed. "I was simply concerned for his well-being. I do so wish to have a healthy husband. Speaking of, how is your prostate?" she asked.

Finn looked about ready to faint right then and there—his skin pale, his brows pinched, and sweat starting to bead up on his brow and neck.

"I believe the procedure to check the health of it involves one inserting a finger—" she said, holding her pointer up then making a jabbing motion.

"All right," Henry interrupted. His voice was too loud, and he clapped his hands hard enough to make Iris jump. "Perhaps, from this point on, your education should involve immersing yourself in the surface world, not watching documentaries. That will . . . better help you understand . . . appropriate topics of conversation."

"I would be happy to lead her around Manhattan," Monty, recovered from his laughing fit, declared.

"Fine," Henry said. "Just keep her out of trouble. And out of the tabloids. I'll wait for you at the office," he added, nodding his chin toward Finn.

He couldn't get out of there fast enough, leaving them alone with Finn, who looked like he was still trying to recover from her comments.

He cleared his throat awkwardly and shook his head. "It's all right. You'll . . . pick things up pretty quickly."

Iris was reasonably certain he was even less sure than Henry, before he turned and walked away.

"What? You're not going to offer to inspect his manhood yourself to make sure he is cleaning it properly?" Monty asked when Finn was gone.

"Do you think it worked?"

"Making them think you're barnacle-brained? Maybe. But the important thing is, we are allowed to leave the apartment. As much as I love penthouse living, we can't deny this wonderful city the pleasure of my presence any longer. You get some shoes. I will get some cash. And then we are going to go have some fun. Without getting into too much trouble."

Oh, she was looking to get into trouble. As much as possible, in fact, so long as she could maintain plausible deniability.

Finn had no idea what lengths she was willing to go to so she could find a man who didn't want to try to dull her shine and turn her into someone she didn't even recognize anymore.

She wasn't just running from what Finn wanted her to be.

She was still searching for someone who would see all of her—tangled hair and loud voice and sensual gait—and think she was enough just as she was.

Iris

"Do you smell that?" she asked a few minutes later as they walked down the street, and she could have sworn she caught the scent of salt water washing down the streets.

"Huh? Oh, it's probably the sewers," Monty said. He was too busy gawking at everyone he passed in the hopes of brushing shoulders with someone who 'was someone.'

Whatever that meant.

Iris was okay with his distraction, though. It allowed her to really start to absorb the city and its people without getting distracted by Monty's monologues.

She felt it all in her bones—how alive everything was here. The hum of traffic, the pulse of magic tucked between shop doors, the messy tangle of human and paranormal life bumping elbows on the sidewalk.

It wasn't the cage she'd seen it as at first blush. It was chaos. Freedom. The opposite of court formality.

And for the first time since she stepped on land, she didn't feel like she was drowning.

They passed by vendors on the street corners. Some sold food—much to Monty's delight and never-empty stomach—but others specialized in premade spells from the witches and wizards or sticky rollers for the werewolf professionals who didn't want to show up to important meetings covered in fur from roaming around their homes in their wolf form, shedding everywhere.

"Oh!" she gasped. Up ahead, she saw a small woman with bright pink hair and a rainbow dress and a basket overflowing with flowers, shiny gemstones, and bits of stained glass. "Is that a fairy?" Her voice was full of the same wonder she heard people use when asking others if she was a mermaid as they passed.

"Let's see. Bright hair and clothes. Bits and bobs. Big eyes. Mischievous smirk. Yes, I'd venture a guess that she is of the fair folk."

"Wait, where did she go?"

"Subway." At her blank look, the bird shook his head. "Remember the bus that passed us a few blocks ago?"

"Yes."

"Under our feet, there is a giant, very fast bus that runs along the city to take people where they need to go without all the traffic.

"There are also all the tunnels down there for the vampires and wraiths to travel during the day without fear of bursting into flame or becoming completely powerless. Come on, stop gawking. Still lots to see. I'd bet my third flight feather that we could run into some celebrities up at the café on the corner—"

"Actually," Iris said, spying a sign just a few doors down

that had her heart leaping. "Would you mind if I hung out at the bookstore instead? I won't leave. Or cause a scandal. I promise."

"Bookstores don't have shirtless celebrities or reality stars crying into their salads. Priorities, Iris!"

"I'll tag along tomorrow, I promise."

After a lifetime of only having a few books to read, she was giddy at the prospect of a whole store full of them.

"Fine. Go sniff binding glue and ink. But just remember, no one in a bookstore has ever been invited to an impromptu yacht party with a billionaire!"

He reached into his bag that he must have packed along with the sunglasses he currently had perched on his beak.

"What's this for?" she asked, folding the paper in her hands.

"Money, my sweet sea spawn. We had the money talk, remember?"

"Right. Of course." Though she was reasonably sure she still didn't quite understand the math involved.

"Keep it hidden in a pocket. The human pickpockets have nothing on some of the paranormals and their quick fingers."

"I'll be fine, Monty," she promised the bird, leaning down to plant a kiss on his giant beak.

"Lucky," a man passing murmured.

Monty shot the man a hard look. "Stay away from the men."

"I have no plans on being near any men." Least of all her fake fiancé.

"I will be back in a few hours to pick you up," Monty said as they moved in front of the bookstore doors. "Feel that?"

"Feel what?"

"The wards," he said, doing a full-body shiver. "A witch owns that bookstore. Be careful around her."

"I'm literally just trying to buy some books," she reminded him.

"Where did I go wrong with her?" Monty asked the universe, making Iris smile before he waddled off.

Turning, Iris looked at the glass door and the funny charms hanging from it. When she reached forward, she could feel a certain pulsing in the air around them. Perhaps that was what Monty had mentioned. She found the sensation kind of comforting instead of shiver-inducing.

Weird.

She pushed the door inward, hearing a pretty tinkling noise as it moved.

The air smelled like ink and chamomile tea, with a faint trace of nag champa clinging to the rafters. Books were crammed into every possible space—on shelves, stacked in windowsills, even teetering on chairs. Fat candles flickered near a display labeled *Curses & Cures*, and tiny glowing runes danced across the spine of a book that growled as she walked by.

A few customers milled about. A tall, lithe woman with waist-length locks browsed the table featuring new queer romance reads, her hands shimmering with subtle magic. A stooped older human leaned heavily on his cane as he perused the bookmark sections. Two college-aged fae giggled at something in one of the books, their rapid-fire Spanish drifting over toward Iris.

"Please don't tell me you came all the way to the surface to look for true love," a voice called as the door closed behind Iris.

"Not at all," she said, glancing over to where the voice was coming from behind a tall wooden counter. Was this witch a mind reader of some sort? Or was it a common occurrence for other paranormals to leave their homelands behind in the hopes of finding love?

"Thank the goddess. Well, if you're here for a romance book, note I have them shelved under: Emotional Propaganda. Right next to the Unverified Folklore shelf."

The owner of the store popped up then, a huge pile of books in her arms.

The proprietress was a short woman with long, straight, royal purple hair framing a heart-shaped face with sharp cheekbones, pretty honey-brown eyes, and a smattering of freckles in an unnatural shade of purple to match her hair.

Glamour magic.

Iris had read about it before but had never seen it up close.

"How did you know I was a mermaid before you saw me?"

Of all the creatures on the surface, Iris was most fascinated by the witches and warlocks—who practiced nature-based and 'lower' magics—and sorcerers and sorceresses—who performed higher ceremonial magics.

"Your smell."

"My smell?" Iris yelped, leaning down to sniff her arm.

"It's not a bad smell. You just have a salty, lightly citrus scent."

"Oh, that's the soap."

"It's not," the witch corrected. "All mermaids have a citrus scent. Sometimes it's more grapefruit, lemon, or lime. But you are definitely a lemon-lime mixture. Are you royal?"

"Wow," Iris said. Did all paranormals have a signature scent? As far as Iris could tell, most humans smelled like whatever scented products they slathered all over their bodies. "Yes. I'm Iris."

"Princess?"

"Second born."

"Obviously."

"Why obviously?"

"Your older sister would be next on the throne. Your younger sister would be kept for an important political placement. Which leaves you. On land. So, the question is . . . why are you here?"

Iris immediately liked this woman and her bluntness. It was refreshing. Nothing fake about her. What she thought, she said. It was night and day to Finn's carefully constructed mask.

"I am being married off."

"Ah, yes, nothing says 'romance' like contractual obligation."

"Right?" Iris said, shaking her head.

"I'm Selene. Witch, obviously. If you didn't feel the wards."

"Yeah, speaking of, what are you warding against? It felt okay to me, but my companion shivered."

"It's warded against superficiality and optimism."

Well, that explained Monty perfectly, didn't it?

"Shallow and positive people can still come in, but they don't feel *encouraged* to."

"Well, I'm certainly not feeling very positive right now."

"What woman being traded like chattel would?" Selene asked. "So, who are you getting shacked up with?"

She probably wasn't supposed to admit to who it was.

She wasn't supposed to be creating any scandals. That said, she could claim ignorance if it somehow got back to her mother.

"Don't worry," Selene said, shooting Iris a knowing smirk. "I don't have any friends to tell. Unless Gerty counts."

She waved into the shop, but when Iris looked, she saw no one. "Is Gerty here?"

"In spirit. Literally. She's the former owner. She refuses to leave."

"She's a ghost?" Iris asked, whispering. She'd read about them in books, of course. But she'd kind of always imagined they were figments of the writers' imaginations. She wasn't sure if she was intrigued or unnerved by their existence.

"No need to lower your voice. She knows she's dead. Right, Gerty, you obsessive-compulsive kook?" she asked. "She must have been suffering from memory loss near the end there. Every single night, she takes all the books off the shelves to, I guess, do inventory. Guess who gets to put them all back *every* morning?"

"Can you use your magic to help?"

"Sometimes I do. So, spill. Who is the groom?"

"Finn Westrock."

"Finn *Westrock*? The man who has starch in his soul?"

"That's the one." Though she wasn't sure she knew what starch was.

"Huh. When one thinks of romantic chemistry, one definitely thinks of a sea goddess and a sentient campaign poster. But who am I to judge? Maybe you're into guys who use spreadsheets to plan foreplay."

Iris couldn't stop the laugh from bubbling up and bursting out.

"You have him pegged perfectly. I've known him for all of two days and have yet to find anything genuine about him."

But then again . . . she'd seen a crack in his mask. Just the once. That look in his eyes when she'd worn the camisole. She'd tried to convince herself it was just lust. But maybe it was something more.

"So, what? His campaign manager thought a mermaid would help him get elected? Did he lose faith in the toothpaste ads disguised as campaign posters he has plastered all over the city?"

"Apparently, they don't think a single man can win over a family-oriented candidate."

"He's probably right about that. But what's in it for you? Most mermaids don't want to be this far away from the water."

"It seems Finn is promising to push through very strict regulations against pollution that is wreaking havoc on our oceans."

"Huh."

"What?"

"I dunno. I thought Finn was already running on a green platform. Maybe I was mistaken. So, you're just willingly here? I'd be kicking and screaming."

"What am I supposed to do?"

"Run. Run fast. I'll cast you a distraction spell and tell him you eloped with a troll."

To that, Iris let out a laugh.

"Wow, that's practically witchcraft," Selene said.

"What is?"

"That laugh. I mean, your voice in general is hypnotizing, but that laugh is something else entirely. I half expect for the whole male population to come charging in here. And a quarter of the women."

Iris's gaze shot to the door, concerned. But no one even glanced inside.

"You said you've met other mermaids?" Iris asked.

"A handful, yes."

"I thought we didn't live in the city."

"Live? No. Visit? Occasionally. Though, most of you come in with hats and sunglasses, trying to lay low. Especially Caprica."

"Caprica," Iris repeated, the name ringing a bell.

"Caprica Coraline. The author."

"Wait, what? Caprica Coraline is a mermaid?" Iris asked, thinking of the stories in the royal library she'd read. They were some of her favorites. But it seemed like she'd stopped writing just before Iris was born.

"Of course she's a mermaid. Don't you have her books in your library?"

"Well, the ten of them in print."

"Ten," Selene snorted. "She's written seventy-five books. And counting."

"Seventy-five? Why haven't I come across more?"

"Because Caprica came to the surface, what, twenty years ago. To stay for good. And she's been writing ever since. I guess the books just never got, what, shell-bound and printed on . . . kelp?"

"Yes, exactly. Though, apparently, magic can be used to send books below. Finn did so for me."

"Did he now? That's surprisingly thoughtful for a robot."

"I guess he didn't get it done here."

"I mean, I could do it. But this isn't a spell shop. I sell books."

"Why?"

"Why do *you* read books when your people are usually socializing or having lots of confusing mermaid sex?"

"Fair enough," Iris agreed.

"My mother was one of those all-spells-all-the-time kind of witches. When I was old enough to go my own way, I decided to lean away from magic. Well, aside from the wards. And the spells to keep my coffee warm. And flip my book pages when I'm too lazy to do it myself."

"Priorities," Iris said.

"Exactly. So, if you're looking for Caprica, she has her own section," Selene said, moving out from behind the desk.

She didn't know why she looked, but Iris glanced down to see a book sitting open and pages down on the counter. The cover was an illustrated couple standing back-to-back, arms crossed, in what had to be a clear hate-to-love rom-com.

Catching her looking, Selene's eyes widened.

"It's for, ah, research," she insisted. At Iris's scrunched brows, she rushed on, "About emotional manipulation and unrealistic expectations."

Iris hid her smile until Selene was walking ahead of her through the stacks.

"Is this building spelled?" Iris asked as they walked deeper and deeper. So long, in fact, that it seemed impossible that they were in a normal Manhattan building—where everything felt somewhat narrow and shallow, but tall.

"It is," Selene admitted. "It took me months to get the spell right. But there isn't a single building in Manhattan that would be big enough to house all the books I wanted to be able to offer."

She did have an enormous selection. Iris noted sections

for each paranormal creature, with history texts, species-specific self-help, and shelves featuring authors of that species.

On top of that, she had every genre of fiction written by human authors. Though some of her labeling took some getting used to.

Swords, Spells, and Poor Life Choices was where all the Fantasy lived.

Space: The Final Tax Bracket was Science Fiction.

Plotless, but Award-Winning was what she called Literary Fiction.

And, perhaps Iris's favorite was the New Adult section that Selene dubbed *Apocalypse, but Make It Horny*.

"Here we go. You get the comfy chair too," she said, waving toward an oversized round chair. "And I even have the newest Caprica right here." Selene pulled a thick hardcover off a shelf. "It's actually about a mermaid. It's the first time she's written about one in her career. Though, given your current situation, maybe you want to avoid all things gilled and free."

"I'm trying to sabotage my engagement," Iris admitted, knowing she shouldn't. But something about Selene told her that she could be trusted.

"Good for you. That's my favorite section, by the way," she said, gesturing over toward a three-bookcase-wide section: *He Had It Coming*. "Though, that's usually when she ends up killing a dude who had it coming. I'm assuming you're not going to murder the mayoral candidate."

"He might be a walking campaign ad, but I don't think he deserves to die for it."

"That's debatable," Selene said, dragging a laugh out of Iris. "So, what's the plan?"

"To make myself so undesirable from a political standpoint that he has no choice but to call it off."

"Which lets you get off without being in trouble with the queen."

"Exactly."

"Have you made any progress?"

"Well, he looked about ready to pass out when I asked him about the health of his prostate this morning. That's why I'm out in the city. Henry, Finn's campaign manager, thought that immersing myself in the city might teach me more appropriate lines of conversation."

"And, unfortunately for him, you ran into me. Someone who thinks helping to sabotage a high-profile political marriage is a public service. Do you want to stage a scandal? I know a guy. Actually, I *am* the guy."

"I have some ideas. But I have three months, give or take, before the actual marriage."

"Okay. Well, how many times are you going to see him between now and then?"

"Only constantly. After I poured my drink on him at our first meeting, my mother made me move in with him."

"No way. Wait, don't tell me there's only one bed."

"There's only one bed."

"No way. I would have thought with all the settlement money from the city, he would live in some giant penthouse or something."

"He does live in a penthouse," Iris said. "But there's only a bedroom and a small office. My companion has claimed that as his own. What settlement?"

"Oh, huh. I thought that would have been in your welcome packet or something. Finn's father was the D.A."

"What's a D.A.?"

"District Attorney. They prosecute crimes in the city. He was killed in the middle of a really ugly inter-species court case. Before she passed, Finn's mom sued the state for not having better protections in place. I mean, what good was a human security guard going to do when paranormals started warring in the courthouse?

"Anyway, the family was awarded a boatload of money. And, I guess, Finn is using a chunk of that to get his own seat at the table."

She'd learned more about Finn from a *stranger* than Finn had told her himself.

"It makes sense, in a way, that he chose you, then, if you think about it."

"How so?"

"Because if *he* is able to not hold a grudge against the paranormal communities in the city after all he's lost—and is actually *marrying* a member of one—then those same communities should be able to trust that he will be fair to them."

That did make sense. Even if Iris hated to admit she understood the motivations for him to force this engagement upon her.

"Anyway, back to getting back to hexing your happily ever after. Metaphorically. Or . . ." Selene trailed off with a warm smile. "I mean, say the word and I'll summon three very inconvenient exes and a major scandal."

"It has to be subtle," Iris insisted.

"Not my strong suit, but I'm sure I can help you come up with a plan. Okay. You shop. I'll plot the end of your relation—goddess, Gerty. It's rude to walk through people," Selene said, doing a whole-body shiver. "I'll be at my desk if you need me."

Where she would totally, absolutely not be reading that rom-com on the counter, Iris thought as she started to browse the books.

She got lost among the stacks for hours, trying to debate which books to buy and which she would have to come back for when she had more money on her. Though it was a lot like deciding which child to leave behind, when she made her way back up to the counter, where Selene was bent over a notepad, dutifully writing a list while an enchanted pen doodled in the margins.

"This is it. I've got the ultimate sabotage—but make it discreet—list."

"Let me hear it."

"One. Be *alarmingly* honest. Especially in public. Say everything you're thinking. Especially observations about Finn.

"Two. Develop odd human hobbies. Taxidermy comes to mind. Collecting antique dental tools or creepy dolls.

"Three. Make it musical. Break into sea shanties. Constantly. The raunchier the better.

"Four. Compose him love poems. Terrible ones. And then share them. Publicly.

"Five. Get really into human conspiracy theories. Secret alien laboratories included. Be very concerned about the rights of those fictional aliens. And swear that when Finn gets elected, you are going to get to the bottom of it.

"Six. Ocean puns. Constantly. Make it really embarrassing.

"Seven. Give him gifts. But make them unsettling. A pickled fish in a jar because it 'made you think of him.' Braid a lock of your hair into a shape that looks a little too much like a noose and leave it on his pillow. Or inside a heart-shaped box labeled 'romance' . . . I could keep going."

Iris's smile threatened to split her face. "You're a mastermind."

"Finally," Selene said with a bright smile, "someone recognizes the brilliance behind my weaponized cynicism. We can . . . is he here for you?" she asked, nodding toward the front door.

Turning, Iris found Monty waiting for her. He might have been celebrity-watching, but he'd clearly also gone shopping. His wings were loaded down with bags, and he had a fancy tie hanging down his chest.

"That's Monty. He's that companion I mentioned. Your wards work too well on him."

"All right. Let's get you checked out. I'm going to stick your list inside the new vampire thriller you got. Guard it with your life."

"Got it. Thanks for your help."

"I'll be here anytime you need to revise your plan. Or vent. Or, you know, buy more books."

With that, after Selene handed her a tote bag with the store's logo, Iris made her way outside.

Monty eyed her bag but said nothing as they started the long walk back to the penthouse.

"Hey, Monty?"

"Yes, my charming sea witch?"

"Where might I find vintage dental devices?"

Finn

"What the hell is that?" Henry's voice was tight and horrified, making Finn turn to find him looking at the jar that now sat proudly in the center of his island.

"Exactly what it looks like," Finn said, exhaling hard.

"Those are teeth. You have a jar of teeth on your counter."

"Indeed, I do. Fangs too. She's an equal opportunity collector."

"This is Iris's doing?"

"Well, I certainly didn't discover some new obsession with teeth all of a sudden." He wasn't even going to bring up the torture device that was sitting next to their toothbrushes in the bathroom, which had been used to keep mouths open in early dentistry.

"But why?"

"Good question. If you ask her, can you also try to figure out why she's taken up entomology too?"

"Entomology?"

"She collects dead bugs and pins them to a board. I suspect she only got into it because I told her I didn't think there was anywhere nearby that taught taxidermy classes."

"When did this all happen?" Henry asked.

"Seems like she got a whole life going while we were out of town for that golf tournament." He wasn't sure if he was freaked out, intrigued, or completely charmed by it, to be honest. On the one hand, he loved how she was settling in and finding hobbies and interests. On the other, he did kind of wish her interests weren't so unsettling.

It had only been two and a half days. But that was long enough for Iris to really spread out.

And Finn wanted her to feel comfortable, to start to think of his apartment as her home as well. To that end, he found himself charmed by the piles of books all around, her coral comb that was always left somewhere random after one of her many daily hair brushings, and her random kicked-off clothes on the bedroom or bathroom floor.

Those things were familiar and domestic.

The teeth and bugs, though, that was just as creepy as an undead subway rat making eye contact.

To be completely honest, he had purposely not done the research on the taxidermy thing. He wasn't sure he could stomach coming home to find a bunch of stiff, dead animals scattered all around his home, staring at him with unnerving glass eyes.

"I thought mermaids were supposed to collect shiny things," Henry said.

"Whatever you do, don't say that to her."

"Why not?"

"Because I made that mistake right when I got home

and saw them. She told me I was being speciesist and ran to the bathroom and cried. Loudly. For hours."

It was strange how fragile she seemed to be. This woman in his apartment, integrated in his life, barely resembled the fiery-eyed woman who'd dumped a drink on his head when he'd come off as a bit of a jerk at their first meeting.

"Well, could you lightly *encourage* less morbid hobbies?"

"I barely know the woman, Henry. I can't start dictating what she does for fun."

"Well, maybe you need to get to know her more. Take her to an art class. Or pickleball. Anything but this," he said, shaking the jar of teeth. "You have no engagements until tomorrow afternoon. See what you can do with that time."

With that, Henry was off.

"Do we have any more push pins?" Iris called, walking into the apartment a few minutes later, holding a dead caterpillar in her hand. "Willow found this around the roots of her tree, so she gave it to me."

Great.

Another dead bug.

This one was huge, too.

"I think we're out. Maybe we can just set this guy outside for the birds to eat."

"Why? Don't you think he's beautiful?" she asked, shoving the thing in Finn's face.

It took every bit of media training Henry had forced him through not to wince. Or gag. Possibly both.

"Yeah, it's a . . . fine caterpillar."

"Fine?" she asked, her face falling, her eyes hardening. He wasn't sure what about his words had such a dramatic transformation overtaking her, but all the warmth and sweetness he'd come to know her for—creepy hobbies aside—disappeared.

"Well, *fine*. I'll just throw him away, then."

She stormed over toward the cabinet where the trash can lived.

Finn was quicker, grabbing her wrist to stop her from throwing out the fat green caterpillar.

"I will order more push pins," he said. "Why don't we stick him in one of those food containers you saved until then?"

It wasn't just teeth and bugs she collected, but every single plastic container that takeaway food came in. Usually, she could be found scrubbing them while bumbling to herself about plastic pollution and careless humans.

If Finn hadn't been watching her so closely, he might have missed the look of disappointment that crossed her gorgeous face.

But no.

That made no sense.

He was giving her what she wanted. Why would she be disappointed by that?

Maybe he was just bad at reading her. Perhaps mermaids emoted differently. He really needed to find some time to do a deep dive—as it were—into her culture. If he came from a place of understanding, maybe they could avoid some of the growing pains they seemed to be dealing with.

"I have an idea," he said as he dropped her arm, so he didn't give in to the desire to run his thumb across the nearly translucent skin there.

"An idea?" she prompted as he produced a small to-go

container into which she quickly dropped the caterpillar. Almost as if it grossed her out to hold it. She even quickly turned to wash her hands.

Finn's brows pinched as he watched her. "Do you have any plans tonight?"

"Monty is off with his new friends. Why? What did you have in mind?"

"I'm going to keep it a secret."

Iris's head tipped to the side, interest clear in those sea glass eyes of hers. Like she was drawn to the spontaneity.

"Do I need to bring anything?"

"Not even your shoes if you don't want to."

As much as she hated shoes, she did slip into them before following him out of the apartment, into the elevator, then down, down, down.

He wasn't sure Iris even knew about the basement of the building. If she did, he felt like she would be spending a lot more time there than in the apartment.

"Wait . . . where are we?" she asked as his hand pressed to the small of her back, leading her out of the elevator.

"That thriller you're reading giving you all sorts of ideas about basements, huh?" Finn asked.

"No one mentioned a basement."

"Because Monty is too busy trying to rub shoulders with the elite. And Willow wants nothing to do with more concrete. Right through here," Finn said, typing his passcode into the locked door and then pulling it open.

"Is this some sort of—*oh*."

Finn was captivated by the surprise and pleasure on her face as her gaze landed on the Olympic-sized saltwater swimming pool.

He watched, too, as tears flooded her eyes when she

stepped closer, kicking off her shoe and dipping her toe into the water.

She had nothing else to say right then as she reached down, shoving her shorts to the ground and then reaching to yank up her top.

He knew he should excuse himself, give her privacy. At the very least, look away.

But his feet stayed rooted in the same spot. And the world could have started to fall apart around them, and nothing would have made him look away as Iris pulled off her camisole and, finally, her panties.

He wasn't sure what he wanted more—to touch her, or to deserve to.

She was so free, so unguarded. Like she didn't know her body could be a weapon. Or maybe she did, and didn't care.

Either way, it made him feel clumsy and crude by comparison. Like every glance was a violation.

Her long waves protected most of her modesty, but, God, he memorized each inch of exposed skin.

His palms itched with the urge to reach out, to run his hand over that subtle curve of her hip, up over her ribs, cup one of her full breasts as she . . .

No.

He had to stop.

But before he could even begin to clear his mind, Iris dove into the pool, disappearing under the water with a splash that coated his clothes.

For a moment, all he could see were the ripples of the water and her long pink hair.

But then her tail flashed.

That same urge to reach out and touch overcame him

again, but this time in a less sensual way. He wanted to know what that tail felt like, if it was cold or warm like her skin. *If she'd react to him touching it the way she did when he rubbed her feet.*

Iris swam from one end to the other and back again before she surfaced, her face a mask of pure pleasure as the water cascaded down her face.

Wet, the scales near her hairline were more prominent and colorful. And the marks on her neck that looked like scars had split into subtle gills.

The shell bra, though? That was apparently something mermaids put on. Because she was bare from the waist up. He tried like hell to keep his gaze on the area of her above the water.

"You've been keeping this from me?" she asked, her voice even more musical in her mermaid form. Sure, she sounded sad that he'd kept the one thing from her that called to her blood, even if a salted pool was a poor replacement for the sea.

"Honestly, I forgot," Finn admitted. "I've never been down here except when I had a tour of the building before I moved in."

"You don't like to swim?" she asked, her tone suggesting that didn't seem possible.

"I *can't* swim," he corrected.

"What? What do you mean?" she asked, her brows furrowed.

"I mean I was born and raised in Manhattan. I was never really near water."

"Manhattan is surrounded by water."

"Yes," Finn agreed, "but no one swims in that water."

"Are you afraid of the water?"

"I think I have a healthy fear of anything that could be dangerous. Large bodies of water, heights, too-fast vehicles . . ."

"You could just put your legs in," Iris suggested. "It's the perfect temperature."

She seemed determined to see him enjoying the water. And some part of him really wanted to please her.

"I can do that."

He sat down on the edge of one of the chaise lounges, untying his shoes, then removing them and his socks. He was barely paying attention to what he was doing, though, as Iris broke back into a swim, cutting through the water, going end to end far quicker than any human could ever move.

There was something undeniably beautiful about seeing someone in their element.

Suddenly, he felt a little crack form inside.

How could you take someone meant for salt water and currents . . . and ask them to stay still on solid ground?

And yet that was exactly what he was doing, wasn't it?

Asking her to perform. To behave. To shrink.

He'd told himself it was for optics, but maybe it had been about control, too.

And that made something twist in his gut.

After rolling up his pant legs, Finn moved over to the edge of the pool, lowering himself down, then slipping his legs into the water.

Iris was right; it was the perfect temperature. And there was something calming about the way the water sloshed around his skin as Iris swam her tireless laps.

Over the next twenty minutes or so, her movements

slowed until she stopped entirely and floated on her back on the surface of the water.

Her hair offered a peek-a-boo effect with the swells of her breasts, but offered more than enough to tantalize.

Desire pinged off his nerve endings, making his chest feel tight as he started to harden.

Still, he couldn't look away.

She was so peaceful then, her face relaxed, her tail lazily undulating in the water to keep her afloat. The movement made the muscles in her stomach tense and contract.

Iris took a deep breath, making more of her chest appear above the water.

Finn was close to getting up and moving away to try to get some distance, some control over his desire.

But then Iris was slipping under the water.

And the next thing he knew, she was surfacing between his legs, her arms resting on his legs, soaking the material through.

He hardly noticed that, though. Not with her so close, so bare to him, her face so lit up with joy.

"Isn't it nice?"

"Perfect," he said, knowing she meant the water. When he meant her.

"There's nothing like it on the surface."

"Can't argue with that."

It was a city of millions of women—humans and paranormals alike. Not a single one held a candle to Iris.

"There's a shallow end, you know."

"Yes."

"You should come in. Sit on the steps."

If that was what she wanted, he'd do it. Happily. Even if it was the last thing he did before he drowned.

"But you'll need to take these off," she said, her hands rubbing up and down his thighs. Which was not helping the whole desire thing.

"Right," he agreed, voice tight.

"I'll meet you over there," she said, sinking back below the surface and swimming away.

Finn sighed as he pulled his legs out of the water. He turned away from the pool to remove his belt, then his pants. He left on his shirt and jacket, knowing full well how ridiculous he looked, but figuring it would hide the raging hard-on he was dealing with as he walked over toward the shallow end of the pool.

His hand had a death grip on the metal railing as he went down one step, then two. And finally, three.

Once there, he lowered down to sit on the second stair, the water covering his thighs but not coming up to his waist. Which felt safe enough to him.

Besides, if he somehow slipped under the water, he had the world's best lifeguard to save him.

Finn watched with a swooping sensation in his stomach as Iris swam toward him.

"There," she said, reaching out to grab the railing to hold herself still as she stopped right in front of him, flicking her hair back and sending the sopping strands over her shoulder.

He couldn't tell if the move was deliberate or accidental, if she was even aware of her exposure. If she even cared if she was.

His mermaid knowledge was lacking at best, but everyone knew that mermaids were very free and comfortable with their bodies, that they were sensual by nature and had no shame about their sex drives.

It was entirely possible that Iris had no idea that she had him rock-hard and aching just by being nearby, exposed, and looking so incredibly tempting to touch.

The cool temperature of the water had her nipples twisted into points, and Finn had the almost uncontrollable urge to pull her closer and suck one into his mouth.

The only thing keeping him from acting on his urges was the dubious amount of consent between the two of them. He hadn't ever gotten around to asking her about her involvement in their engagement, about how willing she'd been to come to the surface.

It was a conversation they needed to have. Preferably when they were both fully clothed, so he could think straight.

"Aren't you glad you came in?" she asked, seemingly oblivious to what she was doing to him.

"Yeah," he agreed, if for no other reason than to get close to her happiness.

"Swimming is great exercise. Though, it might not do much for your calves." Her hand moved out, fingers teasing up one of his calves.

There was no way to stop the small rumbling sound that escaped him at the soft touch.

He was sure it was too low for her to hear until her head tipped to the side, her gaze cutting to his, curiosity in her eyes.

"Does Henry have an issue with your thighs?" she asked, her hand drifting up over one of his knees toward the body part in question.

"I . . . n-no," Finn stammered.

"I've always thought tails were most attractive on a man," she went on, her gaze dipping to watch as her fingers grazed over the raised muscle of his quad. "But these muscles are interesting."

Nothing about her tone suggested her touch and interest were anything other than curiosity. But there was no telling his body that right then.

As her fingers trailed up his quad, heading dangerously high, he couldn't seem to keep himself from squirming. Unfortunately, the motion made the material of his boxer briefs graze across his hardness, dragging a hiss out of him.

He wasn't sure where her hand may have continued to explore if given the chance. But just then, Finn heard the beep as someone's card was scanned at the door, making him jump up a step and adjust his shirt so it covered his lap more fully.

"For goodness' sake, this is a public pool, you—" the woman who entered started to rant as she looked at Iris's bare upper half. Until she caught sight of her tail. "Oh, sorry," she murmured. Her gaze skirted away.

In response to her words, though, Iris quickly wrapped her hands across her chest, shielding her body from view.

Suddenly, Finn hated modesty standards in society, simply because they made Iris ashamed of her nakedness.

"We're just about done here," Finn said. He shrugged out of his suit jacket and draped it around Iris's shoulders.

"Thanks," she murmured as she slid up onto the top step, then pulled her tail out of the water so it could dry.

He watched, fascinated, as shimmering scales gave way to flawless skin. Every version of her was pure perfection.

Iris pulled his jacket down, and Finn reached out to fasten the buttons as more and more skin appeared.

While Iris waited for the rest of her tail to fade away,

Finn gathered her scattered clothes, then helped her to her feet.

"All yours," he called back to the woman who was pretending not to watch them.

He told himself that the way he wrapped an arm around Iris's waist was to sell the authenticity of their relationship when the news eventually broke about it, so no neighbors would say that they'd been living like siblings instead of lovers.

But he just really wanted to hold her.

They were silent on the walk back to the elevator, but as they climbed toward the penthouse, Iris—studying her feet at first—said, "Thank you." Her head lifted, her pretty eyes full of a depth that made it feel like his heart was sinking into them. "Really, thank you. I needed that."

"Of course," he said, his voice choked. "I will leave you the card so you can swim anytime you want."

This wasn't part of the campaign plan. No one had warned him what to do when pretending started to feel real.

"That would be great. But I guess I should invest in a bathing suit," she said as she stepped out of the elevator.

There was no rational explanation for the disappointment he felt at that declaration.

Except, of course, for the one he was trying not to let himself think about.

That he was beginning to have actual feelings for his fake fiancée.

And he had the sinking suspicion that those feelings would not be returned.

Iris

"Morning, Willow," Iris called.

She crouched down to overturn one of the garden stones in the courtyard behind their apartment building. A full-body shiver racked her system at the scurry of a dozen little pill bugs. They left one in their wake, curled up on its side, long dead.

Iris gagged as she reached down toward it.

"I think, at this point, if the bug boards aren't working yet, they're not going to," Willow said. She walked over to her tree, lovingly stroking the hanging leaves.

"He looks pale each time he has to pass them by. It might be wearing him down."

"How many are there now?"

"Four. It nearly takes up the whole hallway. Mostly spiders. There's an almost alarming number of dead spiders around the building."

"Something to bring up at the next tenants' meeting,"

Willow said, walking over toward the parlor palm she'd rescued from the lobby, where it had been dying a slow and preventable death. "Are you feeling better?" she asked it as she poured water from a pot of rainwater she'd collected.

"Do all the plants talk back?" Iris asked. She dropped the dead bug into a container she carried around in her bag for just that purpose. But, yeah, she was starting to agree with Willow; the bugs and teeth didn't seem to be working.

The medical devices weren't doing much either. Though Finn had had a visceral reaction when she'd held up a speculum and spread it while telling him what it did.

She was seriously debating starting the creepy doll collection. She'd only been putting it off because she also found them almost unbearably unnerving.

"Some are chattier than others," Willow told her. "And it's always the ones with far too many opinions on me that never shut up. I used to dance in the moonlight with all the willows. Now, I get unsolicited dating advice from a ficus in the dentist's waiting room."

"Is that one happy you saved it?"

"It was pretty fond of that guy who lives in 8D. And since he never comes back here, it's a little salty about its new—much healthier—home. I've told you time and time again that I will bring you back into the lobby when the appropriate lights and misters arrive," she told the plant. "Anyway, how goes the engagement sabotage?"

Yeah, while she *probably* shouldn't have told Selene about the plan, she definitely shouldn't have told someone living in the same building, who was also fond of Finn.

The beauty of Willow, though, was how well-grounded

she was. It was in her nature to stay steady and neutral, no matter what chaos erupted around her.

Besides, after the third time she caught Iris looking sick as she collected dead bugs, she almost *had* to give the dryad an explanation.

"Finn hasn't been home much this week," Iris confessed. She went ahead and ignored the little sloshing sensation in her stomach as she said that. Surely, the thought of Finn simply made her sick to her stomach. Nothing else made any sense. "He and Henry have been holed up researching and practicing."

"Oh, right. He has that big debate coming up."

He did.

And he looked unusually stressed about it. She was so used to the man being nearly unflappable that seeing him, well, flapped, was interesting.

It gave her a small glance into the man himself, not the facade.

"Where's Monty?" Willow asked as she dropped down onto the ground by her tree.

"Oh, well, he is off to brunch with a guy whose girlfriend is cousins with someone who is married to some big-time reality TV producer."

I am on my way, Iris! On my way, I tell you. I can practically taste the sweet, flaky flavor of success and calculated flattery.

"I, for one, can't wait to see him get his first coming attractions poster."

"Right? He will be insufferably smug," Iris agreed.

"But no one could say he didn't bust his feathered butt to get to the top."

That was very true.

As much as he claimed to be both her emotional support pelican and her Head of Surface Affairs, he'd been about as MIA as Finn had been the past week.

To be fair, he always invited her on his little outings. Then lectured her about her preference to stay home to read and swim.

Her old friend was starting to slip away from her, little by little. She took for granted how much she'd had him to herself for most of her life. Her constant, caring companion. She selfishly never stopped to consider that he might have his own dreams and goals, that his connection to her—and her steadfast determination to remain in the sea—had been holding him back. As much as she missed his nearly ever-present figure in her world (especially in this new world), she knew she had to let him go. She had to be happy for him and his new adventures. Even if she felt a pang at his absence.

"I have a yoga class today, if you want to come," Willow said, unfolding from her spot under her tree. Iris could swear her skin looked more glowing and her hair more green just from being near the tree.

"After falling on my face the last time? No, thank you. Outside of the water, I fully respect gravity and the hold it has on this form," Iris said, waving down at herself. "I think I'm heading to the bookstore today."

"Oh, fun. Have a good time."

She technically still had one book from the first trip to read. She was telling herself that she was being proactive, going to get more before she ran out. But the fact of the matter was, she was almost soul-crushingly lonely.

As vast as the ocean was, she had never been truly alone.

There were the other merfolk, sure, but also millions and millions of other creatures.

In her steel, cement, and glass surface prison, with Finn gone with Henry, and Monty rubbing shoulders with the latest Who's Who, it was just Iris and Checkers in the apartment all day and most of the night.

Well, Iris, Checkers, and all the dead bugs.

And as much as she adored the cat—and his innate ability to sense her tide-touched moods, coming to purr on her lap or make biscuits on her—he wasn't someone she could talk to. Or, at least, expect a response from.

It wasn't just the silence that unsettled her. It was the stillness. The ocean always moved. Even when she was alone, the current would tug at her, would whisper reminders that she belonged to something fast, real, and alive.

Here, the air didn't speak. It just sat. Thick and quiet.

And there were only so many books she could read before her thoughts turned inward. Before she started wondering what would happen if she never managed to go back.

She was just about to make her way back inside the building when a loud *caw* sounded from above.

"Go away," she grumbled at the seagull. She was not in the mood for her mother's spies. "What do you want?" she snapped when he just kept squawking at her. Glancing up, she noticed a small box hanging from his beak. "A present?" She stood up and reached to take the package from the bird. "Thanks," she called, but the bird was already flying off.

She wasn't sure if she was excited or nervous. Coming from her mother, there was no way to tell if it would be something thoughtful or some sort of warning.

When she reached inside the box, though, it was Shelly's swirly handwriting on the note:

> I stole two of Mother's shellphones.
> Give me a call. I need to hear everything.

Shellphones weren't common in the ocean. The magic that created them was incredibly rare, so most mermaids accepted that only the very influential would be able to make calls to one another from across the ocean.

Even though her mother used shellphones almost daily, Iris had never been allowed to even touch them.

This particular shellphone was a giant pink conch shell.

Iris pulled it close, taking a long sniff of it, smelling salt and seaweed and *home*. Tears pricked her eyes and it took her a long moment to blink them back before she finally pressed the phone to her ear.

"Hello? Shelly?"

"Iris!" Her sister's voice shrieked in her ear, making Iris yank the shell away from her ear.

"You are going to be in so much trouble for this."

"Only if I get caught. Mother was just gifted a new shellphone from one of the sirens. It's a worn snail shell. Very sleek. It's hideous. Mother loves it, though. She won't notice these two are missing. And now we can talk. So, spill. What is the city like? Have you met a vampire yet? Are they as beautiful as everyone claims? What's your favorite food? Favorite place to visit? Tell me everything. I'm drowning in a sea of sameness. I'm living vicariously through you right now."

Iris's lips curved up even as her heart ached. She was so homesick it was hard to breathe. "I've seen vampires from afar. And, yes, stunning. Hot pretzels are basically the best food ever invented. But pizza is a close second. Oh, and pasta. There are so many ways the humans have learned to make pasta. You have to come visit sometime and we will taste-test them all."

"I'm worried Mother will never let me come. But maybe if we can put it under the guise of some sort of human wedding tradition. So, what have you been exploring?"

"Um, well, I really like the bookstore."

"The *bookstore*? You have this big, sprawling city full of untold marvels—both human and otherwise—and you've been spending your time in a stuffy old bookstore?"

Shelly had never understood her sister's love of the written word. There was something oddly comforting about the fact that it hadn't changed.

"Well, if it helps, the bookstore is run by a witch. She's hilarious."

"I'm not at all jealous," Shelly said. There was a dramatic sigh on the other end of the shellphone. "So, tell me about Finn."

"There's not much to tell."

"Oh, come on. You are living with him. A human. A human *man*."

"I think you're imagining it to be a lot more interesting than it is."

"Oh, come on. You have to tell me something. Does he have any strange habits?"

"He sings in the shower."

"What does he sing?"

"Showtunes, according to Monty. He's actually kind of good."

"So . . . you're taking showers with him?"

"What? No!" Iris just hoped her sister didn't pick up on the slight hysterical edge to her voice. She really didn't need anyone else to know that she spent a lot of time thinking about Finn in the shower. Naked. Soap running down those . . . no. Nope. Her mind could not go there. "But the sound carries through the apartment."

"You know what I think?"

"What?"

"That you are going to totally fall in love with your fiancé."

"What? No. Absolutely not. That is never going to happen."

"Oh, come on. I don't think I know anyone who wants to fall in love as much as you do."

"I do. More than anything. Which is why I am trying to get Finn to break off our engagement, so I can find my true love."

"Would it be so horrible for your true love to be Finn?"

"Of—"

"Barnacles! Mother is calling me. I have to hide this shellphone before she comes in. But call me back, okay?"

Iris wiped a tear off her cheek. "Absolutely."

"Love you bigger than the ocean," Shelly said. The call dropped before Iris could offer her little sister the same sentiment.

Iris took a few moments to collect herself before she made her way back up to the penthouse. She wasn't sure if the call had healed or hurt. On the one hand, hearing from her sister felt like getting a part of herself back. On the other, it was just a reminder of everything she was losing by continuing to be on the surface. Her sisters, sure, and her mother. More than that, though, the familiar sights, sounds, the vastness of the ocean, her *tail*.

The surface wasn't all bad. There was a lot of freedom on land. In the city, there were no royal duties, no endless, soul-sucking meetings, no speeches she needed to prepare, nothing to study. Her time, for the first time in her life, was her own to do what she pleased with.

Whether her little sister understood it or not, what pleased her the most could only be found between the pages of books. So she collected her beloved tote and more of the money her mother had sent her to the surface with—enough money, Monty claimed, to live comfortably for months—ready to head out.

She'd barely managed to locate her shoes, though, before there was a knock at the door.

Expecting Willow, she pulled the door open without looking out the peephole like Finn had instructed her to do, while giving her a speech about personal safety in big cities.

But it wasn't Willow at the door.

It wasn't anyone she knew.

Whoever this stranger was, he was almost shockingly tall and on the lean side without looking too gaunt.

He had a classically, almost darkly, handsome face with a strong, wide jaw, a straight nose, and a stern brow over deep eyes that conjured up images of the bruised sky after a storm.

His black hair was styled back away from his face, and his gray suit was quite a bit tighter than the ones Finn wore.

And speaking of that, Henry would never allow Finn to don a tie that featured a bunch of black and gray hearts on a white background.

There was an energy about him that screamed paranormal, but she couldn't quite place it. His energy felt almost dark and bright at the same time.

A warning pulsed low in her gut—predator energy, maybe. But layered over it was a kind of seductive charm she'd only ever seen used by sirens back home. The kind that made you want to follow, want to please. Even to your own death.

She wasn't sure whether to slam the door or invite him in.

"I'm not interested," she told him with a firm nod.

She'd been hit on too many times to count since coming to the surface. She found a firm refusal was usually the most effective way to handle the situation.

"As absolutely breathtaking as you are, Iris," the man said, his gaze sweeping over her in a way that reminded her a bit of Henry, just less judgmental, "you're not my type."

"Who are you?" she asked, narrowing her eyes at him, not ready to let go of her aggressive outward demeanor until she knew she was safe. "My boyfriend is on his way home," she added, remembering one of Monty's podcasts saying men respected you more as a possession of other men than as an individual.

"He is not," the man said. "He is at his office with his campaign managers and about half a dozen PR interns, everyone giving him a spit-shine so bright that even the terrible lighting at the debate could catch."

So he not only knew her but also knew Finn and Henry.

"Did Henry send you?"

"Interesting you would ask that instead of Finn. But no. Your mother sent me."

"My mother? But you're not merfolk."

"Alas, the queen has many connections to all sorts of people. Both human and paranormals alike."

That was fair. Iris attended many meetings in her life, but there were others that she and her sisters had been locked out of that were held away from the palace. While Iris had always assumed those meetings involved other sea creatures, it did make sense that the queen would need to meet on land with other high-ranking officials as well.

"I would say Her Majesty sends her warm regards, but . . ."

"But she probably sent you with a stern warning about my behavior."

"Precisely. But she also sent me with all this money for you," he said, pulling an envelope out of his breast pocket and handing it to her. "So you can't be too mad. You can use it to buy more . . ." he scanned the room ". . . teeth?"

The jar sat dead center on the kitchen island, catching the morning light like some morbid shrine. Nearby, one of her partially completed bug boards leaned against the wall, a dead, leggy spider pinned at a slightly crooked angle.

She should probably clean up.

Or at least move the jaw spreader from the bathroom sink.

"I'm sorry, but who are you?"

"Arden Laurent. Lower demon. Connoisseur of love. Planner of soul-binding contracts." At her blank look, Arden shot her a wicked smirk. "I'm your wedding planner, love."

"Oh! Okay. I mean, since you talked to my mother, I'm assuming you know this match is, uh . . ."

"As romantic as political red tape can be," he supplied. "No worries. The love interests don't have to like each other at first. That's what banter is for."

As he said that, Arden pulled a heart-shaped notebook out of his pocket. Then he pulled the heart-printed pen out of the spiral binding, popped it, and got ready to write.

"So, you're a summer."

"A summer what?"

"Season. Your coloring. Your fiancé seems more like an autumn to me. But, let's face it, it's your beauty we want to accentuate on your wedding day. Do you have any preferences on gown styles? Because with a body like that, you could wear last week's headlines and still be the talk of the town."

"I don't really know much about dress styles," Iris admitted. "I'm new to the surface," she added.

"Dress shopping is . . . scheduled," he said as his pen raced across the page.

"Out of curiosity, how loyal are you to my mother?" Iris asked, hating the idea of Arden putting a ton of work into her wedding, only to find it canceled.

"I am bound to the royal family to plan all their weddings for the next fifty years. But if you're asking if I'm going to tell the good queen that her darling daughter isn't a starry-eyed virgin in her white gown, your secret is safe with me. I like the love story. But I'm here for the money."

"Do you still get paid if the wedding gets, you know, canceled?"

To that, Arden's lips curved up, and a dark glee spread across his stormy eyes. "Oh, I have witnessed quite a few engagement collapses in my time: runaway brides, grooms sleeping with the maid of honor, a rogue troll coming to object and steal the bride away. You name it, I've seen it. And have gotten paid."

"Oh, good."

"Trying to get out of your arranged marriage, are you?"

"Yes."

"Can I ask why? Because I have lived through five centuries, two hundred and seventy-five wars, eighty-six vampire scandals, and still *that man's* jawline is the most dangerous thing I have ever seen."

"Because he's . . . a mayoral mannequin. He's full of scripted sincerity and PR-approved charm. I don't think there is a single genuine thing about him."

"Ah, yes. He does come off as Mr. Electable. Because he, as crazy as this may sound, wants to be elected."

"Hey, whose side are you on?" Iris grumbled.

"Yours, love, always yours. I support a woman's rights and her wrongs. I will let you decide which category this falls into."

"I don't belong on land," Iris said, her barely contained emotions drifting to the surface.

These were the real ones.

Not the over-the-top dramatic ones she pretended to have in front of or around Finn.

She'd hurt her own throat from pretend-sobbing over that thing he'd said about collecting shiny things.

To her horror, he hadn't been turned off by the display, either. He'd been waiting with a cup of tea and what seemed like a real apology. She tried to tell herself he was so good at spin that it was impossible to tell if he was being real or not.

"Oh, you pretty thing," Arden said, producing a pocket square that featured—of course—a heart pattern. "Heavy is that coral crown," he said, patting the tears on her cheeks. "Well, just because there won't be a wedding doesn't mean we can't have fun planning the most fantastic one imaginable."

"Fun how?"

"Well, we can go visit venues, for one. I was thinking, given who you are, something near an ocean would be ideal."

"We could visit the beach?" she asked, spirits rising.

"Of course we can. You know *you* can, right? You're not a prisoner here."

"I wouldn't even know how to get there."

"That's what GPS is for."

"I don't have a phone."

"You don't have a phone." Arden repeated it as if she'd declared she didn't have bones or lungs.

"No. I wouldn't know how to use one if I did."

"What is this fiancé of yours doing to help integrate you into the surface, exactly?"

Iris squashed the sudden, unwelcome urge to defend Finn. Because what the heck was that about?

"He gave me the card to access the saltwater pool in the basement."

At Arden's blank look, she shrugged. "Monty volunteered to show me the city. So I guess Finn thought that was enough." She couldn't really blame Finn for the fact that she had turned down the pelican and his desire to 'hobnob with the rich and scandalous'—whatever that meant.

"Right. Because a social-climbing pelican should be in charge of making sure you know how to function like an adult in a big, overwhelming, sometimes dangerous city."

"You know Monty?" Iris asked as Checkers came sauntering into the kitchen.

His tail had been swaying until he caught sight of the wedding planner.

His fur stood up.

His back arched.

And a hiss Iris had never heard before escaped him.

He looked almost possessed.

"Checkers, what's wrong?" Iris asked, trying to pet the cat, but he only hissed harder as he stared holes into Arden.

"Oh, don't mind him." Arden waved a hand, unbothered. "All cats react like that to demons. It's because of the drop of demon blood in your veins, isn't it?"

"What?"

"Yes. Cats have demon blood. It's very watered down, of course. But they don't want their humans to know they're sharing their homes—and tuna—with partially evil creatures. The times have changed, cat; the humans know demons aren't all wicked now.

"Now, back to your wedding. Do you think Mr. Mayor would be willing to sacrifice that blue suit of his for something that better works with our color palette?"

"I think you'd need to pry that thing off his cold, dead body."

"Right?" Arden asked, letting out a deep chuckle. "I picture him sleeping in it so he is media-ready at any time of day or night."

"He sleeps in a pair of sleep pants."

"No top?"

"No top."

She hated how even the thought of that made her belly slosh around again. And how much harder it was to try to blame a stomachache when she knew very well how strongly her body had reacted to Finn's partial nudity the first time. She'd just come out of the bedroom to get a glass of water, and there he'd been, stretched out on the sectional, his arm thrown over his eyes, so he at least couldn't see as she stood there ogling him. While some very unsettling sensations overtook her body that left her overheated and tingly.

If she were being honest with herself, she'd admit that she'd felt those same feelings down in the pool, when his gaze had been moving over her and her fingers had been slipping up his thigh.

But she was choosing to delude herself instead. It worked better for her plan.

Besides, desire was base. It was just chemicals and the animalistic instinct to mate, to reproduce, to keep the species going. It didn't *mean* anything. Even if she felt it. Which she totally hadn't. Not for a man who was all fins and no current, as the saying went.

Arden let out a little whistle. "I bet he works out."

"He does. Daily. He's usually at the gym before I'm even waking up."

"We love a healthy groom. Unless we're marrying for money, in which case we want them ancient, addicted to fried foods, and dealing with a five-pack-a-day habit."

To that, Iris let out a laugh.

She might have come to the surface determined not to like anything about life on land. But she had to admit that there were some perks. The endless supply of books was at the top of her list, of course. Then, the food. Monty had been very right about that.

But most surprising was the people.

While she had her family in the ocean and some acquaintances, she was always a bit of a loner thanks to the fact that other merfolk tended to walk on seashells around members of the royal family.

On land, it seemed as though no one really cared about her title.

She'd found deeper connections with Selene, Willow, and Arden in hours than she'd developed in a lifetime with others in the sea.

That was somehow both comforting and off-putting in equal turns.

"Anyway, back to the colors. No blue suit. Because, quite frankly, no one escapes my color palette, not even the future mayor of the city."

"Should we even bother planning things like this?" she asked as Arden kept scribbling in his notebook.

"What happens if you, I don't know, fail on your little mission?"

"I won't. I can't."

"Or what if you, perhaps, fall in love with your fiancé?"

"That's even more impossible."

"Forgive my doubt. I once witnessed the wedding of a storm elemental and a fire sprite. They literally extinguished each other. It was *electric*. I'm just saying, if there is even a minuscule chance that this is fate, I say you may as well embrace—and monogram—it."

"Fine, you can plan it. But I don't really care about any of it."

"But if you do end up falling for Mr. Tall, Dark, and Delectable—I mean *Electable*—and want a ceremony to celebrate that . . ."

"It's not going to happen."

"You know who else ran from love? A minotaur named Kevin. He ended up alone in a maze, eating sad cheese."

"What is sad cheese?"

"The kind you eat to ease the sting of knowing you left

the love of your life at the altar because you got a little tummy ache on your wedding day."

"Finn is not the love of my life. The love of my life would know how to *swim*. And emote."

"What can I say? I am a true romantic. Always rooting for the unlikely couples. Judging by this," Arden said, picking up one of Iris's books, "you are too."

"I'm starting to think Selene is right."

"About what?"

"Not believing in love. Except the kind that shows up in chapter fifteen after a near-death experience and grand declaration . . ."

"And pray tell, where did the inspiration for that story come from?"

"Fantastical thinking."

"I see you are determined to live under your own personal storm cloud of doom and gloom—as is your right. But you'll forgive me for not doing the same. This is dry-clean only," he said, waving down at his suit. "So, what do you think about incorporating coral and shells into your traditional floral bouquet?"

It sounded perfect.

If her relationship were real.

And if her wedding was going to happen.

Which it wasn't.

No matter how perfect Arden's palette was.

Iris

"It's time," Henry declared as he strode into the apartment first thing the morning after the long-awaited debate. It seemed like there were more and more 'very important events' as the deadline to the election—and her upcoming wedding—drew closer with each passing day.

Iris didn't even know how that went. She was pretty sure she'd rather watch coral grow than tune in to a political debate.

It was bad enough that she couldn't escape it every time Henry was in the apartment. She wasn't going to volunteer for more of it in her free time.

If Henry was expecting her to ask what it was time for, he would be waiting a long time. She focused on making her coffee—what could she say? She'd grown fond of the pressed bean juice. She hadn't had a word to give Henry since the time she'd overheard him refer to her as 'the accessory.'

"Don't you want to know what it's time for?" he pressed, since Finn hadn't appeared yet.

Her answer was to loudly stir her coffee.

"It's rude to do the silent-treatment thing."

Iris's hand slapped down on the counter. "Oh, so now you're concerned about what is rude?"

"What's that supposed to mean?"

"It *means* it's not okay for me to not talk to you, but it's totally fine for you to refer to me as Finn's *accessory*?"

"Hey, no need to get emotion—"

"I *dare* you to finish that sentence," she cut him off, taking a step closer to him. "Dare you."

"What's going on out here?" Finn asked, walking out of the hallway in a pair of hastily pulled-up slacks. No top. Because that's what she needed right then. Half-naked Finn.

"A small misunderstanding," Henry claimed.

"Right. Because I couldn't possibly comprehend your meaning with my tiny little female merfolk brain, right? So clogged up with emotions that a thought can't pass through."

To that, Finn's head cocked to the side, his brow raised. Almost—dare she think it—annoyed.

But no.

A real emotion from Finn?

That wasn't possible.

"Care to explain why Iris seems to think you're insulting her?"

Something in Finn's tone had Henry holding up both hands in a placating gesture.

"Iris overheard something . . . uncharitable I said to you. She is understandably upset about it."

Finn glanced between them.

"He thinks I'm as useful as cufflinks."

"That's not what I said."

"They're an accessory, aren't they?"

"Oh, that," Finn said. He exhaled hard. And Iris absolutely did not notice the way his chest widened and his abdominal muscles contracted. Nope. Not her. "Iris, I already had a talk with Henry about that comment. You are not an accessory. You are a valuable member of this team."

Well, then.

If he'd wanted to douse the flames of her growing desire, he'd certainly accomplished that.

"Well, as *teammates*," she said, biting off that last word, "Henry has some sort of announcement."

Finn watched her for a second, brows furrowed like she was a puzzle that didn't quite make any sense.

"What announcement?" he asked, finally looking to his campaign manager.

"It's time."

"Really? So soon after the debate?"

"It's the perfect time. We're still riding high on the good press coming from that. It's the perfect time to go public."

When neither of them thought to clue her in, Iris gritted her teeth and asked, "Go public with what?"

"Your relationship," Henry said.

Some part of her wanted to ask: *already?*

The other part, though, was surprised it had taken so long.

Clearly, she was slacking with her sabotage plans if Henry was so confident about Finn parading her out in public.

Maybe she should have pulled out all the stops. Dyed

her hair tentacle-green. Gotten a large tattoo of Poseidon riding a narwhal. Insisted on wearing seaweed robes. Or piercings. Lots and lots of visible piercings. With seashell chains connecting them.

"What did you have in mind?" Finn asked while Iris tried to figure out what she could wear to mess with the date.

"That new supper club."

"The one run by a banshee?" Finn asked.

"Yep. The ambiance? Terrifying. But the lamb shanks? Divine."

"Why there?"

"Because it's mildly controversial. Your appearance there is likely to cause a stir. Even without a mysterious woman on your arm."

"Why is it controversial?" Iris asked, ready to take up for a fellow paranormal, even if she didn't know them.

"The rumor is the waitstaff is almost unbearably rude. And most people leave with a migraine thanks to all the screaming. But when some people bring up the very real flaws of the establishment, others start saying people are just being judgmental of banshee culture. So on and so forth. It will look good that you are eating there. It will look better if you come out afterward seeming pleased with the experience and at the very beginning stages of being in love."

"Did you have any plans tonight?" Finn asked, looking at Iris.

She'd been planning to hit up the bookstore since Arden had monopolized her entire day once he'd shown up. But she couldn't let it get back to her mother that she was being difficult.

Her first instinct was to protest. Loudly. She barely knew how to navigate her feelings in private. How was she supposed to parade around the city on Finn's arm like she wasn't a walking, spiraling identity crisis?

But if she pushed back too hard, it might get back to her mother. And that, frankly, was worse than any dinner with banshees.

"Oh, well, I *was* going to attend my first Necromancy For Beginners class . . ."

"Necromancy For Beginners?" Henry repeated.

"*How to Raise the Dead Without Raising Eyebrows,*" Iris said. It was a real class. She'd used the phone Arden had insisted they go out to buy—then learn how to use—to track it down, wanting to have it in her back pocket if the conversation called for it.

"Necromancy," Henry repeated, giving Finn a look she couldn't quite interpret.

"I'd hate to cut into your new hobbies," Finn said.

"So long as I don't miss next week's class . . ."

"What's that one?" Henry asked.

"*Séance & Song: Summoning the Dead with Showtunes.*"

"So we can expect necromancer singing in the future," Henry observed. "Great. Anyway. Tonight. Eight. I already made the reservation. Finn, wear the slacks and a shirt but no jacket. Iris, I will have something sent over."

"Why can't I pick out my own clothes?"

"Because I'm half afraid you will find something in a material printed with vintage torture devices or something. Eight. Happy faces. So in love. I can't be there to coach you. But make me proud."

With that, he was gone.

Iris felt like the air got instantly thinner once he left

the room. She couldn't quite decide if Henry was that insufferable, or if she was viewing him through a lens of principled hatred. He was the man behind Mr. Mayor. She couldn't help but wonder how much of Finn's utter lack of personality was because Henry claimed his likes and hobbies didn't pass muster with a focus group.

"I'm sorry he springs things like this on us," Finn said when Henry was gone. "He forgets that people have lives."

"Maybe because you don't have one."

That was mean. And she even regretted it the moment it was out of her mouth. But things couldn't be unsaid.

Finn watched her for a moment. Then his mouth opened and closed before he gave her a tight nod. "That's fair."

It really wasn't.

But Finn was already moving past it. "Do you have any concerns about this part? The possible paparazzi . . ."

"Not really, no." How much worse could it be from the usual gawking she got?

"You may have some concerns about Henry's outfit selection."

"Why?"

"The shoes. He's not going to send over flats."

"Ugh," Iris grumbled, looking down at her feet that seemed to be in a constant state of minor pain if she so much as slipped them into anything other than the sandals that Monty had brought home as some sort of swag gift from a party.

"Kind of speciesist to go with shoes with a toe loop," he'd said, waving down at his own feet. "Not all of us have toes."

"We'll be sitting most of the time," Finn reassured her now. "I'm going to go get dressed."

There was a knock at the door about an hour and a half later, interrupting a scene in her book that was getting steamy.

"I'll get it," Finn said, holding up a hand at her and making his way to the door, returning a moment later with a garment bag and a box of shoes. "Told you," he said.

"How high are they?"

In answer, he draped the garment bag over the arm of the couch and opened the box for her.

They were surprisingly casual espadrille jute-wrapped wedges. With a closed toe, of course.

"Well, at least they don't have those icepick-thin heels," she decided.

"Henry is not without mercy."

"Oh, come on. You and I both know he went with wedges because he's afraid I'll fall on my face and embarrass you."

"I know you're determined to dislike him," Finn said, closing the box lid and handing it to her. "And he has earned some of that. But if you give him a chance, he's not all bad. He just wants the best for us."

Henry wanted the best for Finn.

She only factored in for image purposes.

"No, not on the table," Finn said. His voice was tight as Iris tried to set the box there.

"Why not?"

To that, Finn winced a little as he rubbed the back of his neck. "Superstition," he admitted. "My mother always said it is bad luck to put shoes on the table. Or a purse on the floor. Or not to throw salt over your left shoulder if you spill it. She was full of superstitions. Most of them stuck somehow."

That was an interesting tidbit that made him seem just a little more like an actual human being, not a campaign cutout of a man.

"My aunt Lydia is full of them too," she admitted. "Though we have very different ones."

"Like what?"

"Never brush your hair on a full moon, always swim clockwise around a shipwreck. Oh, and finding two pearls in a clam means you're going to have twins. Or someone is coming to visit. She could never keep that one straight."

"Do you follow them?"

"Well, one time, I *did* brush my hair on a full moon. And it got so tangled that night that it took me a week to get the knots out. I haven't done that since."

"And no more tangles?"

"Not like that."

"Better safe than sorry tends to be my motto," he said, reaching for the garment bag. "I'll go hang this up so it doesn't get wrinkled."

Iris finally finished her book as Finn sat watching videos of his political opponents on his laptop, until she couldn't take it anymore and got up to go get ready for their night out.

It wasn't until she was out of the bath and dripping wet that she realized she hadn't grabbed a towel from the hall linen closet.

"Barnacles," she grumbled, squeezing as much water out of her hair as possible, then using her hands to squeegee the rest of the water from her arms and chest.

Then, without stopping to check, she flew out of the bathroom, stark naked, to get a towel. And ran right into Finn.

"Whoa," he grunted, his arms automatically going around her. At the feel of her bare skin, his whole body stiffened. And when he seemed to realize that one of his hands was firmly placed on her butt, another part of his body started to *stiffen* too.

There was no stopping the strange little whimpering sound that escaped her. Though she tried to do some mental gymnastics to convince herself it was simply from the delicious steamy scenes in her book, not the man whose body was pressed to hers.

"You okay?" he asked, the huskiness in his voice making her belly flip-flop. "Did something happen?"

"Yes," she said, finding her own voice breathless.

"What was it?"

"I forgot a towel."

To that, Finn let out a small rumbling chuckle.

She expected him to do the politically correct thing. To turn away, to give her privacy.

Instead, one arm stayed around her—the one with his hand on her butt—as the other reached out to open the linen closet and pull out a towel.

Before his arm fell away, his hand grazed over her round cheek in a way that no one could claim was accidental.

The desire grew, spread, started to burn through her as Finn took a step back to unfold the towel.

His gaze wasn't on his task; he was drinking her up, his eyes tracking up and down her body for a short moment before he wrapped the towel around her back. He pulled the material forward, tightening it around her chest, his knuckles grazing her breasts in the process.

Another one of those needy sounds escaped her.

Something about that seemed to undo him, to loosen the control he kept such a tight hold on.

Iris found herself pushed back against the wall.

Then his hand was sliding up her thigh under the towel. There was the slightest pause as his fingers grazed the soft skin of her inner thigh, giving her a chance to change her mind, to say no, to move away.

But she wasn't capable of moving right then, with the need coursing through her, with the passion in his eyes—something she couldn't help but be transfixed by.

She wanted this.

And she wasn't going to overthink herself out of it.

Iris's hand slipped down, covering his, and pressing his hand between her thighs.

Her moan mingled with his hiss as he felt the proof of her desire.

Iris's hand slipped away, letting Finn have full control. Her hand slid up his forearm instead, holding on to his bicep as his fingers moved upward.

A soft whimper escaped her as his thumb circled that pearl of her desire. The sound had Finn's eyes burning as he watched her. He did another circle. Then another. Slow, deliberate. Over and over. Until her thighs were shaking and her nails were digging into his arm.

Only then did his movements pick up pace. Every brush of touch was a tide rising, every moan that escaped her the sound of waves cresting.

"Finn," she whimpered, her hips rocking against his touch, begging—demanding—more.

Finn was happy to give her exactly what he sensed she needed.

Two of his fingers skimmed down, then slipped inside her.

He pressed her more firmly against the wall like he was bracing her for a storm as his fingers started to thrust.

The need was swelling, driving her up higher and higher, leaving her clinging to him, bracing for the fall, for the crash.

Her walls tightened around his fingers, dragging a groan out of Finn as his thumb continued to circle, as his fingers thrust.

"There you go," he murmured. His voice was both rough and soft at the same time as her body tensed, as her head tilted up and a long moan escaped her.

The climax moved through her, a deep, throbbing pleasure that pulled her under the surface over and over, leaving her clinging to him, letting him anchor her as the waves kept pulling her under.

Her head fell into Finn's chest, breathing in the scent of him that she'd grown so accustomed to.

She hadn't known the notes at first, being earth scents.

She knew them then: bergamot, sandalwood, and vetiver.

They're the most universally liked scents, Finn had told her when she'd mentioned his cologne.

That alone was enough to break the spell of her post-pleasure contentedness.

What was she *doing*?

How could she let Finn, of all humans, touch her that way?

She grabbed his wrist and pulled his hand from between her thighs. Then shoved her hands against his chest for good measure.

She couldn't blame him. She knew that logically. She'd wanted that. She'd encouraged it.

She was madder at herself than anything.

"Iris . . ." Finn called, gently grabbing her wrist as she started toward the bathroom again.

Was that regret in his voice? Remorse? Confusion? A combination of all three, maybe.

"That's never happening again," she told him, clearing his conscience but making it clear that it was a momentary lapse in judgment.

She closed herself in the bathroom, slumping against the door and trying to pull herself together.

She wasn't supposed to *like* him. That hadn't been part of the deal. She was supposed to sabotage the engagement, not sink into his touch like it was a riptide dragging her under. Worse still, she didn't even know *who* she liked. The real Finn? The one who touched her like she mattered? Or The Suit Finn, built from campaign promises and perfect smiles?

Her feelings had always been a mess, but now her body had joined the rebellion as well.

And tonight, she had to fake a fairy-tale romance, knowing it was all lies. Knowing her skin still tingled from the truth.

Both her body and mind felt tugged in a dozen different directions.

On the one hand, she had wanted that more than she even wanted to admit to herself, had enjoyed every second of it. But on the other . . . what in deep-sea disaster was that?

Yes, Finn was an almost devastatingly good-looking man. And, sure, she could understand her body having a biological attraction to him physically.

But that face and body of his belonged to a man who was more political talking points than personality.

Her desire shouldn't have been able to overpower her common sense. Or standards.

That was it.

No more spicy books.

No matter how much she loved them.

The last thing she needed was to let that happen again.

As it was, she had no idea how she was going to be able to go out to dinner with him and pretend to be all lovey-dovey—to sit across from him at a table, all the while knowing that just hours before, he'd had his hand between her thighs; he'd felt her falling apart for him.

This was going to be a nightmare.

But there was no way out of it now.

Iris

"Where is my sweet sea spawn?" Monty called as Iris stood in front of the bathroom mirror, fully dressed but stalling for time.

"Getting ready to go out for our first official date," Finn told the pelican. "Do you think you could . . . nudge her along for me? We really need to get going if we want to keep our reservation."

"Beauty cannot be rushed," Monty said dramatically. "But I'll see what I can do."

Iris heard the flap of his feet down the hallway.

"Darling, your human is twitching. And you are beautiful enough."

Iris opened the door, getting a whistle out of the bird—who was now wearing a ridiculously loud turquoise vest.

His gaze moved over her floor-length baby-pink dress with its sweetheart neckline, thin straps, and dainty floral embroidered design.

But the second his gaze got to her face, his head cocked to the side.

"What happened?"

There was a lot she shared with Monty. Her intimate life was not one of them. At least not in detail.

"I don't want to go," she admitted. It was true enough.

"I didn't want to let Priestess Alana pluck my feather for a spell, but alas, we have to suffer for our dreams."

"But this isn't my dream."

"Dining at one of the most buzz-worthy restaurants in the city is absolutely the dream, my darling girl. I'm not at all jealous. Now, chop chop."

"What are we even going to talk about for an hour and a half?"

"Talk about your hopes and dreams. Your tragic pasts. Your favorite seaweed dish. Or just stare at each other longingly over breadsticks. Isn't that what the humans do?" He gave her a wink. "Though, I'll admit, your guy's a bit . . . stiff. Like someone carved him from a block of dry salt. So, if all else fails, ask him about his political platform. We both know he can talk for hours about that."

"True," she agreed, sucking in a steadying breath. "Do I look okay?"

"No. You look stunning. Now go let the whole city be jealous."

Not having a choice, Iris walked out of the bathroom and down the hall.

"Wow," Finn said when he turned at the sound of her heels on the floor.

She liked the look in his eyes a little too much. So she rushed to grab her bag instead of letting herself soak in his admiration.

"We're late," she said.

Finn said nothing as he followed her to the door.

"Monty, don't eat the cat," she called.

"I'm going out too," Monty said, waddling out with them. "I can't help my nature. I would never actually eat him. His fur tastes funny, by the way."

"Because I started using a perfume spray on him to stop you from putting your beak on him."

"Rude," Monty said, fluffing his feathers. "Do I look ready to party?" he asked.

He'd changed into a suit jacket instead. Iris had no idea where he even found clothes to fit him. But he did look pretty adorable all dressed up.

"Absolutely. You'll be signing autographs in no time."

"Of course I will," Monty said, walking out of the elevator.

"Let's take a cab," Finn said, throwing a hand up in the air.

He tried to hide how he'd checked his watch again. "I'm always late," she said, sliding into the back seat of the car. "My mother probably should have told you that."

"We can still make it there in time."

The restaurant was only a few blocks away. It was a brick building that had been painted black, with black awnings and a small number of outside seating surrounded by wrought-iron fences.

There were dozens of people standing outside, looking around, likely waiting for tables.

"We have to sell it," Finn reminded her.

"I remember," she said as Finn slipped out.

His hand extended to her, and she had to force herself to slip her hand into his.

They made their way through the crowd.

Cameras clicked. Phone screens lit up. A whisper floated by: "That's the mermaid, right?"

Iris kept her chin lifted and her eyes forward, but it felt like barnacles were attaching to her skin.

It was impossible to tell if the stares were full of curiosity or judgment. Probably both.

"Henry will be pleased," Finn said as they moved into the restaurant. And at those words, her heart felt like it deflated a bit in her chest. "Those pictures and videos should be circulating any moment now."

Finn talked to the hostess as Iris turned around, taking in the surroundings.

Henry had been right about the ambiance. The entire inside of the restaurant was bathed in black, with occasional pops of red. Even the abundant overhead chandeliers and tabletop candles did nothing to brighten the cavernous-feeling space.

"Right this way, Mr. Westrock," the hostess said.

Finn's hand pressed to the center of her back, and she pretended to ignore the way her skin felt warm at his touch as they moved through the tight space between tables until they reached their own.

"I'm not sure how we're going to read this," Iris said after the hostess handed them their menus and moved away.

"You can't really go wrong with steak."

"Is steak good for optics?" Iris asked.

To that, Finn's head tipped to the side, his gaze curious as he looked at her, making her feel suddenly exposed.

Whatever he was about to say, though, fell away as he closed his menu.

"Yes. Research shows that eating meat is popular among humans and most paranormals. So long as I am also willing to be seen at the occasional vegan restaurant as well."

"Isn't that exhausting?" she asked.

"What?"

"Always wondering what people think and want from you?"

"That's the job," he said, shrugging.

The server interrupted them then, taking their orders, and then pausing when there was an ear-piercing scream from somewhere deep in the building. Around them, several water glasses shattered, making the bussers rush over to clean them up.

"Our chef," the hostess said with a strained smile. Iris was sure she could see pain behind the woman's eyes, like she had a headache from the screaming.

"Of course," Finn said, his press-conference smile firmly in place.

"I'll be right back with your drinks."

"What does wine taste like?" Iris asked after the hostess walked off.

"You've never had wine?" Finn asked, brows rising.

"No. We don't have grapes in the ocean."

"Of course. We probably should have put some wine tasting in your training. You can pretend to sip it if you don't care for it. It's . . . an acquired taste. Henry forced me to learn to like it over the course of six months. I ordered a pretty sweet one, so it's a decent introduction."

"Why can't you just drink what you like?" Why couldn't she?

"It's more about proper etiquette. You never know what you are going to be served at various events or someone's dinner party. It would be rude to turn something down or not at least taste it."

"I guess that makes sense. I feel that way about fish eggs."

"You don't like caviar?"

Iris couldn't help the full-body shiver at just the idea of the eggs. She was surprised by the laugh that escaped Finn—the sound making a different kind of shiver move through her. And that smile he shot her? It almost looked real.

"Did you try to get out of it when you were younger?"

"There was a particularly disastrous time I tried to hide them in my bra, only to have them float out in front of important company."

He was laughing now—really laughing—and the sound made something in her crack open.

Maybe he wasn't just a mouthpiece in slacks. Maybe, under all the polish and platform language, there was still a person in there.

She could almost see it in the way his eyes lit up when he mentioned his parents, the way his voice softened when he asked about her sisters.

"My mother was furious," she concluded.

"It sounds like she's hard on you."

"She has high standards. And my older sister effortlessly meets them. So it tends to be a bone of contention that I don't or can't."

"You have a younger sister too, right?"

"Yes. Shelly isn't like me or Juna. She's kind of obsessed with the surface. She was very upset that she didn't get to be the one to come here with you."

"What is in her future? Juna is meant for the throne, I assume."

"Yeah. Actually, I don't know. I don't know if my mother knows yet, honestly. She's still pretty young. She's definitely in her 'defiance, then moping when she doesn't get her way' phase."

"That makes sense."

"Did you ever have one?"

"One what?"

"Defiance phase."

"Oh, no."

"Of course not," Iris mumbled under her breath, disappointed that she couldn't at least imagine that a much younger Finn had been a human being with thoughts, desires, and dreams.

"My father was killed just around the time when I would have been heading into that phase of my life," Finn said. "Then, well, it felt wrong to misbehave in any way. My mother was already going through so much."

"You were too," Iris said, just barely resisting the urge to reach out and put her hand over his.

"It wasn't the same."

"How so?"

"She was trying to fight the city to get them to take accountability for their part in what happened."

"A lack of security, right?"

"Yes. There should have been paranormal security guards at the very least. But she was fighting for wards in the courthouse, so it would be impossible for anything like that to happen again, no matter how sensitive the cases they were working on were."

"Did she accomplish that?"

"She didn't live to see it implemented, but she definitely got the ball rolling. It became a law about a year after she passed away."

"How old were you when you lost her?"

"Two weeks shy of my eighteenth birthday. We'd spent the night before packing all my belongings to head off to college."

"You were the one to find her?" Iris asked, this time reaching out and giving in to the urge to put her hand over his.

"Yes. It seemed . . . peaceful. I hadn't even known she was sick. Her attorney said she'd known but hadn't wanted to worry me."

"But knowing would have given you time to prepare."

"I don't know if anything could have prepared me for losing both of them so young."

"Should I not have brought it up?" she asked, noting the tension in his body.

"No, I'm glad you did. I get asked about my father quite a bit. But everyone forgets my mother. It's nice to talk about her. She was a wonderful woman."

"Was she in politics too?"

To that, he shot Iris a smirk that did not make her suddenly want to slip out of her panties. Nope. Not her.

"No. No, my mother was in public relations."

"Oh, come on," Iris said, helpless to fight the smile that spread across her face.

"Yep. Had her own firm. Can you guess where Henry's mother and father worked?"

"So you guys go way back."

"We went to college together. He brought me home to

his family on the holidays so I wasn't alone. He comes off as cold, but there's a heart under there somewhere."

"I will have to take your word on that."

The server came back with their wine, making her suddenly aware that she was still holding his hand. She snatched it back and thanked the server, then reached for her wineglass.

"Yeah, smelling it probably won't help," Finn said when she put the glass toward her nose. "A quick sip is probably the smartest bet."

She followed his instructions, deciding it was arguably much better than fish eggs, but not anywhere near as good as her newly beloved coffee.

"I think I can learn to sip this to be polite—barnacles!" She gasped. Her whole body jolted as another scream wailed from the kitchen.

"Seems like this restaurant is a good test of nervous system regulation," Finn said.

Finn, as usual, was unflappable, no matter how often or how loud the screaming got.

Meanwhile, Iris felt like every nerve ending was frayed by the time they finished their meal and rose from the table.

"You all right? You've looked a little pale for the past few minutes."

Iris chose not to think of the way her belly swooped as he said those words directly behind her, his breath tickling the shell of her ear.

"Yeah," she said. She sucked in a steadying breath as they moved outside, where everyone gathered around seemed oblivious to the siren calls within. "Much better now," she said. Her breath caught as Finn's arm slid around her, curling her closer to his body to move her out of the way when some guy stumbled backward toward them.

He kept her close as they made their way through the crowd and toward the edge of the sidewalk.

"Don't look, but we have company."

"The paparazzi?" she asked, her mind conjuring up images of catching Monty talking to his reflection in the bathroom one night. *No paparazzi. Please, I'm just trying to live my life!*

"Yes. What do you say to really selling this?" he asked, his hand tightening on her hip, his arm pulling her more firmly against him.

"How?" She was going to pretend not to hear the breathlessness in her voice. Or the way the closeness was setting off little wildfires of need across her skin.

In answer, his head lowered down, his forehead pressed to hers.

"A kiss," he suggested, gaze watching hers, waiting for her answer.

"Okay," she whispered. Totally *just* for the cameras. No other reason.

That rumbling sound moved through Finn again as his hand rose, sliding along her jaw gently as his head angled.

Then his lips were on hers.

If she'd expected something performative and stiff, she was wholly mistaken.

He kissed her like the sea claimed the shore—slow at first, then all-consuming. Her breath caught, a gasp tangled in the pull of the undertow.

One of her arms wrapped around the back of his neck. The other grabbed the material covering his bicep.

But even as she sighed against his lips, Finn's mouth moved from hers.

His forehead was on hers again.

"That should be on the front of a bunch of gossip papers tomorrow," he said, making her heart sink.

"Oh, goodie," she said, turning away from him to hail a cab.

To an onlooker, she probably looked like a woman desperate to get home to continue the intimacy they'd started on the sidewalk.

Only she knew that she wanted to get home and as far away from him as quickly as possible.

She'd thought they'd made some sort of strides over their meal. The conversation got easier, even if the topics became a lot less intense after speaking of the loss of his parents and his motivation to go into politics.

Clearly, though, it had all just been part of the show for him.

If the man was able to fake a *kiss* like that, if he could so convincingly manufacture intimacy, there was nothing about him that she could trust.

She'd been a fool to think otherwise for even a moment.

She needed to get home, get changed, get some sleep, then wake up in the morning and kick her plans into overdrive.

But she was going to need some reinforcements.

Finn

"You've forgotten your talking points five times in a row. What is going on with you?" Henry slapped his notepad on the desk.

"I don't know." Finn dropped down onto the couch, slamming his head back to stare up at the ceiling.

He did know.

He just couldn't tell Henry.

He'd waltzed into the office that morning brandishing a pile of website printouts, beaming over the quality and angles of the kiss on the street outside the restaurant.

Apparently, the people were 'eating it up.' He'd gone on and on about the talking points in the articles on each website.

Since no one knew Iris's identity yet, they were dubbing them *The Mer and the Mayor*.

"Are you getting sick?" Henry asked. "We can go get you hooked up for some fluids. Maybe one of those immunity cocktails like we did last year."

"I'm not getting sick."

"Are you sure? Because we can't afford to have you down and out for a week at this point in the campaign."

"I'm sure. I just can't focus today."

"Maybe you need to hit the gym. That usually helps to shake out the cobwebs."

"Maybe."

Henry watched him for a moment, then sighed.

"All right. What is it? Not campaign manager to political hopeful. Friend to friend."

He knew better than to believe they could separate the two. But he had no one else to talk to.

"It's Iris."

"Did she pick up throat singing? Séances? Collecting werewolf claws?"

He could bring up the incredibly creepy vintage porcelain doll that had been sitting in the bathroom first thing in the morning. Or the fact that he was reasonably sure he heard a musical laugh out in the hallway when the sight of it made him let out a yelp he wasn't exactly proud of.

"Not yet. But I wouldn't be surprised."

"What is it, then? Just her weird hobbies? Those can be . . . guided. Smoothed over."

Finn sighed. He'd always appreciated Henry's ability to view a situation as an objective outsider. But they were talking about Iris now, not some abstract idea. He didn't want to hear all the ways she could be altered to better serve a preferred image.

"I'm not trying to change her."

In fact, the problem was he liked her a little too much just as she was.

"What, then?"

"Tell me more about the arrangement."

"What do you mean? You get married. After some carefully chosen and executed events. Pretty simple."

"I mean the process of setting it up. Did you speak to the queen herself?"

"No. From what I understand, Tatiana doesn't come to the surface."

"Why, then, would she want a princess to?"

"We've covered this. Pollution regulations."

"Who did you speak to?"

"Maria. She's the queen's land dignitary."

"What did Maria say the queen said about the situation?"

"That she was open to it. What are you trying to get at here? What are you digging for?"

"Information."

"About what?"

"If Iris was forced into this or not."

"Oh." Henry's shoulders slumped a little. "That, I don't know. But I'd venture a guess that the merfolk are a lot like many other paranormal royal families."

"Meaning?"

"That there is an expectation of . . . advantageous weddings for the princes and princesses."

Finn mulled on that for a moment. "Was Tatiana's own marriage arranged?"

"Oh, absolutely. That was a big to-do. They'd never even met until the day of their wedding. Tatiana's consort was an important political figure from a merclan from somewhere off the shores of Greece. So, I would venture to guess that Iris knew her whole life that she might end up married for political gain."

Maybe that was true.

But she'd likely never considered that her marriage would end up being on *land*.

His mind flashed back to Iris diving into the pool in his building, the enthusiasm of her movements, the joy on her face.

She clearly loved the water.

It was in her blood.

Every time she looked at him instead of the sea, she was reminded of what she was losing, of what he had stolen from her.

Something sacred.

Her very *nature*.

"Is she complaining?" Henry asked.

"No. She never complains."

Except about the temperature of the air conditioning. And why human beings had yet to develop a comfortable shoe. And the fact that her favorite Chinese food place closed too early on Tuesday nights. And, of course, that the sequels to certain books weren't even written yet, let alone close to publication.

She said almost none of those things directly to him, though. Most of it was things she'd grumbled to herself or confessed to Monty. Or, even on occasion, to Checkers. To his credit, he was happy to warm her lap anytime she wanted it.

Iris rarely, if ever, spoke to him, unless she absolutely needed to. It was something that bothered him more with each passing day. Even if, admittedly, he'd never been great at bringing up random topics of conversation, unless they had to do with politics or his campaign.

He'd been coached on who to be for so long that he was

starting to worry he'd forgotten who he *was*—under the talking points, beneath the plans.

"Then why are you asking about the arrangement?"

"I want to know if she agreed to it. Or if she was forced into it."

"I think, in a way, it would be both, wouldn't it?"

"Maybe."

"Why these thoughts all of a sudden?"

"I dunno," he lied. "I guess it's just the first time I've slowed down enough to really think about the situation."

That may have had a small part in it.

But Finn knew what had changed was the dynamic between the two of them.

Anytime he thought about the incident in the hallway, he swore he could still feel her, could still hear her moans.

Then the kiss on the street.

The reason for it may have been manufactured, but the passion itself was all organic.

But after both instances, when he'd maybe been expecting softness and sweetness, he got coldness and guardedness.

It wasn't that she hadn't wanted him—he'd felt it. But something always snapped shut afterward. Like desire for him was dangerous. Like it cost her something. And he didn't know why.

It was hard not to worry that he'd overstepped some line, even though in both instances, he'd had enthusiastic 'yeses' from Iris.

Because if Iris *wanted* to be there, if she'd agreed to the marriage, why was she having such severe reactions to the relationship between them evolving into something more real?

It made no sense.

"I can put some feelers out, but I doubt we will be able to get any kind of straight answer. It will all be spin about how the princesses are overjoyed to improve ocean and surface relations."

That was true.

Finn wasn't the only one with a PR team.

"I have a radical idea. Why don't you ask Iris?"

"Would she give me a straight answer? If her mother somehow made it clear that she *has* to do this, would she tell me that she didn't want this and risk whatever consequences her mother might have for her?"

"I don't know. She's certainly had no issues telling me her opinion."

"Because she thinks you're nothing but an empty suit. Who is always judging her."

"I'm trying to help improve her image," Henry said, brows pinching. "Like I've always done for you. Do you feel judged?"

Not anymore, he didn't.

But maybe that was just because there was nothing left of him that hadn't been gone over with a fine-tooth comb and a high-definition media lens.

He could remember a time, many years back, though, when Henry had scoffed at his sci-fi movie posters and had helped him box up his comic books and stick them in storage.

In their place, he'd been instructed to invest in artists from all the different boroughs of the city—and to make sure he represented humans and paranormals alike in his collection. In place of his action heroes who saved the world, he was urged to read non-fiction books on history, species, and political policy.

Finn hadn't seen the last ten big-budget superhero movies that had come out. Nor the many comics that had been released. He'd forgotten about them for the most part. And the nerd inside him died a little more at that realization.

Henry watched him, sighing.

"Tell you what? Why don't you take the afternoon off? Go do something relaxing. Get a massage. Take a walk. Come back here tomorrow with your head on straight."

"Yeah," Finn agreed, getting to his feet.

"And don't forget to tell Iris about the fae cultural parade. She has to be there."

"Got it," he agreed, making his way out of his office, then the building.

As he moved out onto the street, he had the depressing realization that he had no idea what to do with himself if he wasn't focusing on work.

All he knew was he couldn't go home and be confronted with Iris's coldness while trying to battle his own desire for her.

So he did what Henry suggested—as he almost always did.

He walked.

And walked.

Until, at some point, he turned to look where his feet had automatically taken him.

Back to a store he'd spent too much time in—and far too much of his parents' money—as a kid and teen.

The comic book store.

He hated how he paused, how he looked around to see if anyone was watching him, recognized him, and what they might be thinking of him if they did, if they saw where he was going.

"Screw it," he mumbled to himself and moved inside.

The bell jingled over the door, the same way it always had. The scent hit him first: ink, new paper, a whiff of sugar from the vending machine someone still stocked with off-brand candy.

It was a temple. One where younger versions of himself had debated plot twists, stacked issues like sacred texts, and dreamed of being the kind of man who could save a city with nothing but conviction and a cape.

No platform.

No polish.

No talking points.

Then he spent an afternoon lost in the old worlds he'd let slip away from him, having adventures, seeing the good guys be tested but prevailing.

And the thought that came to mind as he walked out later?

He wished he could tell Iris about those stories, knowing from her book selections that she enjoyed a good action plot.

He wanted that. He wanted to share something with her, to relate to her, to show her that maybe they weren't so different after all.

It was with that thought in mind that he walked into a building and signed up for a class.

If she'd given up the sea to stand beside him, the least he could do . . . was learn to swim.

14

Iris

"Look, I'm not claiming he's your soulmate," Arden said. He opened the door of Selene's bookshop. "I'm saying I ship it so hard that the postal service is going to file a complaint."

Iris rolled her eyes at him.

He'd been like a dog with a bone since he'd shown up at her doorstep with cut-up pictures of her kiss with Finn all glued together into a collage on the front of a thick red binder.

And he absolutely would not listen to her insistence that the kiss was just for the cameras.

"It was *fake*," she insisted once again.

"Oh, please. You two have so much unresolved tension, it's giving me chest pains. And I don't even have a heart."

"Wait, you don't have a heart?" she asked, gaping at him.

"Nope."

"Is that why you're so obsessed with heart-shaped things?" she asked as they stopped just inside of the door.

"Fun fact," Selene said, coming up from somewhere in the back of the store. "The modern heart shape we see all over is actually the shape of a woman's butt when she's bent over."

Selene seemed even more ethereal than usual. The air seemed to sparkle around her. Like she was, Iris didn't know, recharged.

It took her a long moment to realize that the late-night howling from the werewolves wasn't the only thing that happened on a full moon. All across the surface, covens and solo-practicing witches alike gathered under the moon to dance, to sing, to set intentions.

Iris had no idea what kind of magic Selene had been working on, but the witch was glowing. Even her hair seemed shinier.

"Well, what's not to love about that?" Arden asked, eyes sparkling as he shot one of those devilishly charming smiles in Selene's direction.

"Oh, don't bother with that," Selene said, waving at his face. "I'm immune to your charms. Tried, tested, and *vaccinated*."

Arden was unfazed.

"That's not immunity, darling. That's denial with extra sass." The charm was practically oozing off him. Iris wasn't even in the path of it, and she could swear she felt some of it clinging to her.

"Who is this?" Selene asked, nodding her chin at Arden.

Was it just Iris's overactive imagination, or was her witchy friend staying a deliberate distance from the demon?

"Arden. My demonic wedding planner. Arden, this is Selene, my co-conspirator."

"Ah, yes. The witch trying to ruin my wedding."

"I believe their utter lack of compatibility is what is ruining it. But, technically, I'm only ruining their *engagement*; the wedding is collateral damage." Her chin jerked up, everything about her primed for an argument. Iris could already hear her spiel about the suffrage movement, bra burning, and the ever-present problem of the inequitable division of labor in households. Minus, of course, orcs. Who, apparently, were brutes in the streets, but lovingly attentive husbands and fathers at home.

"You know what? I think I sense *longing* buried deep in that cold, jaded heart." Iris watched as Arden stepped closer toward Selene. Even though everything about her friend was sparking warning signs.

"You're mistaken. That's just the echo chamber where I keep my apathy." Selene stepped closer to a display table, pretending that she needed to straighten the stacks. When Iris knew she was simply putting some space between herself and the demon who perhaps saw a bit more of her than she liked.

"Are you sure you're not just scared of love?" Arden asked.

"No. I'm scared of glitter, huggers, and overhyped books. Love just has terrible PR."

"Love is the most potent magic of all."

Iris almost wanted to snort at that. Sure, mermaids were of the romantic sort. But that was cheesy even for her kind.

"Love is a neurochemical betrayal wrapped in bad poetry and cheap flowers."

"You really *don't* believe in love, do you?" Arden asked, the charm slipping to genuine concern.

"I believe in books, caffeine, petty revenge, and the inevitable heat death of the universe. Love is somewhere below those." Despite her words, Iris could swear she heard a false note in her friend's voice.

Arden watched her for a moment. "You know, if I planned your love life, I bet you could actually have one."

"If I let you near my love life, I'd have to be fumigated. So, progress?" Selene asked, looking away from Arden to give Iris her full attention. Like if she tried hard enough, she could pretend the demon and his keen observations didn't exist at all.

"Well, he hates the bugs and teeth. And the doll almost made him wet himself. But, no. No, he's just . . . the same old Finn."

"Oh, I don't know about that," Arden said, pulling the binder from his chest to flash it toward the two women.

"Oh, yes, a carefully orchestrated pap shot. How romantic. That campaign manager of his probably even tipped off the press."

"Thank you," Iris said, vindicated. Even if her heart did a little flip each time she saw the pictures of the kiss.

"Oh, come on. Even you have to admit that Finn is leading man material," Arden insisted. He gestured toward the table of romance novels she'd just straightened.

"Sure, if he is the main character in a cautionary tale about the subjugation of women. I mean, look at her," Selene said, flinging an arm at Iris. "She's from a matriarchal culture. Even her own true form is, at a biological level, matriarchal. Her body has to be excited and willing for there to be any sort of sex. And you want to force her to become the pawn in some scheme among surface men?" Selene's tone was tight, borderline angry.

"Darling, it's only a scheme if she doesn't like him. And I, for one, see the look in her eyes when she talks about him. That's not hate. That's a spark.

"I'm not some mustache-twirling villain. I happen to think they're perfect for each other. And if I'm right, that makes me a romantic, not a conspirator."

"A man who was perfect for her wouldn't force her to leave the ocean." Selene, in her anger, took a step closer toward Arden. Iris swore the air sparked between them. She wasn't sure if that was the witch's magic or something more.

"I believe that honor belongs to Her Majesty the queen, not Finn." Arden tucked his chin to look down at Selene.

There was a silence following that. Because they all knew he was right. Sure, Finn had wanted an advantageous marriage to a paranormal figure. But it had been Tatiana who'd volunteered Iris for the position, whether she wanted it or not.

"Anyway," Arden said. His voice sliced through the tension in the store. "For the seating chart for your friend here, I think we should place her somewhere strategic," he said, opening up his binder. "Close enough to witness true love conquering in the end. Far enough that her scowling won't ruin the photos . . ."

Despite trying to keep her lips in a firm line, Selene's smile and snort indicated that she wasn't quite as immune to the demon's charm as she'd claimed.

"I mean, I'd consider putting her at the singles table. But we don't want to risk her sparking an anti-romance rebellion mid-toast."

To that, Selene rolled her eyes. "Why is he here?" she asked, her arms crossing as she nodded her head toward the demon.

"He shows up randomly and insists we talk about fonts and centerpieces." Though why he wanted to keep her in the loop when she was so insistent on there not being a wedding was beyond her.

"Hmm," Selene said. "Hey, we could use that."

"Use what?"

"The wedding planning as a form of sabotage."

"No, we cannot," Arden insisted.

But Selene ignored him. "You could insist on absolutely unhinged centerpieces. Bioluminescent fungus comes to mind. It glows *and smells*."

"Absolutely not," Arden interjected. His handsome face was horrified.

"Set the color scheme as 'rotting kelp' or 'barnacle gray.'" The tension slipped from Selene's body as her ideas took shape.

"The palette is *soft summer*." Arden hugged his binder closer to his chest.

"Insist on inviting every ex he's ever had. With a plus-one. Say it is traditional that they regale you with stories of their first time being intimate."

"That's unhinged," Arden said, reaching up to loosen his tie when Iris didn't immediately agree with him.

"Have a signature scent for the event. Eau de Old Aquarium Water would be a good choice. Instead of a DJ, maybe consider a pod of melancholy dolphins . . ."

"Ooh, I know an eel barbershop quartet!" Iris said.

"You can't be playing along with this," Arden grumbled. "We have plans in place. Good, non-smelly plans."

"Don't listen to him. This is all gold," Selene said.

"There's an obvious flaw here," Arden insisted.

"What's that?"

"That if we get all the way to the wedding, nothing is going to stop it from happening."

"Ugh," Selene grumbled.

"It's okay, darling, you can admit that I'm right." He seemed immune to the concept of being cursed for life, because the guy shot a wink in Selene's direction.

"I'm not your darling." She turned back to Iris. "Okay. What plans do Finn and the PR guy have lined up now after your hard launch?"

"I'm not sure, but I do remember Finn mentioning that this was the crunch time, from now until the election, and that Finn's calendar is jam-packed. I guess I assumed it was just Finn's calendar. But it might be mine too, now that I think about it."

"Well, it seems like the usual things will involve town halls, late-night TV shows, charity events . . ."

"And cultural events. The fae parade is coming up," Arden supplied.

"I thought you weren't helping," Selene said.

"Hey, so long as we continue to do the wedding planning as we agreed, I'm willing to toss out some ideas. Even if I still believe you guys are going to fall madly in love. Which reminds me, this was supposed to be a quick stop to stock up on books on our way to taste-test cakes."

"Cakes?" Selene asked, perking up even more at the thought of sweets than she did over sabotage. Which was really saying something, since the woman was an evil mastermind when it came to dismantling a political marriage.

"I don't remember actually agreeing to the cake testing," Iris said. "You just assumed." Even if it would be really hard to turn down such a treat. Iris had to admit that the surface people got one thing right. And that was food. Especially if it was deep fried or covered in icing.

"Oh, no. We're cake testing for sure," Selene said, rushing behind the counter to shove various items into a big crossbody bag.

Just before she moved out, Iris saw her grab a book—this one with a shirtless alien man embracing a human woman—and shove it in a cabinet drawer that was labeled *Cursed Journals: Do Not Touch*.

"Come on. Grab your books. Can I interest you in a steamy . . . where is the romance section?" Arden asked.

"I don't want romance. I think I'm going to peruse the *Good for Her* section. Maybe some thrillers . . ." She glanced back between the two. "Can I trust you to behave without me for a few minutes?"

"Define behave," Arden said.

"I'll try not to turn him into a frog," Selene shot back. "But no promises."

Iris moved deeper into the bookstore, the sounds of Arden's and Selene's voices drifting away, the stress of the past day easing from her shoulders.

As much as she claimed she hadn't agreed to cake testing, Iris was glad for a distraction.

She'd lucked out that Monty had been home that morning and full of stories about the exciting things that went down at the star-studded party he'd attended.

His never-ending talking had allowed her to avoid speaking to Finn as he got up and got ready for his day.

She wouldn't even let herself look at him as he moved around the apartment.

Part of that was her frustration with him for forcing her to remember that their date had been fake all along—despite the very real feelings it had evoked in her.

The other part—the one she was desperately trying not to acknowledge—was that no matter how annoyed she was about how effortlessly Finn could fake real feelings; she couldn't deny that there was still some definite yearning on her part.

Fine.

It was more than yearning.

It was the kind of aching that had kept her awake all night, tossing and turning and tangling in her sheets, leaving her feeling overheated and unsatisfied.

She couldn't help but remember the way he'd kissed her, how his hands had teased and tantalized, how he'd been able to read her body so well, to give her exactly what she needed.

Iris was no stranger to all the lovely ways her own body could feel. While she had never really found a love match in her past, she'd been as curious as the next woman when it came to casual dating and exploration with the opposite sex. Everything from that first awkward, uncertain fumbling to a few lovely weeks enjoying the company of a man she knew would never be more than whispered moans and gentle caresses. But no one had ever been able to make her sing the way he could.

And it was just so disappointing that the man who could make her feel those things was the one with whom she could never have a real relationship.

She wasn't sure Finn was capable of having a genuine connection with anyone.

Iris reached for the first cover that caught her eye. Then another. And another. But as she made her way back toward the front of the store, she couldn't seem to stop herself from grabbing another of Caprica Coraline's books, even though she knew it was a romance. A spicy one that was only going to compound those needy feelings inside her.

She couldn't help it. Despite her current situation, she was a hopeless romantic at heart. She craved those warm and tingly sensations she got from seeing two characters fight for their love.

Sure, when she finished one of those books now, she was filled with a deep well of sadness at the idea of not being able to experience her own love story anytime soon. But she could live vicariously through the characters on the page.

"You sure you want this one?" Selene asked as she rang her order up. "This is extra romantic. I mean, they have a bunch of roadblocks, but it's a pretty epic love story."

"And how would you know that?" Arden asked, shooting her a devilish smirk. "It's hard to take your anti-love campaign seriously when it sounds like you devoured that book in one sitting."

"I skimmed it. One must understand the battlefield to dismantle the war machine."

"Admit it. You can't get enough of books where people kiss and cry and feel things."

"I read it for purely academic purposes. I was studying the psychological repercussions of unrealistic expectations."

"There's nothing unrealistic about love and love stories."

"Grand romantic gestures come to mind."

"They exist in real life."

"Oh, please. *Real* people don't do grand romantic gestures. They forget your birthday and track dirt in on your rugs."

"You're kind of cute when you're cynical."

"And you're kind of tolerable when you're silent. So, let's focus more on that. Anyway. Cake."

"Don't you have to worry about the store?" Iris asked as she hauled her tote bag onto her shoulder, grimacing a bit at the weight of it.

"Nah. Business is slow today anyway. You hear that, Gerty?" she called to the ghost. "You can start your inventory early today."

"Wow, that's rude," Arden said.

"What's rude?" Iris asked, looking behind her, where Arden's gaze was, but not seeing anything.

"Your little old ghost lady just flipped you a double bird."

"You can *see* her?"

"You can't?"

"No. She walks through me sometimes, but that's it."

"She thinks that's hilarious," Arden said. "Also, she says you were reading a spicy romance and that you cried when the duke proposed at the masquerade."

"I had something in my eye," Selene insisted, chin jerking up. "It's called *disbelief*."

"Sure, sure, sweetheart," he said, heading toward the door.

Selene turned back to the store in general and hissed a quiet, "Snitch!" at her ghostly predecessor.

"She wasn't dealing with dementia at the end of her life, by the way," Arden said.

"Then why is she always doing inventory?"

"Darling, what makes you think she's doing inventory? She's just screwing with you."

Selene stopped to gape at him. "But why?"

"Something about a cash register."

"Seriously? The ancient thing didn't even work anymore!" Selene yelled into the store, making a book fall off a shelf. "Real mature," she grumbled.

"She says you could get it fixed. In fact, she demands it." As if to emphasize her point, another book flew off the shelf, whacking Iris in the shoulder.

"Ow," Iris grumbled, leaning down to grab and right the book.

"It was her father's cash register. She says it belongs on the counter he built, where you read your smutty books." That last part made Arden's lips twitch.

"Fine, you old bat. I'll get the thing fixed. But I can't actually use it. It doesn't take credit cards. Let's go. I need all the cake."

With that, they were out.

"What's wrong?" Selene asked when Iris hesitated at the top of the stairs that led down to, she assumed, the subway platform.

"I've never been," she admitted.

"Really? What have you been doing since you came to the land? Walking everywhere?"

"I haven't been going out much now that Monty has started his social climbing and networking. I've mostly been just getting food from local places and reading. And, you know, collecting bugs and teeth."

"And trying to learn how to use her cell phone," Arden added. "That accidental dial while you were belting out a Celine Dion chart-topper was hilarious, by the way."

"Gee, thanks," Iris said, wincing at the memory of realizing she hadn't 'been alone' while she got dressed, like she thought.

"We've got you," Selene said, sliding her arm through Iris's and leading her down the steps.

"Are there *vampires* down here?" she asked.

"No need to whisper. It's not a bad word," Selene assured her.

"Do we have to . . . worry at all?"

From what Iris understood from her studies, history with more predatory paranormals like vampires had been vast and confusing. There'd been uprisings, assassinations, and many attacks and killings.

"Not anymore," Selene assured her.

"They have to carry bite consent cards now. It's all very gauche," Arden supplied.

"I've seen those in a bunch of stores," Iris said. "How do they work?"

"Vampires and donors alike have to carry cards. If the two parties agree to a feeding, each has to sign the other's card to show they consented to it," Arden explained.

"But . . . can't vampires *compel* a human to sign even if they didn't consent?" Iris asked.

"It's not a perfect system," Selene agreed. "But it was a major piece of legislation to make sure there were no more instances of anyone being drained. This way, the government can enforce punishments if a vampire does something bad."

"They had to build specific prisons for vampires," Arden went on as they walked into the mezzanine. "No windows. Blood banks. They're very sleek."

"Anyway, if they drain a human now, they get a

'remainder of life' sentence. So if they drained a twenty-year-old human who should have lived to eighty, they get the remaining sixty years in jail."

"Actually, isn't that the law that went into place after Finn's father was killed?"

"Yeah, I think that was what got it pushed through, but it was working its way through the courts for a while before then," Selene said. "You go with Arden through the turnstiles," she said. "I have to use the booth." She gestured toward where a person was sitting inside a booth.

"Why?"

"So I don't use spells to avoid paying. Meet you on the other side."

With that, they made their way onto the subway platform, where Iris tried not to gawk at a crew of vampires—dressed in stereotypical all-black—as they made their way off of a subway car and into the dark tunnels in the walls that allowed them to move through the city without exposure to the deadly sunlight.

Iris comforted herself with the fact that even many of the other humans and paranormals watched the group disappear.

They clambered onto the train, and Iris checked out the enchanted graffiti that shimmered and shifted as the subway whooshed forward, making her stomach feel like it was taking off ahead of her body.

*

"Yeah, I think I'd rather walk," she declared as they made their way up the steps at their stop. She still felt like she was moving, even when she stood still.

"You get used to it," Selene assured her. "Now, let's go eat a whole red velvet cake before we decide it's the wrong choice for your wedding that isn't going to happen."

And that was exactly what they did.

Even though they were all operating under the assumption that the wedding would not take place, they'd all agreed to a white cake with vanilla bean frosting.

"Seashells and stars instead of flowers, obviously," Arden had told the baker.

Iris felt a little churning in her stomach at the idea of never getting to see that cake.

But she went ahead and blamed the tummy ache on too many sweets.

Iris

"Just remember to smile for the cameras. Don't ever let your face fall. If you look miserable for even a second," Henry warned, "they will catch it and publish it. Along with some story about how you hate fae."

"I don't hate fae!" Iris insisted.

"That won't matter. That's the spin they will put on it. Finn went to a siren poetry reading once, and the siren in question hit a painful note that made him wince. What followed was an entire week of articles claiming Finn was not only speciesist to sirens but hated women's stories and women in general."

"That's absurd."

"That is the media," Henry told her as he handed her the garment bag with her outfit for the event.

Iris suddenly felt a little apologetic about all the times she'd thought the two men were overly concerned about what the media might print.

"When in doubt, let Finn lead with the answers."

"Just smile and look pretty," Iris drawled.

"Exactly," Henry agreed, missing the sarcasm. "Okay. I have to go. I gave you flats," he said, starting to lower the shoebox onto the counter.

"No! Not there," she said, grabbing it out of his hands. "Finn said it's bad luck."

Henry's raised brows had a lot to say. All of which she ignored as she took her outfit and made her way to the bathroom to get dressed.

Media nonsense aside, she was really excited about the event. She'd asked Finn no fewer than a hundred questions about the parade, learning that it started out as a lunar alignment ritual, now turned annual fae flaunt-fest. He said it was not as flashy as the banshee lantern walk, but ten times louder.

She'd also inquired about what to expect and what might— or might not—be considered appropriate from a bystander.

It was the most she'd ever spoken to Finn since moving in with him. She tried really hard not to be charmed by his easy smiles. Or, you know, turned on by the smooth sound of his voice.

"Wait . . . that's what you're wearing?" Iris asked when Finn walked out of the bedroom, changed out of his usual blue suit. In its place, he had on knee-length tailored tan shorts, a lightweight brown cable polo shirt, and suede loafers.

It was casual yet screamed sophistication.

"It's important for me to look put together at official events. But this isn't supposed to look like an official event. We're just supposed to be having a fun day out."

Iris held in her sigh.

Nothing in Finn's mind was ever *just* one thing. It always called back to the campaign and his image.

"Besides, I've worked hard on these calves. I'm tired of hiding them."

That dragged a little laugh out of Iris. At the words, sure, but mostly at how genuine he sounded.

"I don't know what the original calves looked like, but these look very mayoral. What?" she asked when he grimaced.

"The current mayor has chicken legs," he said. "Don't jinx me."

"Can I hope my outfit is that casual?" she asked.

"Only one way to know," he said, waving toward the bathroom.

It was his subtle way of trying to hurry her along, knowing she was always late and that he liked to be on time.

Iris went into the bathroom, combing her hair for a few moments longer than it truly required before opening up the garment bag.

It was too much to hope that Henry would let *her* wear a T-shirt and shorts. But she was pleased by the simple cream-colored A-line midi dress with a square neckline and wide straps. The back was low enough that it wouldn't allow her to wear a bra.

Would she have preferred a more colorful outfit? Absolutely. But she was pleased with the soft fabric and the flowing skirt.

And the shoes?

Simple black ballet flats.

She knew when she slipped into her clothes and looked in the mirror that her outfit had been chosen explicitly to go along with Finn's outfit. Did that make her feel a bit like the accessory she'd once been called? Yeah. But not even that could ruin her excitement about the event.

"Read—" Finn started as he heard Iris coming. But his

voice fell away as he turned and looked at her. "Damn," he said, exhaling hard as his gaze slid over her.

Each inch his eyes moved over felt like it warmed. And Iris couldn't help but press her hand to her belly as it flip-flopped.

"We'll be the picture-perfect couple," she said, though she was pretty sure she was saying it to remind herself that this was a publicity stunt, not just a fun day out.

"Of course," Finn said.

Iris was sure it was just her seeing what she wished to see, but she could swear she saw something sad cross his eyes.

"That's the point," he added, his voice deader than just a moment before. "Do you want me to carry anything for you, so you don't need to bring a bag?"

"Oh, my phone. I want to take pictures. To show my sisters. If, you know, I see them again."

"Of course you will see them again." Finn's certainty eased the ache at her sisters' absence.

He shoved her phone in his back pocket, and then the two of them were off.

The barricades were already up to keep cars off the street, and thousands of people were on the sidewalks.

Iris was at once assaulted by the scents of hot pretzels, hot dogs, gyros, and the sickly-sweet smell of cotton candy coming from the dozens of food carts hanging around, just waiting for hungry spectators to stop by for some food.

"I forgot to ask Willow if she was going to be a part of this," Iris said as she spotted a float parked down a side street, waiting for the parade to start, that featured several tall trees and a few potted little ones. She couldn't help but imagine adult dryads and little baby ones popping out of their trees as the float started to move.

"She told me last year that her tree is still too fragile to try to uproot it. But I'm sure she will be here. I'm surprised Monty isn't here. This seems right up his alley."

"Oh, he's going to be here, all right. He got himself on a float."

"A float? But he's not fae."

"Nope. But he has charmed the fae royal family. They invited him to ride with them."

"I think I underestimated that pelican," Finn said. "He really does seem to be going places."

"He has always been a determined bird."

"How did he come to talk?" Finn asked as they moved close to the barricade to secure their spots, as the crowd started to grow.

"Well, when I was a little mermaid, I was really lonely."

"Really? Why?"

"Well, I guess I was a bit awkward. I kind of preferred to stay in the royal library and read. And no one else ever wanted to discuss books or anything like that, so I always kind of felt like an outsider."

"So you befriended a talking pelican?"

"Well, actually, Monty didn't speak then. He was just a bird who I swore had really knowing eyes. I used to sit on a rock and talk to him, tell him about my books, about my hopes, about what my mother was angry with me about that week."

"How did he gain the ability?"

"Well, I remembered the stories of the Echoing Tides from my studies."

At Finn's blank look, Iris went on.

"Beneath the twilight tide, it was said that there is a species of rare oyster that absorbed not just seawater and minerals, but songs, stories, and secrets.

"Every hundred or so years, just after reproducing, the oyster travels to the harp coral and dies. And if you're really lucky, you can find the pearls.

"So one night, I snuck out during one of my mother's dinner parties and went in search of the pearl. It took me all night and part of the morning, but I finally found one.

"It was so neat. It shimmered like nothing I'd ever seen before. And, well, I'm a mermaid. I know all about shimmer."

To that, Finn shot her a smile so warm that she felt like she could bask in it.

"So I took the pearl and offered it to Monty. The second he swallowed it, he started talking. And he has never stopped. He's hardly slowed to take a breath," she added with a little laugh.

"And you weren't so lonely anymore."

"Exactly," she agreed.

Until now, she thought. Though having both Arden and Selene helped fill the space left by her hobnobbing pelican.

She glanced down the street, seeing a magnificent centaur in a vibrant green dashiki adjusting one of the sound boards just before music started to play.

"Oh, it's starting!" Iris cheered, bouncing up and down as the first float started to move into the street.

It wasn't the dryad one.

It appeared at first like a rolling garden—lush and vibrant. Roses, poppies, daisies, and lavender tumbled over its curved surface in a dazzling explosion of color. The petals swayed in some unfelt breeze.

Then—just as the float started to slide past them—the flowers appeared to shiver.

A collective gasp rippled through the onlookers—Iris included—as hundreds of tiny petals floated up into the air.

They weren't plants after all.

They were flower sprites.

Their petal-wings fluttered in the air, fast and shimmering like dragonflies.

Iris's head angled up, her lips parted, eyes wide, her heart thudding. The shimmer of wings echoed something deep and wordless inside her. It felt ancient—older than her frustration with Finn or the obligations to the surface world. This was joy in its purest form. She wanted to bottle it, to drink it like sunlight through sea glass.

They lowered back down to the float, everyone moving in perfect choreography until they formed a sign out of their soft, vibrant bodies.

First, we pollinate.

Then, we party.

The onlookers erupted into cheers and whistles as music blasted from speakers built into the float, and the sprites indeed started to party.

"I think that was the most beautiful thing I've ever seen," Iris declared when the float moved on.

"I agree," Finn said, making her turn to find him watching her.

But before she could let herself analyze that, there was a chorus of voices, drawing her attention back to the street where hundreds of small red-hat-clad gnomes marched.

Each marched in a perfectly timed formation, wielding sparkly tools like hammers, garden spades, and rakes.

Just when Iris was starting to think that was all they would do, they stopped in the middle of the street and broke into a dance, using their tools the way a color guard troupe would use flags, as they broke into some sort of song—only, there were no words.

"What is that?" Iris asked, not even glancing at Finn because she didn't want to miss a second of the display.

"Beatboxing," Finn supplied.

As the gnomes walked away, Iris spotted the dryad float moving down the street, the bright green leaves waving in the wind, their limbs swaying.

Then, so slowly that it almost seemed as if your eyes were playing tricks on you, they emerged from their trees—adults and children alike—and broke into a song about protecting the woodlands. It was so beautiful that Iris found herself blinking tears from her eyes.

Another garden float was next, this one lined in rows of dirt, with vegetables sticking out of the tilled rows.

Then, with a growing rumble like an impending storm, the root fae pulled themselves out of the ground to show off their colorful and shapely bodies.

"I forgot there were so many kinds of fae," Iris said as a group of female fairies in rainbow outfits and lots of hair ribbons came down the road doing backflips and cartwheels.

"Hundreds," Finn said, his arm shooting out to grab her as someone to her side rammed into her.

"Do you know them all?"

"Individually? No. But the types? Yes, absolutely. And it looks like the elves are up next."

Finn's arm didn't leave her lower back as the group of men with gossamer wings and barely there flesh-colored shorts—and nothing else—came marching down the street like an army, their bows in their hands.

The group stopped suddenly, half of them turning in the opposite direction.

Then, in perfect unison, they reached for arrows, nocked their bows, and shot the arrows into the air.

Where they exploded into floral confetti that rained down on the delighted crowd.

Iris, like just about everyone else, leapt up and reached out, grabbing for some of the falling petals.

But her heart shot up into her throat, and her belly hit the floor, as she lost her footing and started to fall over the barricade.

Before her gasp could even fully escape her, Finn's hands were on her hips, dragging her back against his firm body.

This time, as her heart tripped into overdrive, it was for entirely different reasons.

His arm draped across her lower stomach, keeping her against him. His face was against the side of her head.

All she could think about was how perfectly their bodies fit together, how nice it felt to be held.

She even let herself get caught up in those feelings for a few moments before she caught sight of a news crew across the street from them.

Knowing what she knew of Finn, he'd noticed them and decided to play it up for them.

Why she found that disappointing, when it was literally *the plan*, was beyond her.

She stayed in his arms, but she was a lot tenser than a moment before.

Thankfully, the next performance was making its way down the street.

Tall, ethereal fae seemed to float across the pavement, their skin, hair, and wings matching shades of magnificently translucent white.

There was a twinkling sound in the air, and it took her a moment to realize it was coming from the fae as they sang and slowly broke into a dance that had their bodies swaying and their wings gently flapping in the wind.

The song and their movements pulsed, grew, until suddenly, they hit a high note as they floated up into the air like angels.

Not even the planned paparazzi could dull her amazement at the performers moving down the road.

"I think this is the last one," Finn said, his fingertips teasing upward, stopping just shy of decency. She barely resisted the urge to slouch ever so slightly until his fingertips brushed the underside of her breast.

Even just the idea of it had a delicious ache building in her core.

Her breathing went quick and shallow; her pulse quickened.

She was pretty sure if the last float hadn't drifted up right then, she would have done something humiliating—like grind herself back against him.

But its wheels came to a stop before them, revealing a lush, gorgeous garden. Reds, pinks, yellows, and blues covered every inch.

At first, Iris assumed the movement across the flowers was the wind blowing down the street.

Then, suddenly, the movement intensified. It wasn't wind. It was fluttering.

All at once, all the winged creatures drifted up into the air. Bright, colorful wings danced, then shifted around until they formed a perfect rainbow above their float.

The crowd erupted in cheers at the sight of the fluttering rainbow.

The show wasn't over yet, though. They transitioned from a rainbow to flowers, and finally, the date.

Then they drifted back down to their flowers, and the float chugged on down the road to the sound of loud clapping and cheering.

"I thought you would like this," Finn said. His lips were close enough to her ear for his breath to warm the shell of it.

"So much," she agreed, not having it in her to lie.

"Mr. Westrock," someone called, making him turn the two of them as a unit toward the sound of the voice.

His arm drifted down to a more neutral position low on her hips as he pulled her in at his side.

"Marsha Grand," the speaker said. She was statuesque, with a distinct gray tone to her skin, two large horns erupting from her forehead, and massive wings she had pulled in close at her back.

This, Iris was reasonably sure, was a gargoyle.

"Miss Grand," Finn said, reaching out to give her a firm but friendly handshake that Iris was sure he'd practiced a thousand times before implementing. "Spokeswoman for the Gargoyle Rights Council."

"You remembered," Marsha said. Her head tipped to the side as she shot Finn a charmed smile.

"How could I forget?" Finn asked. He was practically oozing charisma—thick, heady, and completely off-putting to anyone who knew how fake it was.

Iris just barely managed to keep her lip from curling.

"It's nice to see you again, Miss Grand."

"Marsha, please," the gargoyle said. She was all smiles, having gone from collected—if not a bit cool—to on the verge of giggling schoolgirl in close proximity to Finn.

Iris watched as the woman's gaze triangulated from Finn's eyes, down his body, then up again.

Heat flared behind Iris's ribs—sharp and fast, like a jab from a trident's tines.

What was that?

A random case of indigestion?

"Marsha," Finn repeated, pearly whites all on display. He was in full-on eye-crinkle territory while looking at this woman.

As her stomach twisted, she had a sneaking suspicion it wasn't indigestion. Oh, no. It was something far more unwelcome.

Not jealousy, exactly. Just some sort of mild disgust at witnessing someone mentally unbuckle a man's belt while his arm was clearly wrapped around someone else.

Not that she *cared*. Truly.

But it was weird to watch a public display of desperation like that.

And so what if she noticed that Marsha's perfume had the same chemical profile as the bathroom cleaner they used at the local coffee shop she frequented? That didn't mean anything. It was just an observation.

The woman tossed her head back and laughed at something Finn said.

Iris's eye twitched—literally. A full-on involuntary tic.

Finn leaned into the sound, bending toward the woman, his smile threatening to crack his stupidly handsome face.

Her jaw locked so tight, she could have cracked a clam between her molars.

That strange heart lurch she felt? It didn't mean anything. Hearts just did that sometimes. It had absolutely nothing to do with the fact that Finn was smiling at this woman like he actually *meant* it for a change.

It wasn't jealousy.

It couldn't be.

She didn't *want* Finn. That was the point. But he couldn't be playing into the hands of someone who clearly wanted him, right in front of her.

It was a matter of respect.

Of morals.

Of freaking campaign optics!

"I almost forgot about that," Finn said, shaking his head as the two of them shared a memory that left Iris standing there as an outsider. "So, Marsha, what can I do for you today?"

"Well," Marsha said, her gaze cutting to Iris like she just noticed her. And didn't want her there.

"Oh, I'm sorry," Finn said, pressing his hand to his chest. She hated that move. It was so practiced but meant to look natural. A pure 'my bad' gesture. "Marsha Grand, this is Iris."

This is Iris?

That was how he introduced her?

She didn't get a last name, let alone a title? Or, heavens forbid, a connection to him.

"Nice to meet you, Iris," Marsha said. Her tone turned to granite. And there were no smiles for Iris like there were for Finn. "I'm sorry, but this is a bit of a . . . sensitive topic."

Oh, please.

A 'sensitive topic?'

What—was she about to request a private audience to discuss his . . . legislative *package*?

Did she want Iris to walk away so she could pitch her bedroom re-election campaign?

She wasn't going anywhere.

"Iris, would you mind?" Finn asked.

Oh, he didn't.

He did.

And he'd said it so gently, like she was a child being ushered out of the room before the grown-ups could speak in peace.

Anger snapped—hot and potent, threatening to burn it all to the ground.

"Oh, absolutely," she said, snark slipping into her tone. "I don't want to stand in the way of political networking. Or whatever they're calling it these days."

She lurched out of Finn's hold, forcing her chin up, and walked away like there wasn't a strange crushing sensation in her chest.

Of course, that was the exact moment a news crew moved directly in her path, making it impossible for her to sidestep them without making it look deliberate.

"Porsha DeWinter. Channel 16 News," the woman with the perfectly styled brunette hair announced. "We saw you with mayoral hopeful Finn Westrock. Can we ask you a few questions?"

Oh, they could bet their asses they could.

He wanted to embarrass her in public?

Fine.

Two could play that game.

"Ask me anything you want."

Then she did something she swore she would never do: she plastered on the fakest smile imaginable.

And threw any trace of media training out the window.

Finn

He'd looked for her for over an hour after Marsha finally let him go.

He genuinely couldn't stand the woman. She was pushy and backed up all of her *suggestions* with something that sounded a lot like a threat.

But he couldn't afford to tick off any of the paranormal organizations. They had a lot of influence. And while he was leading in the polls with humans, he was still trailing behind with paranormals.

He had to play nice.

He had to shake hands, smile, and laugh while making soul-crushingly polite small talk.

While all he wanted to do was find Iris. Because there'd been something in her eyes before she'd walked off that had his stomach tensing.

Something heated, but under that, vulnerable?

Or maybe he was just projecting what he wanted to see there.

"Finn, finally!" Henry said, rushing up to him, his tablet in his hand, a panicked look on his face.

"What are you doing here?" Finn asked, looking past his campaign manager to scan the streets for Iris.

"I need to talk to you."

"Can't it wait? I'm trying to find Iris."

"Oh, I can tell you who *did* find her. Porsha DeWinter from Channel 16."

"What?"

"Yeah, she gave a full interview to a news station. Without you present. Talking about you and your relationship."

"That can't be—" he started to object. Iris knew the rules. She was only supposed to speak to the media with him about their relationship. It was important for them to present a united—and in love—front if they wanted to be able to sell their marriage to constituents.

But Henry was already bringing up the video and hitting play.

"This is Porsha DeWinter, Channel 16 News. And I'm standing here at the Fae Pride Parade with Princess Iris Marivelle. Princess, I saw you standing *very* close to mayoral hopeful Finn Westrock."

"Did you?" Iris asked, a telltale glint in her eye that answered the question without words.

"I have to say, the two of you make *quite* the pair. How did you like the parade?"

There was a spark of something in Iris's eyes right then. But it was gone before he could pin it down.

"I think it was totally fin-tastic."

"Did she . . . did she just say *fin*-tastic?"

"Indeed, she did. Just wait." Henry looked seconds away from passing out.

"I mean, they were really krilling it out there. I was completely hooked. Ten tentacles *way* up."

Oh, good gods.

Was she making fish puns on live TV?

"Great. Love that," Porsha said.

Why, *why* did it have to be Porsha DeWinter to catch Iris alone?

Sly and cunning were her very nature, being a fox shifter. If she scented a story, she would do everything in her power to charm it out of someone.

And Iris didn't have nearly enough media training under her belt yet.

"So, back to Finn Westrock. Do I sense . . . love in the air? What an unlikely duo," she went on. "A royal mermaid and a politician."

"How does that saying go? Opposites attract," Iris said, her smile peeled back so tight, it looked like it hurt. "You know, like barnacles to a hull."

"Oh, no," Henry groaned.

"This is bad," Finn muttered, running a hand through his hair. The last thing he needed was a viral soundbite full of fish puns. Not when the Pixie Council was still on the fence and the Vampire Syndicate was watching his campaign like hawks. They wanted stability and tradition. Not chaos and pun-loving sea royalty.

"I'm not sure which of you is supposed to be a barnacle in this scenario of hers. But either way, it's not good," Henry said.

"I mean, a mermaid and a politician," Iris went on, reaching up to flip her hair. Even the cameraman lost focus for a second, zeroing in on the silky strands and the way the sun hit the shimmering scales up near her hairline. "It's all uncharted waters," Iris said.

What was with all the ocean references? He'd been living with the woman for a while now and hadn't ever heard her use fishy puns or ocean metaphors.

Was she just nervous?

"I think we're going to be making waves, though, that's for sure."

"No doubt about that," Porsha cut back in. "Well, you heard it here, folks. One of America's most eligible politicians has clearly been *reeled in*. This is Porsha DeWinter, Channel 16."

"What," Henry started, turning off his tablet, "and I can't stress this enough, in the *hell* was that?"

That was a good question.

Finn had never seen Iris act so fake.

He didn't like it.

Even if he knew it was exactly what he and Henry were constantly demanding of her.

"I don't know. But we can't figure that out until we find Iris and ask her."

"No, we have to figure out how to get ahead of this. There are going to be hundreds of calls, people asking for comments, for interviews. And memes. There are going to be so many memes."

"I need to find Iris."

That look in her eyes before she'd walked off was still bothering him.

"No. We're going back to the office. Now."

As if on cue, both of their phones started to ring.

It had begun.

"You get two hours," Finn offered. He fell into step with Henry as he answered the call from one of the interns.

Finn could hear her tight, frantic tone, likely overwhelmed at having to hold down the fort alone.

"We're on our way. Don't answer until I get there and give you our comment."

They spent the rest of the walk trying to come up with something to leak to the news stations and gossip accounts.

"You know what happens next, right?" Henry asked after they had spent a few hours putting out the fires.

"A joint TV interview."

"I'll see what I can get—daytime or late-night. Daytime is traditional. Late-night will pin you as the fun, relatable new couple on the block. I'm going to poke around and see who might be interested."

"Okay."

"You need to find your fiancée and inform her that she is going to be on round-the-clock media training from now until we put this fire out. And tell her not to speak to anyone without you again."

"Yeah, I heard you the first twenty times," Finn grumbled, raking a hand down his face.

It was supposed to be a nice day.

A turning point.

A simple win.

Maybe a moment Iris would look back on and think: *Okay, this wasn't so bad*.

Instead, it was unraveling by the minute.

Now, he had to ruin what was left of it by lecturing Iris about talking to the media.

"Get that look off your face before you hit the street.

The last thing we need right now is someone snapping a picture of you walking alone, looking miserable. After being called a barnacle."

"I'll talk to you later, Henry," Finn said, turning and walking away.

He did force his lips to tilt up before he started walking, but it took a lot more effort than usual. His face hurt by the time he got back to his apartment.

"Monty!" he snapped when he opened the door to find the bird standing on the arm of the couch, looming over Checkers as he slept, his giant beak open wide.

The pelican jerked, just barely managing to stop himself from face-planting on the cat.

"What?" the flustered bird asked, fluffing his white feathers. "I was *yawning*. Big yawn. Stretching my jaw hinge. Totally normal." At Finn's raised brows, he added, "This is why no one trusts birds anymore." He dramatically waved out a wing. "One open beak and suddenly I'm a menace."

"You can't eat the cat, Monty," Finn reminded the bird with what little patience he had left after a long day.

"I wasn't going to *eat* it. I was going to cradle it. Gently. In my beak. Like a cozy little emotional support snack—I mean friend!"

Checkers had woken up and was eyeing the pelican with totally earned suspicion.

"Have you seen Iris?"

"You mean your resplendent, glittering, camera-ready-on-a-random-afternoon fiancée? She mumbled something about saltwater therapy. Wait," he called as Finn went to head back out to check the pool.

"What?" Finn asked, hearing a strange whooshing sound coming from the shell sitting on the coffee table. Was that some kind of spelled gift, something that reminded her of home? Spelled conch shells, trips down to the saltwater pool. She was crying out for connections to her roots, to the salt water that was in her veins. Their schedules were jam-packed with the election creeping closer, but he had to find some time for her to reconnect with the ocean, to get to be a mermaid, not just his future wife.

"Can you leave that pretty gold card of yours? I'm feeling peckish."

Monty was going to charge at least five hundred dollars' worth of sushi to his card. But it beat him trying to eat Checkers again. So Finn left his card on the island before leaving the apartment.

He hadn't been down to the pool since that first night with Iris.

He was surprised to walk up to the door that had once just been glass to see a new screen on it.

Mermaid Privacy Screen was scrawled across it.

Huh.

That was nice.

Though he wasn't sure if someone had asked the super to put it up out of genuine concern for Iris's privacy. Or because they'd been upset that their kids or husband had witnessed some unexpected nudity.

Finn felt an unexpected jolt of possessiveness, not wanting anyone to see Iris like that. Even if he knew it was natural for her and her culture to be comfortable with their bodies.

He reached for the door and moved inside.

The moment he opened the door, the air shifted, smelling unmistakably briny and wild, like a storm rolling off the sea. The humidity wrapped around him like a memory. Somewhere in the distance, he thought he could hear a whale song. Or maybe that was just in his head, stirred up by the presence of the woman he couldn't get out of his blood.

Iris's tail slapped the water when she dove under.

She swam away from him, so he had just a moment to watch how perfectly she moved through the water. Like the two of them recognized each other. Like they were meant for each other.

And, of course, they were.

He felt a pang as he sat down on a chaise, suddenly feeling like he'd stolen something sacred from the place she belonged.

But, of course, she was a grown woman. If she didn't want to be there, she didn't have to.

She'd chosen land.

He hadn't stolen her from the ocean.

"Did Monty tell you I was here?" Iris asked, her sea glass eyes glaring at him from the side of the pool.

"He was trying to schmooze my credit card out of me, so you can't be too mad at him."

"That's to be determined," she said, pushing off the wall of the pool to float on her back.

Finn tried not to notice the way her breasts peeked out from between the wet strands of her hair.

Clearly, he failed.

And this was not a good time to be having desire burning through his veins.

"Why are you here?" Iris asked, gaze still on the ceiling.

"We need to talk."

"I'd rather not."

"I'm afraid it's not optional."

Iris swam to the edge of the pool, effortlessly hauling

herself out onto the cement, her tail glistening. He had an almost overwhelming urge to reach out and feel it for himself.

So he curled his hands into fists.

"Why do you sound like my tutor when I wasn't paying attention to my lessons?" she asked, reaching toward her bag to pull out a shell comb and start the process of brushing out her long strands. The motion made that citrus-salt scent of hers drift over to Finn. It wasn't helping the whole desire thing.

"We need to talk about that interview you did."

"Why would we need to talk about that? I thought that was what you wanted. To go public."

There it was again.

A tightness and coolness to her tone.

Completely different from the faux enthusiasm in her little news interview.

"Yes," Finn agreed. He took a steadying breath, his gaze watching as her tail slowly disappeared, leaving perfect legs in its wake.

Finn shifted in his seat, his pants brushing against a part of him that refused to listen to reason, nearly dragging a groan out of him.

"Then what's the problem?" she asked. Her voice pitched higher. Almost as fake as it had been in the interview.

"We needed to go public in the *right way*."

"Oh, yes, optics. How could I forget?"

"It's important that we project the right image."

"Triton forbid anything real interrupts the narrative."

"It's not that it's fake. It's—"

"What did Marsha want?" Iris interrupted.

"I'm sorry?"

"What did Marsha Grand want?"

"It was just . . . campaign stuff."

"Campaign stuff," she repeated. Her voice grew tight. "Was it some big secret?"

"Not especially."

"Can you ever just . . . give a real answer?" she snapped, making Finn straighten.

"That was a real answer."

"It's always perfectly twisted so you don't make anyone unhappy. Mr. Electable," she said, turning onto all fours, then slowly getting to her feet. "Manicured messaging in a suit. All optics. No authenticity. I mean, when's the last time you felt anything real?"

His hand shot out, closing gently around her wrist, drawing her closer.

"I'm feeling something real right now."

Could she read the sincerity on his face?

Did she hear the thickness in his voice?

Iris's gaze cut to his, surprise crossing her pretty face for a moment as he applied pressure. Not exactly pulling her, leaving the ball in her court.

It felt like an eternity before she made the decision. But then she was stepping closer. One foot at a time. Until she was standing at the foot of the chaise.

Given their positions, his face was level with the core of her.

He tried to control himself, to think of all the reasons this was a bad idea.

But he leaned forward, his forehead pressing into her lower belly.

Iris sucked in a breath, and he felt the way she melted against him.

Her free hand rose, lightly resting on the back of his head, her fingers sifting through his hair.

It was all the encouragement he needed.

His head shifted, lips grazing her stomach and dragging a shaky little mewling sound from her.

He moved across her soft, water-cool skin, the barely there touch making her breathing quicken and her fingers tighten in his hair.

His hands drifted up from the sides of her knees, over her thighs, her hips, then shifted back to sink into the curve of her ass.

Finn's mouth trailed from one hip to the other, lips pressing warm kisses to her skin until Iris was rocking restlessly, silently begging for more.

His hand grazed back down her thigh, sinking in just behind her knee and pulling up.

Her leg lifted until he rested her foot against the chaise beside his leg, the position opening her up to him.

His head shifted, lips pressing a kiss to her inner thigh, tasting the salt on her skin, before his tongue flicked out, tracing the seam of her thigh, then moving greedily between.

The sound she made nearly undid him. It went straight down his spine. Lower.

Her fingers curled in his hair, holding him against her. As if he had any intentions of moving away when he had her like this.

Soft.

Sweet.

Practically vibrating with need.

For him.

His tongue traced upward, finding her clit, and working slow circles around it.

She gasped his name, making heat flood through his chest.

That was *his* name on her lips.

Those were his whimpers and moans.

Her hips rocked against his face, chasing every flick of his tongue as he drove her higher and higher.

Her body tensed, her thighs starting to shake as she got closer.

Those sharp, breathy little sounds she was making? He wanted to hear them a hundred more times.

But her body had other ideas as she tensed, as her breath caught.

One more flick and she shattered for him, body shaking, voice wrecked—and he never wanted to hear anything but that sound.

He shifted his head, pressing another kiss to her inner thigh, then reaching for her hips, pulling until she lowered down onto his legs.

His arms went around her body—trembling and breathless—holding her together as she fell apart.

Her body shifted closer, and a ragged groan escaped him as the thick press of him met the core of her.

The little whimper that escaped her had his hips rocking up against her.

Iris's face turned into his neck, her warm breath teasing over his skin as she ground down on him.

His need pulsed against her, hot and impatient, desperate for release.

Iris's head lifted, and Finn got to watch the depth of desire on her gorgeous face for a moment before her head angled—lowered.

Their mouths collided—not soft, not slow, just heat and teeth and ravenous need.

The kiss was hard and frenzied, like they'd been holding back for too long.

She was trembling with need, and her hands were everywhere, as if she couldn't decide what part of him she needed the most.

Her fingers slid down his back, slipped under his shirt, her palms flattening on heated skin.

Their bodies moved together like they forgot there were still clothes between them.

Her hips rocked against his, chasing friction like oxygen as he ground against her—pure instinct taking over.

Each roll of her hips made his breath stutter, the pressure building with nowhere to go.

It was an almost humiliating kind of need, and he gave in to it willingly.

They both rocked into the rhythm their bodies demanded, lost in the moment, lost in each other.

It was unrestrained, clumsy, desperate. They were shaky, sweaty, panting.

The shudder moved through Iris, and his lips swallowed her long, deep moan as the orgasm moved through her.

His control snapped, yanking her hips down and rutting against her until he was coming with her.

Neither of them moved. The only sound was the quick, shallow gasps of their breaths.

It wasn't just his body that felt shaky. It was something deeper, something he wasn't ready to name.

He felt the shift in her slowly, then all at once.

She hadn't said anything. Not a word. Her breathing slowed. Her hands went still. Her mouth, moments ago fused to his like she couldn't get enough, was pressed shut now.

Finn didn't move, didn't even blink, like he might spook

her if he shifted wrong. But something inside him had already started to crack open, letting in the cold.

The realization started as an ache just under his ribcage.

But before he could decide if it was just insecurity about dry-humping like teenagers, or something darker, uglier—something that looked a lot like regret—there was a slamming on the door.

"There's a time limit, you know!" a woman's voice called, loud and annoyed. "I know you're a mermaid and everything, but we all deserve access to the pool."

Iris was off his lap before he could even try to reach for her.

She scrambled away, grabbing her clothes and yanking them on.

He reached for her towel, draping it over his arm to hold in front of his body.

But by the time he managed that, she was out of the room, and the woman was moving inside.

"Mr. Westrock," the woman greeted. "I don't mean to be rude or anything . . ."

Just once, he wanted the right to be frustrated or annoyed.

But he didn't have that luxury.

"No, of course not. You're absolutely right; it's your pool too. If you'll excuse me."

By the time he made it back to the apartment, Iris was locked up in the bedroom with Monty, leaving him to go into the bathroom, strip, and clean up in the shower.

The taste of her lingered.

But he had the sinking feeling that her sighs, her moans, her shivers, and kisses would be nothing but memories soon.

17

Iris

"So, you gave in to a biological need," Selene said as the two of them walked down the road after Iris showed up at the bookshop for an emergency meeting after a conversation with Monty devolved into a dramatic plotline in one of his dramatic romance shows.

She needed to call in reinforcements to talk it through. Because what the hell was that?

Not bad enough that she'd let him go down on her, but then she'd climbed on him, and they'd humped on the chaise like a couple of horny teenagers.

"It's not the end of the world. You're both adults. And, I mean, you *are* a mermaid."

"What's that supposed to mean?" Iris asked over a mouthful of soft pretzel. Her third one. Thankfully, Selene was the kind of friend who didn't judge her for trying to bury her feelings with food.

"That you're, you know, innately sexual. It's part of who you are."

"It's part of who we *all* are."

"Yeah, but to a lesser degree. I mean, even if this is all complete nonsense, you can *claim* that's all it was if he decides to confront you about it."

"True," Iris agreed, feeling a little of the tension in her shoulders lessening. They'd been inching up since she'd run out of the pool room. She was starting to worry she might need to get them surgically removed from her ears if she didn't calm down.

Not just because of what happened, but what it meant. Or didn't mean. She couldn't stop herself from obsessing over what Finn might be thinking about it. Was there regret? Was he brushing it off? Did it even register as a mistake to him . . . or was it just another political complication he had to manage?

And, worse, why the hell did she care so much?

"I have to ask," Selene said as they approached the entrance to the park.

A large sign hung from the wrought-iron fence.

No werewolves in the dog park.

There was a big wolf-man in the background with a red X across his body.

"Ask what?" Iris asked, scrunching up the piece of parchment paper her pretzel had been wrapped in and tossing it in the trash.

"Well, how *was* it?"

How was it?

Spine-tingling.

Soul-shattering.

Consuming.

Devastating.

But more than all of that: stupid. So incredibly stupid.

"It was fine."

"Fine?" Selene asked, brows shooting up. "Huh. I had him pegged for one of those repressed guys who are animals when you peel them out of their stuffy suits."

That was exactly what Finn had been.

Demanding, unrestrained.

Real.

For just a few moments, with their bodies moving together in an ancient rhythm, he'd been real with her.

"Well, I don't know why you showed up at my doorstep all frantic over *fine*. I was about to get to a very important part in my book."

"Were the enemies about to become lovers?" Iris asked, shooting her friend a smile.

"The villain was about to bang the heroine in all sorts of steamy ways. Then, I imagine, declare his undying love for her. At least the former part is believable. I've always found that the bad boys are the only ones who know what they're doing in bed."

Iris may have agreed with Selene in the past. But she had to admit that Finn was, objectively, a good man. And that good man? He really knew what to do with his tongue.

"So, what were you hoping to accomplish on this walk? Aside from bolstering up the local pretzel-vendor economy?"

"I don't know. I guess I just need to figure out what to do next. I mean, we've hooked up now."

"Barely. Look, most guys don't want to make a big thing out of a little dry-humping. If you go on acting like it's no big deal, I'm sure he'll do the same. Now, what we really need to do is talk about that little interview you gave," Selene said, shooting Iris a smirk. "That was brilliant."

"Finn doesn't think so. And I'm sure Henry is likely drafting up some story about me having heat stroke or land-sickness or something."

"Does land-sickness exist?"

"No, but I'm sure he's willing to create a disease just to cover up a story about my awful fish puns."

"I think it's more the barnacle thing they're objecting to."

"Well, whatever it is, I have 'a period of intense study' ahead of me."

"Who said that—Henry?"

"Yeah."

"The man sounds like a robot."

"I'm pretty sure he's made up entirely of ambition and empty campaign promises."

"And he's Finn's best friend. Says something right there. Oh, goddess. What is *he* doing here?" Selene asked, sighing hard as she stared at someone off in the distance.

Following her gaze, she saw Arden standing near the bend in the road.

"I have no idea." Sure, Arden was known for dropping in on his own schedule, but that was at the apartment. She had no idea how he'd tracked them to the park. Or why he looked so excited.

"We could just turn around and walk away," Selene suggested.

"He would totally follow. He has some kind of soul contract with my mother."

"Demons don't have souls."

"A blood oath, then."

"Are we talking about me?"

"We're discussing the mediocrity of men in the bedroom. So . . . probably."

"Darling, why do you think all the most delicious things in life are associated with the wicked and sinful?" Arden asked, shooting her a look that could be called nothing short of devilish. "Trust me, we throw down in the bedroom."

"My experience suggests that the men who claim to be good in bed are always the ones who can't find the clit with both hands and a map."

"Wanna test that theory?" Arden asked, taking a step closer to Selene, everything about him sparking sexual energy.

Even the usually unflappable Selene seemed a bit, well, flapped.

If Iris hadn't been watching her friends so closely, she might have missed it.

The strange static in the air that had the hairs on Iris's arms rising. Then the flash around Selene's hand. Like a dozen itty-bitty fires.

She lifted her hand and pressed it into Arden's chest.

Anyone else would have jumped, yelped, tried to get away from the heat.

Arden leaned in, giving Selene eye contact—his eyes blazing red around the irises—that gave Iris secondhand trembles.

"I didn't think you liked it kinky," he said, lips teasing up at the edges.

Defeated, Selene dropped her hand. "Huh. I didn't know you like women," she said, brows scrunched.

"Oh, my sweet summer witch, I'm pansexual. Anybody can get this," he said, waving down at his body.

"Interesting. Learn something new every day," Selene said, but Iris noticed how she put some distance between them. She was clearly more affected by that intense, flirty little interaction than she wanted to admit.

"Arden, what are you doing here?" Iris asked.

"A little pelican told me he saw you heading in this direction. He was having brunch with a *very* famous movie star, by the way. That bird is going places."

The sting of his absence ached less with each passing day. And as much as she loved that bird more than almost anything, she found that as her world broadened, as her circle widened, she felt less in need of her emotional support pelican.

"And doesn't his ego know it," Iris said with a smile. "Is this—"

She trailed off, distracted by a group of small children running past them, their hands reaching for tiny glowing orbs as their laughter spilled out, tinkling like wind chimes.

"One way to get their energy out," a woman said as she passed them, her hand flicking in the air, making the orbs change directions suddenly.

"Is this about wedding planning?" Iris asked, finding her last train of thought.

"No, actually. I got a call from a very bossy campaign manager with a sexy-as-hell voice."

"What did Henry want?"

"There is a charity event coming up in your schedule. I'm supposed to get you gowned up for that. And work on your walk in heels."

"Oh, yes. Nothing says female empowerment like strapping your feet into medieval torture devices and waddling like a baby deer." Selene rolled her eyes.

"She has a point," Iris agreed.

"I'll give you that heels aren't easy. But who doesn't like a nice gown?"

"Let me guess," Selene said. "Floor-length, strapless, and designed by a man who has never needed to wear a bra."

Arden's gaze appraised her. "Iris won't need a bra."

"Totally not the point."

"Don't listen to her," Arden urged Iris. "You're going to look a-mazing."

"Like a gorgeous, reluctant sacrifice," Selene piped in.

"Maybe we should ditch her before we get to the boutique," Arden suggested.

"Nope. I'm coming. The last thing she needs is another man on her case about something. She needs someone to stand up for her."

"Barnacles," Arden said, grimacing.

"Yeah, I'm in trouble. My punishment is a million hours of media training."

"As usual, I think Henry is overreacting," Arden said. He gestured for the women to start walking, steering them back out of the park. "From what I'm hearing, people were really charmed by the silly puns. I believe the most liked comment under the video I saw was: *'Who knew mermaids were so adorable?'* So, I think it's fine."

If Arden saw that, no doubt Henry had as well. Maybe he would change his mind about all the media training.

"Here we go," Arden said. He pulled open the door to a boutique with blacked-out windows. "You," he said to Selene. "Behave."

"No," she said, pushing past him and into the store.

Iris followed, waiting for her eyes to adjust to the dark. With no natural sunlight, all the light was coming from several large, ancient, black candelabras, and long streams of red wax dripped down the center columns.

"How are we supposed to shop for dresses in the

dark?" Iris whispered to Arden. Her gaze took in the lush black velvet curtains and the extravagant arrangements of blood-red roses.

"My sweet, innocent sea princess," Selene said, moving in close. "This is a vampire dress shop."

"Really?" Iris asked. She wasn't sure if the way her pulse skittered was excitement or fear.

"Indeed," another voice joined them, arriving a half a second before the speaker herself.

Iris had begun to see that each type of paranormal had its own specific kind of beauty.

Witches, she felt, had a seductive, defiant kind of appeal.

Shifters had an untamed, golden-hour beauty. It was wild around the edges—fierce and majestic.

Demons, Arden included, had that wicked beauty. Sinful by design. All temptation and teeth.

And the fae, well, they had an ethereal beauty. Like a dream that didn't want to let go.

This was her first up-close-and-personal interaction with a vampire.

But her immediate thought was they had a cold, sculpted kind of beauty—polished, practiced, *timeless*.

This vampire had flowing red hair spilling over the shoulders of her crushed velvet black gown that hugged each of her dangerous curves.

Her face was all sharp cheekbones, pale skin, and keen blue eyes.

"Arden," she purred. She made her way over toward the demon. She pressed her body to his. A little too close, a tad too intimate, for a quick peck on each cheek. "How long has it been? Fifty years?"

"Carm," Arden greeted her. "At least seventy-five," he

said. "We were at the opera. You were in the opposite balcony, on your knees, feasting from the femoral vein of one of the actresses."

"I remember her. Bouncy brown hair. Big, golden eyes. She was delicious."

Iris didn't realize that her face had betrayed her, until the vampire's gaze slid in her direction, a sly smile toying at her lips.

"Just a taste, not a full meal. In the good old days," she went on. "Before the bite cards."

"You can't blame humans for wanting protection," Selene—always the one to defend others—said.

"Can't I?" the vampire asked. She moved closer to Selene. "I believe I can do anything I like," she said.

Iris was close enough to see how the vampire's pupils dilated, but far enough not to get a direct hit of her glamour like Selene did.

Her usually controlled friend wavered on her feet, leaning closer to the vampire, her eyes full of wonder.

"I believe you would let me do anything I want, wouldn't you?" the vampire intoned.

Selene's lips parted, and her head tilted to the side, opening up her neck.

Iris's fists clenched at her sides as she watched Selene fall under Carm's glamour. A part of her wanted to rush forward and pull her friend away. Another part of her wondered if this was just how things were. Paranormal or not, weren't they all just constantly being seduced, pressured, and manipulated into giving themselves over? The pool. The chaise. The way she'd melted under Finn's touch.

Was every interaction with another person just a form of glamour?

"That's enough, Carm," Arden said. He dropped an arm on Selene's shoulders. "This one is under my protection," he said, curling Selene into him.

"Like hell, I am," Selene objected. She tried to wrench away from Arden, but he held her tight as Carm shrugged and moved further into her store.

"Don't be an ingrate," Arden said. He gave Selene a raised-brow look. "If I hadn't stepped in, you would have been pants-free, spread-eagled on the chair over there, begging for Carm to bite you. And as much as I may have enjoyed that image, I know you're the high priestess of personal boundaries and wouldn't appreciate that."

"I thought glamouring was illegal," Iris whispered.

"It's . . . a gray area," Arden admitted.

"There's nothing gray about it. The current lawmakers are just too chicken to stand up to the vampires."

"But not *her* future lawmaker," Arden said.

"Really?" Iris asked.

"Yeah, Finn's platform includes a ban on glamouring outside of consensual relationships and vampire clubs," Selene explained. "Right now, the only law on the books is that vampires can't compel someone against their will to commit crimes or have sex. The new law would be a lot more far-reaching."

"Which is why Finn is not very popular among the vampires," Arden concluded.

Iris distinctly remembered overhearing Finn and Henry having a heated debate in the kitchen while she had been trying to ignore them in the living room as she read her book.

It had been about the vampires.

With Henry trying to get Finn to bend on the issue. And Finn putting his foot down.

It stuck with her because he always seemed to roll over and do whatever his campaign manager said. It had been kind of hot to see him have his own opinion and the backbone to stick to it.

"I didn't climb out of the coffin at this sun-cursed hour for chit-chat," Carm said, waving a fine-boned hand toward a rack of dresses. No, not dresses—gowns.

"Carm, we talked about this," Arden said, striding toward the vampire. With his arm still around Selene, he pulled her along with him.

Iris followed. She was excited about the gowns, even if she wasn't exactly looking forward to a formal charity event.

"About my impeccable taste? Yes, yes, we did."

"Carm. Everything here is black."

"Nonsense, this is navy blue," she declared, waving toward the only gown on the rack that wasn't midnight black.

"And it is lovely. But it doesn't work with Iris's coloring. We want her to stun in a soft summer palette: mauve, rose, soft blue . . ."

Carm mimed a yawn but sighed and threw up a hand. "Fine! Come with me."

With that, all three of them followed the vampire to a back room where the colorful gowns were hidden.

Arden pulled Selene down on the couch beside him. Iris watched as Selene scooted an inch away, a move so small that it was almost imperceptible. Her friend was ruffled. And Selene hated to be ruffled.

But before Iris could read more into it, Carm was making a beeline for her, her heels clicking on the stone floor. She shooed Iris into a curtained-off dressing room and shoved gown after gown at her.

Both she and Arden had been ruthless with their criticisms of the gowns, with Selene throwing in her usual clap-backs and support.

Iris knew it the moment she moved out from behind the curtains when they finally landed on the right gown—and thank the seas, because there were only three left.

It was a satin halter gown with a gathered waist and a pooling hemline in a stunning shade of 'Sienna rose.'

"Wow," Selene said, nodding. "That's the one. For sure."

"It is so close to perfect. But do you have it in blue?" Arden asked.

"Why does it have to be blue?" Selene asked.

"It goes with the whole mermaid thing."

"The whole mermaid thing being, you know, her entire identity? For goddess's sake, you don't have to keep shoving that down everyone's throats."

Arden considered her words. "I don't know if Henry will agree with that, but he's not here. All right, Carm. Let's ring this up."

With that, Arden's arm finally fell from Selene's shoulders. Iris could have sworn there was something akin to disappointment on the witch's face.

"Come on," she said, fighting through those feelings Iris imagined she wanted nothing to do with. "Get back in your street clothes. You must be ready for another hot pretzel by now."

"And a good book and comfy clothes," Iris agreed. "And about a week of nothing to do."

Fate—and Henry—had other plans for her.

Iris

"What, exactly, is a town hall?" Iris asked, still only half-awake after staying up until almost sun-up reading the Caprica Coraline novel Selene had handed to her as they parted ways at her shop.

It had been a giant mistake.

She really needed to be avoiding romance. Especially ones that got spicy.

She'd lain there afterward, pulse pounding, desire thrumming, just trying to talk herself out of walking into the living room and climbing on top of Finn.

"It's a meeting with various constituents," Henry explained as she dropped down on one of the island stools, leaning forward to rest her head on her arm. "In this case, it will likely be heads of various paranormal interest groups. It gives everyone a chance to ask Finn about his stances on certain subjects. Or request he focus on problems they and their communities are facing. I imagine there is something similar in your kingdom."

Iris's memory flashed back to endless meetings sitting in the throne room, listening to her mother and the advisers work through issues various merfolk were facing.

"Something like that," she agreed. "Why do I need to be there?"

She knew she was being surly. She had a book hangover and hadn't had a cup of . . .

A mug dropped down in front of her face, making her head angle up to see Finn giving her another of his tight, fake smiles.

"Look like you needed that."

"Thank you," she said, perking up from just the scent of it.

"The short of it is . . . Finn's opposing candidate's wife goes everywhere he goes."

Oh, Selene would have a field day with that.

"And Finn has mostly been alone. If you two are engaged, you need to be seen there supporting your fiancé."

"But we're not officially engaged."

"You are."

"I don't have a ring."

"Oh," Henry said. He frowned at her empty finger. "Right."

"I have a ring," Finn said.

"You do?" Henry asked. "Since when?"

"When you came up with this idea, I got my family's jewelry out of the safety deposit box. When I met you, I knew which ring it had to be."

There was something soft in his gaze that had Iris's heart fluttering.

"Can I see it?"

"Come on," Henry said. "Get the mermaid her shiny thing."

"Hey," Finn snapped before Iris could say anything.

"It's a fact that mermaids enjoy shiny things. It's like saying that the fae are repelled by iron."

"I don't care. It comes off as condescending," Finn said. "I'll get the ring," he told Iris.

Despite her desire to really dislike the man, she felt her lips tipping up at his swiftness at jumping to her defense.

"I genuinely meant no offense," Henry said. He put a hand to his heart. It was a practiced move. It was probably a practiced apology. Still, he wasn't a man to apologize often, so she wasn't going to be ungracious.

"Okay. Thanks."

Finn was back in a moment, like he'd been keeping the ring close, looking for a chance to give it to her.

There was a dainty cream-colored leather ring box in his hand as he walked toward her. He set it down next to her coffee, allowing her the pleasure of opening it up.

Henry wasn't exactly *wrong*. She loved shiny things. And she really loved gifts. Gifts of shiny things? Best of both worlds.

She reached for the box as her heartbeat skittered around in her chest.

She flipped the lid and found what had to be the most perfect ring.

It was a rectangular emerald-cut aquamarine stone on a platinum band.

"We might need to get it sized," Finn warned as she pulled it out and slid it on her finger.

"No, it's perfect." She wiggled her finger, watching the way the light blue stone caught the light, casting sea glass shadows across her knuckles. A flicker of homesickness pulsed through her so fast, so sharp, it made her breath catch. The color was the ocean. The setting was not. The contradiction felt heavy on her hand—like a gift, and a chain, all at once.

"This made you think of me?" she asked, uncomfortable with how strong she had to blink to keep the moisture from gathering in her eyes.

"Is it not right?" Finn asked, looking genuinely concerned. "I have a whole box of—"

"No, this is mine," she said, covering it with her other hand as if he was going to reach over and snatch it off her finger. The move made Finn's lips curve up. "I like this one," she added.

"Good. I'm glad."

"Good, that's handled. Back to the event. Yes, you need to be at the town hall like a doting spouse. Or, in this case, future spouse. You will just be standing with Finn, smile on your face. Don't let the media catch you frowning. Especially when Finn is talking to different groups. They will spin it that you have some sort of bias."

"The job is . . . arm candy?" Selene had taught her that phrase. She hated it.

"Pretty much. We're hoping no one asks you anything directly."

"Triton forbid I have an opinion or personality."

"We've seen what happens when you go rogue."

"All right. All right," Finn said. He held his hands up. "Can we not go there today?"

"What packaging are you putting me in?" she asked.

Henry didn't bite the bait. She saw his mouth part to do just that, but a glance toward Finn's uncharacteristically hard face had him closing it again.

"Arden will be dropping off an outfit later. It's not a formal event."

"Do I have to wear heels?"

"In the interest of not having a meme of you falling on your face, we're going with flats until you get more practice in the heels."

"Really looking forward to that."

Iris reached for her mug, getting momentarily distracted by the way her new ring shimmered in the light.

"After the town hall, you will have media training," Henry said.

It was hit after hit, and she hadn't even finished her coffee yet.

"Fine."

"You all right?" Finn asked.

"Tired," she admitted.

"Saw your light on at three."

"I was reading."

"The books I gave you?" Henry asked, surprised and hopeful.

"By the tides, no. It was a Caprica Coraline book."

"The mermaid?" Finn asked.

"You know her?" Iris asked, head snapping up. Was she pleasantly surprised? Absolutely. Was she happy about that? Debatable.

"I do. She's incredibly prolific."

"Finn here has been brushing up on his mermaid customs. Her name came up."

"You have?" Iris asked. She wasn't sure if she was

meant to be flattered by that. Because it was likely some ploy to know how to manipulate her better.

"I didn't even have to suggest it," Henry said, moving out of the kitchen at the sound of a knock at the door.

Iris glanced at her fiancé, trying to read something real beneath all the political polish.

"There's my gorgeous little mermaid mannequin," Arden greeted, breezing into the room in a pair of black slacks and a tight button-up black shirt patterned with little red hearts. He held a garment bag draped over one arm and a leather bag in his hand.

"Ugh," she grumbled.

"Oh, you love playing dress-up, and you know it." Arden reached up to pull the sunglasses off his face, folding them, then slipping the arm into the neck of his shirt. "Wow. You look like hell. And I know hell."

"Gee, thanks. I really needed a pep talk today."

"You look fine," Finn assured her.

Fine.

What a leg-quivering compliment.

"Can you do something about . . . all that?" Henry asked, waving toward Iris as a whole.

"Charming as ever, Hens," Arden said, shooting the other man an eye roll.

"Well, can you?"

"I'm still in the room," Iris grumbled.

"She needs nothing to be absolutely stunning. But I will have her done up and dressed for the town hall."

"On time," Henry insisted.

To that, Arden snorted.

"As much as I can control Iris being on time, sure."

"Good. Come on, Finn. We have to go over talking points."

Finn moved to follow his campaign manager but paused. "Don't slap a ton of makeup on her," he said. His gaze cut to Iris. "She doesn't need it."

"Oh, baby," Arden said after tugging her into the bathroom. "I am about to combust from that secondhand longing."

"What are you talking about?" she asked. She watched as Arden hung up a garment bag on the back of the door, then pulled about half a dozen items out of his bag, spreading them across the counter.

"That look, my sweet sea goddess. That look."

"What look?"

"The one your fiancé shot in your direction before walking away."

"I have no idea what you're talking about. What is all of that?" she asked, waving.

"Wait," Arden said, mouth falling open. His hand shot out, grabbing hers. "Is this the ring? *The* ring?"

"Oh, yeah. Finn just gave it to me."

"Oh, Iris," he said. He pulled it up for a closer look. "It's stunning."

"Yeah. I really love the stone."

"Of course you do. Kudos to Finn for being a great jewelry shopper. That's an important trait for a husband."

Was it, though?

Sure, she liked pretty and shiny.

But she wanted more than superficial things. She wanted someone to ask her about her feelings, to inquire about her hopes and dreams, to give her their own depths and vulnerability.

And that man would never be Finn.

So as Arden spent the next few hours slathering things on

her face and hair as he took her from grudgingly awake to (in his words) an 'ethereal sea stunning,' she tried to think of ways she might make Henry and Finn second-guess her as a political wife at the town hall, without being offensive to anyone or making a complete fool of herself.

She wanted to talk to Selene about it. But by the time Arden thrust the garment bag at her, they only had five minutes left before Henry started nagging.

Alone, she slipped into the light-pink pencil dress that hugged her figure but had a modest neck and hemline.

The fabric slid over her hips like a second skin, soft and smooth and nothing like seaweed wraps or the scratch of coral-polished shells. Too soft. Too easy. Too . . . human.

Though, she had to admit, Arden definitely knew how to dress her.

As she turned in the mirror, she had the strangest, most stomach-dropping thought.

She was starting to like playing dress-up more than she liked forever sporting her tail and shells.

The thought was so shocking, she walked out of the bathroom on stiff legs, her spine ramrod straight, feeling like her very mind was betraying her nature. The dress was simply something she *wore*. Her tail was part of who she *was*. How could she possibly think for even a moment that she preferred window dressing to her true form?

"Arden does good work," Henry said with a nod.

It was high praise from him, but Iris was too stunned by her own mind to react.

"Hey, are you all right?" Finn asked, reaching out toward her arm. Like he thought she might need support.

She did.

But she yanked her arm away.

She wasn't upset with him this time. She was mad at herself. For becoming so land-oriented. It had been so easy to slip into this new world, this altered version of herself. There were things on the surface that felt like pieces she'd been missing all her life.

The books came into mind first. After a lifetime of reading the same stories, the world had opened up to her. There were endless stories within countless books. There were places she could only visit between the pages of books she would never be able to read under the water.

It was more than the books, though. It was the fascination that came with exposure to other cultures, other people. She hadn't been ignorant of the surface. But it had existed as an abstract, almost like bedtime stories instead of reality. But almost as soon as she'd surfaced, she could see how narrow her own world had been. Always the same faces, the same sights, the same language and customs. While the land was bursting with people and experiences she never could have even imagined.

They were strange and wonderful things. Reality television. Soap operas. Taco Tuesdays. Next-day delivery. Fuzzy socks. Escalators. Balloons. Tiny dogs in sweaters. The scent of rain. The sparkle of magic in the air after a spell. The way humans argued passionately about pizza toppings. Intricate designs on long plastic nails. Glitter eyeshadow. Hot pretzels.

Without realizing it, without meaning to, she'd come to love thousands of little things she could only find on the surface.

She was terrified she was beginning to prefer it to her home, the place she loved so much, the thing that sang in her very veins.

It was terrible of her to think after just a few weeks on land that she could possibly choose it over her home, her ocean, her people. How could she abandon herself like that? She had to go back, to fall in love with all the things that had made her never want to step foot on the surface world in the first place.

And to do that, she had to get out of this engagement once and for all.

"Fine. Let's go."

She needed to get this event over with so she could get back to her original plan.

To get herself out of this marriage.

To get back to the ocean.

Before she became someone she didn't even recognize anymore.

Nothing else mattered.

Finn

It was a packed town hall. Everyone stood shoulder to shoulder, barely having enough breathing room.

Werewolf musk mingled with banshee perfume and something spicy an eagle shifter had smuggled in from a street vendor outside.

He should have been going over points and scripted answers in his head.

But all he could do was keep gazing over at Iris.

What happened in that bathroom?

Sure, she'd been in a bit of a grumbly mood when she'd gone in there with Arden. But she'd been tired. And Henry had been his usual self toward her.

When she'd emerged, though, she'd looked gorgeous. But pale. And those lovely eyes of hers? Haunted.

Had Arden said something to her?

He got the impression that the two of them were close. Maybe not as close as she clearly was with the witch, but close enough that he didn't think Arden would do or say something to make Iris look like that.

He tried to catch her gaze, to mouth her some reassurances.

Before he could untangle himself from Henry, though, he was being announced.

They had to go out.

To her credit, Iris slipped a mask over her face, hiding all that vulnerability behind it.

Even if he hated that she had to do that.

They moved out in sync toward some enthusiastic—and just as many reluctant—claps.

Finn waited for Iris to be seated in the chair on the raised stage before he took his own.

He glanced at her once again, finding her sitting exactly how Henry had told her to.

But her spine was ramrod straight.

Her smile was plastic.

He started to address the crowd even as he reached out, placing a hand on her knee and giving it a reassuring squeeze.

When he glanced around the crowd, he noticed her smile had relaxed slightly. Though he wasn't sure if he could take credit for that, or if she was just fascinated by the crowd.

Living in the ocean, she'd had a very sheltered life, only being exposed to other sea-dwelling creatures. She'd never gotten a chance to meet all the paranormals that he'd known all his life.

She'd met fae and a gargoyle with him. The witch from the bookstore, Arden the demon, and a vampire dress shop owner. But it still left so many other paranormals she hadn't been in direct contact with.

She was trying to be subtle, but he could see her looking at the people gathered, likely trying to figure out what kind of paranormals they might be. Her gaze caught on a man near the front—tall and fit in his casual gray tee and jeans, his sable hair styled kind of shaggy.

He was a werewolf, but Finn couldn't help but wonder if Iris's interest was just because of his shifting abilities or if it was a different kind of interest.

A cold pit formed in his stomach, heavy and undeniable. For the first time in his life, he felt the urge to get up and square up to a stranger. For no other reason than he suspected that Iris might find him attractive.

"Yes, Miss . . ." he prompted, pointing toward an ethereal high fae with white-blonde hair and a sharp triangular face.

"Folk. Hi. I actually come with an issue my kind and I have been struggling with for our whole lives."

"I'm sorry to hear that. What is the issue I can hopefully help with?"

"The fences," Miss Folk said.

"Which fences?"

"Just about every fence around the city. But especially those around Central Park. They're wrought *iron*," she explained. "We would like to have them replaced with something less . . . murdery."

There was a chorus of claps from her peers.

"If we're speaking about those sorts of requests," an older male werewolf said, moving forward, "my kind would like you to commit to changing all of the silver door handles in public buildings. It's an accessibility issue."

"While we are talking about accessibility . . ." Another woman stepped forward. She was a shifter of some sort, but nothing about her suggested what kind. "I would like for you to commit to adding larger stalls to public restrooms. It's impossible to shift comfortably in the current ones."

"Hell, it's impossible to comfortably take a leak in the current ones," some human in the back of the crowd piped in, getting a chorus of laughter.

There were dozens of other questions, concerns, and demands for change from the crowd.

Finn answered to the best of his ability, prepped well with all the talking points he and Henry had discussed all morning.

There were a few who threw him for a loop, of course; you couldn't prepare for everything. But he'd been coached for so long on how to answer things with confidence, charm, and just a little bit of humor—when situationally appropriate—that he managed to answer those questions and calm those concerns with ease.

This was the part that made all the rehearsed press conferences and long television interviews with talking heads worth it. This was why he was running. To be a man of the people. All the people. To learn more about the issues that other communities faced, and try his best to make a better, more equitable world for them all.

"Hello," a woman said. She was tall, with long braids that hinted at green when the light hit them right. A dryad, Finn guessed. "I actually have a question regarding your pollution initiatives."

"Of course. That's an issue near and dear to my—*our*—hearts," he corrected, giving Iris's knee another squeeze. It made her smile stretch wider for the audience, but he was acutely aware of how it didn't reach her eyes.

All eyes shifted to Iris, who looked wide-eyed under the attention.

"I, uh, yes, of course," she said, slowly pulling herself together. "Ocean pollution is at an all-time high. The last time I took a swim, I got a candy wrapper and a fishing line stuck in my hair. I've seen so many examples of carelessness when it comes to disposing of waste properly. And I know the roadsides and forests are dealing with similar issues."

The dryad nodded along as Iris spoke. Finn could swear everyone in the room leaned into her, found themselves drawn to her. She wasn't a siren. She didn't have the ability to lure people in. Still, they found themselves entranced by her.

Finn couldn't blame them.

He felt a similar—stronger—tug toward her. Even if she seemed to do everything in her power to avoid him. When she wasn't buried in a book, or going out with Arden or Selene, she was behind a closed door with Monty.

Whenever he passed those closed doors, he would feel a tug of envy as Iris's real, twinkling laugh filtered out into the hall.

The more he was around Iris, the more he realized that he almost never got that real part of her. She was always guarded, masked, watching him with pinched brows and eyes that always seemed to find him lacking.

He only caught glimpses.

Like when she'd been excited over the ring.

Or, of course, when his hands and lips were on her, when they were lost in sensation and each other.

But since that night in the pool, she'd made it a point not to so much as brush his shoulder in the hall.

All he did was replay that scene over and over in his mind.

There were more questions for Iris, despite her not having the power to make changes. It seemed like everyone was just charmed by her and wanted to be in her orbit.

And Iris, to her credit, easily warmed up and lost her tension. Despite being new to land politics, she clearly had experience speaking to large groups of people.

It struck him, as he watched her, how little he actually knew about her life and upbringing.

Being a princess, there must have been royal duties. She surely had training in decorum and composure and had been forced to sit through never-ending ceremonies and meetings.

She handled it like a pro.

Before he knew it, after answering a few final questions, the whole thing was over.

They made their way off the stage but somehow lost track of each other in the crowd.

He wanted to look for her, to bring her back to his side. Not just because it was important for them to show a united front and a happy relationship. He just wanted her there.

He was pulled in a dozen different directions then, shaking hands and making connections. Henry was right there with him, taking down numbers and making promises for private meetings.

At this rate, Finn wasn't going to get a moment to himself until election day.

Then, if he got elected, it would be endless as well.

And if he didn't?

Honestly, he didn't even have a backup plan for that scenario. He'd lived, breathed, eaten, and slept this campaign since college. There was no vision that didn't involve politics, making changes and helping the people of all the communities.

His father had been killed trying to protect the old laws. Finn wanted to help create newer, fairer ones—ones that would benefit everyone, not just the select few interest groups who could afford to buy off the former corrupt politicians.

If he couldn't do that, he had no idea what his life would be like. Where would he work? Would he lose Henry to some different campaign in another state? Would Iris feel compelled to follow through with their arrangement?

That last one gave him the biggest gut punch of all.

Once the rest of the constituents had cleared out, Henry ushered Finn into the staging area, going over all the meetings they would be setting up, how he thought things had gone, and which paranormal groups they'd gained.

"Unfortunately, at this rate, I don't know if we have a chance of winning over the vampires," Henry was going on as Finn craned over his shoulder to see if he could spot Iris anywhere.

Where could she have gotten to? Especially once everyone was gone?

He wanted just a couple of minutes alone with her to tell her how well she'd done, how impressed he was with her grace and kindness.

And ask her about her background, what royal duties she liked, and which ones she couldn't stand.

He also would like a chance to ask her what she saw in her future. In *their* future. Was she planning on being a political wife? Arranging charity events, doing community outreach, hosting lavish parties at their home?

Did she have dreams of her own career?

"Especially not after that whole fiasco." Henry waved out toward the stage.

"What fiasco?"

He and Henry were usually on the same page when it came to how successful an event was or not. They'd been working so closely for so long, sometimes he swore he could hear the exact words about to come out of his campaign manager's mouth just seconds before he uttered them.

His surprise was enough to make him stop looking for his fiancée and focus on Henry.

"With Iris," Henry said, scrolling through something on his phone, then rapidly typing with one hand. Finn could just picture his calendar filling up in real time.

"What are you talking about?"

"The way she went on and on about the ocean," Henry said, tapping away.

"She's *from* the ocean."

"Yes, fine. But this town hall was not about her. None of this is about her."

Taken aback, it took Finn a moment to sort through his thoughts.

"I know you're not aiming to be an ass, but you really hit the mark," Finn said, watching as his head lifted, brows raised.

"You know I didn't mean it that way. I meant that you need to be the focal point of these types of events, since these people will be voting for you, not her."

"Still. Watch how you talk about her. She could have overheard and misinterpreted."

"Understood. Now, let's go over—"

"Not tonight. I'm going to find Iris and get her home. She's had a long day. We can start early tomorrow."

Henry watched Finn for a long moment. He wasn't accustomed to Finn making the rules and setting the pace. Usually, trusting Henry like he did, Finn allowed him to hold the reins.

Just this once, though, he was going to put his foot down.

He was going to find Iris.

The problem was, she was nowhere to be found.

Not at the town hall venue.

Not at the bookstore.

Not at any of the hot pretzel carts.

Not in the pool or penthouse.

Minutes ticked to hours as Finn's anxiety grew. It wasn't like her to be out late. She was getting used to the city, but not enough to feel comfortable out alone at night.

And she was alone.

He'd spoken to Selene, Willow, and Arden. No one had seen her.

Had she gone out with someone from the town hall?

Had it been that werewolf she'd been staring at?

His stomach coiled, but he forced himself not to let those thoughts take root.

He needed to focus on finding her, not on what she was potentially doing. Or with whom.

It was the darkest part of night when he heard a rattle at the penthouse door, shocking him out of a near sleep that left him feeling more disoriented than before.

"Iris?" he called, jumping off the couch.

"Alas, no. It's not the stunning sea wench," Monty called. He waddled in with a wing holding several swag bags, like he'd attended multiple events in one night. And, given his social-ladder-climbing ways, he probably had. "She probably went out for coffee. Or a pretzel."

"No, Monty. She's been gone all night."

"All night?" he asked, some of his usual lightness falling away.

"We were at the town hall together. But she disappeared. I haven't seen her since."

"You mean to tell me that a sweet, sheltered stranger to the land is lost in this sprawling metropolis and there isn't a swarm of police in this apartment? Where are the federal agents? The National Guard?"

"Monty, I get the panic. Really, I do. But I need you to focus. Try to figure out where she might have gone. I've checked the usual places."

"Was she feeling particularly tide-turned?"

"What does tide-turned mean?"

"Moody. Off."

His mind flashed back to her face when she'd come out of the bathroom.

"Maybe. Yes. Yeah, definitely. Why?"

"She may have gone to the closest body of water, then. To clear her head. I'll go see if I can track down some gulls and ask," he said. He dropped his bags then moved toward the door. "You stay here."

Finn wasn't sure if trusting a pelican was his best bet. But, then again, no one in the city knew Iris as well as her 'emotional support pelican.'

Alone again, Finn went into the bathroom, cranking the water to cold, then stripping and climbing in, wanting to shock himself fully awake.

It wasn't until he climbed out that he saw it.

The ring box on the sink counter.

The ring nestled inside like a closed promise.

He knew she'd been wearing it at the town hall.

Its presence in the penthouse meant she'd come home afterward.

He rushed down the hall, pushing open the primary bedroom door and looking with fresh eyes.

There.

Half kicked under the bed was the light pink dress she'd worn to the press conference.

Along with her strapless bra.

And her panties.

All crumpled like a shed skin.

Monty was right.

She'd gone to the water.

Likely in nothing but a sundress or cover-up, so she could easily strip and slide into the waves.

As he glanced more around the apartment, he realized that while she had left the ring, she had taken something else with her. The book. His book. The one he'd spent hours picking out and getting spelled for her.

Its absence gave him hope that it wasn't too late to change her mind.

She was running.

Not just away from the pressures of his future office.

But also from him.

Though, he was crossing his fingers that taking the book with her meant she wasn't completely done with him.

Because he needed to bring her back.

And it wasn't about appearances, or strategy, or trying to salvage the relationship he'd mapped out like a campaign.

This had nothing to do with optics.

It was her pillow-creased face first thing in the morning. It was her late-night laugh when Monty regaled her with stories of his adventures. It was the way she challenged him without flinching. It was how she cried happy tears when the characters in her books finally got out of their own way and fell in love. It was the way her hair fell into her face when she laughed, and her eyes warmed when she shot him one of those rare, precious smiles.

It was the way she made him want to do better, to be better. Not for the views, not for the headlines, not for the votes. But for her.

It was because she'd only been gone a short while and his world already felt darker and colder.

He had to bring her back because he knew somewhere deep in his marrow that what had started out as a strategy had become the only thing in his life that felt real.

Iris

She'd gotten a little turned around in the crowd.

It seemed like everyone wanted a minute or two with her after the official questioning was over.

One or two of them genuinely wanted to discuss things like the ocean and pollution.

As a whole, though, she mostly felt like they just wanted proximity to her.

Was it because she was royalty?

Or simply because she was a mermaid?

She had no idea.

But after the fifteenth face got in hers, she was finding it hard to maintain that fake smile.

Suddenly, she had a lot of respect for Finn for being able to fake it so well. Even if she deeply disliked it about him at the same time.

It took a lot of self-control not to roll her eyes or sigh at some of the things people said, the wild accusations they threw, the borderline conspiracy theory ideas they'd cooked up in their heads.

Finn faked peace and understanding perfectly.

She, as much as she hated to admit it, was going to need more practice.

When she'd finally untangled herself from that werewolf she'd been momentarily fascinated by when she'd first seen him, but quickly found him a little pushy and inappropriate one-on-one, she'd gone in search of Finn.

She was ready to go home, get comfy, and get to sleep early for once.

She'd just been moving toward the staging area when Henry's voice carried out to her.

"This town hall was not about her," he said. Her stomach clenched at his words. Because she thought she'd done well. It wasn't like she wanted to be there. She'd been forced. And she'd done her part. "None of this is about her."

Iris froze.

Say something, she implored. *Defend me.*

But all she heard following Henry's words was silence.

With a strange catch in her throat, she turned and ran back through the front of the building, then out onto the street.

She walked aimlessly for a few moments but felt a tug in her heart, a sensation that pulled her in, crashed, released, then pulled again.

The tide calling her home.

She nearly ran back to the penthouse, stripping out of her clothes, then throwing on a simple, lightweight cotton dress.

She only paused after changing when her ring caught her eye.

A cry caught in her throat at seeing it there—an anchor tying her to a man who couldn't be bothered to defend her.

She ripped the ring off her finger, unable to see it sitting there for another second. No matter how much she loved the thing.

She placed it back in its box and set it in the bathroom, where she knew Finn would find it eventually.

And understand the message.

She was done.

She couldn't be forced to marry someone like him.

Sure, her mother would be furious. She might even find some old, undesirable merman for her to marry as punishment.

But at least she could be at home.

At least she would be among people who understood who and what she was, who wouldn't constantly be trying to shape and change her.

She grabbed her bag on the way out, before doubling back to find the one thing she wanted to bring with her. She went ahead and didn't let herself wonder if there was any deeper meaning to that item being the book Finn had gifted to her. Then she slipped into a taxi and headed out of Manhattan.

She fought the burning of tears at the back of her eyes the whole way, not daring to name the feelings crowding her chest.

Sure, she would miss Selene, Arden, and Willow. But she could visit them. Now that she was comfortable on land.

It wasn't them, though. She knew it in the weird tightness in her chest. The sadness had nothing to do with her friends.

Thankfully, the taxi pulled up to the beach before she had a chance to analyze that sensation any further.

Iris waited until the taxi was nothing but headlights in the distance before kicking off her flip-flops and making the long walk across the beach toward the sandbar. The sand crunched underfoot, warm and familiar, as the sound and scent of the water filled her with hope.

That she could shift and swim away the uncomfortable feelings she didn't want to face.

Under the mostly full moon, she stripped out of her dress, tucking it carefully into her small purse and setting that on top of her shoes.

She didn't know why she was leaving anything behind. She wasn't planning on coming back to land anytime soon.

With a sigh, she lowered herself into the water, feeling her tail shift and flick in the current.

She dipped under the surface.

Then she swam.

Hard and far, setting a punishing pace until her body ached and exhaustion tugged at her eyes.

Only then did she finally swim back toward the palace.

She was met immediately with all the familiar sights: the whalebone gate, the lush kelp gardens teeming with fish, the coral columns of the palace itself.

She waited for the sensation of *home* to return. But even as she drifted down the hall to her old bedroom, it never came.

"I thought I heard your door," Shelly said, appearing in her room just a few moments later.

It hadn't been long, but she would swear her sister looked older, more mature, less like the angry girl she'd left behind to go to the surface.

"What are you doing here?"

"I want to come home."

"Oh," she said, pressing her lips together. She thought about her next words. That was so mature, so careful, so very *not* like her little sister. What had been going on since she went to land? "I'm not sure our mother is going to go along with that plan."

"Oh, I'm sure she's going to be furious. But she'll get over it. And marry me off to Osiren or someone, as punishment."

"No. Not Osiren."

"Why not?"

"Because Osiren is engaged—"

"Oh, good for him."

"To Juna."

"To *Juna*?" Iris yelped. "Rule-following, serious, duty-bound, future queen Juna? *Our* Juna?"

"Yes."

"When?"

"A few days after you went to live in the city."

"Was it mother's choice?"

"It was a joint decision. As much as anything can be a joint decision when you're a princess."

"But they're just so . . . different."

"I never bought into the whole opposites-attract thing until I saw them together," Shelly said. "She brings out a less vain, more sincere side of Osiren. He brings out a playful side of her."

"Playful? Juna? The same Juna who used to use her toys to hold court? That Juna?"

"He got her to jump on the backs of dolphins and race for bragging rights. And 'borrow' the royal chariot. Only to get caught making out in it. Oh, and he got her to play a game of Truth or Dare. And she had to sing opera in front of visiting dignitaries."

"But Juna can't sing."

"No, no she can't," Shelly said, eyes and smile warm.

"I'm sorry I missed that."

"What have you been up to?"

"Trying to ruin my engagement," Iris found herself admitting.

"Is he that awful?"

"No. No, he's not awful. He's just . . ."

There was a loud giggle coming from Juna's room, then a shushing sound.

"Oh," Iris said, pressing a hand to her mouth, her cheeks feeling warm at the idea of her sister having a man in her room.

"You have no idea," Shelly said, wincing. "I needed to make makeshift noise-canceling headphones out of giant clamshells. That whooshing sound almost drowns out the . . . other sounds. Almost."

"I'm happy for her." She was. Juna deserved to be loved for who she was, while also having someone at her side who could show her depths to herself that she might not know existed otherwise.

Iris couldn't help but feel a little envious.

That lack of connection was why she was back home in the first place. She didn't have that with Finn.

"Me too. But tell me why I can't be happy for you too."

"He's just . . . he's all surface, no depth. And you can never know if he's being real or not. He's been so coached all his life that I'm not sure there is anything about him that's genuine anymore."

"Hmm."

"Hmm? That's all you have for me?"

"Well, I have more. I just don't know if you're ready to listen to it or not."

Iris sighed, making a trail of delicate bubbles spiral

upward like tiny pearls, shimmering near the ceiling before they popped.

"I feel like it's wrong to be getting advice from my baby sister. But, sure, I'll listen."

"The way I see it is . . . you're happy for Juna because Osiren saw the parts of her that even *she* couldn't see, and he put in the time and work to bring those parts out."

"Yeah . . ."

"But you're not willing to do that for Finn."

Oof.

That was unexpectedly astute.

"It's different."

"How?"

"Because I don't think there are those parts of Finn." Even she didn't fully believe the words as she said them, though.

"If I didn't tell you today, would you have believed that Juna would be capable of singing opera in front of some very important people?"

"No."

"Exactly. Look, I'm not saying you can *change* someone. I don't think that's possible. But maybe you aren't seeing beneath the surface because you aren't looking."

"Maybe." She had been focused on finding fault in him because she desperately didn't want to be condemned to a life on land.

"So, now the question is: are you choosing not to delve deeper because you genuinely don't care for him, or because you're afraid you could want him and a future on the surface with him?"

Huh.

"When did you become so wise?"

"Mother has focused on me now that you've been gone, and Juna has been . . . indisposed."

"I don't know how I'm supposed to feel about that."

"Well, she's training me to become a possible land liaison."

A land liaison. Iris had never given the position a second thought before, let alone wondered what kind of mermaid would be right for that job. But as soon as her sister told her, she knew that Shelly was the perfect woman for the job. Even if her heart pinged a little at the idea of her baby sister being suddenly old enough to be considered for such an important role.

Perhaps she'd never given her mother enough credit in the past. She'd been aware of parts of her daughters that even they might not have seen. How her eldest needed a man like Osiren to bring out a buried, playful side. How Shelly couldn't go live on the surface because she would be a vital bridge between the deep and the land. And, yes, how her middle daughter who never saw a future outside of the ocean would come to love so much about the world above.

"That is the best of both worlds," Iris said.

"Exactly."

"Can I tell you something that I'm almost a little afraid to admit to myself?"

Shelly mimed locking her lips. "You can trust me."

"There's a lot about land life that I'm beginning to enjoy."

"Told you!" Shelly said, shoving her shoulder. For just a second, she was the little sister Iris remembered. "It's totally the books, isn't it?"

"I'm not going to lie, that's a big part of it. I've been reading like eight books a week. Did you know Caprica

Coraline moved to the surface and has been writing like crazy ever since?"

"I didn't. But I've never been into books like you. What else?"

"Well, the food."

"Yeah, nothing beats the food. I always eat like a million street hot dogs when I go up."

"Hot pretzels are my downfall."

"Solid choice too. Anything else?"

"I've made a couple of friends. Selene, she's this hilarious, jaded, sarcastic witch. And Arden—"

"The demon wedding planner?" Shelly asked.

"You know him?"

"I met him once a while back. He's a trip."

"He is. He's planning a 'summer season' wedding for me. And then there's a dryad in the building named Willow."

"I'm happy for you. You never did have a lot of friends down here. Juna and I always worried about you."

"Juna never had any friends either."

"That's not true. She's always been close with the other children of the council members."

"I didn't know that."

"Because you were always doing your best to escape."

"Escape?"

"Into your books. With Monty. On long swims by yourself."

Shelly was silent for a few beats, seeming to sense that Iris needed a moment to absorb what she'd just said.

She'd never seen her life that way. Like she'd been trying to get away from it or avoid it. But maybe that was because she'd been in the thick of it.

Perspective was easier to gain from a distance.

And now that Shelly mentioned it, she had spent most of her life avoiding not only her duties as a princess but also the other merfolk, even—at times—her own sisters.

She'd always believed that she loved nothing more than the ocean and her life there.

But if she didn't have any friends, close relationships with her family, or even any dreams or ambitions of her own, could she truly claim she loved it as much as she thought?

"It's part of the reason why I was so surprised you objected so hard to going on land. I figured it was a chance for you to experience all those things in books: adventure, travel, friendship, love."

"I love the ocean."

"Of course you do. We're *mermaids*. I love it too. But I also really love the surface world. I mean, have you *seen* how hot those shifter men are?" Shelly fanned herself with her hand. "No one is making you choose between them, you know. You can love the ocean and spend time in the ocean but also live on land."

"I guess."

It hadn't exactly taken a lot of work to get herself driven out to the beach so she could swim and see her family. No one was preventing her from doing that each time the urge struck.

If she wanted that balance, she could have it.

The question was: did she want it?

And if she were to dig a little deeper: did she want that with Finn?

There was no denying that there was some physical chemistry between the two of them. That said, she knew that attraction didn't mean anything. It was just chemicals, just bodies that recognized they might do some fun things together to a mutually enjoyable end.

Could she be content with that? A physical connection, but not a soul one? A marriage with passion but no connection?

"What has you most conflicted?" Shelly asked.

"I don't know if I can spend the rest of my life plastering on plastic smiles and pretending I don't see Finn being fake. Or flirting with gargoyles in front of me."

"Come again?"

"He was talking to a gargoyle, and it was . . . flirty. For sure on her side. And then Finn dismissed me."

"Dismissed you? Why?"

"So they could flirt in private, I imagine."

"You imagine or you know?" Iris was sure her sister could read that answer on her face. "Well, what did you say to him when you confronted him about it?" At Iris's silence, Shelly sighed. "Did you expect your fiancé to be a mind reader? Because I'm pretty sure Mom told you he was human through and through."

"It was rude. I shouldn't have needed to tell him for him to know that."

"Or maybe you just saw it that way because you were upset about what you perceived was flirting."

"Listen, I don't like this version of you. I want the sister back who always spoke before she thought."

"Even she could see that you're looking for reasons to dislike Finn."

"Maybe," Iris conceded. "But there are also some legitimate concerns."

"Then how about I suggest you sit down and talk them

out like two partners in a relationship would do? Instead of just tiptoeing around it and hurting your own feelings?"

"We'll see. I'm not even sure I'm going back yet."

Just then, there was a slam in the hallway, making both sisters straighten. They knew that slam. That was Tatiana herself. And she was unhappy about something.

"Oh, no," Iris whispered. "Juna has Osiren in her room."

"He's been in her room every night. She doesn't care. Actually, I think she's happy about it. If anything, I think she figured out that you—"

"Iris Lanae Marivelle."

"Uh-oh," Shelly said, shooting her sister a grimace.

"Hello, Mother," Iris greeted the queen as her bedroom door flew open.

"What have you done?"

"What?" Iris asked, stomach twisting. Had Finn said something? Had another news outlet published something embarrassing about her?

"The only reason you could possibly be here is if you bungled your relationship with Finn Westrock."

"That's not true. I could have gotten myself in trouble with the law and needed somewhere to hide out," Iris quipped.

But her mother was in no mood to entertain jokes.

"Out with it. What did you do?"

"She didn't do anything, Mom," Shelly said. She swam next to her sister, her chin jerking up.

"Then why is she here at this hour?"

"She missed us. And the ocean. Isn't she allowed to visit?"

Tatiana's gaze moved between her daughters—suspicious but not closed-minded.

"Is that so?"

"Yes," Iris said. She *did* miss the ocean. And she *had* been wanting to reconnect with her family. The only variability was how much time she meant to spend down there.

It wasn't a lie. Maybe just a small omission.

"In that case," Tatiana said, holding open her arms.

The queen was not an overly affectionate woman. When she was offering a hug, you took full advantage of it.

Iris swam into her mother's arms, letting herself be held, be loved. And for just a moment, she felt the cracks in her heart filling in.

"It was lovely to see you. But you need to get back to your fiancé before he misses you."

Right.

She was relatively sure Finn wouldn't miss her until Henry said they needed her for something. Like a real-life doll they could dress and prop up whenever it suited their needs.

"I haven't been able to see Juna yet."

"Yes . . . well." Tatiana shook her head. There was a ghost of a smile on her lips. "I believe your sister is going to be indisposed until the morning. Perhaps the next time you visit, you can send a message with one of the gulls, so we can be sure to be available to you."

It was then that it finally sank in that home would never actually be home again.

At home, you didn't need an appointment; you didn't need to tell people you would be around, because it was expected.

There was a little wobbling feeling in her heart at that realization. Even if she'd always known that Juna would be the only one of them who would live in the palace for her whole life. She and Shelly would be expected to move on, marry, have children, and lives of their own. They were meant to make new homes.

It was up to her to figure out where home was now.

Unbidden, the penthouse flashed into her mind. Her books cluttered the surfaces. Checkers was keeping her legs toasty. Selene and Arden were sniping at each other good-naturedly. Monty was perched on the coffee table, telling her the latest scandal involving the rich and famous.

Somehow, between mourning the loss of her life in the ocean and trying her damnedest to get back to it, she'd created a whole new one. With new faces. New connections. New hopes.

She wasn't sure if Finn simply wasn't there, or if she was choosing not to allow him to be.

One thing was for sure, though.

Whatever she decided to do with the rest of her life, it no longer involved the palace.

It was time to leave.

This time on her own.

She stayed for a while longer before saying her goodbyes. She visited the kelp gardens, her favorite shipwrecks, and soaked up all the things she loved most about the deep.

Then she made her way back toward the surface.

When she finally broke the surface, it wasn't just her purse and dress on the sandbar.

It was Finn.

She watched the relief play across his face.

Then he was suddenly moving, reaching into the water, grabbing her at her sides, and pulling her up out of the water.

He looked at her like she was storms and shipwrecks.

But he pulled her closer anyway.

Iris

Water cascaded down her body as Finn pulled her against him, her cool skin meeting his warm body.

There was no stopping the little whimper that escaped her as her bare breasts pressed against his wide chest.

Finn's fingers flexed on her hips in response to the sound as his gaze held hers for just a moment, looking, searching, and seeming to find the answer he was seeking.

The second their lips met, it was over. For just that moment, she was his. He kissed her like he knew it.

He kissed her like the tide—fierce and impossible to resist.

Iris's hands slid up his strong arms and wrapped around his neck, letting her press closer as Finn pulled her fully out of the water.

He pulled her with him as he lowered down to the sand, situating her across his lap as the water dried on her tail.

His hand slid upward, framing her face as the kiss grew deeper, rougher, needier.

He caught her lower lip between his, sucking gently before adjusting the angle and devouring her.

His hand tentatively touched the side of her tail, dragging a little sigh out of her, urging him on.

His palm moved upward, gliding over her scales even as her tail was slowly starting to disappear.

By the time his fingers were at her hip, he was touching her human skin.

Need crashed through her body as his tongue swept over hers—tentative at first, then filled with hunger as a moan escaped her.

Iris pressed her thighs together, trying to ease the ache growing between them.

He wouldn't need to look to know how consumed she was. She was all pulse, heat, and slippery need.

Iris shifted up onto her knees, and Finn's hungry gaze slid down her body, taking in every exposed inch of her.

When his gaze reached hers again, her hands moved out, grabbing Finn's wet shirt and drawing it up and off his body.

She slid closer, dropping down onto his lap, feeling how he ached for her. Their chests brushed, making her nipples peak and ache.

A rumble moved through Finn.

His hands slid up her back, pulling her until her chest met his, making both of them gasp.

Finn leaned down, his lips meeting the column of her neck, making a tremble slide down her spine.

There was no stopping the way she rocked against him, feeling the hard length of his desire against her heat.

His tongue teased out, tracing over the pulse in her throat before moving downward.

His lips dragged like silk across her skin as he moved between her breasts.

She swore she could feel his breath in her bones—each soft exhalation a match strike.

He leaned her backward so he could move down, his tongue tracing around her nipple.

Goosebumps rose in a rush at the sensation just before his lips closed around the peak, sucking it into his mouth.

Her thighs clenched around his side as need sparked between them.

Finn sucked and licked and grazed until she was rocking against him, desperate for relief from the ache growing in her lower stomach.

Finn moved across her chest, and she arched without thinking, her spine bowing to invite more.

Time hiccupped—every second stretched thin with wanting, with sensation.

Just when she was sure she couldn't take another moment of sweet, soft torment, his head shifted between her breasts. Then he was moving down.

Their bodies moved together until she was flat on the wet sand and he was shifting her legs over his shoulders as he slipped lower and lower.

"I want you to come apart," he murmured. His lips pressed a kiss to that delicate crease of her inner thigh. "Slow," Finn went on. His soft hair teased her sensitive skin. "Sweet," he added, lips pressing to the triangle above her sex. "And all over my mouth."

His lips closed around her clit then, dragging a ragged moan out of her as pleasure bloomed in her core.

Her pulse fluttered deep in her throat. Her breath hitched in halves, like her body had forgotten the rhythm.

Iris's hands went downward, fingers curling into Finn's hair as his tongue started to trace a maddeningly perfect path around her clit.

Finn's hand grazed up her thigh, slipping between them, then pressing into her.

Her breath caught and flipped, like tripping over her need at the feel of his touch slipping inside.

His tongue flicked, steady and teasing, and his fingers followed, deeper now.

Her body pulsed.

Her moans poured out into the night, the sound as primal and desperate as the tide crashing against the shore.

The pressure built to a fever pitch.

Then she was there.

Right at that precipice.

Her body clenched around the promise of it, every breath a gasp, every heartbeat a countdown.

Then everything inside her seized and spiraled, the pleasure flooding out in helpless, rhythmic bursts.

She cried out as the orgasm pulsed and pulled her under over and over, leaving her shaking and breathless in the aftermath.

Finn's head shifted, kissing across one thigh, then the other, before moving across her hips, belly, between her breasts, then her neck.

"I could stay between your legs all night," he murmured against her ear.

A pained sound escaped her as another rush of need coursed through her.

She'd just been satisfied, but she was shaky and aching once again.

Her hands drifted down Finn's back, sinking into his ass, finding herself riding against his hardness.

That sexy rumble moved through Finn again.

"Not done with me yet?" he asked, lips kissing the corner of her mouth.

"Finn, please," she moaned, rocking her hips against him.

"Tell me what you want," he demanded just before his lips sealed over hers.

With her mouth otherwise occupied, she showed him what she wanted. Her hands grabbed the waistband of his shorts, dragging them down.

Finn pushed up to allow her to work his pants down.

Her hands sank into his ass, dragging him against her, then grinding against his hard length.

A groan moved through Finn as he pushed up to watch her with molten eyes as she rocked against him.

"You're so wet for me," he murmured. His hips ground down on her cleft, dragging a ragged moan from deep within her.

Her stomach coiled, tight and expectant as the air between them crackled—too thick to breathe, too sweet not to taste.

But before she could feel the pulse of release, Finn was pulling up, sitting back on his heels, his gaze moving over her for a moment as he reached for his wallet, finding the foil, then making quick work of protecting them.

"Look at you," he said, his hands drifting up and down her legs, "trembling just at the thought of more."

"Finn," she whimpered, reaching for him and pulling him down on her again. "Please. *Please*." Her legs wrapped around him, her body shaky with her need.

"Shh," he murmured, breath near her ear, "I know. I've got you."

He rocked against her.

The press of him felt like a promise.

For more.

For everything.

Finn's hips shifted.

Then she felt the press of him again, the push, the slide as he moved into her.

She was strung taut, every nerve lit, her body begging for the release that was just out of reach.

They both gasped at the sensation as he slid deep, her walls closing around him.

"I've been dreaming of this," he told her, his voice thick with need. "About how you would sound when I'm buried deep inside you." He rocked his hips just a little deeper, dragging a ragged moan from between her lips.

There was nothing then but sensation as he started to move.

Iris felt strung up, every inch of her wired and waiting, sure that the very next touch could detonate her.

"You feel so good," Finn groaned as their bodies moved faster, growing more desperate.

Pleasure tightened, gathering low and hot like a wave about to crest.

Her breath came in frantic gasps.

"That's it," Finn murmured. "Let go. I've got you. Just let go."

And so she did.

She came like a storm breaking, like a tidal surge swallowing everything but the sensations.

Everything clenched as she came, gasping, clawing, wrecked.

Finn groaned as the orgasm continued to roll, taking him with her, his body tensing, his breath catching, his weight coming down on her.

She wrapped him up in her arms and legs, satisfaction humming through her body.

The pleasure—that was easy. The quiet after, limbs tangled, heartbeats in sync, her mind clear to wander—that was another issue completely.

She lay still, careful not to breathe too deep, knowing any slight change would crack the fragile spell they'd fallen into.

It wasn't long before thoughts surged that had something sneaking its way in. Not regret. But something like its quieter cousin. It was a sense of unease.

She wasn't supposed to want him.

What did it say about her that she craved someone who never showed her anything real?

Except, of course, his desire.

But desire was fickle and fleeting. It could trick you into thinking you knew who someone was.

Finn lifted up, and she took the opportunity to curl away from him. Slowly. Quietly. Not because she wanted space, but because closeness could start to tell her a lie that she couldn't afford to believe in.

It seemed as if the ocean itself sighed as the distance grew between them, as the connection dissipated like the sweat on their skin.

"How did you find me?" she asked, still naked, but she pulled her walls tightly around her, shielding everything important.

"Monty."

Of course.

No one else would have known where she'd come out of the ocean but the pelican she'd been with at the time.

"Why did you run?"

"I was homesick."

"You could have told me."

"I wasn't sure you'd notice."

"You disappeared from the town hall. Of course I noticed."

This was her chance.

To rein in her pride.

To confront things head-on.

She sucked in a steadying breath.

"I guess that makes sense," she said, rolling up. She reached for her dress, yanking it down over her body, not ready to have this conversation while naked. "Since I stole the whole show, right? Made it all about me?"

Her gaze cut to his, watching her words land with impact, making his head jerk back slightly.

"Henry never should have said that."

That was it. No explanation. No assuring her that he wasn't going to stand for that kind of disrespect moving forward.

"Do me a favor," she said, grabbing her bag and shoes. "Tell Henry that the next time he wants to criticize me, he can do it to my face. That way, I can stand up for myself."

Unlike you, she added silently before walking away.

She left him to scramble to get himself dressed.

She hauled it across the sand but realized her mistake as she walked down the empty road.

She wasn't in Manhattan anymore. Taxis weren't just milling about all the time. She wasn't even sure if there was a subway system to use. Not that she was a fan of those. But it would be better than being stranded.

"Iris?" Finn's voice was soft and coaxing.

"What?" she asked. She turned to him—arms crossed, body language closed.

"I have a car down at the corner," he said, gesturing.

"Oh."

"We're going to the same place. Might as well go together. For the environment," he added with a smile that she could only call self-deprecating.

"Well, it wouldn't be good optics to say one thing and do something different."

She hadn't meant for that to be cutting. But there was a slice of something across Finn's eyes that made her wish she could suck the words back in.

They climbed into the car and drove in silence back to Manhattan.

He dropped her out front of the building so she wouldn't have to walk back from the parking garage where Finn kept his car.

She was glad for the distance—both physical and metaphorical.

"Monty!" Iris yelped when she walked into the apartment—trailing sand—to find Checkers at his bubbling water fountain with the pelican walking up behind him, beak open.

"I wasn't going to eat him."

"Then why do you keep checking to see if he will fit in your beak?" she asked, scooping up Checkers.

"I was trying to measure him. For science." Monty fluffed his feathers and lifted his head—giant beak and all—appearing above such a thing as eating house cats, despite the evidence otherwise.

"What kind of science is that?" Iris pressed, placing the cat down on the back of the couch.

Monty ignored that, deciding to change tack. "I see your handsome human found you."

"Yep," Iris said, popping the '*p*.'

"He was worried about you, you know," Monty said. He followed her down the hall and into the bathroom, where she sat down in the tub and used the shower wand to wash the sand off her legs.

Her tail emerged half-heartedly before she started to wash off.

"He has a lot invested in me," she said, reaching for a towel.

"Oh, my sweet sea child," Monty said. "No. That was not a politician worried about his campaign. That was a man upset that the woman he cares for was missing."

"Sure, Monty," she said, rushing toward the bedroom in a towel.

She heard Finn come home as she slipped into her clothes, half-listening to Monty tell her about the day's escapades. She had every intention of avoiding her fiancé for the rest of the night.

Until there was a loud crash followed by a curse.

She sighed before making her way out, only to find Finn on his knees beside a large box, his shoulders hunched, his breath coming in fast, shallow bursts.

"Finn?" she called, concern slipping into her voice. "Are you all right?"

"Fine," Finn panted out between ragged breaths.

"What happened?"

"Was putting that box down," he said. "Threw out my back."

Iris wasn't familiar with the sensation but judging by how badly Finn was sweating and how red his face looked, she figured it was painful.

"Do you need to go to the hospital?"

"No. No, this happens once in a while. I just need to rest it."

"Iris can help you get up," Monty offered.

Iris shot him a look, but the bird was right. She had to help Finn off the floor.

"Yeah, here," she said, moving closer. "Take my hands."

Finn huffed out a few more breaths before reaching out. His hands were clammy in hers, and he looked about to faint as he slowly let her pull him to his feet.

"Are you sure you don't want to go to a doctor? You went from lobster-red to angelfish fast."

"It'll pass. Help me over to the couch."

"You'd think a mayoral candidate would have better lumbar support," Monty mumbled.

"Not helping," Iris chided.

It was a painstaking process, but she eventually got him over there, then let him use her body as leverage to lower down.

But the second he leaned back, a loud howl escaped him.

"Perhaps he needs to be in bed," Monty suggested. He got another look from Iris.

"I just need to be flat. These cushions won't work. Can you help me to the floor?"

"The floor?" she repeated.

"You can't let him sleep on the floor," Monty insisted.

Of course she couldn't.

"You can take the bed."

"Nonsense," Monty said, waving a wing. "You can share. It's plenty big for the two of you."

"It's fine. The floor will work."

"Oh, for Triton's sake," Iris said, reaching down for his hands again. "Come on."

It was a slow process down to the bedroom. By the time she got Finn into the bed, he looked exhausted.

He reached into the nightstand, shuffling around with a familiarity that reminded her that this was once his room, his bed, his nightstand.

A bottle of pills rattled as he opened it. He threw back several without a drink before collapsing against the pillows.

Iris stood there, feeling helpless.

Mermaids didn't typically suffer from 'thrown-out' backs. She had no idea what to do, but felt like she was supposed to do . . . something.

"I'm all right," Finn said, patting the space beside him. "Get some sleep. You've had a long day."

When she hesitated, Finn sighed.

"Iris, can we just . . . not tonight?"

Iris moved to the other side of the bed, then climbed in.

She slept on the left. He slept on the right. And the tension rested somewhere in between.

Finn

He didn't even know how Henry found out about his back. But he woke up to half a dozen texts about a massage therapist and acupuncturist scheduled for later that morning.

The campaign trail didn't stop for a busted back. And he and Iris had that damn late-night show to film that day.

He'd been hoping in those few, perfect moments after they'd both found their release, surrounded by sea, sand, and sky—all their walls and masks forgotten—that things had changed between them.

Until he felt her tense, felt the air shift with her.

Back were all her defenses, the anger he didn't quite understand. All he knew was it was directed at him. That when she looked at him, there was something that not only bothered her but pissed her off, too.

He wanted to know what it was.

He wanted to tell her he would work on it, that he thought what was growing between them was worth fighting for.

The problem was, he'd spent his entire life since his parents passed pushing down his real feelings when they pushed up, covering them up with a smile and a quip and some surface-level charm.

He barely knew how to acknowledge his true feelings, let alone how to discuss them with someone else.

When he turned his head on the pillow, he found Iris turned toward him, her cheek resting on her hand. Her pale hair was spilled across the pillow, the morning light making it glow. The pretty pastel scales up near her scalp seemed a little more prominent in sleep.

He couldn't seem to stop himself from reaching out to touch them.

But as his hand lifted, his back spasmed.

And he promptly slapped his hand right down on her face.

She came awake with a start, bleary-eyed and confused.

"I'm sorry. Iris, I'm so sorry," he said. He pulled his arm back, no matter how much his back screamed at the motion.

Iris's hand rose, rubbing her sore face.

"I was reaching out to . . . tuck your hair behind your ear," he lied. "And my back seized up. My hand just fell."

He didn't know what he expected in response to that, but it wasn't the way her eyes warmed and her lips tipped up.

"Not any better, huh?"

"Oh, it will be."

"What do you mean?"

"Henry."

"I'm sure Henry is great at a lot of things: making interns cry in the supply closet, memorizing weaknesses and weaponizing them, choking on his own smugness . . ." The bite of her words was softened a bit by the humor in her eyes. "But I'm pretty sure he's not a doctor."

"No. But we've been here before. Massage therapy and acupuncture usually help. If not, I can get a steroid injection that should provide some short-term relief. In extreme situations, magic will fix it temporarily."

"Why can't you just rest for one day? Do you really think your whole career will go up in smoke if you take a single day off to take care of yourself?"

It was a valid question.

Finn knew she didn't want the real answer.

"Unfortunately, we have an engagement today," he said.

"Ugh." Iris threw herself onto her back. Her arm went dramatically over her eyes. "What now?" she grumbled.

That was possibly what he liked best about her: her willingness to openly display every emotion. She was just so fully . . . herself all the time. Frustration and annoyance included.

"The late-night show," he reminded her.

"Already? But I haven't had my fifty thousand hours of media training. I was *so* looking forward to that."

A little chuckle escaped Finn. "It wasn't supposed to be so soon. But according to Henry, we are 'trending,' so the talk show wanted to ride that momentum."

"And if massage, acupuncture, and a shot don't work?"

"We'll be seated the whole time. I can fake it."

"Yes, I guess you can," she said, her tone getting a little colder as she climbed out of bed. "I'll make coffee."

And just like that, she was gone. Literally and figuratively.

Finn sighed, frustrated that she was beginning to take some of her training to heart, that she was becoming less genuine because that was what he, Henry, and the political sphere demanded of her.

He managed to slowly get himself into a seated position by the time he heard a knock at the door.

"Where is he?" Henry's voice asked, already moving through the house to look for him. "Oh, great," he sighed when he got a look at Finn, sweaty and pale, face contorted in pain from the movement.

"It's been this bad before."

"Not when you had an engagement the same day."

"It's a seated engagement."

"You're seated now and look like you're on day two of the flu."

"Always a ray of sunshine, Henry," Iris said, moving into the room to bring Finn a cup of coffee.

"Thanks," Finn said, frustrated with how his back spasmed just from raising his arm.

"Why is your face red?" Henry asked, zeroing in on Iris.

"Oh, Finn slapped me."

"He *what*?" Henry asked, eyes widening.

Finn hated that he couldn't tell if Henry's gaze went serious because he was horrified that his friend was capable of slapping someone . . . or if he was trying to figure out how to minimize the blowback politically.

"Accidentally," she added.

"Thank God," Henry sighed, visibly relaxing. "A little ice or makeup should hide that from the cameras."

"It doesn't hurt, by the way," Iris said, never willing to

let Henry's callousness slide. "I know you were very concerned about it."

"Is that the massage therapist?" Finn asked when there was a knock at the door.

"Arden. To get Iris ready for tonight. Between him and the bird, they should be able to shape her up."

"Like a piece of clay," Iris grumbled under her breath.

"Which allows me to focus on you and your talking points," Henry said, ignoring her.

"Looks like a miserable day for both of us," Iris said, moving out of the room. "But at least my teachers aren't you," she added. She shot Henry a saccharine smile. "It's always good to look on the bright side."

"Huh," Henry said as she walked out. "She was snarkier than usual."

"She overheard what you said last night," Finn told him. "And was upset enough to go to her family. She'd left her ring behind." Even just the memory of seeing it there had his heart twisting. All over a few careless words from a man who knew how much weight words carried. Henry's career relied on knowing the right things to say, the right *way* to say them. It was frustrating that he so rarely thought to use that insight to mind his own words. "I know you don't intend to hurt her, Hen. But that doesn't stop it from happening when you're so careless."

That managed to get through to his campaign manager. Was it because he was having a truly human moment of regret? Not likely. But a broken engagement this far into his campaign would be a nightmare.

"I forgot how emotional mermaids can be."

Finn sighed. "I don't think *she* is being emotional. I

think you're being an ass. And it needs to stop. I don't want to lose her."

Henry's head tipped to the side, watching him with eyes that Finn knew saw him all too well.

"Are you catching feelings for your fiancée?"

"Isn't that the goal of a relationship?"

"I guess. But it complicates things."

"How?"

"Because if you're falling for your fiancée, your focus will be more on her."

"This far into the campaign, Henry, I don't think we have that much to worry about."

"My polls don't suggest you should feel so confident about that."

Henry handed him his tablet, letting him look through the polls as well as the compiled document of social media comments one of the interns had put together.

Henry excused himself for a phone call as Finn scrolled.

The thing was, this time, Finn wasn't convinced that Henry was right. The more he read, the more he saw things that he'd heard Iris grumble about: him coming off as fake, as surface-level, as a PR shell.

The people didn't relate to Finn on a personal level, even if they did agree with his politics.

The deeper he dug, the more he saw what Henry had been hiding from him when it came to issues with his image.

In fact, the only gushing comments he could find had been on the pictures that had been posted of him and Iris at the parade.

He actually looks relaxed and happy was the most liked comment beneath the article.

All during his massage and acupuncture, all he could focus on were the comments saying that they'd seen him a hundred times and still couldn't get a feel for who he was as a person.

The scariest part was that Finn himself was starting to lose those genuine, human sides of himself as well.

He didn't have time for hobbies, for leisure, for nurturing the side of him that was a person, not just a politician.

He was able to move without excruciating pain by the time the acupuncturist—who used magic-infused needles for an extra oomph—left, but Henry still insisted on the shot before he headed out with Arden and Monty to pick out an outfit for Finn that would make him seem casual and approachable while still trustworthy.

He imagined Iris was spending her few stolen moments reading, so he went into the bathroom, took a shower, then stood in front of the mirror in his towel, practicing answers to the questions Henry thought would be most likely to come up at the studio.

He didn't realize he wasn't alone until Iris sighed.

Turning, he saw her leaning in the doorway.

"What?" he asked.

"You say all the right things, and it still feels wrong."

"Is it my tone?" he asked, stomach clenching.

"Do you actually believe what you're saying?"

"Of course. It's my platform."

"Do *you* believe it? Not politically. As a man?"

"Yes."

"I don't feel like you do."

"I . . . I don't know what to do with that."

"It feels like you've practiced that answer a thousand times."

"I have."

"That's the problem. People don't want to hear the right words. They want something real."

Finn sighed, shaking his head. "I am real. This is real. This is who I am."

"Okay," she said, turning and walking away.

There was a moment of defeat before she was at the doorway again, this time holding up an old photo album he hadn't seen in years.

"Then who is he?" she asked, opening to a page that featured a teenaged version of himself, decked out in merch for a cheesy show he'd been obsessed with, holding up the action figure his mother had gotten him for his birthday.

His face was unguarded. His eyes were bright. His smile so wide, it made his eyes small.

"I don't know anymore," Finn admitted, feeling the tug of regret. He'd spent so many years becoming the man he now was. He didn't recognize who he used to be.

"Maybe you should try to find him again," she said, closing the album. "Because he is who people want to know. They can relate to him. They like the suit," she added, putting the album down. "But they want to see the *man* under it."

"Oh, yeah?" he asked, lips curving up, eyes going bright.

"Not like that," Iris said with a tinkling laugh. "Though, I bet posing for one of those shirtless calendars wouldn't hurt your chances." Her gaze tracked down him, then back up. "I mean, why spend all that time in the gym if no one is going to see the hard work?"

Her eyes had gone heated as they quickly stole another look at his abs.

The memories of the night before came back with a

vengeance. Her soft skin, her soft sighs, the way she cried out when he was inside her.

Before he could even try to fight it, he felt himself getting hard. And the towel wrapped around his waist? It was doing nothing to hide the issue.

"Maybe you should—" she started, but her gaze slid down again, this time eyeing the shape of his hard length.

"I should what?" he asked, desire pouring through his veins as he saw her pupils blown wide when her eyes found his again. "Drop this towel, push you against this counter, and let you decide if the way I make you feel is fake?"

A sweet little whimper escaped her at that.

He knew he had her; he would bet good money that if he reached out and slipped his hands into her pants right then, he would find her wet and aching for him.

Reaching out, he grabbed her wrist, pulling her into the bathroom, then slamming the door.

"Your back . . ." Iris said as he pressed her back against the sink cabinet.

"To hell with my back," he said just before his lips were on hers.

His hand curled around her jaw as he took the kiss deeper, chasing the taste of her.

His other hand slid up under the hem of her shirt, closing around her breast.

She gasped, and he used the moment to slip inside, tongue stroking over hers, coaxing another moan.

Against his palm, her nipple twisted tighter, inviting his fingers to circle, roll, and pinch.

Her hands slid down the bare skin of his back. Finding the towel, she pulled until the material slid down.

Her fingers were greedy then, palming his ass, digging in.

As her teeth nipped his lower lip, her hands slid to his hips. Then forward. Down.

Her palm curled around his hard length, dragging a groan out of him and a needy little whimper out of her.

His breath stuttered as she started to stroke him. It was slow at first. But when his head fell to her shoulder, she grew bolder, moving faster, hand twisting, driving him up, leaving him rocking into her hand as the need overtook him.

Her own need was growing, though, and her free hand moved out, grabbing his, and pressing it between her thighs.

He wasted no time, sliding under the material to touch her without any barriers, finding her hot and slick for him.

His thumb worked her clit as two of his fingers slipped inside her.

There was no stopping the groan that escaped him when her walls tightened around his fingers.

There was nothing tentative or gentle about him then. He thrust hard and fast, driving her up as she was doing to him.

"Finn, please," Iris whimpered, her hips rocking restlessly against his palm. Needing more. Needing *him*.

He reached past her toward the medicine cabinet, grabbing a foil out of the box, then brushing her hand away from his length.

When his fingers slid out of her, she let out a little whimper that nearly undid him.

He made short work of the protection.

Then his hands were at the hem of her shirt, dragging it up and off.

"Perfect," he murmured, his fingers skimming up her ribs, then across her breasts.

Iris wasn't in the mood for teasing, though.

Her hand went to her own pants, pushing them and her panties down.

She turned, her ass rubbing against his hardness, making him twitch and pulse with need.

His head turned in at her neck as they both watched their reflections, a pink flush creeping across her chest as his lips teased up toward her ear.

"Finn . . ."

His hand slid down her front, slipping between her thighs. He shifted his hips, letting his hardness rock against her slick need as his finger teased her clit.

It wasn't until she was grinding against him—her breathing fast, shallow huffs, her little mewling sounds filling the bathroom—that he shifted back, then slid inside her in one slow, deep thrust.

They both gasped at the sensation, then decided in unison that there was no going slow, no drawing it out.

He started to move, fast and deep.

Iris rocked back against him, demanding more.

Her arms went back and around his neck as his thumb worked her clit and his other hand went to her chest, squeezing, circling, and rolling, driving her closer and closer to the edge.

Iris's breath got fast and erratic as she started to tighten around him.

"Breathe, baby," he murmured, his lips at her neck. "There you go. You're taking it so good for me."

Another moan bubbled up and burst out of her, her whole body tensing and trembling as he got her right to the edge.

Then she fell over.

Crashed.

Shattered.

Fell apart.

With *his* name on her lips.

That sound, and the tensing of her walls around him over and over, had him coming with her, slamming hard and deep, groaning against her ear as he came.

They were still breathless and shaky, bodies close, hearts beating in time, when they both heard the chorus of voices on the other side of the door.

They broke apart, Iris leaning down to gather her clothes, then making a mad dash for the bedroom.

He stood alone in the bathroom a moment longer, heart still racing. Not just from the sex, but from the way she'd looked at him. Like she saw someone worth knowing, not just managing. It was heady, addictive, and terrifying.

Shaking his head, he cleaned up, then slipped into a pair of basketball shorts and a tee before making his way out.

By the time he made it back out, Iris was already there, making a cup of coffee, pretending like nothing had happened. But Finn knew that the flush on her cheeks was from him.

Just like the ache in his back again was from her.

"Those shots usually work like magic," Henry said, frowning. "Well, we're not that far from the filming now. Let's go over—"

"No," Iris said, turning away from where Arden was pulling out an outfit to show her.

"What?" Henry asked.

"No. No more going over anything. Look at him. He

seems relaxed and human for a change. Don't tense him all up again."

Finn couldn't help the flirty smile he tossed in her direction, both of them knowing who could take credit for his sudden change of demeanor.

Henry eyed him for a moment before deciding Iris was right. Miracles, it seemed, were possible.

The next thing they knew, they were in the back of a cab, and Finn was pulling Iris's legs over his lap, finding her closeness grounding, reminding him not to get stuck in his head again.

Anytime during the interview when he found himself automatically slipping back into The Suit, Iris was right there, grabbing his knee or hand, playfully cutting him off mid-spiel to lighten the mood again.

When he watched the footage back later, he had to admit that it was the most *real* he'd ever looked and acted.

He could almost see the boy he'd been, waiting for rune-covered dragon statues, could see the young adult he'd once been, sitting in his college dorm, reading glow-in-the-dark shapeshifter comics. Hell, he could almost see his awkward, bumbling, red-faced attempts at charm.

The real Finn was there, front and center.

And the only person he could thank for that transformation was Iris.

Iris

She didn't even get a chance to bask in the glory of her work.

The second they got back from filming the late-night show, Henry had about fifteen calls that Finn needed to return.

And she watched how all of the tension returned to Finn's shoulders, how his whole demeanor so effortlessly shifted back to the political mannequin he'd spent so many years becoming.

Shelly's words danced around her mind as she spent the next day alone, trying to focus on her reading but failing.

She'd been right that it was possible to bring out a side of Finn that he was keeping under wraps, whether he was conscious of it or not.

The question was . . . did she want to? Was it sustainable? Would it be a constant fight between the real parts of him and the persona he wore like a shield?

If he won his election, he would need to be that shell of a person every day of his life. What were the chances that he would be able to hang up that part of him when he walked in the door and give her the man that she genuinely enjoyed being around?

She wasn't sure she liked the odds.

Iris cradled the shellphone in her hands in the courtyard behind the apartment building as she watched the bees flirt in and out of the flowers she would never see again if she said to hell with this engagement and went back to the sea.

Her heart felt torn in two as she lifted the shell to her ear, hearing the whooshing sound of the sea, and closing her eyes as her blood sang along with it.

"Shelly?" she called.

"I should have known it was her." Juna's voice met Iris's ear.

"What was her?"

"Who stashed a shellphone in with the normal shells in our sitting room. She sent you one too, then?"

"Don't turn her in to Mother. It's been nice to be able to connect with you guys here and there."

There was a slight pause before Juna spoke again. "Why haven't you spoken to me?"

"Well, gee, because I hear you are out spending all your free time with a certain merman."

"Oh. About that. I know you figured he might be your future betrothed, but—"

"I'm happy for you," Iris cut her off. "Truly." And maybe a little jealous at how easy the connection between her sister and her new partner seemed. "You deserve a little fun."

"Are you having some fun?"

"Are you asking me that? You, Miss All-Duty-All-The-Time?"

"I've been finding more balance. I've been keeping an eye on you and Finn. It seems like things have been getting busy as you get closer to the . . . election."

And the wedding.

"They have been. I think there's some big event every week moving forward."

"What else have you been doing? It seems like that pelican of yours has been a little too busy rubbing elbows to hang out with you as much."

"Yeah, Monty has been busy. I've made some friends, though. A witch named Selene, who owns a bookstore."

"That sounds like a tailor-made friend for you."

"I know, right? And then there's Arden, our wedding planner."

"I *adore* Arden."

"Wait, what? You know him?"

"He's going to be planning my wedding as well."

"Oh, wow." So much was going on below the surface without her.

"How do you feel about surface life?"

"Conflicted," Iris admitted.

Because, yes, there were many things she missed about the ocean, but she had fallen in love with just as many things about the surface.

It was to the point that she was considering even staying after the engagement broke off.

Without her mother's good graces, she would need to find her own way. She could do like all the other surface-dwellers did: get a job, an apartment, build a life. One free of any sort of royal or political responsibilities.

"What is it, Iris?" Juna asked. Her voice was gentler than Iris had ever heard it.

"What do you mean?"

"You seem . . . unhappy."

"I'm conflicted," Iris repeated.

"About your engagement? Or your fiancé?"

"Yes."

"Why? Has he not been good to you?"

"No. No, Finn has always been thoughtful and kind."

"And yet?"

"There is a part of him that I have begun to really like. But the other part of him, not so much. And I'm beginning to worry that the other part of him is bigger than the part I have grown fond of."

Juna gave that the usual amount of careful considering Iris knew her for, before speaking. "I know it's hard to see while in the thick of something, but it really hasn't been very long. If there are parts of him you've come to like, don't you think that more time would make you like him even more?"

"I don't have a lot of time. The wedding is being planned as we speak."

In fact, Arden had been texting her pictures of various options for their reception dinner. She needed to pick one so the two of them could go and do a tasting menu in the next few days.

"I'm sure you can find time to carve out for just the two of you. I'm sure Finn is a busy man, but surely his campaign manager can give him an evening off here or there."

"The power is in Finn's hands. It's his choice to go to all these events."

"Perhaps. But have you expressed your desire to have

more alone time with him?" Iris's answer was her silence. "Maybe start there," Juna suggested. "It might help you make up your mind once and for all."

"You're right," Iris agreed. If she wanted to make an informed decision, she needed more than some fantastic sex and one interview where they vibed. "Thanks, Juna."

"Of course. I just want you to be happy, Iris. I know you're worried about Mother's opinion, but . . ."

"But?"

"But you deserve to find your own happily ever after. With someone you like all the time."

With that, they ended their call. Iris sucked in a deep breath and made her way back to the building, her big sister's words still swirling around in her head.

"Oh, good," she said when she entered the apartment to find Finn standing at the kitchen counter. "I was hoping I would run into you."

"You were?" Finn asked, his tone hopeful.

"Yeah, I was wondering if maybe you could find a couple of hours in your schedule for us to be alone?"

"Not tonight," Henry said, coming down from the hallway. "We have that meeting with investors. But you have time tomorrow night." Hope swelled but was quickly dashed. "You have the charity gala."

"That's not alone," Iris griped.

"You'll be together."

"In a ballroom full of other people."

"It's the best we can do. Finn's schedule is booked until election night."

"Finn . . ." Iris implored, silently begging him to listen, to hear the plea for more for the two of them, for a real future.

"I can—" Finn started.

"That's a callback from the Gargoyle Rights Council," Henry said, holding up his phone.

Finn glanced between them. He was clearly torn. But she could sense which way he was leaning.

"Never mind," she said, grabbing her purse and storming toward the door.

"Iris, wait."

"He's right here," Henry announced.

Iris glanced back.

Finn was looking at her, his gaze conflicted.

But he reached for the phone.

And she was pretty sure that was his answer.

She took a moment in the elevator, fighting back useless tears, then picked up the phone to call Arden.

"Hey, gorgeous. What's going on?"

"Any chance we can do the taste test today?" she asked.

"Um, sure. If you're willing to send your mother that bill. And it will be a big one."

"Set it up. But wait. Make it for three."

"Bringing that cynical witch too, hm?"

"Yes." She needed Selene's trademark brand of skepticism and empowerment right about then.

"Name your choice and I'll meet you there in an hour."

Distraction plan in place, she named one of the places at random, then made her way toward Selene's store.

"For goddess's sake, Gerty!" Selene growled as Iris pulled open the door. The witch barely managed to duck in time to avoid a massive tome being hurled at her head. "I put the damn register back, you nasty old crone!"

Another book whizzed through the air, slamming into

Selene's altar behind the counter, sending a small cauldron and little bottles of various herbs clattering.

"Keep it up and I'll have someone come in here to do an exorcism."

"Want to get out of here?" Iris asked.

Selene's head whipped over.

"Hell, yes," she said, jerking as a book whacked the back of her head. "I don't even care if you're dragging me to something nauseating. Like a rom-com."

"We're going to eat a ton of food on my mother's dime."

"It's not all going to be seafood, is it?"

"I think we get to pick from a list of proteins."

"Perfect," she said, grabbing her bag. "Have fun throwing things around," she called to her ghost before moving outside. With a wave of her hand, the door locked and the *OPEN* sign turned.

"What got into her this time?"

"I have no idea. She's more temperamental than my cat."

"We can bring Arden back here after the tasting."

"Ugh. Arden's coming?"

"He is the wedding planner. Besides, I think you like him more than you're willing to admit."

"He's obnoxious."

"He's enthusiastic," Iris countered. "And charming."

"What you call 'charm,' I call a cry for attention in a tailored suit."

"Oh, come on. He saved you from vampire glamour," Iris reminded her.

"I would have snapped out on my own. I think. Eventually. Probably."

"You're just salty because he found out you like love stories."

"They're not *love* stories. They're about . . . tactical alliances. With emotional side quests."

"Have I mentioned lately how much I appreciate having you as a friend?" Iris asked.

"Okay. What happened?" Selene asked, stopping in the middle of the sidewalk.

"What are you talking about?"

"Well, first, the impromptu friendship appreciation declaration. But even without that, the emotional turmoil is popping off of you like sparklers."

"What are sparklers?"

"I forget how green you are sometimes. They're a lot like this," she said. Selene rubbed her fingers together until they sparked and sizzled. "But they're on a stick. Kids usually run around with them. But the little dragon shifters like to bite the tops off, the little stinkers.

"Anyway. That's what your energy is like right now. Add in our little food-tasting adventure, and I'm left thinking something happened with Finn."

Even just the mention of his name had her emotions bursting through her system.

"Wow. Those are some whiplash-inducing feelings," Selene said, taking a step back.

"You can feel them?"

"Sorry. I know; it's invasive. It's not all the time. It comes and goes with the moon cycle. And, you know, my cycle. I can go back and grab a charm to dull it—"

"No. No, it's fine. You're right. I'm all over the place."

"Forced matrimony will do that to a girl."

"Yeah. I mean, yeah."

Selene's head tipped to the side. Almost as if she was listening. Maybe she was.

"Do you have feelings for Finn now?"

Iris sucked in a deep breath and started walking. "I think I have feelings for the parts of him he keeps buried."

"But he doesn't appreciate you coming with a shovel?"

"I don't think that's it, exactly. It's more like . . . I'm worried that I might dig and dig until I can't lift my arms, but he is always going to come back and fill it all in again."

"And yet you're still conflicted."

"I went to see my family, and my sister said something about bringing out hidden parts of someone being worth the work."

"Do you want another voice in your head, or do you just want me to listen?"

Iris exhaled hard. "I think I want all the voices I can get. I'm too mixed up to make sense of anything."

"Now, if you repeat this—especially to that walking warning sign with great hair—I will deny it. But I'm constantly trying to tamp down my hopeless romantic streak with raging skepticism."

"I noticed that."

"That said, I am always secretly hoping someone comes along and proves me wrong. I mean, not me personally," she said, looking horrified at the idea of falling in love. "But those around me. So, if you think there's a chance that things might be real between you two, I think it's worth exploring. And giving Finn some time. I mean, men can be dense. Ask this one," she said, waving toward Arden.

"Ask me what?" Arden asked, turning to look at the women.

"Why men are so emotionally constipated," Selene said, shooting him a big, fake smile.

"Oh, my lovely girls," Arden said. He dropped an arm around each of their shoulders, guiding them toward the door of the catering restaurant. "It sounds like we've been gossiping. And I feel left out. Let's catch me up over some delicious food."

"Good goddess," Selene gasped as they moved inside. "How much does all of this cost?" Her gaze moved over the elegant table setup.

"You don't want to know," Arden said. He pulled out chairs for both women before taking his own.

"Is Finn paying for this?" Selene asked.

"No, Her Highness, the queen of the seas is."

"How rich is your family?"

"If they lived on land, they'd have private jets and mega yachts," Arden explained. "Multiples."

"Where does the money come from?"

"Well, a good chunk of it lately comes from seaweed sheets for sushi," Arden told her.

"Seriously? That creates enough cash for planes and yachts?"

"To be fair, mermaids don't really need or use money much," Iris explained, accepting a glass of water from the server. "The sea provides everything we need. And if there are things we want, we tend to work on the barter system."

"Which leaves a lot of nori money for wedding planning," Arden declared. "Yes, that will do," he told the server, who turned the wine label toward him. "So, what's going on?"

"Iris might have feelings for her fiancé," Selene said.

"Let me guess, you're trying to talk her out of it? Something about love being a lie tied up with a string of empty promises?"

"Hey, I like that," Selene said, lips curving up.

"Actually, Selene was trying to convince me to give Finn a chance to prove himself."

"Wait, you left off the part about men being dense. Like a thick fog of their own emotional cluelessness."

Arden shot the witch a patient, bemused smile. "There's a saying out there about pots and kettles," he said. "You should look it up. Now," he said, turning back to Iris. "We both know I'm so invested in your relationship that I'm seconds away from starting a fan club in the underworld. That said, while love can be work, it shouldn't be hard."

"Whoa, wait. You're going to be the skeptic?" Selene asked.

"Not a skeptic. A good friend. I want you to be madly in love, darling. But I don't want you to feel like your love demands a sacrifice from you. It shouldn't. Because if you give up too much, all that it will breed down the line is resentment for everything you've lost.

"Love should add to your life, not detract. If you're this conflicted, I'm worried you have either already made the decision in your head or you need to explore things more before making any kind of choice for your future."

"Look at you. Being all rational," Selene said, watching the demon's profile as if she didn't recognize him.

"It seems like you've both given me the same advice. I need more time."

"To be fair, most of the time you've had with Finn has been spent trying to get him to break your engagement, not actually getting to know him," Selene said.

"Gee, I wonder who helped her with that?" Arden said.

"I was being a good friend too," Selene said. "At the

time, that was what she wanted from me. Now, she wants something different. And I'm happy to give that too."

"Oh, admit it. You're just dying to slip into a bridesmaid dress and cry as these two declare their love for each other."

"Oh, goddess. You're not going to make me wear something hideous, are you?"

She'd directed the question at Iris, but Arden was the one to answer. "Don't insult me. Nothing hideous has ever made its way into my weddings. Well, there was that intestine necklace once, but we try not to judge other cultures' customs. Even if they drip and smell mildly like rot." Arden suppressed a shudder at the memory.

"And on that note," Selene said with a wrinkled nose, "here comes the food."

They spent the rest of the meal discussing the food and Gerty the ghost, and giving Iris a pep talk about both her relationship and the gala she was dreading.

By the time she made it back to the penthouse, she was feeling calmer, more reasonable, and less emotional about the whole situation.

Even if it did make her heart ache to have to walk through the apartment alone, eat dinner alone, and get ready for bed alone.

She knew it was just her nature, that emotions and connection were something she craved even more strongly than most when she cared for someone. So she wasn't exactly surprised when her eyes flooded with tears or how fiercely she felt the empty space beside her as she started to drift off to sleep.

"I'm sorry I couldn't find time today," Finn's voice murmured in her ear.

His body was curled up behind her, his arm draped across her waist, his legs cocked up behind hers.

"I know you're busy," she said, still trying to untangle herself from the dream world, where she'd been sunning on a beach with Finn, miles away from everyone else, from all his responsibilities. It was just them, the sun, and the sea.

"Still," he said, leaning down to press a kiss to her bare shoulder. "If you want one-on-one time, I will find it."

"I do," she admitted. "I want to see if there's something here."

"There's something here," he said, pulling her closer.

She felt the hard line of him pressed against her ass. "I meant something more than sex."

Finn scooted back and pulled her onto her back. Leaning over her, he watched as his hand slid up to her jaw.

"I meant more than sex too. Though I'm not going to pretend I'm not really enjoying that."

She wouldn't deny it either.

And until he could carve out more time for her, she would be happy to take these little stolen moments of intimacy when they were available.

Her hands slid down his back, sinking into his ass and pulling until he moved over her, sliding between her parted legs.

"Me too," she agreed before pulling his lips down to hers.

It was all need and hunger then.

Lips and tongues and teeth.

Hands grazing, fingers clawing, bodies rocking.

Finn rolled onto his back, taking Iris with him, and he watched as she removed her filmy nightgown while he reached for protection.

But before he could slide it on, Iris was leaning down, pressing a kiss to his throat.

Her tongue traced the pulse point, loving how his heart was pounding for her, how his hands were digging into her skin as she kissed down his chest, his stomach, lower.

An almost pained groan escaped him when she took him in her mouth, sucking down to the base at a pace so slow that his hips were rocking up into her mouth, begging for more.

Taking her cue from him, Iris moved faster, sucking him as his muscles tensed, as his hand curled in her hair, making a pain-pleasure combination sear across her scalp.

And just when she thought he might lose control, he was fisting her hair, pulling until the pinch made him slide from between her lips.

"Get up here," Finn said, his voice rough and commanding.

By the time she'd shimmied out of her panties, he was finished protecting them. His hand went to her hip, pulling until she lowered down onto his lap, trembling at the hard demand of him against her.

Iris rocked against him until she couldn't take the pressure, the clawing need deep within, for another minute.

Shifting up, she positioned herself and lowered down.

She felt him press into her, and a low growl rumbled through Finn as she took him in, inch by inch.

By the time she'd taken him to the base, she was already shaking, the pressure coiled so tightly, it felt like a warning.

A whimper escaped her as Finn's impatient hips rocked up into her, pressing deeper still.

"Show me how you like it," Finn demanded. His fingers dug into her hips like it was taking every ounce of restraint not to take control, not to set the pace.

A little high on her power, Iris started to ride him slowly, soft little rocks of her hips that became faster circles until the need became too strong, until her self-control shattered.

Then she was riding him hard and fast, panting and moaning as she got closer and closer to that edge.

Heat spiraled, coiling tighter and tighter until the pressure alone felt sure to snap her.

"That's it," Finn groaned. "Let go for me."

The tension snapped and her body surged, her head falling back on a moan as the orgasm sizzled through her system.

Finn rocked up into her, dragging it out, making it last, even as she fell forward into him, whimpering against his chest.

His arms anchored across her hips, holding her close as he rocked even deeper, his whole body tensing as he came.

He pulled her onto his chest afterward, both of them spent, bodies lax, too exhausted even to speak.

And if Iris tried hard enough, she could almost make herself believe it was enough.

But morning always came, and the fantasy always faded.

Iris

"But why does it matter if I wear heels, if the dress covers my feet?"

It was a reasonable question.

But none of the men currently looking at her would hear of her wearing flats.

"It's the dress code, darling," Arden told her. He moved forward, carefully placing the subtle coral crown on her head.

She'd tried to insist that a crown would be too much. But both Arden and Henry believed that it was never 'too much' when you were literally royalty.

Finn had held up his hands, claiming he didn't want to be a part of that argument.

"Perfect," Arden declared as he stepped back. "You look like a princess."

"I am a princess."

"Exactly. But now, people will believe it," he said, eyes sparkling.

"Rude."

"But true."

"Fine. That's fair. Any more tips for me?"

"Just be your charming self. I wish I could be there to see it. Alas, I would need an extra comma in my net worth to be invited."

"You're going to Selene's, right?"

"Yep. Gotta ask Gerty what she's angry about now."

"You'll keep me posted? I need something to look forward to."

"Oh, stop. You're going to have fun. Drinking, dancing, good wine, itty-bitty servings of food. Finn, you know where the closest hot pretzel cart is to the venue, right?"

"Enough chit-chat. You're already ten minutes late, and you must drive across town," Henry said, waving toward the door.

"Someone needs to get laid," Arden said, making Iris snort.

"I heard that."

"I meant you to." The demon turned to the campaign manager, straightening his already straight tie. "You're wound so tight. You need to pop," he said, patting Henry's chest.

"The saying is that you're *going* to pop," Henry, a little pink, clarified.

"I believe it means the same thing," Arden said, leaning in close. Then, quickly shifting from sinfully flirtatious to laid-back and easy, he clapped. "Okay. Go be a princess at the ball. I will go talk to a ghost who smells like mothballs and stale cigarettes."

With one last smile, he was gone.

Henry, recovered, ushered them into the elevator, then the waiting town car.

"You're going to do great," Finn assured her, his hand reaching for hers, giving it a squeeze. "We will be together all night, so if you're confused by anything, just give my hand a squeeze."

She didn't imagine there would be much to be confused by.

Until, of course, they moved into the sprawling museum. Everything was dipped in ambiance: candles, chandeliers, fairy lights. It made the space almost cinematic as they moved through the displays of ancient artifacts, following a small crowd toward a wider, open space dominated by a giant Tyrannosaurus rex skeleton.

Music thrummed, low and breezy, from the band near the front of the room. Standing before them, a fae in a brilliant red sari crooned over the music.

"This is the cocktail hour," Finn said, his lips near her ear as he snagged two champagne flutes off a passing tray. He passed one glass to her. "We will walk around, look at the displays, speak to others, possibly bid on items at the silent auction." He waved over toward a long row of tables draped in champagne-colored tablecloths with various items or signs and notepads set in front of them.

"And after that?"

"Everyone will move into the dining hall. We will find our table, eat, and talk with our tablemates. There will be an emcee, guest speakers. And—"

"Mr. Westrock," a voice called.

"Here we go," Finn said. He sipped his champagne, then switched on his PR smile before turning to greet the tall man with ghost-pale skin.

Iris felt a familiar little shiver, could sense the lethal kind of charm leaching from the man.

A vampire.

She was sure of it.

Any hope that the conversation might be interesting or engaging, though, quickly fell away as the men started to talk about policy.

She tried to keep track, really, she did. But it wasn't long before her mind was wandering and her gaze was sweeping the room, taking in the atmosphere and the various humans and paranormals gathered.

Sensing her slipping away, Finn's arm slid around her lower back, curling her closer, anchoring her, silently reminding her that she had to play her part.

One interaction turned to five, then fifteen.

Her champagne flute was empty, and she felt a pleasant thrumming inside her, a lightness she knew came from the alcohol, since she was still having trouble staying present and engaging with the strangers whom Finn seemed to know personally.

"Can we look at the auction items?" Iris asked when a group of humans moved away.

"Sure, we—"

"Finn!" a booming voice called.

Turning, Iris saw nothing but torso until she angled her head all the way up to catch sight of a man with huge, angled horns and a thick gold bull ring in his nose.

He had to be a minotaur.

"Patton," Finn said with a smile, offering his hand.

"Iris," Patton greeted her, ducking his head. "Do you mind if I steal your fiancé for a moment?"

"Of course," she said with her fake smile. Unease at

walking around without an escort spread through her, but she tried to tamp it down.

"I'll meet you over by the tables in a minute," Finn said, pressing a quick kiss to her temple before moving away.

The little belly flip-flop seemed to chase away her discomfort as she dropped her empty glass on a tray, then wandered over toward the auction, being careful to mind her steps without Finn there to balance her if she tripped in her heels.

She moved down the line, looking at offerings of private celebrity chefs, luxury cruises, vacations at the beach, and tickets to sold-out concerts and shows.

Mixed in with those average listings, though, were other—more exciting—ones: a future reading from a high priestess, a 'getting in touch with your inner beast' getaway with a wolf alpha, an aging cask of fae wine, artisanal chocolate infused with true lust magic, and even a haunted mirror (guaranteed friendly).

Caught up in the excitement of it all, Iris leaned down to sign her name for the mirror, loving the idea of a device that might whisper advice and compliments—and, occasionally, cryptic warnings.

And just for fun, she quickly bid on the lusty chocolates.

When she'd checked over all the offerings twice and Finn still hadn't joined her, she'd decided to go and find him. But when she'd scanned the crowd, he was nowhere to be seen.

She spotted Patton and his minotaur friends, but Finn was no longer with them.

She moved around the room, trying not to look like she was searching for someone, but getting a little more uneasy with each passing moment.

Without Finn's hand steadying her, every click of her heels echoed loudly. She couldn't seem to walk or breathe quite right without him at her side.

Her stomach was feeling all sloshy by the time she moved out of the dinosaur room.

The museum was labyrinthine, and everywhere she went, she saw people.

But not Finn.

She was about to give up and try to find her way back to the main gathering area, when she heard the rumble of his laughter.

A shiver worked its way up her spine at the sound, and her lips curved up as she made her way around a corner to find him.

In a little alcove.

With that gargoyle woman.

Her hand was on his chest.

Her body arched too close.

Her laughter just a little too husky.

Iris's stomach bottomed out.

How long had she been standing there, laughing like that? Had he followed her? Or had she led him?

She stood there stunned for a second. But when Finn's gaze found hers, her feet unstuck from the ground.

She turned and rushed away, gathering up her skirt so it didn't slow her down.

She was pretty sure she made her way into a restricted area within a few moments, judging by the lack of mood lighting and people gathered around.

She didn't care.

She just needed to get somewhere private before the stupid tears stinging her eyes overflowed.

Just when she was losing hope, she saw a bathroom sign hanging up ahead.

She beelined for it, pushing the door open. Her heels clicked on the pristine tile floor as she made her way over to the sink, ready to try to put some cool water on her face—to hell with her makeup.

Before the first tear could spill over, though, the door flew open.

And there was Finn.

"Iris, what—"

He trailed off when he caught sight of her face.

Reaching back, he locked the door.

"Why bother following me?" she asked, blinking back the tears. She was more comfortable with the sizzle of anger burning in her stomach. "Go back and let Marsha keep undressing you with her eyes."

"Iris . . ."

"Don't act like I'm being silly. You went with her to some quiet alcove where no one would see you."

"I followed her because she said she was looking for another member of the council. Iris, come on. You don't think—"

"I do. You were all laughing and smiling and letting her put her hands—"

Something moved across Finn's face then. She wasn't sure what to call it, but it made her belly go wobbly. This time, in a good way.

Before she could analyze it, he was moving toward her. He made it there in two strides, grabbing her and turning her away from him, both of them watching themselves in the mirror.

"What are you doing?" She was breathless and throbbing at the fierce, feral look in his eyes.

"Showing you that there is only one woman in this building I'm interested in putting my hands on."

"Finn..."

She barely had time to even think of what to say after that; Finn was lowering himself to his knees and sliding under her long skirt.

Desire pinged across every nerve ending as he yanked her panties to the side.

Her breath caught, then ended on a strangled moan as his mouth closed around her throbbing clit, sucking on it until her legs were shaking hard enough to make her grab the edge of the counter.

Her hips rocked restlessly, riding his mouth as his tongue moved across her.

It wasn't long before she was breathless, spiraling into an orgasm that had a long, low moan escaping her, the sound echoing back to her in the small, tiled room.

Finn slipped out from under her skirt, moving up behind her.

One arm went around her lower stomach, the other slid between her thighs, teasing her desire from embers to flames once again.

"There is no other woman." His breath was warm in her ear, the fierceness in his voice making her heart squeeze. "You are the only one I see." His thumb moved over her clit. "The only one I want." Two fingers slid inside her. "Yours is the only body I want to touch." His fingers began to thrust, dragging a moan from her. "The only voice I want to hear when my fingers are in you, like this." His teeth nipped her earlobe. "And when I'm buried deep inside you, feeling you writhe and whimper and clench around me..."

His dirty mouth had her pushed to the edge, then sent her soaring through another orgasm.

Finn's hands moved, grabbing her, pushing her forward until her forearms were leaned on the counter—the coolness against her hot skin making her shiver.

He hiked up her skirt and pulled down her panties.

Then he freed himself, fisting his length as he pinned her gaze in the mirror.

"See what you do to me?" he rasped. Iris pressed her thighs together to ease the ache growing again. "Only you," he said, stepping closer to rub his hardness against her heat, "do this to me."

He rocked against her as he found and opened a condom.

He quickly slid it on, then rocked against her again.

"And you're the only one I want to feel," he said, surging deep inside her, "like this."

Her moan and his groan mingled, filling the room.

"Look at me," he demanded, watching her face in the mirror. "This is all for you," he told her, rocking his hips. "Only you." He rocked again. "Got that?"

"Yes," she whimpered, her body moving with him as he found the rhythm they both needed.

"And this," Finn went on, pressing deep, "is all for me." A needy little whimper escaped her. "Say it."

"It's all for you."

Nothing had ever been truer than that right then.

She was his.

All his.

There was no more talking then. Just movement. Just pleasure. Just ragged breaths and pounding hearts.

Then, with muffled cries, they came together.

He reached for her afterward, pulling her against his chest.

"I am not, and never have been, interested in Marsha. And any potential interest on her end doesn't change the fact that I'm not interested, okay?"

"Okay," she agreed, feeling that strange flushing sensation move through her insides again. "I don't like how she acts around you."

"I get that," he agreed, turning to tuck himself away. "Next time," he said, "if there is a next time, stake your claim."

"My claim?" she asked.

Finn leaned down, pulling her panties back into place, then dropping her skirt.

"If you think someone is being inappropriate, come over."

"I was there the last time," she said, dredging up the unresolved past. "You dismissed me. After barely introducing me."

Finn reached for her, turning her, then reaching for her chin, tipping her head up.

"You're right. I didn't see it that way at the time, but you're right. I'll do better." He leaned in, pressing a soft kiss to the outside of her lips. "I'm not used to having anyone with me," he went on, kissing the other corner of her mouth. "But I will do better."

With one final quick kiss to her lips, he straightened her dress and wiped a small smudge of her lipstick while she adjusted his shirt and tie.

Then they walked out of the bathroom, hand in hand, and joined the crowd as they moved toward the dining room.

True to his word, he kept her close all evening. His hand held hers, wrapped around her, or squeezed her knee under the table.

He introduced her to everyone with her full title and her connection to him.

This is Princess Iris Marivelle, my fiancée.

Each time he said it, she felt that warm gush move through her.

It was a lovely evening. Even if she had been overwhelmed by the formal table setting that included no fewer than five forks, five drink glasses, four knives, and three spoons.

But Finn sensed her confusion and squeezed her leg under the table before very slowly reaching for the correct utensil with each course of the meal.

As Finn explained, there had been a very charming panther shifter with sleek black hair and lively yellow eyes who served as the evening's emcee. A few speakers got up to talk about the cause: the Paranormal Preservation Fund, which was dedicated to preserving historical landmarks tied to old magic, fae architecture, vampire crypts, and so on.

The only real surprise of the night was when the emcee moved off stage to allow someone else to introduce the surprise celebrity guest.

And *Monty* walked out on the stage, decked out in a custom-made little suit, complete with a snappy bow tie.

"He always said he was destined for greatness," Iris murmured as he charmed the crowd with a few jokes before introducing a siren who was one of the most sought-after and highly paid movie stars in the world.

She had a story about losing some of her own family

history due to the lack of preservation efforts for most paranormal communities.

Before she felt like she could soak up everything, the event was over.

Finn was stopped another eight or ten times on their way back to their car.

But finally, they were sitting in the back of the car, her heels on the ground, her legs up on Finn's lap, and his hands massaging her aching soles.

Her cheeks ached from smiling; her feet throbbed from standing. But her heart? That was somehow lighter.

"You were wonderful tonight," he told her. The praise moved through her like velvet, soft and indulgent.

"I had fun," she admitted.

"You sound surprised."

"I guess I am. I think I was determined to hate all these events on principle. But it was fun. Even if you wouldn't dance."

"We can't have the public learning I have two left feet," he said, wincing.

"We can work on that."

"You know how to dance?"

"Not really. But we can figure it out together. But first, we have a lot to do around the apartment."

"Like what?"

"Like get rid of all those disgusting creepy-crawlers lining the hallway."

"Wait . . . what? You collected those."

"To try to gross you out so you would send me away," Iris admitted, smiling at the shock on his face.

"And the teeth?"

"Another attempt to be unappealing. The vintage medical equipment too."

"For the record, you could never be unappealing. But also, I'm kind of relieved. And impressed. I had resigned myself to a future of dead bugs and old teeth because you seemed so passionate about them."

"Nope. Those ideas were all Selene. She was working with me on my plans to sabotage this engagement."

Finn was silent for a moment, his eyes far away. "I didn't realize that you weren't a willing participant from the beginning. I'd like to believe I would have handled this whole situation differently had I known how much you didn't want to be here."

"I guess I'm kind of glad you didn't know. Because if you'd broken the engagement right at the beginning, I might never have learned how much I really love about the surface."

"Like hot pretzels?"

"And all the books. Taco Tuesdays. TV shows. Memory foam beds."

"And me?" Finn asked, eyes warm.

"I was getting to you. You fall somewhere below fuzzy socks but above next-day delivery."

"An honored position," he teased as they pulled up outside the apartment building. "Here, you hold your shoes. I'll carry you up."

Before she could object, he was sweeping her into his arms. Her belly flipped, dragging a laugh out of her as he spun her in a circle.

Neither had any idea someone had caught the moment on their phones.

But they were all over social media within an hour, and the news cycle by the following morning.

The Tides of Love: Political Golden Boy Meets Actual Feelings—Finally!

They'd been too busy wrapped up in each other to notice. But somewhere in the city, Henry was over the moon.

Finn

The night of the charity gala seemed to genuinely be a turning point for the two of them.

So many of their truths were out on the table. Silly, sweet, or heartbreaking, they were learning to trust each other with their truths. Even if Finn was perhaps keeping the most important truth to himself still. That he not only had feelings for her but was pretty sure he was falling. Hard.

They would get there, he promised himself.

Unfortunately, though, the campaign trail was only heating up all the more. This meant Finn was spending all daylight hours in meetings, doing interviews, or even wearing holes in his shoes going door to door.

It meant Iris was home alone all day. Or, more likely, off wedding planning with Arden, exploring the city with Selene, going to yoga, or taking long walks through Central Park with Willow. And even, on occasion, going with Monty to celebrity-watch.

He knew he had to keep his eye on the finish line, but he couldn't help but be jealous of the many hours her friends got to spend with her. While all he could do was fantasize about a time when he could do more than slide into bed with her at night and get lost in each other's bodies for an hour or two before exhaustion claimed him.

It wasn't how anyone dreamed an engagement would go. It was supposed to be the two of them picking out food, table linens, and flower arrangements. They should have been spending their days enjoying summer in the city or taking off on little weekend trips.

But when Finn had agreed to the engagement, he didn't think it would be real. So there was no need to micromanage the arrangements or find time to spend with his fiancée.

"Finn, focus," Henry interrupted his thoughts.

"We've been over the proposal fifty times this morning."

"I get it. You're riding high on being the gossip rags' darling couple. But that's not going to work on everyone. We need to keep sharp and continue doing outreach to people who aren't falling for the 'Mermaid and the Mayor' headlines."

"Henry, when's the last time you got laid?" he asked.

Henry, so composed, so utterly unflappable, jerked back. His mouth opened and closed like a beached fish.

"What?"

"However long it's been, I think it's long enough."

"Being ambitious has nothing to do with my sex life."

"Go get laid and come back to me. It absolutely has something to do with it. There's more to life than campaign funding and political talking points."

Henry watched him for a moment before shaking his

head. "You went and fell for her, didn't you?" He sighed, slapping his file closed. "That is a monumentally stupid thing to do this close to the election."

He'd more than fallen. He'd sunk under, fully submerged. And he never wanted to surface.

"Just this once, Hen, I don't care. I like Iris. She likes me. I don't give a damn if that isn't ideal for the optics."

Henry sat with that for a second. "I'm not going to lie. Headlines have been a lot more favorable toward you since you and Iris went official. It's made you more relatable and relaxed. There are even some people making up wild stories about you two online."

"Like what?" Finn asked, immediately tense, wanting to make sure no one said anything nasty about Iris that might get back to her.

"Like someone claimed they saw the two of you coming out of a bathroom at the charity gala."

"Oh, that."

"You didn't. Tell me you didn't have sex during a campaign event."

"It's not like Iris is my subordinate. It's not inappropriate to be sleeping with her."

"In your bed, sure. The shower. On the couch, over the kitchen counter, even smashed up against the floor-to-ceiling windows. But not in public. You could nab yourself a public indecency charge."

"It won't happen again." Probably. Unless the right opportunity presented itself.

Henry sighed. "You're a good liar, Finn. But don't forget who taught you how."

"I will attempt to only be with Iris in private places until the election."

"It's not a big ask."

"Oh, by the way, I rescheduled the meeting on Wednesday."

"What? Why? You can't do things like that without consulting me. What if you piss off—"

"We have had long-time support from the hybrid community. They aren't going to be mad that their meeting is pushed back a day."

"Why do you need to push it back?"

"Because I am going to make good on a promise I made."

"A promise to Iris?"

"Yes."

A muscle ticked in Henry's jaw, but he was smart enough to keep his opinions to himself. "What kind of promise?"

"That I was going to make time for us. So all day Wednesday, I'm not going to be reachable. Not even if the entire campaign blows up."

"I see. What are you planning to do?"

"I rented a boat. I'm taking Iris out on the ocean. Just the two of us. No one else for miles."

He'd already checked the projected currents, pored over maps, taken an online course to brush up on boat safety, and ordered food to bring with them.

"All right. I will fence all your calls, so the two of you have a nice day to yourselves without any interruptions. Where are you going to be? Just so I know in case something happens to you."

"Iris is a mermaid. I'm pretty sure if something happened, she could save me."

"Even so. I need to know where you are."

"Fine," he said, producing a map to show him his

projected course, with them ending up somewhere near Iris's favorite sandbar.

He'd been too excited about the outing to pay much attention to his campaign manager.

And he wouldn't know what was coming until it was too late.

To protect Iris.

To protect the delicate bond growing between them.

Iris

"What's this?" Iris asked.

She'd opened the door to find Arden standing there, practically bouncing on his feet, a gift bag held up high near his chest.

"Orders from your fiancé."

"Orders? For what? I thought we didn't have any campaign stuff to do today."

She had her heart set on going to a neat little fae pop-up market where they were selling all sorts of neat trinkets and jewelry.

"No campaign stuff," Arden assured her, moving into the penthouse. "But plans regardless. Open. The anticipation is killing me."

"Is it shiny?" she asked, reaching inside the bag.

"Unfortunately, no. But I promise you'll like it better than a piece of jewelry."

She was dubious about that.

"More clothes?" she asked when her hand met fabric. "How many pieces of clothing does one woman need?"

"All of them, preferably," Arden said, making her snort.

"What in the tides..."

Iris drew out a filmy, long white piece of linen.

"Oh, darling," Arden sighed. He shook his head and took the fabric from her to lift it right side up to reveal...

"Is that a bathing suit cover-up?"

There wasn't much to it.

It was nearly see-through, with a large slit all the way up the front and one pearly clasp right between the breasts.

"Indeed."

"Is there a bathing suit?"

"There's... these." Arden pulled out a pair of barely there white panties.

"That's it?"

"Well, there's also these." Arden pulled out two green-tinted seashell... stickers?

"What are those?"

"Boob stickers."

"Boob stickers? I, uh, didn't realize that's an area that requires accessorizing."

"They're more for modesty. Kind of like your seashell bra. These are specially made for mermaids. They're very water-resistant. Plus, they match your tail."

"Oh, all right. So... is there some sort of beach-themed event going on?"

"Actually, that delicious man of yours is taking you on a date."

"A date? Really?" She was a little embarrassed at how excited she was at the prospect.

"He planned it all himself. And it is good." Arden pressed

a hand to his heart, swooning a bit. "But I'm not ruining the surprise."

"Please don't. So, when do I need to be ready?"

Arden checked his watch—with its little hands tipped in pink hearts. "In about half an hour."

"Wait, really?"

"Finn told Henry he needed the whole day off to woo his lovely bride-to-be. Though, I must say, you seem thoroughly wooed already. Is that a post-coital glow you have going on?"

She doubted it. But the second he said it, her flush betrayed her.

"Was it as good as I imagine it is?"

"Better."

Arden fanned himself. "Better? You're lucky I'm not the jealous type. Except that I am. Viciously so." He paused, squinting at her. "Did you cause the tide to rise with your pleasure? I *felt* something shift. I assumed it was indigestion. But now—"

"You're being—"

"Did he whisper sweet nothings? Or, better yet, *filthy somethings*?"

She opened her mouth.

"Wait, don't tell me. There was intense eye contact and handholding while the universe rearranged itself around your shared emotional climax."

Iris let out a little laugh. "Let's not get carried away."

"Carried away? Darling, I have been waiting for this moment since you met. I am half-tempted to book a skywriting witch to spell out 'Congrats on the orgasms.'"

"Please don't."

"Don't deny me this. I love love. Passion is my passion. Look at you," he said, sucking in a dramatic breath and sighing it out. "Positively phosphorescent. I bet a pod of dolphins applauded at the end."

"You're ridiculous."

"Excuse me. I am *invested*. There's a difference." His gaze softened. "Don't try to act like this isn't the best thing that has happened to this whole situation. You're glowing, the groom is allegedly competent in bed, and I get the satisfaction of knowing I was right."

"I think Selene might disagree about it being the best turn of events."

"Oh, please. Selene is a simp for when the enemies become lovers. She keeps a stash of annotated paperbacks inside a storage closet labeled '*Plague Fungus Studies*.'"

"How do you know that?"

"Gerty the ghost may or may not have let it slip. With a heavy amount of judgment for the numerous explicit scenes where things go inside other things and everyone involved is having a wild time."

Iris snorted. "Sounds like Gerty needs a hobby."

"She does. She is silently judging us." Arden flicked imaginary lint off his sleeve. "Anyway, Selene isn't a lovehater. She's scared. That real-life heroes don't exist. That they won't get to know her coffee order or remember her birthday. That they can't make her clutch the sheets and damn near crack their skull with her thighs as they go down on her. And, perhaps most of all, she's terrified that happily-ever-afters in real life aren't possible. Someday, someone will show her that her romance novels are inspired by real life, not pure fiction."

Iris's head tipped to the side, watching him closely for a moment. "You've really given Selene a lot of thought."

Arden stiffened.

"Excuse me, sweet sea creature, I am merely an astute observer of character. And Selene has that 'secretly soft, hex-you-but-don't-tuck-you-in' energy that demands to be noticed."

"I don't know. I think I sense a spark."

"No spark. I mean, in a purely theoretical, 'if we were stuck in a cursed tower with only one bed' way, who knows. But only in theory."

"Uh-huh."

Arden shook his head. "You get laid, and now you're out here trying to hook everyone else up. Anyway," he sniffed. "Back to you. Have you broken any furniture with your carnal activities yet?"

Iris smiled and laughed her way through his constant—and increasingly absurd—sex questions through the bathroom door as she stripped, put on the nipple stickers, and then the cover-up, before stepping out.

"Be still, my heart," Arden said. His hand went to where his heart should have been. "Where is that bird of yours? He would have a lot to say about you looking paparazzi-ready. But for you and your lady business, let's hope your man has arranged a very private venue so the two of you can commune carnally without violating public decency or accidentally awakening a dormant sea god. Ah," he said when there was a knock on the door. "I believe that is your ride."

Sure enough, there was a driver on the other side of the door, so the two of them followed him down to the street, where the driver waited beside a black car.

"I'm so happy for you and not at all jealous."

"You should go and see Selene," Iris said. "See if she wants to hang out. And maybe make some . . . spicy magic."

"Enough, you," Arden said, poking her in the nose. "Have a shamefully sexy time."

With that, Iris was tucked in the back of the car and driven out of the city. Her curiosity grew as they drove down the shore until they reached the bay marina.

"Are you sure this is right?" she asked, leaning between the front seats.

"Yes, ma'am," the driver said. "I'm supposed to tell you to walk down to the end."

"It was *Finn Westrock* who hired you, correct?"

"Yes, our future mayor, Mr. Westrock himself."

Huh.

Okay, well, it made no sense. But she could practically hear the ocean calling to her.

"Thanks," she said.

Stepping out onto the dock, Iris paused, lifting her head to the sky, feeling the sun beat down on her as she sucked in a greedy breath, smelling the salt water and brine.

She could feel the ocean humming in her veins, just begging her to dip in a toe, to shuck off her cover and dive in.

She resisted the urge to jump in and continued down the dock toward the end, where Finn was standing in a pair of white swim trunks and a blue-and-white-striped top, left open in the front.

The wind kicked up, making his hair flutter and his shirt whip backward, exposing his chest and stomach.

Iris's footstep stuttered as her belly flipped, her desire seemingly always simmering just below the surface.

"You look beautiful," Finn said as she approached.

As soon as she was within reach, his arm slid around her, pulling her flush to his chest, and then he ducked his head to claim her mouth with a long, deep kiss.

"What are we doing here?" Iris asked. Need was humming through her, but there was no way for them to give in to those desires right there.

"We are taking a boat out on the water." Finn gestured toward the side where a new-looking cruiser sat, just waiting for someone to board.

"A boat? *You* want to go out on a boat?" Did *she* even want to go on a boat? Sure, she'd seen thousands of them cutting through the surface of her home before. She'd never considered if she would want to be the passenger on one.

"I want to take *you* out on a boat," he said. He moved away to step onto the boat, then held out a hand for her.

She tamped down her concerns about his safety. She could certainly save him if he fell overboard. Then she placed her hand in his and let him help her aboard.

He led her from the swim platform and into the galley, which featured a table and wrap-around cushioned seats. They moved through to the cockpit.

"Why don't you catch some sun?" Finn suggested. He gestured out to the bow sun pad. "I'll untie the deck lines so we can head out."

Confused yet curious, she did as instructed, moving out onto the bow to lower onto the cushioned sun pad.

She turned to watch as Finn made quick, effortless work of undoing the deck lines, then moved into the cockpit and took off from the dock.

It struck her that there were clearly many things she still didn't know about her fiancé. She was going to enjoy figuring it all out.

The ride was smooth, and she got comfortable on the pad. Acutely aware that Finn had to look past her to see where they were going, she sat up to slowly remove her cover-up, then lowered back down, bare—save for the stickers and the barely there material of her panties.

Even over the roar of the engine, she could have sworn she heard Finn groan.

The marina and the beach became specks in the distance when Finn cut the engine and dropped the anchor with a small splash.

The waves gently rocked the boat as Finn moved out from the cockpit to stand in front of her. He lowered down to his knees at her feet, making anticipation sizzle across her nerve endings.

His hands slid up her calves, then thighs, before snagging the waistband of her panties and drawing them slowly down her legs.

Leaning down, he kissed just inside her knee.

"Go swim," he said.

But his eyes were as heated as the desire blossoming through her system.

"That's . . . not what I thought you were going to say," she said, her voice thick with her growing need.

"No?" Finn's eyes were molten.

Her head shook, and she took a deep breath just to watch his gaze slide to her chest.

Then, slowly, she let her legs drift open, a silent invitation, an aching confession.

This time, she definitely heard his groan as his gaze slid down.

Then he was on his stomach, his face between her thighs, his tongue tracing up her core.

Iris's back arched as her legs slid over Finn's shoulders, her hips rocking against his tongue as he teased around her clit.

Her soft whimpers grew to desperate moans as Finn effortlessly teased her upward. Each slow circle unraveled her a little bit more, until the orgasm pulsed out of her in waves, sharp and sweet, leaving her shaking.

Finn's head shifted, kissing down her thigh, before he moved back to his knees, his fingers drifting lazily up and down her legs.

"Better?" he asked, his eyes still heated.

Iris folded up, her hand sliding down his chest. But his hand caught her wrist, pulling it up and pressing a kiss to her palm.

"There will be time for more later." His fingers slid through hers, pulling her to her feet, then leading her through the cockpit, galley, and onto the swim deck. "Go on," he urged, waving toward the water.

Did she want to climb onto his lap and feel him slip inside her? Yes. But she could practically feel the ocean reaching for her.

Swim now, mutual satisfaction later.

With that, Iris sucked in a deep breath and jumped into the water.

She didn't surface right away. She felt her tail emerge and wave through the water, swimming in dizzying circles, moving halfway to shore, then all the way back.

Only then did she break the surface, watching Finn standing there, his shirt abandoned, his eyes warm as he watched her.

Then, in one quick, heart-sinking move, he jumped into the water.

Iris dove down, her hands desperately reaching for him, but he was already slipping to the surface, where he broke, beaming at her confused expression.

"You're swimming."

"I am."

"But how? You told me you can't swim."

"And I decided that if I wanted to be with a mermaid—and I did—then I should learn."

"You learned to swim for me?" Her voice was a soft whisper as her eyes went watery.

"I did," he said, making his way to her. "I wanted to be able to enjoy the ocean with you. Though I still have some work to do."

Iris reached for him, wrapping her arms around his back, her tail twining instinctively around him, as if it were saying what her heart was singing.

Hers.

He was all hers.

Finn

Iris swam tirelessly, but Finn's arms grew tired after half an hour. He hauled himself back up onto the boat and watched as his fiancée's head and tail dipped up and down into the water, her movements effortlessly beautiful.

Each time she looked out at the sea instead of toward him, he couldn't help but feel guilty for stealing something so beautiful from the place she belonged. Yet he couldn't imagine a future without her.

Maybe, once things calmed down with the campaign, once the wedding was finalized, they could look into getting a little beach house, someplace close to the ocean for them to escape to, where they could leave the big city behind.

He was sure he could sit on the shore and watch her swim for hours and never get tired of it.

Iris surfaced, then hauled her body out onto the lower swim deck. Her green tail and sun-kissed skin glistened with water droplets.

She stretched, reaching upward to squeeze the water from her hair.

She'd never looked more beautiful.

His need grew as he watched her comb her hair, as her tail slowly disappeared, replaced by her lovely skin.

As if sensing the turn of his thoughts, Iris's head shifted. A knowing smile tugged at her lips.

Then she crawled over toward Finn, slipping between his legs and sliding her hands up his thighs.

He'd been aching for her since she slipped out of her cover-up on the bow.

So when she reached to free him, he was hard and straining.

Her warm breath on his skin had his hips bucking up.

But Iris wanted to tease.

Her hand closed around his length, then she leaned down, closing her lips around the base of him, then running her tongue up toward the head, where she teased around the sensitive skin until his hands were fisted in her hair, until he was rocking restlessly.

Only then did her lips close around him and suck him deep.

Finn groaned as pleasure surged through his system.

Everything about her was a revelation. And he was completely and utterly devout.

She worked him slow at first, then faster as his gasps became groans.

His fingers were crushing the back of her skull as she drove him right to the edge, then took him over.

His vision went white with his release, and Iris moaned at the taste of him, working him through it until he was weak and panting.

Only then did she let him slip from between her lips.

Her head rested on his thigh afterward as he tried to bring some order back to his system.

His hands sifted through her damp hair, not ready to break the spell.

In the end, it was Iris's stomach—starving after hours of swimming—that had him pulling away.

"I brought food," he told her. He got to his feet, tucked himself away, then reached to pull her onto her feet.

"Thank the seas," she said.

He led her into the galley, loving how she didn't bother to try to cover up, happy to be bare just for him.

Finn went into the refrigerator to pull out the charcuterie board he'd prepared while waiting for her to show up at the marina.

He poured a little white wine, then the two of them sat entwined, eating cheese, crackers, fruit, and meat until they were both fulfilled. They discussed little and big things—everything from his swim lessons to their feelings on starting a family.

"Go sun yourself," he suggested, waving toward the sun pad. "I'll join you after I clean up."

Iris was happy to oblige, giving him a show as she slowly moved away, her hips swishing, her round ass just begging to be grabbed with each step.

By the time he joined her, though, there was something tender in her gaze as she looked out at the sea.

"What are you thinking about?"

"Would you be willing to go down there with me?" She gestured out toward the water.

He'd follow her down to hell if that was what would make her happy.

"Down where?"

"To the palace. To see my home. My childhood home," she was quick to amend.

"Is that possible?"

"It's a little complicated. But yes. You'd have to go down with me, of course."

"How would I breathe?"

"It's something that would be easier to show you than explain."

"Then show me."

"Really?" Her tone was hopeful.

"Really."

"Now?"

"Right now."

He offered her his hand and they moved back to the swim platform, then jumped into the water together.

"Are you ready?"

"Absolutely."

Iris lifted her hands, and the water between them shimmered. With a whispered word, too low for Finn to hear, the surface tension stretched, gathered, and folded inward—becoming a delicate orb near her mouth.

Her hand lifted, and her fingers brushed his jaw as she moved closer.

They were close enough to kiss.

Then Iris breathed out. Just once. And the whole world changed.

The shimmering sphere spread from her lips, then cupped his face, held.

With it, he could hear her heartbeat. He could smell her citrus and salt.

The bubble was her breath, her life force, and she was loaning it to him.

"You have to stay close," she told him. Her fingers tightened on his. "Or it will stop working."

Finn, not sure he could speak through the bubble, nodded.

"Ready to try it?" she asked, voice soft.

Then they were dipping underwater.

Finn's first instinct was to hold his breath. Iris pressed her hand to his chest, a silent reminder to breathe.

Stomach tensing, worried about sucking in water, he took a short, quick breath.

And got oxygen.

He tried it again, deeper.

Then again.

Iris smiled at him.

Then, hand tightening on his, she threw her body into a swim, pulling him down with her.

The water grew colder and darker as they swam deeper.

All around them, the ocean came alive.

Finn caught sight of another mermaid's brilliant white tail, the bright red of an octopus swimming past; schools of colorful fish parted around them, welcoming Iris home.

She led him past an endless, colorful coral reef, introducing him to things he'd only read about in books: the tiny, mischievous dragonettes, the singing eels, the stunning, almost fake-looking glimmersharks.

Iris paused their swim to nuzzle a few dolphins who seemed eager to see her, though he had no idea if she could understand their clicks, whistles, and squeaks.

Eventually, she pulled him deeper still, until he could reach out with one finger and brush his hand across the sand at the ocean floor.

Before he knew it, she was leading him through a

whalebone gate, then toward a towering castle with coral spires and glowing towers.

They swam down the halls of the palace, sat on the coral throne, and slipped into her childhood bedroom.

"Iris?" a voice called, making them both turn.

Then there was another mermaid in front of them, looking like a younger version of Iris, but with a slight bit of blue in her blonde hair and a deep navy tail.

"Shelly!"

Iris flew at her sister, dragging him along with her with their joined hands. It had him as a one-armed part of a three-way hug as the sisters bounced up and down and twirled in a circle before finally breaking apart.

"And you must be Finn!" Shelly threw both her arms around him, squeezing him like they were old friends. "I'm so happy to finally meet you."

"You too," he said, testing his underwater voice. It had much more of an echo than his land voice, but he didn't choke on the water or anything.

"Finn took me out on a boat today. And I convinced him to give this a try."

"It didn't take much convincing," Finn said.

"I just got the invitation to your wedding yesterday. Mother and Juna are so excited."

"They're coming to the surface?" The shock and hope in her voice had Finn squeezing her hand tighter.

"Of course they are, silly. Arden said he would be by to measure us this week for gowns."

"Has Mother ever been to the surface?"

"That's the same question I had. She didn't want to answer. But Aunt Molly said that when she was a young mer, she would sneak to the surface all the time, drinking and partying with the surface folks. She was constantly in trouble with her parents about it. It only makes me all the more annoyed that she never wanted me to go up."

The bemused look on Iris's face made Finn believe that the queen must be a very serious woman, and Iris was finding it hard to reconcile the woman she knew with the girl she'd been.

"Anyway, I'm so glad you came. I can't wait to come up for the wedding. Please tell me our gowns won't be hideous."

"Have you met Arden? He doesn't do hideous."

"That's true."

"I have to admit that I've loved every idea he's had, even when I wasn't happy about the arrangement." She squeezed Finn's hand to soften the blow of her words. "Is Mother here? We should probably say hello."

"She's not. She had to go tour that new school."

"And Juna?"

"She and Osiren have taken off on a little holiday."

"Juna. On a holiday?"

"I know. She's really softened since her engagement. You seem happier too."

"Things have been good," Iris agreed. She leaned closer to Finn. "You should come visit."

"I have a lot of responsibilities here."

"You?"

"I know," Shelly said with a little eye roll. "Things have changed for all of us so quickly. But for the better, I have to believe."

"Princess?" someone called, making Shelly's posture stiffen.

"Sorry. I have a meeting. If you want to stay, I can tell the staff to prepare more for dinner."

"I wish we could, but I don't know if we could figure out how to get back to shore in the dark."

Finn was thankful he didn't have to be the one to admit that.

"Well, it was nice seeing you," Shelly said. She pulled her sister in for another long hug. Then wrapped an arm around Finn. "And to meet you."

Once Shelly was off on official business, Iris led Finn around the rest of the palace, before she declared that Finn's lips were starting to turn blue.

"Humans aren't meant to stay down here so long," she explained as they moved past the spires, the gates, the coral reefs, the shipwrecks, and past all the beautiful fish, turtles, whales, and stingrays.

When they surfaced, the bubble that had been providing him breath burst.

"What is it?" Iris asked from the swim platform. He hadn't realized he'd been staring. But he also wasn't surprised.

She reached for a towel, quickly drying her tail, and he watched as her skin split and transformed into her long, shapely legs.

Finn hauled himself up, dropping down, and looking out at the water.

"How can I ask you to give all of that up?"

She lifted her hand, pressing her palm to his cheek. "You're not asking. I'm choosing."

"But—"

"And I'm not giving anything up." Her hand slid to the back of his neck. "I can have both. You wouldn't keep me from the sea."

"No. I want to buy us a house on the beach, so we can head over anytime we want to escape."

"Your backstroke could use some work," she agreed, leaning in to press her forehead to his.

Then she tilted her head, sealing her lips to his.

The kiss was long and deep.

Like she was staking her claim.

And, gods, he was happy to be hers.

Iris

Neither seemed in a hurry to get back to land. Or move at all. They just stayed curled together, enjoying the last few moments of solitude, far away from the demands back on land.

"This was the best day," Iris murmured into Finn's neck.

"It really was," he agreed. His lips pressed gently to her hair.

"How much longer do we have?"

"Two hours before we really need to get back to shore."

She never questioned why he had such an exact time. She was just glad that there was no rush to leave.

They spent some time tangled together, a few moments finishing what was left of the charcuterie board. Then Finn sat and watched her swim for a few more precious moments.

She soaked up every moment of it, knowing it would likely be a while until she could visit again, with the deadlines of the election and the wedding looming large.

When she finally made it back on board, Finn pulled the anchor and started to drive.

Iris let herself dry completely right there on the sun pad.

"Iris," he called, making her turn to look over her shoulder at him. "You're going to want to cover up soon," he said, holding out her panties and cover-up toward her.

She reached for them but looked off toward the shore—still quite far away.

But she slipped back into her clothes before joining Finn in the cockpit.

He moved her between him and the wheel, wrapping his arms around her while she pretended to steer.

It was lovely.

Perfect.

Iris stood, transfixed, as Finn backed the stern into the marina, but both of them let out a little chuckle when he bumped the dock.

"Okay, now you take over with the wheel."

"Me?" she squeaked.

"You just need to hold it steady so I can tie us down."

That was a simple enough task. And she got to watch Finn loop the line around the dock cleat with practiced ease. Then he glanced back at her at the helm and shot her a grin.

Iris was still on cloud nine as they walked down the dock with the sun setting romantically behind them.

His hand went around her lower back.

She leaned her head against his shoulder.

Pretty as a picture, Iris thought, her lips curving up into a satisfied smile.

As if her mind had conjured it, the flash of a camera had her heartbeat stuttering.

The smile fell from her lips as one flash met another and another and another.

"This way, Finn."

"Give us a kiss."

"Iris, a little to your left."

"What is this?" Iris asked, her heart plummeting as she wrenched away from Finn.

It really had been the perfect day.

Too perfect.

His timing was too precise.

He'd taken her on a date to set them up for a photo op.

She wanted to see shock or anger on his face, like she felt on her own.

"Iris . . ." he said, his tone placating.

The words were there, hanging heavy in the air around them.

Think of the optics. Don't make a scene.

Campaign over everything, even her comfort.

She was hardly even *dressed*. Which was fine for a stroll down the dock toward the car. It was a complete other thing to have that image plastered all over gossip blogs and magazine covers.

Her hands folded over her chest, trying to cover up some more, painfully aware of the thin fabric and her nipple stickers.

"How was the queen?" a reporter asked.

Iris wrenched away when Finn tried to hold her tighter, tried to get her to play her part, to accept what felt like a betrayal.

Of course, the day had been perfect.

He'd planned it for the best optics.

Because he knew it was going to make the best gossip.

She stared at him for another second, all of her hurt raw on her face.

Then she turned and strode away.

Please follow me, she silently begged. *Show me I matter more than what the public thinks.*

But when she turned back at the start of the parking lot, he was engaged in a conversation with one of the paparazzi.

Her heart ground to dust as she watched him. Plastic smile. Practiced laugh. Never once glancing in her direction.

She'd let him *in*. Let herself believe. Just this once, she thought it might be real. And now the whole day felt like a carefully edited campaign ad.

Just when she thought it couldn't get any worse, there was a flash nearby. It captured, no doubt, her heartbreak.

She whipped away and broke into a run.

She had no phone, no money, no cards, no way to get back to the city.

Once she was sure she was alone, she dove into the water, swimming as hard and fast as she could, making her way back toward Manhattan, where she pulled herself out of the water.

Her cover-up was drenched, almost completely see-through, as she sat there for a few moments, hand pressed to the aching hole in her chest.

It was the laugh from the walkway nearby that had her fighting back her tears.

The last thing she needed was someone snapping a picture of her in her heartbreak.

So as soon as her tail dried and her legs appeared, she pulled herself off the ground and walked over toward a modesty box.

Iris took one of the many pairs of well-worn flip-flops and a large red-and-white flannel that was comically oversized on her.

But she felt a little less exposed as she ducked her head and made her way through the city.

She couldn't go back to Finn's penthouse. She wasn't ready to hear his excuses.

She wanted Monty, but there was no telling where he was or who he might be with. The last thing she needed was more eyes on her.

She felt raw from Selene's cynicism, but she made her way toward the bookstore, knocking wildly on the door until Selene emerged from her attached apartment.

She stumbled toward the door, her wild purple hair pulled up in pigtails, a massively oversized pink sweater swallowing her up.

Selene's hand rose, making the locks disengage before she yanked the door open.

Her gaze scanned her friend.

Then she sighed.

"Well. You look like a woman who accidentally trusted a man. Come on in. I've got tea, tequila, and hex books. Pick your poison."

Iris followed Selene through the darkened bookstore, wishing to feel the usual comfort she did at the scent of paper, ink, and glue binding, but finding nothing but deeper wells of sadness.

"Not now, Gerty," Selene grumbled as a book flew across the store. "Don't you know a heartbroken woman when you see one?"

Selene's apartment was a studio that Iris wasn't sure was real or enchanted. Judging by the small square footage, though, Iris was inclined to believe it was good, old-fashioned Manhattan real estate.

Her friend had fully made the space her own, though. Floor-to-ceiling bookcases lined one wall, soaked in a bright, happy yellow and weighed down with thousands of the romance novels she pretended not to love.

The floors were scattered with various colorful rugs, and the couch and bed were equally mismatched and cozy.

The kitchen was small and tidy, with purple cabinets and dried herbs hanging.

At the furthest end of the space was Selene's altar, featuring storage for spell books, candles, incense, herbs, oils, and salt.

It seemed as though Iris had interrupted some sort of ritual. Supplies were spread across the altar: black crystals, a black candle, a quill pen, and a piece of paper with some writing on it.

Selene moved over toward the kitchen, flicking on the electric kettle, then reaching for two mismatched mugs before turning back to Iris.

"You smell like salt water and disappointment." She waved Iris over toward a small two-chair dining set, the top a mosaic of Moroccan tiles. "Do you want to talk about it, or help me look for a spell to give him an itch he can never quite scratch? Upper back. Just out of reach forever. Or enchant his tie collection to aggressively tighten anytime he is being disingenuous. Or we could keep it simple and make every seagull in the tri-state area see his face as a bull's-eye, if you know what I mean."

"I don't want to hex him," Iris said. Then, after a little consideration: "Yet."

"Attagirl. So, spill. What did The Suit do?"

Iris let it all spill out, this time letting the tears flow when they threatened.

Selene just listened, bringing her tissues, then her cup of tea.

When she was finally done, Selene took a deep breath. "Hmm."

"Hmm? That's all you have to say? Hmm?"

"Well, see, I feel like Finn would have to be monumentally stupid to do something he had to know would upset you just when the two of you had seemed to make some progress. And as much as I hate to admit it, I don't think he's an idiot."

"Are you taking his side?"

"Listen, you know how much it pains me to defend a man," Selene said, making Iris's lips tease up ever so slightly. "I don't think this was Finn's doing. This has that smarmy, self-serving, sneaky-ass campaign manager written all over it."

That did make a certain kind of sense, when she thought about it.

"It still doesn't explain why he didn't come after me," Iris insisted. "Why he chose to stay with the cameras instead of making sure I was okay."

"No," Selene agreed, leaning back in her chair. "No, it doesn't explain that."

Iris watched the steam dance from her cup. "What if he always chooses his career first?" Iris warmed her hand on the mug. "If I want to be with him, does it mean always being second in his heart?"

"I wish I had the answer for that. Maybe what you need is a little time and space to get your mind and heart in check."

"Yeah," Iris agreed.

"You can crash here. I end up sleeping on the couch more than the bed anyway, so it's all yours. And I can loan you something less . . . nipple-prominent to wear."

Despite the sinking sensation in her chest, Iris's lips curved up.

"I'm afraid to take the stickers off," she confessed.

"I think I'd rather drink a truth potion at a family dinner than pull those things off." A full-body shiver racked Selene's system. "But I will soak in a tub until I'm pruny to make a bandage peel off, rather than pull it off myself. Oh, speaking of. That's the bathroom, obviously." She waved toward the only door in the space. "You can touch all four walls from the center. And you have to leave the door open if you want to do something like blow-dry your hair. But it has a pretty nice soaking tub. For elaborate bath rituals, a good cry, or replaying that stupid thing you said twelve years ago until your stomach is in knots."

"I really appreciate this, Selene."

"Don't mention it. I never got to have sleepovers as a kid. This is kind of nice."

"Why couldn't you?"

"You try having a friend circle when your mom summoned a demon to help her bake sourdough, and the thing stuck around and possessed the toaster. Then it whispers things like '*Crumb by crumb, I shall return*,' when you're just trying to make a toaster grilled cheese at two in the morning."

"Are you close with your mother?"

"I moved out of New England to put some buffer between us. Otherwise, she would be dropping in for full-moon rituals every month. Naked. But, yeah, I love her.

And my sisters, aunts, cousins. They're just a lot more . . . magical than I choose to be. I mostly just like my books. And convenience spells. Like the one I am doing . . . right now," she said.

Selene waved her hand in the air, writing something on the air that Iris felt breeze past her, making her hair kick up and a tingle move across her skin.

"What did you do?"

"Cast a spell for a bath that stays at the perfect temperature, no matter what. Go relax. I'll get the bed all changed and comfy. Then you can get some sleep and look at this whole situation from the right side of morning."

Some part of Iris wanted to stay and talk, to hear more about Selene's upbringing and crazy family. To get to know her friend, sure, but also as a distraction.

But the siren call of an endlessly warm bath had her rising and making her way toward the bathroom.

She sank into the water, feeling it warm the muscles that ached from hours of swimming—not to mention pulling Finn along with her to the ocean floor.

"Ugh," she grumbled, sinking under the water.

The bathroom swam around her, and pretty soon, all she could hear was the thump of her pulse in her ears.

It was the most peaceful she'd felt since the boat made it back to shore.

She stayed there in her forever-warm bath for what felt like hours.

Selene came in twice. Once, to drop off some clothes to wear. The second time, to brush her teeth before bed.

When Iris finally dried, dressed, and made her way back into the main area, Selene was passed out with one arm draped over her face and the other hanging off the couch.

The book she'd been reading was on the floor, face down, holding her spot until morning.

Music drifted through the air, soft and sweet, like a music box, though Iris couldn't find the source and had to conclude it was another of Selene's spells.

After grabbing a glass of salt water, Iris made her way back toward the bed.

She hadn't meant to look.

Truly, she hadn't.

Her gaze just so happened to glance down as she moved past Selene's altar. There, she noticed that the spell her friend had been working on had something to do with Arden. Because it was his name written on that paper she'd spotted earlier.

Despite knowing it was rude, she looked at the spell book sitting open on the tabletop.

Open to a page for a banishing spell.

To Douse the Flames of Desire.

Iris glanced toward her friend, who claimed love was a scam, but read romance novels whenever she had a spare moment. It was just then that Iris recognized the song that was playing. Selene played love songs to go to sleep.

It seemed like she wasn't the only one with confusing feelings toward a particular man.

There was something comforting in that as she slipped inside the fresh sheets that smelled like nag champa and patchouli.

But sleep didn't claim her until the sun was already creeping across the sky.

Finn

"Get the hell out of here," Finn snarled as Henry made his way through the penthouse.

The empty penthouse.

Once Finn had untangled himself from the swarming, insensitive gossip reporters, he'd rushed back to Manhattan, rehearsing what he was going to say to Iris the whole way.

Only to find the apartment dark, the bed empty, and no sign that Iris had been back at all.

With a sinking stomach, he wondered if she'd gone back home. To the palace. To her mother and sisters. To the one place where she wouldn't have to tolerate the curious gazes of people who wanted to know about her relationship with an up-and-coming politician.

The look on her face right before she'd turned and walked away had been gutting him endlessly ever since.

"We need to talk about that disaster last night."

"The disaster that you created."

Henry held up his hands, palms out. "Wait. Hear me out."

"I don't think I want to hear you out after that kind of betrayal, Hen."

"I might be an ass," Henry admitted. He ignored Finn's snort. "But when have I ever deliberately set out to hurt you?"

That gave Finn pause.

Yes, Henry could be dogged, ruthless, even. That said, everything Henry did was to help Finn, to benefit his campaign and, by extension, his life. Did he occasionally say something off color? Give him hard truths? Yeah. But he was never cruel. He never went out of his way to do something he knew would upset Finn.

"Are you trying to claim you didn't send the media to the docks?"

Henry sucked in a deep breath. "This is where it gets complicated."

"How in the world could this be complicated?"

"Look, I may or may not have been . . . ranting a little. In the office. Within earshot of a bunch of our very eager-to-please interns."

"Ranting about what?"

"About how you were wasting a perfectly good chance for an incredible photo op because you wanted some time alone with Iris. I was just . . . talking to myself. But I guess one of those well-intentioned interns got an idea in their heads. Then ran with it without running it past me." Henry paused, his shoulders sinking low. "I wouldn't do that to you, Finn. And I kind of hate that you think I was capable of it."

Finn had known his campaign manager for a long time. He'd never seen him look so defeated, so unsure of himself.

"They did so much damage."

"Yeah," Henry agreed. "The news is having a field day with how Iris ran off to—"

"Can you blame her?" Finn cut him off. He raked a hand through his already messy hair. "Iris wasn't even dressed, for God's sake."

"To be fair, she's a mermaid. They're always almost naked."

"*Not* Iris since she came to the surface. I think you forget that she's a person sometimes. With her own thoughts, feelings, and boundaries. While I believe you don't set out to hurt me, it feels like you don't extend that same curtesy to Iris. All you have done is push her."

"To help her become the political wife she agreed to become."

"She was pressured into this marriage, Hen. She spent weeks trying to sabotage it. And both of us were too self-involved to see it. She didn't make any kind of agreement."

"She clearly made some kind of arrangement with you."

"It wasn't an arrangement. It was a relationship. A delicate one. And now . . ." Finn waved a hand, too frustrated to go on.

"This might not be the best time to say it, but if she is going to be with a public figure, she's going to need tougher skin."

"Henry, now is not the time for that. I don't want to hear about optics. I want Iris back."

Finn dropped down on the couch, his elbows on his knees, his head in his hands.

"Where is he?" another voice joined the room. "Where

is the monster who made my charming sea fairy look like this?" Monty came waddling into the room, a phone in his hand. "There you are," he said, making a beeline for Finn. "What did you do to her?" he asked. The pelican shoved the phone into Finn's hands.

He glanced down at the screen, seeing an image he hadn't come across yet.

It was taken near the parking lot. Iris was looking back toward, he assumed, him. Her arms were still wrapped around herself. And her eyes looked completely heartbroken.

His own heart ground to dust in his chest.

"I *trusted* her with you," Monty said, snatching back his phone. "I encouraged her to give you a chance. And this is how you repay that trust? Shame on you. I'll be gathering my things and leaving." He was making his way toward the hall as he spoke. "You can have Iris's things packed up."

"Finn, we need to do some damage control," Henry, not knowing when to let something drop, pressed on.

"No."

"Your image—"

"To hell with my image. With the optics. With this entire damned campaign. I'm losing the love of my life."

"Love," Henry, a realist to his core, scoffed.

"Yes, love."

"Love is . . . inconvenient."

"It always is," Finn shot back. "But it is worth it. To have one *real* thing in my life."

He stormed away from Henry to move into the doorway of Monty's bedroom. Where he found the bird picking up the cat and trying to shove him into one of his many bags.

"You can't take Checkers."

"He likes Iris more than you," Monty sniffed, attempting to zip up the bag around the cat.

"Iris lives in the ocean." Monty's gaze flicked away. Too quickly. "She went to the ocean, didn't she?"

"Where was all this concern for my magnificent sea wench last night?"

"Monty, do you know where she is?"

"I'm her emotional support bird. I always know where she is." He shoved several of his little vests into another bag as Checkers started to wiggle out of the head hole Monty left for him. "Besides, the fish at the aquarium were trying to leap out of their tanks to get to her. One of them was spelling out *HELP* in bubbles, I swear."

"What?"

"The fish were trying to get to her."

"Why?"

"Do you know *anything* about that resplendent creature?" Monty asked, turning to cross his wings and glare at him.

"I know everything she's been willing to share with me so far."

That seemed to soften the bird slightly. His wings fell. "The fish swim to her when she cries. It's some oceanic princess magic, I guess. Which I imagine is charming *in* the ocean. But mildly horrifying on land."

"She was crying?" Finn asked, stomach dropping.

"Of course she was crying. And I hope that witch cursed you with each spilt tear."

"The witch?" Finn asked, grasping onto that with both hands.

Monty sighed.

"She's with Selene?"

"I can't tell you that." Monty lifted his enormous beak. But as Checkers finally emerged from the bag, he turned. "Get back here, you beast, or I'll store you somewhere else much less favorable."

"Do not put the cat in your beak."

"He won't stay in the bag!" Monty threw a wing out dramatically.

"Listen, how about you put a pin in stealing my cat. And in your packing. Let me go see Iris. I want to fix this."

The pelican seemed unconvinced.

"I love her."

"You say that. And yet she was crying last night."

"Please, Monty. I want to make it right. I can't lose her."

Monty stared at him for a moment.

Finally, he gave him a nod and an address.

"But that's the bookstore."

"And Selene's home," Monty said. "Bring her a hot pretzel," he suggested.

"I can do that," Finn said, daring to feel hope for the first time in hours.

"Finn," Monty called.

"Yeah?"

"Bring our girl home."

"I will."

He would.

Whatever it took. Even dropping out of the race, he'd do it. For her.

"Not now," he snapped when Henry tried to stop him.

"Finn, we don't have time for this. You're still lagging in the polls. You have to get your face out there and change public—"

"There's only one thing I need to do right now. And that's try to convince the woman I love to give me another chance. Everything else can wait."

Henry wasn't done, though. He followed Finn into the elevator.

"There's no time—"

"Then we lose the election."

"How can you say that?" Henry shook his head. "This is all you've ever wanted."

"Things change. Now *she* is all I want."

As soon as the doors slid open, he strode out, ducking his head to avoid the hard look from Willow as she watered the plant in the lobby.

"You," a voice said as Finn stepped onto the street. His head jerked up, seeing Arden barreling down the sidewalk toward him.

"I know. I've heard it all from Monty already. And there's nothing you can say to me that I haven't already been saying to myself."

"Good. You should be wallowing. Now go do something heroic and romantic about it. Do you have any idea how hard it is to plan a wedding for two people who have practically been in love since they met but are too stubborn to see it? I'm surviving on caffeine and Firis fan fiction."

"Firis?"

"Finn and Iris. It's your couple name."

"There's fan fiction about us?"

"There's fan fiction about the gargoyle who sits on top of the First Paranormal Bank building and sighs each time one of the tellers shows up to work. Of course there's fan fiction about you two. But I bet after last night's fiasco, a dozen new story arcs are being created as we speak. And I want them all to end in scandalous sex and happy endings. Fix it, Finn."

With that, he walked off.

Finn sucked in a deep breath and strode down the street, stopping only to get a whole bag full of hot pretzels before making his way to the bookstore.

The door was unlocked for business.

But when he tried to enter, he felt an invisible wall slam into him.

"Did it hurt? I hope it hurt," Selene said, appearing out of the depths of the store. "A lot of wards come out kind of rubbery, so they don't do any real damage. I added in some mystical concrete. Not enough to break your nose, but I hope it crunched a little."

He barely resisted the urge to reach up and rub it.

"I deserve it."

"You do. And unless that suit is hiding a grand romantic gesture, a heartfelt apology, or a *soul*, you're not getting in."

"I am sorry, Selene."

"Are you?" she asked, folding her arms across her chest. "Iris deserves fairy-tale-level love. You gave her campaign optics and emotional whiplash. Newsflash: you don't get to be Prince Charming *after* the heartbreak montage. That's not how this works."

"I know I screwed up. I know it seems like all I cared about was my campaign. But that's not true. Trust me, I knew what I had long before Iris was willing to give *me* a chance."

Selene's unmoved gaze said she was going to need more.

"I was willing to accept her asking about my prostate

and sticking dead bugs to the wall. And collecting *gynecological* equipment."

That got a little snort out of the witch.

"That may have been my doing. I had a whole list. We never did get to the best parts."

"My point is, I was happy to accept those . . . eccentricities. Because they were a part of *her* and I knew how special she was."

"And yet you let her walk away last night."

"Selene, if I followed her, the press would have too. There would have been no privacy to talk it out or try to patch things up. I gave her privacy, figuring we could fume about it together back at the apartment."

"So it was Henry."

"Of course it was Henry. I wouldn't do that to her. We had a special day."

She was melting.

But he could still feel the ward radiating in front of him.

"Please, Selene. I don't know what to do without her. I don't know who I *am* without her."

"If you come in here and you hurt her again, I will turn you into a toad. A really ugly, warty one. Who can only eat dung beetles."

"Understood."

Her head tipped to the side, brows drawing together. Any softness she'd been showing him dissipated. When she spoke, her words were cool once more. "You know what breaks this ward?" she asked. "Sincere intentions. Weird how it's still holding strong."

Finn let his anxiety and fear fall away, leaving only the raw, desperate need to see Iris again.

"Fine," she said when they both sensed the ward falling.

"But don't make me hope you're different then prove me wrong. I hate hoping. It's bad for my blood pressure. And my brand."

She waved toward a door to the side of the building, and he could feel her critical gaze on him until he disappeared on the other side of it.

Finn's gaze slid around the room until he found a lump underneath a pile of colorful blankets on the bed.

He took a deep breath, suddenly anxious about what he was going to say. He'd been so focused on finding her that he hadn't figured out what he might say when he did.

He had no grand romantic gestures—just a bag of semi-hot pretzels and his heart to offer.

He had to hope it would be enough.

He made his way over to the bed, sitting down on the edge.

"I don't want to work on a hex." Iris's voice was muffled from the pillow.

"Why not? Haven't I earned it?"

The lump on the bed jolted as Iris dropped onto her back, the blankets falling down to reveal her red-streaked face and puffy eyes.

"What would you do? Give me a tail? Turn me into a werewolf groomer? A vampire tooth-sharpener?"

"I don't want to speak to you," Iris said, not falling for his weak attempt at a joke.

"If you don't want to talk, will you listen?"

Her gaze was guarded, but she didn't object.

"I know you might not be willing to accept this, but I promise you, I did not set us up to be papped like that. I didn't, and wouldn't, invite that kind of invasion. We have enough scrutiny on us. The last thing I want is the media prying into our rare private moments."

Iris's gaze slipped. "It was Henry, wasn't it?"

"In a way. It was more of a misunderstanding. One I made clear can never happen again."

Iris sucked in a deep breath, her soft, vulnerable gaze lifting to his.

"Why didn't you come for me?"

"I knew you were upset. I didn't want them chasing you down. I tried to distract them so you didn't have to deal with that. I thought you would go home. Then we could talk.

"I don't think I realized how hurt you were until I came home and found you hadn't returned. I thought I'd lost you," he admitted, his voice cracking. "I thought you'd gone back down to the ocean floor and that I would never see you again."

"You would have forgotten me in a day. I'd have been replaced in a week."

"Iris," he said softly. "You think you're forgettable? You turned my whole world upside down. You made me question everything I thought I wanted. I haven't been able to stop thinking about you since you threw your drink in my face. And I don't *want* to stop thinking about you. Not in a week, not in a lifetime."

He saw her softening, but the tremble in her lower lip said she wasn't quite there yet.

"Yesterday was supposed to be ours. No plans. No press. Just you and me. I should have made sure our peace was protected. I just . . . underestimated how necessary it was to make my boundaries known."

She looked at him, a glimmer of hope hidden in those

gorgeous eyes of hers. "So what's different now? What stops this from happening again the next time the campaign needs something shiny to parade in front of potential voters?"

"What's different now is that nothing in this campaign—nothing in this whole damn city—has ever felt real until you.

"Everything I say in interviews and on stages is polished and practiced. Every handshake is a strategy based on polling and research. But with you? With you, I have no idea what I'm doing. I don't know the right things to do or say. And it's new and scary. But it's *real*. It's *mine*.

"I can't lose you, Iris." His voice was hardly more than a whisper. "Not to them. They don't matter, not anymore. All that matters is you. And if there's even a chance that you want to give me another chance, I promise I will do everything I can to protect you."

She exhaled shakily, arms wrapping around her bent knees. "I want to believe you." Her voice was quieter, raw around the edges. "I *do*. But you and I both know that the spotlight, the cameras, the questions—they're a part of your life. And I can't fake it like you can. I can't put on a smile when I'm upset or angry. I can't be perfectly polished and know all the right things to say and how to act. And we both know I would be a liability to you."

"You are not a liability. You're the reason I remembered I'm a person at all." His voice shook, earnest and bare. "Before you, I didn't even know I was running on autopilot. Smiling, shaking hands, pretending to be whoever the people wanted me to be. You made me want something for myself. Made me crave something real. You have to see that."

The hope battled the fear in her eyes.

"It could all fall apart," she said. "The optics. The campaign. We both know I'm not meant for public life."

"Good," he said without hesitation. "I don't want someone meant for something as fake as public life. I want you. Wild, wonderful you."

"You're not afraid?"

"Terrified," he admitted, a small, crooked smile breaking through. "But I'd rather be taking risks with you than safe on my own. Because nothing is scarier than a future without you."

Her eyes were shimmering then. He knew she wanted it just as much as he did.

"I can't promise I won't screw up," he said, reaching for her hand. "Because I probably will. I'm still figuring this out—how to be the man you deserve. But I promise I won't ever stop trying."

"I don't need perfect. I *hate* perfect. But . . ."

"But?" he prompted.

"But I love you. I love you enough to be willing to give up everything I thought I couldn't live without."

His heart, so crushed just hours before, swelled in his chest, threatening to break free.

"You don't know what it does to me to hear you say that. I've been chasing approval, applause, votes—and none of it has ever meant as much as this, as you. I love you too. More than I even knew I was capable of. But I don't want you to give up anything to be with me."

"Your life is on land."

"And part of your heart will always be in the ocean. I would never ask you to give that up for me. I want you to have the ocean, with its glimmersharks and eel quartets and endless depths. I will do everything in my power to find a way to bridge our two worlds so you never feel like you are giving up anything to be with me. I want to broaden your world, not restrict it. I want you. All of you. On land, on water, in between. Forever."

He reached for her, and she let herself be pulled across his lap. Their lips met, full of the fear, the hope, the promises, the potential.

And when they broke away, Iris rested her head against his chest, listening to the heart she knew for certain belonged to her.

"Do I smell hot pretzels?"

He grinned. "You think I would risk this conversation without carbs?" He reached for the bag. "I come bearing snacks and sincerity."

"You're lucky I accept bribes."

Oh, he was fully aware just how lucky he was.

"Let's go home," she said, reaching for his hand.

Iris

"I almost gave up my dreams of fame and fortune," Monty said, throwing himself dramatically across her bed, his wing covering his eyes, "to go back to the ocean for you."

"Yes, Monty," Iris agreed, lips twitching. "I am very aware of the sacrifices you might have made for my heartbreak."

"He almost wouldn't let me bring the cat; did he tell you that?"

"To be fair, you keep trying to eat him."

"I have finer taste than that," he sniffed, even if she'd caught him that very morning standing over Checkers while he napped in a sunbeam.

"Why are we discussing ancient history?" Arden asked, looking up from his notebook full of potential centerpieces.

"Ancient history?" Selene asked, rolling her eyes. "It was literally two days ago."

"Exactly. Ancient history."

"This coming from an immortal," Selene shot back.

"When you live forever, you learn quickly how pointless time is. The heartbreak is over. Let's focus on the future now. And the future does *not* have votives sitting in sand inside a *mason jar*," he said, ripping a page out of his binder.

"Hmm," Iris, heart light with love, started to tease, "how about synchronized seahorses in fishbowls? They could perform slow-motion water ballets!"

Selene—seeing Arden's disgust—piled on. "Oh, how about prophetic goldfish? They could interrupt bits of conversation to offer relationship advice."

"Oh, we don't need goldfish for that," Willow said, bringing a tray of snacks over to the table. "I have a ficus that we could propagate that could do that without all the water."

"Oh, or miniature shipwreck dioramas," Selene suggested.

"Yes, because nothing says 'romance' like death and destruction," Arden, tugging at his collar, grumbled.

"How about a pair of doves?" Selene said.

"Doves?" Arden asked, brows pinching. "How would you keep them on the tables?"

"Well, they'd be taxidermied, of course."

"Right. Dead birds. That's what everyone wants to look at while they're eating."

"It's the *symbolism*."

"Death is not the symbolism of a long and happy marriage."

"Fine. Glass snow globes. But with sand instead of snow."

"That's . . . not horrible."

"And inside each one is a tiny scroll," Selene said, making Iris's lips twitch.

"With a love poem on them?" Arden asked, hopeful.

"No. With a little prenuptial agreement."

"You're hopeless," Arden said, laughing.

"Better hopeless than hopelessly cliché." She leaned over his chair, flipping through his binder. "Candles? Potted plants? Yawn. I mean, you could just drop down a few really pretty copies of classic romance novels and call it a day."

Arden's head tilted, and his eyes went warm. "That might actually be charming. And I suppose you have someone in mind to make the suggestions for the books?"

"Well," Selene said, trying to act nonchalant about the topic. "I mean, I do own a bookstore."

"Right," Arden said, wrapping an arm around her waist and dragging her down onto the chair next to him. "Purely professional recommendations. Has nothing at all to do with your secret stash of dark prince smut."

"I do not . . . what is this?" Selene asked, pulling a shiny book out from under Arden's binder.

"Don't look at me," Arden said as Selene looked at the comic book.

"I'm a cozy mystery kind of girl," Willow said when gazes slid in her direction.

"It's Finn's," Iris said, reaching for it. She couldn't stop the smile that teased her lips as she took the glossy book and looked at the muscled group of men and women on the cover.

"I did not have him pegged as a comic book guy."

"Henry did his best to hide this side of him," Iris said. "The comic books and his sci-fi movies."

They'd been watching those movies every night. Admittedly, Iris spent most of the run time watching Finn watch the movie, loving how his face lit up, how his words tumbled together when he was trying to explain some part of the plot to her. But she enjoyed every moment of it.

"Why?" Selene asked. "This interest would get him the nerd vote."

"It makes him so much more real," Willow agreed, taking the comic book. "My nephew eats these things up. I got him a digital comic book subscription for his last birthday."

As a whole, Willow—for obvious reasons—tried to avoid paper products when she could. While not all trees were dryads, all dryads felt very connected to the trees.

"That's what I told Finn," Iris agreed. "People like being able to connect with their civil servants. He's done a million interviews, and I don't think I ever heard him claim to like a hobby that wasn't exercise-related."

"Well, we can all agree that we appreciate his dedication to exercise," Arden said, smirking. "I know it was a bad night for you, but those images of him on that dock where the moon cast all those stomach muscles in shadow? The whole of Manhattan swooned."

"If you want to compliment him, tell him his calves look good," Iris said, her smile soft. "He worked hard on those."

"Noted," Arden agreed. "No, absolutely not," he said when Selene pointed to something in his binder.

"Why not?" the witch asked.

"Because those are for *Halloween* parties, not weddings."

"We're getting nowhere with these plans," Selene

grumbled, reaching for Iris's copy of one of Caprica Coraline's books.

"Oh, speaking of. Did I tell you she RSVP'd?" Arden asked.

"Who did?" Iris asked, but she was half distracted by Finn's comic book. She'd been trying to read some of them in her free time so they could talk about them.

"Caprica."

"Wait, she RSVP'd? Caprica? Who never does public appearances? Not even for book releases?" Selene asked. "Even when asked very nicely," she added, her tone sulky.

"She even sent a little personal note," Arden said. He flipped through his notebook, looking for the note. "She said she's been watching your story since you first came to the surface. And that you have . . . oh, what was it?" he asked, finding the note. "Right. She said you have 'greatly inspired the plot for her next book.'"

"What?" Selene snatched the book out of Arden's hand. Her eyes went round. "This is an actual handwritten note from Caprica Coraline? *The* Caprica Coraline?"

"It is." Arden was watching Selene with a warm light in his eyes.

"You have her contact information?"

"Oh, sweetheart, I have everyone's contact."

Iris felt a similar thrill of excitement, but it was quickly overwhelmed by an entirely different sensation as Finn came sweeping into the penthouse. He was already tugging at his tie, eager to shrug off The Suit.

It seemed that once he fully became aware of how much the persona of a politician had overtaken him, he'd been working hard to separate that from who he really was.

He made a beeline toward the table, his gaze moving

around everyone gathered, then the items on the surface of the table.

But before he even bothered to greet them, he stepped behind Iris's chair, reaching around her to grab her chin and tilt her head backward.

His lips were on hers then, kissing her hard and deep and entirely too briefly. She could never seem to get enough of him.

"Hey, guys," he greeted the table. "How is the planning going?"

"Slowly," Arden said with a pointed look toward Selene.

"Hey, you're the one who wanted my input," Selene said, quietly tucking the note from Caprica into her purse.

Iris was fairly sure Arden didn't actually want Selene's help, just her company.

"Don't worry," Arden said, looking back at Finn. "Everything will be planned and perfect for your big day."

The day was closing in.

Just a few weeks away.

Instead of feeling trapped by the deadline like she had been, all Iris felt was excitement, a bone-deep sort of *rightness*.

A lifetime with Finn—good, kind, selfless, attentive, smart, gorgeous, generous, and slightly nerdy Finn—was all she could think about these days.

Pretty soon, it was going to be her reality.

"Shouldn't you be getting dressed?" Finn asked, making Iris's eyes go round.

"Oh! Whoops. I lost track of time." She popped up out of her chair to rush toward the bedroom to grab her outfit.

"She does that," Selene agreed.

"She showed up at my yoga class ten minutes short of it being over," Willow piled on.

"In my defense, I knew I would be terrible at it," Iris called from the bedroom.

"She knocked over a row of advanced yogi women like dominoes," Willow explained. "And a snake plant that actually hissed about the disruption."

"She's making it sound worse than it was," Iris insisted. She yanked on a vintage T-shirt from some obscure comic book that featured a mermaid-vampire hybrid that she had never read but thought would be perfect for the day's event.

There was a time she would have wanted to wear a shirt to embarrass him. Now, all she wanted to do was match him and make him proud.

"Okay. How's this?" she asked as she emerged.

"Where did you find that?" Finn asked, eyes bright.

"In the same store where we found your wedding present," Selene announced.

"It's perfect," Finn told her, heading past her in the hall.

"Where are you going?"

"To get changed."

"I thought we had to leave at eleven."

Finn's smile was sheepish as he turned to look at her. "Yes, I did *say* that."

"You gave me a fake time?" she asked, pretending to be shocked.

What could she say?

She knew she was always late.

And that Finn was really excited about this outing.

"A necessary evil," he said, shooting her a smirk before slipping into the bedroom.

By the time he came out, Arden, Selene, and Willow had seen themselves out. So there was no one there to admire his casual outfit of black shorts and a T-shirt featuring a ton of different comic book covers with the words *I've Got Issues* printed above.

It was the most casual she'd seen him dress for anything that involved leaving their home.

"I love it," she declared, beaming at him.

"Are you ready for this?"

Given what she'd seen about these giant comic book events online, no, she was not.

"Absolutely," she agreed, taking his hand.

It was a short ride to the venue, and they made it out front just as the doors opened.

"You're actually *on time*?" Juna asked, mouth falling open as Iris and Finn approached.

"Finn lied to me," Iris admitted.

"Smart man," Shelly, standing beside Juna, declared with a nod.

Iris wasn't sure what had gotten into the queen to allow all three of the Marivelle sisters to be on land at the same time, but she was over the moon to be able to spend some time with her siblings.

"I still can't get used to seeing you guys with legs," Iris admitted.

"I still can't get used to having them," Juna admitted.

"My feet hurt all the time," Shelly said.

"That's where fiancés come in handy," Iris said, leaning her head into Finn's shoulder.

As if on cue, Osiren came bounding over, his legs as enormous as the rest of his body, handing each of them their lanyard badges.

"Ugh, no thanks," Shelly said, lip curling.

"Remind me to introduce you to my friend Selene," Iris

said, shooting her baby sister a smile as Finn slipped her badge over her head.

"Ready?" he asked, practically bouncing on his feet.

Iris watched her sisters disappear into the building. "Abso—"

"Mr. Westrock!" a voice called, making Iris fight to keep a smile on her lips. She knew a paparazzo trying to get Finn's attention when she heard one.

"Richard," Finn said, his professional voice and posture taking over.

Iris felt her belly tighten.

But then Finn's arm slipped around her lower back, pulling her close.

"Right now, I'm off the clock and spending time with someone special," he said, giving Iris a small smile. "But I'll be happy to answer your questions at the press conference tomorrow night. Or you can send them to my office for a statement." Richard looked disappointed, but Finn's next words made it hard for him to press. "I really appreciate you giving us a little space."

With that, he turned and led Iris into the building.

Her heart was a balloon in her chest, pumped up to full volume, making her feel like she was floating.

Sure, he'd already made it clear to Henry that he wouldn't tolerate any more interference in his personal life, that there were some matters in which he didn't want his campaign manager's input.

But this felt different.

He'd set the boundary with an outsider.

He'd prioritized her and them.

"No way," Finn said, stopping dead and staring up at something hanging from the high ceiling.

Iris followed his gaze, finding a two-story poster for a new action and mystery movie.

Featuring none other than Montague Featherington, wings flared, tuxedo flapping. And just beneath, the dramatic tagline: *JUSTICE TAKES FLIGHT!*

Iris's smile spread until her cheeks hurt.

"He always said he was going to be a star," she said. "Looks like he got his wish."

Iris leaned into Finn.

Yes, he had.

But so had she.

Epilogue

Election Night

Iris

"I heard you're the mermaid to talk to about the best book club around," someone said behind Iris as she grabbed a flute of champagne off the platter of a passing server.

Turning, Iris saw a tall, lithe woman with long sable hair and two small horns poking out of her forehead. Clearly some kind of shifter, though Iris had yet to figure out an appropriate way to ask someone that particular question.

"I'm Fawn. You knocked me over at yoga once."

"Oh, oops. Yeah, I'm still getting used to walking on two legs. Doing yoga on them was probably a bad idea. I hope I didn't do any damage."

"Wasn't the first time I took a tumble in class. And won't be the last. At least I could blame you for that one. So, this book club. I heard Montague does readings at them . . ."

Oh, Monty.

He would be insufferably delighted to know how many rooms his name was spoken in these days.

"He does. He does voices and everything."

"Do you have room for one more?"

They were going to have to move the book club from Selene's store to an event venue if too many more readers got wind.

But Iris was happy to extend her circle.

Her gaze scanned the room, smiling when she saw Caprica Coraline talking to Willow near the buffet table.

Monty was fashionably late, as always. *I can't show up on time, like some common pigeon.*

Both Arden and Selene were suspiciously absent. And Iris secretly hoped they were off making out behind a floral arrangement or something.

"Of course we do. We're reading that new vampire thriller that just shot up the charts."

"I'm so excited. I can bring a cheese board."

"Excuse me," Finn said, moving in at their sides. "Mind if I steal my wife away for a dance?"

"Of course!" Fawn said, beaming at Finn. "I just *know* you're going to win tonight," she said.

"Either way, we will have a great party," Finn, ever the diplomat, said. "Have a great time."

With that, Iris was swept into his arms and out onto the dance floor.

"I have to give it to Arden," Iris said, glancing around the room, "he can really pull together any kind of party, can't he? It's beautiful."

Not as beautiful as their wedding, all beachy and surrounded by their loved ones, but, again, she was a little partial to that event.

"Haven't been able to look at anything but you. Did you paint this dress on?" His hand ran down her exposed back that, she'd insisted to Arden, would be too risqué for an election night watch party. But with the wonder in Finn's eyes, she knew it had been the right choice.

It was a floor-length silk gown the color of sea foam that hugged every curve of her body.

It was worth it. Even if she had to wear those blasted boob stickers again to pull it off.

"You like it?"

"It's been . . . problematic," Finn admitted. He pulled her in close, his face pressed to the side of hers. "I've been trying to listen to the speeches from the donors and heads of the various organizations, and all I've been able to think about is how with one swipe of my fingers, that dress would be a pool on the floor."

"You were out of bed so early this morning. I wanted to . . . give you a little good luck on such an important day."

"Oh, really?" he asked, his voice getting thick.

"Mmhmm. Wait, what are you doing?" she gasped as Finn spun her, their bodies moving across the dance floor toward the side of the room.

"Well, the numbers are rolling in," he said, taking her hand and quickly pulling her down a narrow hallway. "I could use a little luck."

The polls had finally closed.

Votes were being counted.

Henry was popping antacids and looking a little gray.

But Iris wasn't worried.

And Finn no longer based all his happiness on the results of the election.

He yanked open a door, pulling Iris into the darkened storage closet.

Finn reached up, pulling the string, the harsh yellow light buzzing above them, illuminating the room full of cleaning supplies.

He moved closer to her, intent burning in his eyes.

When his hands lifted, he made good on the fantasy he'd mentioned, brushing the barely there straps off Iris's shoulders until the material of her dress spilled from her body.

Cool air kissed her flushed skin.

She was left in nothing but her heels and panties, and Finn's appreciative rumble had her need building quickly, overtaking her so entirely that she didn't even think of objecting.

The party was in full swing.

There was music thumping loud enough to vibrate up through the floor. Conversation and laughter strained to be heard over that.

No one could hear.

So she didn't even try to soften her moan when Finn grabbed her and pulled her back to his front so his hands could drift up her stomach to cup her breasts.

Her head fell back, and Finn's lips pressed to her neck, making a shiver course through her.

His hands were as greedy as her desire, squeezing, his fingers circling, rolling, twisting.

Her soft whimpers deepened to throaty moans as one of Finn's hands slid down her stomach to slip between her thighs, stroking, circling, teasing her desire from a flicker to a flame.

Her hips rocked as Finn's fingers slipped inside her.

"So wet for me already." Finn's voice grazed down her spine.

"Finn, please."

"Love the sound of you begging."

His fingers turned, stroking across her top wall, driving her closer and closer to the edge.

Impatient, Iris reached back, tracing the rigid line of him through his pants until he was rocking into her touch, until his breathing went as ragged as her own.

Then his fingers were slipping out, and he was pressing her forward until her forearms were pressed against the wall, her ass arched out toward him.

His hand traced down her spine, teased across her hips, over her butt, then dragged her panties down.

She heard the slide of his zipper, then felt the press of his hard length against her.

Iris wiggled back against it, shameless with her need.

A low chuckle moved through Finn as he teased himself against her. A pressure. A press. A pause.

Iris pushed backward, gasping as he started to fill her.

Her gasp turned into a moan as he sank deeper, slow and steady. He gripped her hips, steadying her, anchoring himself.

Iris's arms pushed harder against the cool wall, her breath catching with every inch. The stretch, the heat, the dizzying closeness. She felt split open and stitched back together at once.

Finn rocked into her, his rhythm building gradually, deliberately. But unhurried. Like he was trying to memorize every sound she made, every shiver that moved through her.

Iris tried to bite back the sounds climbing in her throat

but Finn's hand grabbed a handful of her hair, pulling her back against his chest, his lips in her ear. "Don't hold back. I want to hear you."

A breathy cry slipped from her lips, and he groaned in response, sinking in deeper.

She could feel it in the way his fingers flexed on her hips, in the tension coiled tight in his body, how close he was to losing control.

She felt the same urgency building inside her.

But Finn kept the same agonizing pace, each slow thrust sending sparks ricocheting through her.

Finn's teeth nipped her earlobe. "Tell me what you need."

"You," she whimpered. "All of you. Don't stop."

His curse was a reverent thing, nearly a prayer. And then he gave in.

His stroke deepened, his grip tightened as he moved harder, faster, chasing the edge for them both.

His free hand slid down her body, pressing between her thighs, teasing her closer and closer.

Iris turned her face into his neck, overwhelmed by sensation.

Close.

She was so close.

His hips rocked.

His finger circled.

She tensed, shuddered, spiraled.

"Iris," he gasped, voice breaking as she shattered around him, breathless and undone, finding his bliss with her.

Their breaths tangled, their bodies spent afterward, just leaning into each other, enjoying the tingling aftermath.

She felt boneless, floating, tethered only by the strength

of his arms around her as their plans for the future tumbled from between their lips. A house by the beach. Monthly trips out on a boat and to visit her family. A saltwater hot tub for the apartment so Iris didn't always have to go down to the pool if she wanted to connect with her roots. A guest room for her sisters, mother, or Monty. Vacations to explore all the beautiful oceans of the world together.

He promised her hot pretzels.

He promised her separation between politics and personal life.

He promised her his truth, his heart, his future.

They were still lost in those soft, floating sensations when there was a sudden silence, then an eruption of cheers and applause from the party.

The results, it seemed, were in.

"Congratulations," Iris said, smile soft, "Mr. Mayor."

His arm slid around her belly, pulling her closer still.

"You got what you wanted."

"I did," he murmured, kissing her throat, then her jaw, the curve of her cheek. "And I'm never letting go of her."

Acknowledgements

To Amy, whose guidance, encouragement, and creative instincts helped this story find its true heart—thank you for believing in me and for making the process feel like magic.

To Maddie, Jessica, Jess, Emily, and the rest of the incredible team at Avon UK—thank you for bringing such vision, warmth, and care to this story. I feel so lucky to have a home with you.

To Helena and Daniela, for your keen eye and all the attention to detail that makes the words shine—thank you for helping this book become its best self.

And to the readers—you are the reason these worlds keep growing. Every message, review, and late-night reread reminds me why I do this. Thank you for letting me tell you a story.

Loved *Mermaid in Manhattan*? Don't miss Jessica's next book, coming soon!

Don't miss the wedding of a lifetime!

The addictive, fake-dating vampire romance, perfect for fans of Lana Ferguson and Jenna Levine.

Something witchy this way comes . . .

Don't miss this ultimate sapphic, academia spicy romance!

Gilmore Girls meets *Charmed* in this cozy, small-town, second-chance romance!

Perfect for readers of *Pumpkin Spice Cafe*, Erin Sterling and Lana Harper.